# A MEASURED SEDUCTION

Gellir hesitated only briefly. Then he eased forward. Closed his eyes. Slanted his mouth across Merraid's in the gentlest, most tentative of kisses.

Soon his feather-light caresses tempted her to answer. She moved her mouth beneath his, deepening the kiss, drawing closer to let her tongue explore the inner recesses of his mouth.

His tongue circled hers in a slow and sultry dance of desire. But with each moment, the dance grew more eager. More fervent.

What she remembered of his kiss before was nothing like this.

That had been the quick peck of a lad.

This was the measured seduction of a man.

LAIRD OF STEEL

Glynnis Campbell – Publisher
P.O. Box 341144
Arleta, California 91331
Contact: glynnis@glynnis.net

Cover design by Richard Campbell
Formatting by Author E.M.S.

ISBN-13: 978-1-63480-138-6

Published in the United States of America

# LAIRD OF STEEL

The Warrior Lairds of Rivenloch, Book 1

GLYNNIS CAMPBELL

# DEDICATION

For everyone who admires
a proactive Cinderella,
one who doesn't just wait around
for Prince Charming

# OTHER BOOKS BY GLYNNIS CAMPBELL

# ACKNOWLEDGMENTS

A gracious thank you to

The Ladies of the Carlsbad Author Retreat
for kick-starting my rejoyvenation

My awesome production/marketing team of
Jill, Amy, and Kirby

Becca, Skye, Alessandra, David, Nicholas, and Derek
for keeping me on track

My family
for their understanding of the creative process

Surprised Eel Historian, PhD
for his narrow focus and broad appeel

Alexander Dreymon and Jessica Chastain
for their inspiration

# PROLOGUE

*Castle Darragh, Scotland*
*Autumn 1156*

Fifteen-year-old Merraid stood on tiptoe, peering between the merlons of the castle parapet. She gazed into the distance, waving her kerchief. How she wished it were the silk scarf of a titled lady instead of a maidservant's nubby linen rag. Despite her brave salute, her chin trembled. Her eyes filled with tears.

Gellir Cameliard of Rivenloch, her beloved champion, was leaving her. Going home.

But home was a hundred miles away, near the east coast of Scotland. He might as well live on the moon.

Her spirits sank. How would she survive without the dashing warrior who'd stolen her heart? Would she ever see him again? If by some miracle their paths did cross, would he even remember her?

Her throat tightened. She choked back a sob.

She knew she should be glad for the time they'd had together. Gellir's clan had helped return the castle to its rightful ruler, Laird Dougal mac Darragh. After a fierce battle, the grateful Laird Dougal had even married Gellir's cousin—the beautiful and clever Lady Feiyan—uniting the two clans.

The marriage had been a godsend for Merraid. It meant seeing more of Gellir. The Rivenloch folk lingered at Castle Darragh for several fortnights, helping the newlyweds set their household to rights. And seventeen-year-old Gellir was put in charge of training Darragh's new army.

In that time, Merraid had fallen helplessly in love with the Rivenloch warrior. Not only for his brave and thrilling fighting skills. Not just for his dark and dramatic looks that took her breath away. But for his chivalry and kindness. His unmatched courage and heart.

She'd made up her mind to make him fall in love with her.

Unfortunately, she was not well-schooled in the art of persuasion. Despite her best efforts, summer passed in the wink of an eye. In the end, she found herself no closer to winning his affections.

If only she could turn back time, she'd do things differently.

She wouldn't waste time hiding behind doors. Stealing peeks at him. Lowering her eyes with shy blushes. Stumbling over her words in his presence.

Instead she would speak her mind. Reveal her heart. Bare her soul.

What she felt was nothing like her brief and childish infatuation with Laird Dougal. Nor her crushes on several other clan lads. Her affection for Gellir felt real. Lasting.

From the battlement, she watched her hero ride slowly away.

Curse her timid blood! She should have seized the moment. Acted on her impulses.

Now it was too late.

Even at this distance, within the retinue of his clan, she could recognize Gellir. His noble bearing was unmistakable.

His back was straight. His shoulders were broad. The early autumn breeze flirted with his lush, dark hair.

"Farewell!" she sobbed out. But her voice was weak and thin. Faltering with heartbreak. He'd never hear her.

Her throat ached. This must be how noblewomen felt, watching their knights ride off to war. Uncertain of their destiny. Tormented by longing. Haunted by...

"He'll be back," came a wry voice behind her.

Merraid gasped as she whirled toward Gellir's cousin, her laird's new wife. "M'lady." She clapped a startled hand to her chest and bobbed a curtsey.

It was troubling the way Lady Feiyan could steal up on a person. Doubly troubling was the knowing smile that graced the lady's face.

Merraid had done her best to hide her feelings for Gellir. But she was sure her adoration was obvious. As obvious as the orange hair on her head.

She forced a casual shrug. "Will he?"

"Of course." The lady's silvery gaze softened. "One day."

Merraid carefully lowered her eyes to hide the spark of hope. *One day.* Maybe not next month. Maybe not next year. But if *one day* he'd return, she'd wait for him.

Lady Feiyan nodded toward the departing travelers. "Keep an eye on them till they're out of sight, will you? Make sure they get away safely into the woods."

"Aye, m'lady," Merraid dipped her head.

The lady's command was laughable, of course. The Rivenloch clan hardly needed Merraid's protection. Only a fool would attempt to cross the renowned warriors. Besides, there were a dozen tasks she should be doing instead. Polishing the oak chests. Sweeping out the rushes. Harvesting herbs for supper.

Lady Feiyan had taken pity on her. She probably dismissed Merraid's affection for Gellir as trivial. The fleeting sentiments of a lovestruck lass. She probably figured there was no harm in letting Merraid feast her eyes upon her hero one last time.

The lady was wrong, of course. Merraid's affection was anything but trivial. Her love for Gellir was true and everlasting. Merraid knew it. She could feel it in the depths of her soul.

"When they're gone," Lady Feiyan continued, "come to the courtyard. I have a gift for you. Something my cousin thought you should have."

"A gift?" Merraid was so astonished, she stared at the lady like a gape-mouthed salmon.

A gift from Gellir? What could it be? Her heart soared as she contemplated the possibilities.

A ribbon for her wild hair he complained was always escaping its braid?

A new apron to replace the one he'd torn when he'd saved her life in battle?

A ring inscribed with the Rivenloch motto, *Amor vincit omnia,* Love conquers all, and a promise to return for her hand in marriage?

She bit her lip. She mustn't let hope make a fool of her.

"I'll see you below." Lady Feiyan gave her a secret smile as she slipped down the steps.

Merraid turned back to the departing company in the distance. Summoning all the intensity of her passion, she narrowed her eyes. She stared hard, sending a formidable message of desire toward the target of her love. She fired it across the grassy sward like an arrow aimed at his heart.

To her surprise, he turned her way.

Her breath caught. He'd received her message.

There could be only one reason for that. There was a *connection* between them. A mysterious *bond.* Their love was *meant to be.*

He was too far away to hear her call out. But he gave

her a wave and a nod. Then he reined his mount about again and plodded into the trees.

Her pulse was still pounding as he vanished into the forest. She was left with a thirst that would fever her dreams and remain unquenched until that *one day* when she saw him again.

She wiped away a stray tear. But her sorrow was softened by a thrill of hope in her heart. She clambered down the stairs, eager to discover the gift her magnificent champion had left for her.

Gellir was eager to get home to Rivenloch.

It wasn't that he disliked Castle Darragh. It was exciting to train warriors who admired him. Men who didn't scoff at the fact he was only seventeen summers old. Not even a proper knight yet. Warriors who welcomed his instruction. Who worked hard to improve. And it had been rewarding to know that in just a few short months, he'd molded Laird Dougal's clansmen into a respectable fighting force.

But he missed his brothers, Brand and Ian. He missed Hew and Adam, his oldest cousins. And he missed the challenge of sparring with knights who could actually best him.

Aside from the fierce Laird Dougal, none of Darragh's men could put up the kind of fight he liked. A fight that made his heart race. Fired his blood. Imbued him with a healthy fear for his life.

The remote Westlanders simply didn't face the kind of battles Gellir had grown up with at the Borders. Where he lived, war was a way of life. Gellir may have taught them the skills to hold off an English army. But the Darragh clan weren't likely to tussle with more than an occasional band of Highland reivers.

Indeed, Gellir feared if he lingered much longer in the

peaceful, boring, impressionable Westland, he'd grow fat and lazy, inclined to rest on his laurels.

Already he was treated like a paragon among men. Dogged by packs of wee lads who wanted to be just like him.

Wee lads weren't the only ones hanging on his every word. Following him about like orphaned pups. That sweet-faced, redheaded maidservant Merraid was never far away. Gazing at him with adoring eyes and a dreamy smile.

He'd been kind to the lass, of course. Chivalry had always come as naturally to him as breathing. In the great battle to save Castle Darragh, he'd comforted her when a brute had broken her nose. He'd protected her from villains who sought to have their way with her. He may have even given her a harmless, celebratory kiss or two in the heat of victory.

Afterward, she'd brought him breakfast every morn. Made sure his armor was always polished. Listened to his strategies for war. Bandaged his battle nicks.

In turn, he'd given her his protection. When lads gaped at her, Gellir barked at them to mind their eyes. When drunken sots snapped at her to fill their cup, he poured ale over their soused heads.

She'd worshipped him like a hero. And he'd become like a big brother to her.

Bright and clever for her age, Merraid was full of spirit and courage. A hard worker, willing to learn and eager to please. It would be a lucky lad who won the heart of such a loyal and loving lass.

But Gellir was not that lad. He had no time for courting. No patience for the sundry tasks it required. Writing verse. Picking flowers. Extolling virtues. He was far too loyal to his first love—warfare—to take a serious interest in a lass. Any lass.

His cousin Hew was the sort to heap spontaneous praises upon every damsel who caught his eye. But "Grim Gellir," as Hew called him, was uninterested in practicing his charms.

Especially on a fiery-haired, freckle-faced, wide-eyed wisp of a maidservant with whom he could have no possible honorable intentions.

As far as *dis*honorable intentions... Other lads his age might wave their flags and cast their seed about indiscriminately. But Gellir would never compromise a woman's virtue. Not even a maidservant's.

He was the son of the Laird of Rivenloch. Namesake of his noble Viking grandfather.

When the time came for him to be shackled to a wife, it would be to one of the king's choosing. She would be the daughter of a laird. Or a widow with valuable property. Or a nobleman's sister from a land with which the king wished to form an alliance.

It didn't matter to Gellir.

His path was clear. He might have to wed. But he was a warrior at heart.

Who needed a woman in his bed? He was perfectly content with a sword in his hand and a horse between his knees.

Maybe for lads like his cousin Hew, happiness came in the arms of a pleasing wife. A woman with a bonnie face and childbearing hips. But for Gellir, the prospect of bairns...

He blinked as a comical image careened through his head. A wild horde of children with Merraid's orange hair and blue eyes. Wee beasts running loose through the halls of Rivenloch. Wreaking havoc. Sowing chaos.

He shuddered, curling his lip in a combination of amusement and horror.

He'd father his own brood one day. It was his duty, after all. But his progeny would possess his discipline. His decorum. His dark hair and serious gray eyes.

Merraid's eyes weren't serious. Not at all. They sparkled with frivolous joy. Irreverent ideas. Clear and blue as a summer sky, they were disruptive, disturbing, distracting.

Her tresses were distracting as well. Startling, like a marigold in a field of violets. Full of unruly curls. It had been a surprise how soft to the touch they were the first time he kissed her brow during the battle for Darragh.

That vivid memory suddenly struck his heart like a bolt fired from a bow. Why would that occur to him now?

A strange prickling along his shoulders made him turn around to cast one final glance toward Castle Darragh.

Even at this distance, her bright pennon of long, loose hair was unmistakable. Merraid was watching him leave. He shook his head and smiled to himself. Of course she was.

In truth, he was going to miss the lass.

He waved at her, wondering who the funny wee maidservant would obsess over when he was gone.

It didn't matter. Aye, it was dangerous for a young lass to wear her heart on her sleeve the way Merraid did. But he'd tasked his cousin Lady Feiyan with looking after the hapless maid in his absence. Feiyan would keep her safe enough.

One day the right lad—a lad deserving of her sweet nature, her quick wit, and her unreserved devotion—would come along to claim her hand.

With that assurance, he nodded a silent farewell. He steered his mount and his mind toward Rivenloch. And he completely forgot about the wee lass with the orange hair.

For four years at least.

# CHAPTER 1

**Spring 1160**

O ne day had arrived. Merraid's champion, Sir Gellir
Cameliard of Rivenloch, was at long last returning
to Darragh.

Fifteen-year-old Merraid would have been elated.

Nineteen-year-old Merraid was not.

She was mightily peeved.

The knave couldn't have chosen a worse time.

Even the measured movements of the *taijiquan*—the
morning ritual of martial arts Lady Feiyan had taught her,
the ritual Merraid currently performed atop the western
wall walk—couldn't calm her ire.

She bent her knees and slowly circled her arms with
as much grace as she could muster. But her mind roiled
with exasperation. With an angry puff that made fog in the
chill air, she blew back the tendril of fiery hair that kept
dripping down over her brow.

Why now? Why, after four years of avoiding Castle
Darragh, had Gellir chosen to return at this particular
moment?

Four years ago, Merraid would have given Gellir everything. Her heart. Her body. Her soul. But that had been

once upon a time. When she was a young and foolish lass.

How she'd raced to the courtyard on the day Gellir left to find the gift he'd given her. She'd discovered Lady Feiyan waiting for her, empty-handed. Gellir's gift, the lady said, was protection in his absence. The lady intended to train Merraid in combat.

At first, she'd been confused. Protection? Did Gellir think she was a child? Completely helpless? Or was it something else?

In the end, she convinced herself it was a sign of his devotion to her. He'd come from a clan full of warrior lasses, after all. For Gellir, such a gift was surely the greatest expression of love a Rivenloch man could bestow.

He must be readying her to join his clan. Making certain she was worthy of the Rivenloch name. Once she was brought up in the ways of a warrior lass, he'd return to claim her as his own.

Her heart full of promise, she'd thrown herself into training. Mirroring Lady Feiyan's movements. Following her intellectual pursuits. Learning to read and write and do sums. Molding herself into the kind of woman Gellir could respect and admire. A woman like his cousin Feiyan. Fierce. Brave. Educated. Independent.

When he came back, she meant to impress him with her accomplishments.

But he never came back.

In that first year, she'd been so sure she'd see him before Yuletide. After all, over the magical summer they'd spent together, every time a lusty lad looked at her sideways, Gellir had charged to her rescue. Surely he'd return to be sure his ladylove was safe.

When he didn't appear, Merraid decided it was due to his turning eighteen and preparing to be officially knighted. No doubt he was preoccupied with earning his spurs.

In the year following, when he still didn't return, she figured it was because he was fighting. Defending the border, which Lady Feiyan grumbled was ever shifting at the whim of King Malcolm.

In the third year, it was clear he'd become singularly focused on his reputation. Obsessed with winning a name for himself on the tournament field.

At that, he'd succeeded. Sir Gellir Cameliard of Rivenloch's prowess in the lists had become the stuff of legends.

Merraid had heard the tales. Everyone had. News of his latest exploits reached the castle every fortnight, it seemed. The magnificent son of Rivenloch was undefeated. In every tournament in the past year, he'd emerged as champion.

There were some saying Grim Gellir was the greatest warrior who'd ever lived.

There were rumors the king might reward him with his own Border holding. Land. A castle. A wife.

It was those rumors that awakened Merraid to the harsh truth. And it felt like a hard slap across the face. After years of pining, Merraid realized Gellir wasn't coming back for her. He'd never meant to. He probably didn't even remember her.

A common maidservant like Merraid had no possible future with the son of a laird. A tournament champion. A noble warrior. She'd been daft to ever believe that.

She wasn't daft now. She'd come to her senses. Listened to reason instead of her heart. And to her surprise, the surrender to the truth had come as a relief. It seemed the chains binding her heart had been broken.

So now that she saw the future more clearly...now that she was beginning to find her own path forward...now that she'd scrubbed his image from her mind as thoroughly as she scoured soot from the hearth...

*Now* he was returning to Darragh.

She sighed, staring across the silver-blue firth with its white-tipped waves. A pair of gulls circled in the sky.

His timing was deplorable.

Merraid had practiced her combat skills all winter. She meant to compete for the first time in Darragh's spring tournament. In secret, of course. A maidservant couldn't legitimately enter a tournament.

She'd come up with an elaborate plan. She'd disguise herself as a youth. Persuade a scribe to forge papers of nobility. If she proved herself in the lists, perhaps Lady Feiyan would let her join the fighting force of Darragh.

But now there would *be* no spring tournament. And it was all Gellir's fault. Lady Feiyan had delayed the competition. Instead, she'd arranged a clan feast in honor of her illustrious cousin. A celebration for the hero returning home from battle.

Merraid tried to quiet the frustration simmering inside her. She brought her hands together, palm to palm. She gazed out at the sea. Drew in a deep breath of crisp, cleansing air. Finished the *taijiquan*.

In a way, she owed Gellir her thanks, even if he'd all but abandoned her. She would never have learned warfare at all were it not for his gift of training. She certainly wouldn't have acquired the abilities to enter a tournament.

That training had proved useful in strengthening her body. Giving her confidence. Balancing her temper—most of the time. Best of all, Feiyan's martial arts made her able to defend herself.

In the past year, she'd had to do more of that. Some men assumed that, as a woman grown and a lowly servant, Merraid was theirs for the taking.

They rarely made that mistake twice.

Now she had an arsenal of skills with which to guard her virtue. Skills that would have made her a shining star in the tournament.

She sighed. Turning away from the firth, she pulled her tucked skirts out of her belt. She shivered them back into place. Then she hurried down the stairs.

With Gellir's retinue arriving, it would be a busy day. She was eager to get an early start. She was also impatient to catch a glimpse of Gellir. Despite her irritation with him, she couldn't help but wonder... Had his youthful good looks matured into manly proportions? Had he grown taller? Larger? Did battle scars riddle his handsome face? Was his countenance as grim as they claimed?

Much could change in four years. She smiled as she thought about the awkward, starry-eyed innocent lass he'd waved to as he'd ridden off to Rivenloch. There was little left of that Merraid. She wondered what he'd think of her now.

Stiff from the long journey, Gellir and his men were glad to finally arrive at Darragh. They dismounted and handed their horses off to a pair of stable lads.

Young Campbell, now sporting a downy beard, approached to greet Gellir. He had apparently been promoted to Master of the Stable. "Good to see ye again, sir!"

"Campbell." Gellir nodded. "How's Urramach?"

Long ago, Laird Dougal had been forced to abandon the noble black steed. It was Gellir who had purchased Urramach and returned the animal as a wedding gift.

"Still runnin' like the wind," Campbell said with a grin.

Gellir nodded. Laird Dougal said Urramach was too skittish for battle. But he was a demon for speed.

"Cousin!" Feiyan hurried forward to meet him. Fresh-faced and heavy with her second child, she looped her arm through his to guide him across the yard. Marriage and motherhood had imparted a wise glimmer to her gray eyes. "'Tis been far too long."

19

"Where's my nephew?" He had yet to meet Feiyan's three-year-old son.

"Och, staying with the Ferguson clan for the spring. He's found a fast friend in the laird's firstborn. But what news from Rivenloch?"

He shrugged and furrowed his brows. "Seven new babes in the clan since winter. A minor skirmish with Firthgate. Looks to be a good year for salmon." He wasn't quite ready to discuss the dilemma that called him to his cousin's castle. "What about you?"

"Staying busy," she said with a chuckle. She absently rubbed one hand over her swollen belly as she gestured to the workers around them.

The courtyard buzzed with activity, proof of her efficiency as the lady of the keep. Maidservants scurried past with baskets full of fragrant bannocks. Sweaty blacksmiths melted ore on a great forge. Laundresses transported bundles of fresh-washed linens. Woodworkers shaving trees into planks stood ankle-deep in curls of oak.

"You know," Feiyan confided, jostling him with her elbow, "they're calling you the finest knight in the world."

Gellir grunted in reply. In truth, he was growing bored of battles that granted him gold and glory, but little else. Even the craftsmen around him seemed to have more purpose than he did. Still, he'd rather deal with the drudgery of the tournament circuit than the herculean task he now faced.

She pinched his arm in irritation and murmured, "I was looking forward to seeing you do battle. Why did Laird Deirdre bid me delay the tournament? Was she afraid one of my trusty knights would best you?"

They both knew that was unlikely. Feiyan's men were stouthearted. But they were hardly equal to a Rivenloch warrior. He gave her a derisive snort.

She gave his arm a punishing punch for that snort.

"Oaf." Then she arched a brow. "Come now. Confess. What's going on? Why have you come?"

"Since when do I need an excuse to visit my dear cousin?"

She narrowed sly eyes. "Since you're missing *several* lucrative spring tournaments to be here."

He sighed. She was right.

"I'm...biding time," he told her.

"Biding time?" She laughed. "You? When have you ever been willing to idle away hours you could be fighting?"

She was a fine one to tease him about fighting. She'd spent most of her childhood at the heels of her mother's ancient instructor Sung Li, practicing combat from the Orient.

Now, however, as the lady of a castle, Feiyan was more concerned with keeping the peace. Beside the courtyard well, a pair of wee lads clouted each other with sticks. She barked their names sharply. Sent them away in opposite directions.

Without missing a step, she asked, "So why do you need to bide time?"

Gellir supposed there was no point in beating around the bush. He muttered under his breath, "The king may be hunting down a bride for me."

"What?" Feiyan stopped abruptly. She faced him with raised brows that quickly lowered in a frown. "Wait. That's a *bad* thing? You don't *want* a bride?"

"Of course I want a bride." He moved out of the way as a woman herded a flock of geese past them. "Just...not now."

Feiyan gave him a look that would freeze mist. "Gellir. You're one and twenty. You're a man of means. From a clan loyal to the crown. How long did you expect the king to wait?"

"'Tisn't that."

21

"Then what is it?"

Gellir scanned the courtyard for gossips. When he was sure no one was listening, he confided in a murmur, "I'm sure you know King Malcolm has been rather... friendly... with the English of late."

She nodded and arched a disapproving brow. "He's ceded a good deal of Scottish land to Henry."

"And aided the English against the French."

"The siege at Toulouse."

"Aye."

Gellir scowled. For once, he was grateful the Rivenloch clan was currently defending the border. Not fighting alongside the king. The Rivenlochs were loyal subjects, to be sure. But for King Malcolm to join forces with England, their arch enemy, against their long-time ally France? It was ill-conceived and dangerous.

There were some who claimed the king had formed the alliance purely for vanity. Young Malcolm liked to brag about the fact he'd been knighted at Toulouse last spring by King Henry himself.

"What does this have to do with you?" Feiyan asked.

"The king may be looking to strengthen that alliance."

"Strengthen it?"

"With marriages."

She gasped in realization. "He might wed you to an Englishwoman?"

He nodded.

She let out a slow whistle. "'Twould be a travesty. The Rivenlochs have held the English at bay for generations. Protecting Scotland and the crown."

"Exactly."

"A Sassenach wife," she said with a shudder. "We can't allow that. You'll hide here at Darragh."

Gellir scowled. *Hiding* was exactly what it felt like. A shameful, cowardly act. He didn't like it one bit. But under the circumstances, he couldn't afford to call undue attention to himself.

She quietly voiced his thoughts. "Roving across the countryside. Winning every tournament. Your name and your exploits have surely reached the king's ear. We don't want to draw his attention here."

"Right. Which is why I need to lie low. And why the tournament must be delayed."

"But what will you do? You can't hide here forever."

He grimaced at her use of that reprehensible word again.

"Sooner or later," she said, "the king will recall there's an eligible bachelor in the Rivenloch clan."

"Two."

"Two?"

"Hew was sent away as well. He's staying at a castle betwixt here and Glasgow." Laird Deirdre had sent their cousin Hew to a remote spot. A place where none could hear his hotheaded bellows of rage over the ludicrous possibility of marriage to an English lass.

Feiyan stiffened. Her brow creased with worry. "What of Adam?"

"Your brother should be safe enough," he assured her. "He's young. Besides, he can always make himself invisible."

Adam was a master of disguise. Able to disappear in plain sight. Or impersonate royalty. Traveling with Gellir, he'd once feigned to be the king's right hand man.

"But then what?" she wanted to know. "Will you just wait? And hope the king's fascination with the English fades?"

"Nay. 'Tis worse than that."

"Worse?"

Gellir stopped before the doors of the great hall. He took a deep breath and let it out again. Steeling his

23

expression to grim determination. It was the expression he donned before challenging an opponent in lethal combat.

"Laird Deirdre has commanded me to secure a bride. Before the king does."

For a moment, Feiyan didn't speak, waiting for him to continue. "Is that all?"

He frowned. "What do you mean, is that all?"

"You just have to...find a bride?"

His scowl deepened. "'Tis a grave quest."

She fought back a grin tugging at her lips. "Is it?"

He straightened, towering and glowering down at her. "Do not make light of my situation."

Despite his foreboding scowl, she burst into uncontrollable giggles.

"You find my quest amusing?" he demanded.

"'Tis hardly a quest," she said, "when half of Scotland is in love with you."

That was nonsense.

He cursed and turned on his heel. But as he stalked away from her, headed to the armory, looking for a fight, Feiyan's mocking laughter echoed in his ears.

Perhaps crossing swords with one of Darragh's warriors would temper his aggravation with her.

The instant he stepped into the armory, he was welcomed with cheers and claps on the back. These were men he'd trained four years ago. They gathered round, begging him for tales of his tournament victories. What honors he'd won. Which challengers he'd defeated.

Primed to do battle, Gellir had no interest in singing his own praises. But he supposed he should oblige them. It was his duty as a champion, after all, to inspire others.

Urged on by the insistent young knights, he planted one foot on the bench, crossed his arms over his knee, and began to regale them with his adventures.

A half dozen stories in, the men's rapt eyes shone with

dreams of glory. They pleaded for more. Gellir was feeling better already. Less ashamed. More self-assured. Less of a fugitive. More of a hero.

Besides, he told himself, it was a good thing he did for the men of Darragh. He remembered how rousing a knight's tales of courage could be. Especially to unseasoned warrior lads.

He told the tale of how he'd fought a French knight at Stirling for a full hour. How the knight finally fell to the ground, exhausted. Then he related the story of his unlikely triumph in Edinburgh after he broke his blade mid-battle. Then he gave his account of the Roxburgh melee, where he singlehandedly took down five swordsmen.

After several stories, his throat began to grow dry.

From the corner of his eye, between the gathered men, he spotted the swish of a servant's faded woad-blue skirt.

"Fetch me an ale, lass, will you?" he called out. "All this blathering has left me parched." Then he turned his attention back to the warriors. "As I was saying... There I was. Knocked to my hands and knees. My sword just out of reach. And there stood the Moor, looming over me like a mighty oak. But then I thought to myself, oaks are meant to be felled, aye? So I picked up my shield in both hands," he said, miming his actions, "and, swinging it like an axe, I—"

He froze as the men parted, revealing the most beautiful serving lass he'd ever seen. Wordless and breathless, he could only stare at her with his arms aloft, ready to vanquish the imaginary Moor.

The maid's lush coppery locks were swept back into a braid that fell seductively over one shoulder. Her lips were rosy temptation. Her breasts swelled above her linen shift like two soft loaves of rising bread.

She sauntered forward with a seductive smile. Her hips moved with a sinuous grace that stopped his breath and roused the beast in his braies.

His foot suddenly slipped off the bench and hit the ground with a thud.

"Good morn, Sir Gellir," she purred. "'Tis been a long while."

Who was this vision? And how did she know him?

He narrowed his eyes at her face. Her eyes sparkled like blue crystals. A frisson of recognition suddenly stirred his memory. "Merraid?"

Like a magic incantation, reciting her name released a torrent of memories. Memories he hadn't recalled in years.

The battle for Darragh. The wee orange-haired waif sneaking him into the castle. Rescuing him from the dank gaol beneath the keep. Bringing him his sword so he could join the fray. Waving goodbye from the parapet.

"Ye *do* remember me," she said, a twinkle in her eyes.

But this was not the Merraid he remembered—the funny-looking, freckle-faced lass with the marigold hair who hung on his every word.

This was a beautiful woman with tempting curves. A dangerous woman who could wrap him around her finger. Leave him speechless. Make him forget his thoughts. Rattle his world. And steal his soul.


Merraid had been watching Gellir from the shadows of the armory for nigh an hour. At first sight, she'd felt stunned, as if she'd been struck on the helm by a war club. Her heart fluttered. Her breath caught. A girlish blush warmed her cheeks.

He was even more handsome than she remembered. He'd grown several inches and broadened at the shoulders. His voice was deeper, his face seasoned with manhood.

For a long, delicious moment, passion gushed through her veins. Desire blossomed in her heart. Lust bloomed betwixt her legs.

Then she gave herself a sobering shake. She no longer had designs on Gellir of Rivenloch. The days of foolish yearning for her hero's return were gone.

Inside, Merraid was not the same awkward lass. And by the way he gazed at her now—his mouth agape, his nostrils flaring, his eyes smoldering—he saw that as well. He could no longer dismiss her as an infatuated maidservant worshiping at his feet. Indeed, it seemed he didn't quite know what to make of her.

As for Merraid, she was still peeved at him for appropriating her tournament. And hearing his lofty tales—injected with equal amounts of stirring bravado and feigned humility—made her roll her eyes several times.

A season of uncontested triumph and glory had obviously gone to his head. What self-assured, swell-headed Gellir needed most was someone to humble him. Someone who remembered the beardless lad he'd once been. Someone to knock him off his high horse. To remind him that even the mighty could fall.

Merraid turned up the corner of her mouth. She could do that.

It was time to bring the braying braggart back down to earth.

She planted her hands on her hips and faced him with a confident smile. "If I do fetch ye an ale, sirrah," she promised in a voice that was hardly that of a lovelorn lass, "'twill be to pour it o'er your swollen head."

He coughed in disbelief. "What?"

The Darragh knights gaped at her as if she were mad.

"For nigh half an hour," she said, "I've listened to your boasts and brags. Heard all about how ye knocked this knight from his saddle. And flung that warrior's sword across the field. How ye outwitted Sir Clever. And outlasted Laird Tireless. How ye pummeled Sir Forget-Me-Not into oblivion."

Gellir was struck dumb.

"But 'tis all talk," she said. "Why not put your mettle where your mouth is? What good are words without deeds? Tales are only tales. The proof is on the field o' battle. Wouldn't ye agree?"

The lads silenced, awaiting his response with bated breath.

She expected Gellir to stammer out an excuse. To refuse the challenge. Instead, she was surprised by the glittering star that sparkled in the stormy sky of his eyes.

The wily devil had been hoping for this. A challenge. A dare.

Of course, she thought. How could she have believed otherwise? Gellir was a warrior. A person of action, not words. He didn't want to talk about fighting. He wanted to fight. He had always preferred to speak with his sword.

"I do agree," he announced. "So who will fight me?"

Merraid knew no one would pick up the gauntlet of "the greatest warrior who'd ever lived." To do so would guarantee a humiliating loss. Perhaps even worse, it might incur the magnificent Gellir's disappointment.

"Come on, lads," he coaxed. "Surely someone thinks they can best me."

The men shuffled uncomfortably.

"Is there no one up to the task?" he asked.

The warriors murmured amongst themselves.

Merraid smirked.

Only one person was not afraid of losing.

Only one person didn't crave the high-and-mighty Gellir's approval.

Hers was a bold decision. Daring. Brazen. All the things that would have mortified fifteen-year-old Merraid.

But it was time Gellir met the saucy woman she'd become. The Merraid who could keep scoundrels at bay with a smoldering glance. Who could cut knaves to pieces with a sharp tongue. Who could lay villains flat on their backs with a single blow.

Summoning the courage of the Rivenloch warrior maid who had taught her all she knew, Merraid smiled and said, "I'll fight ye."

# CHAPTER 2

"**Y**ou?" Gellir scoffed. "Don't be ridiculous. I won't fight a..."

Merraid lifted a brow. Was he going to say "a woman"? Surely, coming from a clan full of female warriors, he didn't dare.

"A maidservant," he finished.

"Why not?" she said, scornfully crossing her arms. "Are ye afraid?"

The Darragh warriors scoffed at the notion.

"Hardly," he said.

"Then why not fight me?"

"What will you fight with?" he asked. "A broom and a mop bucket?"

The warriors laughed again.

Merraid did not. She could actually do quite a bit of damage with a broom and a mop bucket. "If ye like. Ye choose the weapon."

He smirked.

The men waited to see what he would do.

"Fine," he finally agreed with smug assurance. "Then I choose *no* weapon."

She lowered her eyes, amused. He thought he was being clever. But she didn't need a weapon. She *was* a weapon.

"You choose the time and place," he said. "I'm sure

you'll want a few days to prepare." *And to reconsider and back out of the challenge* was his unspoken thought.

But she had no intention of backing out. She smiled. "Here. And now."

He blinked.

"Ooh," cooed the men, eagerly scrambling out of the way to make room for the fight to come.

Gellir let out his breath on a whistle. "Are you sure you want to do this?" he warned. "I don't want to hurt you."

"Ye won't," she said, widening her stance, bending her knees, raising her arms. "Have ye forgotten the gift ye gave me when ye left?"

"Gift?" He furrowed his brows. Clearly he *had* forgotten.

"The promise ye extracted from Lady Feiyan?" she prompted.

"I asked her to look after you."

It was Merraid's turn to blink. "Look after me?" She lowered her hands. "Is that what ye said?"

"You were young and vulnerable," he explained. "'Twas the least I could do, knowing I was returning to Rivenloch and leaving you defenseless."

Merraid was mildly vexed. So Gellir had never meant to mold her into a warrior maid at all. It had been Lady Feiyan who had decided Merraid should learn how to defend her*self*.

On the other hand, she had no right to be angry. Lady Feiyan may not have followed Gellir's wishes exactly. But because of her, Merraid had become strong, stealthy, capable, independent.

"Well, I'm not defenseless now," she said, making her hands into loose fists before her.

Reluctance twisted his mouth. He obviously thought she was at a serious disadvantage. And it went against his sense of chivalry to wage an uneven battle. So he did the noble thing. Facing her, he stood with his arms at his sides.

"Fine," he said. "I'll give you the honor of the first blow. But see you take care. I don't want you to bruise your lovely knuck-"

Before he could even finish the word, she twisted sideways and snapped her foot into his chest, knocking him forcefully backwards.

Gellir hadn't been caught off guard in a long time.

Unprepared, he staggered back into a group of men, who caught him and levered him upright again.

"Well done," he said with a cough, rubbing his chest and chiding himself. "I should have seen that coming."

"Now ye," she said, lowering her arms.

He scowled. He couldn't attack a defenseless lass. It wasn't that he hadn't fought a woman before. He'd been raised by a warrior maid of Rivenloch, after all. But the womenfolk of his clan were daughters of Vikings. This lass was half his size. How could he bear to scratch that delicate face? Bruise that luscious body?

He came at her with slow, careful, exaggerated movements. He aimed to catch her gently about the waist, giving her time to work up a defense.

She didn't need time. She immediately struck both of his arms aside with the heels of her hands and clenched his tabard in her fists. Turning, she thrust into him with her right hip, nudging him off-balance. Using momentum, she levered him up. Rolled him over her shoulder. And dropped him onto his back on the flagstones.

The men gasped. But he was more thunderstruck than hurt. He gazed up at her from the armory floor. How had she done that?

She smirked down at him, clapping the finished task from her hands and quipping, "Och, how the mighty have fallen."

By the Saints, she was breathtaking. Literally. She'd knocked the wind out of him.

But she was also beautiful. Even when she mocked him. Her hair looked like an angel's bright halo, at odds with her devilish grin.

"M'laird," a young knight urged. "Ye've got to get up."

The others joined in.

"Ye can't let her get away with that."

"Show her who's the best warrior in all Scotland."

"Ye'd best watch out, lass. He's a champion. He could break your neck like a twig."

"Go on, m'laird. Don't let a maidservant get the best o' ye."

Gellir gave his head a shake. He rolled up to his feet. This time when he faced her, he wouldn't misjudge her.

The men shouted encouragements as he circled her like a wolf stalking a lamb, searching for a weakness.

Her knees were flexed. Her hands were loose. Her breath was calm. Her gaze was locked on him.

The instant she blinked, he charged forward, planning to gather her in his arms.

Somehow she was ready for him. She deftly stepped aside, and he sailed past her, crashing painfully into the armory grinding wheel. The men groaned at the dull thud he made as he struck the rock. Even the maidservant sucked in a sympathetic breath.

But he didn't need her sympathy, no matter how his shoulder throbbed. He pinned her with a smug expression. Half grimace. Half grin. Then he lunged forward, trying again to trap the wee minx.

She instantly captured his forearms and pulled him aside. Sweeping a foot behind his heels, she knocked him off his feet. She eased him down to the flagstone floor, like a nursemaid putting a babe to bed.

Gellir should have been furious. A vicious slam to the

ground was one thing. A gentle, controlled drop like this was a bald insult.

But he was too fascinated for anger.

She released his arms and smugly held a hand out to help him up.

He took her hand. Her palm was warm within his, triggering another pleasant memory—making their way through the dark of the sea cave, holding her small hand in his. It had been warm. Soft. Trusting.

For an instant, they exchanged tender glances. He savored the sensation.

Then he narrowed his eyes and gave her hand a sudden, brisk tug.

He was surprised she fell for the trick. It was one of Feiyan's favorites. But in that instant of lusty distraction, she'd let down her guard.

Pulled forward, she landed in a graceless sprawl atop his body.

The men cheered. Part of him gloated in triumph. The other part realized he'd made a serious tactical error.

This close to her, he could see astonishment in her sky-blue eyes. Count each delicate freckle standing out in blushing relief from her pale cheeks. Feel her velvety breath upon his face.

If he eased an inch closer, he'd be able to capture her plump, rosy lips between his own. And he had an unruly urge to do just that.

But that wasn't the worst of it. She no longer seemed like that little sister he'd once thought her to be. Her breasts were soft and pliant where they were crushed against his chest. Her legs entwined with his in a sensual tangle. And despite the audience and the inappropriate situation, his loins immediately began to respond to the wicked, warm weight of a woman pressing down upon them.

Quickly, before she could detect the bulge in his braies, he rolled her over onto her back, trapping her between his arms.

The men crowed and whistled over his manly triumph.

But when he looked into Merraid's eyes, triumph wasn't what he felt. Not at all.

The brave maidservant had challenged him when no one else would. She'd been unafraid to put him in his place. Fierce and fearless, she didn't care a whit about his reputation or his status or how many tournaments he'd won. She treated him as an equal.

Unfortunately, while he was reflecting upon that, the sneaky wench used her knee to give him a swift jab in the ballocks.

He yelped and recoiled at once. Rolling off of her onto his back, he clutched his offended manhood with a groan. Now he remembered why he hated fighting women.

The men winced, making empathetic grunts.

Merraid popped up to her feet and dusted off her skirts. As he grimaced in pain, she crouched beside him, arching a brow and whispering, "He who tries to fly among the gods gets burned by the sun."

He narrowed smoldering eyes up at her. He probably deserved that. But he wasn't quite ready to forgive her.

"Sung Li?" he guessed, croaking. It sounded like something Feiyan's teacher—that wizened old relic from the Orient—would say.

"Nay," she replied. "Icarus's da."

He sighed. Of course. Icarus. The cocky Greek knave who had thought himself invincible and had fallen to his death.

Maybe she was right. In some ways, success had spoiled Gellir. Flush from a year of praise and glory in the lists, he'd forgotten how to be humble. Maybe a sobering slap in the face—or a punishing knee to the groin—was just the thing to remind him he was a mere mortal.

35

Still, it was unpleasant to receive such comeuppance from his cousin's maidservant. One who could quote Greek mythology.

By their grumbling, the Darragh warriors were just as disgruntled as he was. But their remarks, mostly aimed at Merraid for what they perceived as dirty brawling, made him realize her precarious position. Whether by fair means or foul, the men's appointed champion had fallen. They would naturally seek retribution for that slight. Perceiving Merraid as the source of their affront, they would target her for insult. Or worse.

He couldn't allow her to suffer for what was essentially his failing. It was up to him to frame her battle for the victory it was.


Merraid expected the sweetness of her conquest to be short-lived. As Feiyan had warned her long ago—and experience had verified—men hated to be bested by women.

The slurs muttered around her were familiar and unsurprising. A few of the Darragh warriors had met their own demise at her hands. They were doubtless relieved to be in good company. She expected Gellir would have a few choice names to call her as well.

Which was why she was taken aback when his brow softened. His stormy gray eyes melted into fog. And the corner of his mouth lifted in a conspiratorial grin.

"Well executed, m'lady," he said, applauding her even while wincing from the blow she'd inflicted. "See, lads? You should never let your guard down. Always be prepared for the unexpected. The noblest lion can still be lamed by a rose with thorns."

She was so shocked by his praise, she didn't even hesitate when he reached out a hand for her assistance.

This time he didn't betray her trust. He allowed her to help him to his feet.

"Let this be a lesson to you all," he continued, still clinging to her hand. "Never underestimate an opponent."

While Merraid stood in open-mouthed wonder, he raised her hand to his lips, and brushed her fingers with a gentle kiss.

"I thank you for the challenge, m'lady."

The men of Darragh, baffled at first, soon joined in with cheers.

Merraid was left speechless. The back of her hand tingled where his lips had touched it. Her cheeks flushed. Her heart throbbed. For a moment, she was reduced to that naïve fifteen-year-old lass again. Stumbling over her words. Blushing with desire. Overwhelmed by passionate yearning.

She thought she'd left that lovelorn lass behind. She was so certain her heart, once broken, was now safely encased in steel plate.

Yet here it was, pounding again for Gellir of Rivenloch with the force of an armorer's hammer. Softening under the twinkling light of his amused eyes and proud smile.

"Well, why are you all standing about?" he called out to the men. "Someone bring the lady an ale!"

A cup was passed forward through the crowd. He handed it to her. Then he went down on one knee before her. "Go on then, champion. Pour it o'er my head."

She had no intention of doing any such thing. Not now. Not since he'd shown her such knightly courtesy.

He may have arrived four years too late. Basking in the light of his grand achievements. Heralded by tales of unmatched glory.

But she knew now that Gellir Camelliard was the very same young man who'd won her heart all that time ago. Humble. Brave. Chivalrous. Self-sacrificing. He possessed the lofty trappings of a hero. But under them, he was still the simple lad whose only wish was to use his sword arm. Defeating evil. Defending honor.

She thought she'd locked her affections for him away. But God help her, they spilled forth from her heart like an uncorked cask of wine. Preserved. Mellowed. Aged to a complex and delicious elixir. One with the power to render her helplessly drunk on his love.

Her fingers trembled on the cup. Her face glowed with admiration. Her pulse raced. Her heart melted like butter.

Somewhere in the back of her thoughts came a whisper of warning.

She couldn't let this happen.

She dared not fall in love with him.

Nothing good could come of it.

They lived in different worlds.

He'd already broken her heart once. She couldn't let it happen again.

Yet the tender feelings were all too familiar and completely unavoidable.

As he knelt before her, her eyes swept over his shaggy hair—the dark color of wet wood, and his swarthy face—shaded with manly stubble, and lingered on his wry mouth.

Then she made the mistake of letting her attention drift up to his steadfast, beautiful, honest gray eyes.

She was lost at once. Falling into the deep, silvery pool of his gaze. Drowning in the strong currents of temptation, where nothing could save her.

For a moment, she considered extinguishing the flames of longing by pouring the ale over her own head.

"Merraid!" came a bellow from the back of the crowd. Tom the kitchen lad made his way forward. "Merraid!"

Someone needed her. She quickly downed half the cup and wiped her mouth with the back of her hand. "Aye?"

"Ye're needed in the hall. The cook says ye're to help set up the feast for Sir Gell-..." He stopped abruptly when he noticed Gellir at her feet. Unsure what to make of the situation, he backed away, muttering, "Ye're to come at once."

For Merraid, the command was a clear and painful reminder. Sir Gellir might be kneeling before her at the moment. But that was only for show. He was a nobleman. The son of a powerful laird. And she was but a servant in his cousin's household.

With a quick bob of her head, she pressed the half-drained cup back into his hands. Then she picked up her skirts and fled the armory.

Gellir watched her go. He still couldn't believe the dazzling beauty was Merraid. Gone was the timid, scrawny, wide-eyed maidservant. She'd grown into a woman who was lovely. Self-assured. And undeniably tempting.

He was unaccustomed to noticing such things. In the last two years afield, he'd enjoyed a sampling of lasses—from lowly camp followers to titled ladies. They swooned over him. Showered him with tournament favors. Begged for his affection.

None had turned his head.

He'd been too centered on improving his skills in the lists to care about the ladies who filled the spectator stands.

To be distracted by a woman was a novel experience for him.

One of the men nudged him from his thoughts. "Ye let her win, aye? I mean, the greatest warrior in all o' Scotland couldn't be defeated by a wisp of a lass."

Gellir looked up. All the men were staring at him, waiting for his answer with a mixture of hope and disappointment.

"Of course," he replied. He wasn't altogether certain that was true. But if he'd unleashed the full measure of his power from the very first, he might have squashed her like a flea. "Trouncing her would have been discourteous, aye? Chivalry is a warrior's guiding principle. A knight's foremost duty is to protect the helpless. Never forget that."

Merraid was far from helpless, as he'd discovered. But the men seemed satisfied with his answer.

"M'laird?" A servant entered the armory with a bob of his head. "Lady Feiyan is requestin' your company."

Gellir left the men musing over his advice as he followed the servant up the stairs to his cousin's solar.

Feiyan's chamber looked more like a private armory than a lady's sitting room. There were the requisite chairs and even a plate of sweetmeats on the table. But on the wall opposite the east-facing window hung a collection of exotic weapons from the Orient. Curved blades. Steel stars. Sharpened forks.

"You summoned me?" He sauntered toward the dish of sweetmeats and popped one into his mouth.

Feiyan frowned as she scanned him from head to toe. "You haven't bathed yet."

"I've been busy," he said, chewing the sugary treat. "By the way, when I asked you to look after Merraid, I didn't mean for you to teach her to fight."

Feiyan shrugged. "I don't have time to watch over every maidservant. 'Twas the best way to protect her."

He grunted.

She waved away his conversation. "Look, I've invited a guest for supper. You should look your best."

He stopped chewing and lowered his brows. "A guest?"

"A marriage prospect."

He choked on the sweetmeat. Between coughs, he ground out, "Well, you've certainly wasted no time."

She clapped him on the back, which did absolutely no

good. "There's no time to waste. Who knows how soon the king will make his move? You should secure a wife as soon as possible."

He glowered. But he supposed she was right. "Who is this prospect?"

"Her name is Lady Forveleth. She's the daughter of Laird Aengus mac Donald of Maybole, just south of here. She's quite lovely. Of an appropriate age. According to Dame Joan, she—"

"Dame Joan?"

"Joan is my...well...she knows everything. She keeps me abreast of the town gossip."

Gellir sighed. Women were curious, scheming creatures.

He ambled to the hearth and picked up the poker to jab the glowing embers to life.

"Anyway, Joan said if you don't care for Forveleth, she can send word to Lady Godit. Lady Godit is unfortunately pox-scarred and a bit long in the tooth. But she's newly widowed and comes with a considerable fortune."

"Which I don't need."

"Which you don't need. But there's no point in turning it away if you like her well enough. Then, if Lady Godit is unappealing, Joan knows of a third—"

"There's no need for a third," he said, replacing the poker. "I'll take the first willing maid."

Feiyan scoffed at that. "Don't be ridiculous. You're going to be chained to the lass for a lifetime. 'Tis bad enough you have to make a swift decision. At least examine a few options."

"I've always known mine would be an arranged marriage. I expect no more. As long as the lass can give me bairns, it doesn't much matter what she looks like or how much coin she has."

Feiyan let out a simmering sigh of frustration. "I swear you'd take more care in choosing a sword than a wife."

"Is that so strange?" He shrugged. "My very *life* relies upon a good sword. One that stands ready to defend me. Sharp. Trusty. Strong. True. A tool fitted so well to my hand that I don't know where one ends and the other begins."

"Like a good wife." Feiyan arched a brow.

Gellir arched a brow back at her. Feiyan only thought that because she'd had the luxury of wedding out of love. She and Dougal had a marriage based on mutual respect and affection. They were lucky.

But when you were the firstborn son of a laird and a warrior without peer, your fate was not your own.

"In any event," Feiyan said, "your prospect deserves to meet a bridegroom who doesn't smell like horse sweat. I'll have water heated and a tub brought up. You can bathe here."

After she left, Gellir stared into the fire a long while.

For his cousin's sake, he'd acted nonchalant about the matter of his marriage. He didn't intend to burden her with the responsibility of finding him a wife. But the truth was, even though the eventuality of taking a bride had always been an inevitable part of his life, he suddenly felt as if it had been thrust upon him.

The details had never seemed to matter before. But now that his destiny was fast becoming a reality, he had questions.

What *would* his wife be like? How would she feel about *him?* Would she be sweet and gentle? Or hot-tempered and bitter? Cruel? Or kind? Given to laughter or tears? Clever or dull-witted? And though he'd said it was of little consequence, he had to wonder... What would she look like?

Unbidden, a vision of lush gingery hair, dainty freckles, and sky-blue eyes stole into his mind.

He couldn't help but smile. Merraid might not fit on

Feiyan's list of prospects. But she'd make some man a happy bridegroom indeed.

She was charming and challenging. Spirited. Brave. Beautiful. Who would not wish to be wed to such a lass?

She was also blessed with soft skin. Tresses that tickled his cheek. Full lips that had once yielded to his in a sweet kiss.

He sighed. It was a fool who dwelled on things he couldn't have.

And Gellir was no fool.

All the way to the kitchens, a silent battle raged inside Merraid's head.

She thought her passion for Gellir had grown cold. But a tiny ember must have been glowing inside her all these years, for now she longed to melt into his arms.

He'd shown her the uncommon chivalry and respect she remembered from long ago. He'd accepted his defeat with grace and dignity, humility and honor. And he'd reignited memories of the brave and forthright young warrior she'd once adored.

"Merraid!" the cook barked, startling her from her thoughts. "Linens for the table. And wine. Thyme and rosemary from the garden. Take Swannoc and Ede."

Setting aside for the moment all thoughts of whom the preparations were for, Merraid took refuge in busying herself with the tasks at hand. She brought four dusty-shouldered bottles of French wine from the buttery. Then she snagged the two wee lasses to assist her in arranging linens atop the trestle tables.

But her hopes of distraction were short-lived. Young Swannoc and Ede were bursting with excitement over the guest of honor.

"Did ye see how wide his shoulders are?" Ede whispered as she folded a napkin.

"Aye," Swannoc replied, smoothing the tablecloth. "He's grown since he was here last."

Ede gasped. "Ye remember him from before?"

"Oh aye," Swannoc said. "I was twelve, but I remember him well."

"I was only nine." Ede sighed. "I wish I could have seen Grim Gellir fight for Darragh."

"'Twas brilliant," Swannoc gushed. "He was like lightnin' with his sword and—"

"Less tongue-waggin' and more napkin-foldin', if ye please," Merraid scolded.

They obliged, but it wasn't long before Ede asked, "Do ye remember Sir Gellir, Merraid?"

Before she could answer, Swannoc replied, "Oh aye, Ede. Don't ye know? 'Twas Merraid herself who brought him a sword for the big battle."

"Ye did?" Ede squealed.

"Aye," Merraid admitted, straightening the tablecloth.

"And did ye see him fight?"

"I did."

Ede's eyes lit up. "What was he like?"

"He was..." Fierce. Powerful. Brave. Magnificent. "A good fighter."

Swannoc scoffed. "The men o' Darragh say he could best Laird Dougal."

Ede gasped again and turned to Merraid. "Were ye friends with him then?"

"Aye." They might never have been more than that, but they had definitely been friends.

"So he spoke to ye?"

Again, Swannoc answered. "O' course he did. He looked after Merraid when she got her nose broken."

Ede's mouth went round. "He did?" She clutched a napkin to her chest. "What was he like, Merraid?"

He'd been kind. Gentle. Chivalrous. And self-sacrificing. He'd offered to look after her, even though he would have much preferred to join the battle.

But she wasn't about to tell them all that.

"He wasn't so very grim, if that's what ye want to know."

Ede hid a smile behind the napkin and murmured, "I wish I had a broken nose so he'd look after me." She giggled.

Swannoc smacked her arm. "Put your eyes back in your head," she scolded. "Ye're only half-grown. Besides, he's a noble knight. He has no use for a wee servin' lass like ye."

Merraid's jaw tensed.

Ede pouted. "Ye're a mean old killjoy, Swan."

"Swannoc is right," Merraid told her, snapping a napkin in the air. "'Tis a muddle-headed maid who'd waste her breath makin' such a silly wish."

Merraid's harsh words and the ugly truth might hurt Ede at the moment. But in the end, the lass would be glad she hadn't spent years as Merraid had, feeding an imaginary beast. It was much better to face reality now than to cling to false hope.

Merraid briskly folded the napkin and placed it on the table.

Everything was put in its place now.

The tablecloths.

The napkins.

And the maidservants. *All* of them.

"Fetch your shears, and meet me in the garden," she said. "We need to cut herbs for the cook."

Moments later, crouching beside the thyme, Merraid still had trouble letting go of her own silly wish. With each snip of her shears, she tried to sever her long ago memories of Gellir.

His devotion to her as war blazed around them. Snip.

His protectiveness when he'd confronted her attackers. Snip.

The joy they'd shared when the enemy was defeated. Snip.

His shame when he'd loaned Feiyan his clothing and was forced to stand before Merraid in nothing but his...

"Merraid!"

She jumped, narrowly missing her fingers with the shears.

Ede was running full-tilt toward her, shears in hand.

Swannoc caught Ede by the scruff of the neck. "Don't run with shears, ye ninny."

Rather than slow to a walk, Ede dropped the shears, pulled free, and continued running.

"I have news!"

"News?"

"Aye." Ede relayed her tale in breathless bursts. "I heard Lady Feiyan...and Dame Joan... talkin' about Sir Gellir."

Swannoc came up then and swatted Ede on the back of the head. "Were ye listenin' at doors again?"

Ede elbowed Swannoc in the ribs. "How else am I supposed to find out what's goin' on?"

Swannoc rolled her eyes.

"Anyway," Ede continued, "they said Sir Gellir came to Darragh...for a bride."

The shears drooped in Merraid's fingers.

A bride? At Castle Darragh? She entertained the brief, foolish possibility that Gellir had returned for *her*.

But reason quickly slammed the door in hope's face. That was only the fantasy of an infatuated fifteen-year-old lass. Gellir would marry a noblewoman.

Swannoc held out the shears she'd retrieved for Ede. "He didn't come here for *ye*, Ede, if that's what ye're thinkin'."

Ede snatched the shears from her. "I know that."

Swannoc began cutting sprigs of rosemary. "I wonder who he's marryin'."

Merraid didn't want to think about it. The idea left a bitter taste in her mouth. It was bad enough that Gellir was going to wed. But if it was someone in the Darragh household... If she had to see him arm-in-arm with his bride every day...

"Och, that's the thing, Swan," Ede said. She plopped onto her bottom beside the rosemary. Using both hands, she closed the shears around a tough stem. "He hasn't chosen a wife yet."

"Nay?"

"Nay," Ede confirmed. "Lady Feiyan is sendin' Dame Joan to find him a proper bride."

"What?" Merraid exploded, startling the lasses. "Dame Joan?"

Ede tossed the rosemary stem into Merraid's basket with a shrug. "She's found three ladies so far."

"Three?" Swannoc said, impressed.

Merraid clenched her jaw as she pruned the thyme. Had Gellir just impulsively decided it was time to acquire a wife? And now he was letting the town gossip choose a suitable spouse for him? God's bones! She hoped he took more care when purchasing a blade.

"Aye," said Ede, "and the first one is comin' to supper tonight."

Merraid's breath caught. So soon?

Apparently, Gellir didn't intend to tarry long at Darragh. With Dame Joan setting up a brisk courting schedule, he might well be wed and gone by the end of the sennight.

Maybe that was a good thing. Maybe the sooner he left, the better. Life would go back to normal, and she'd prepare for the deferred tournament. She could banish Gellir of Rivenloch from her thoughts once and for all.

And he could go on his merry way with his new bride. A bride found hastily by the castle wag-tongue.

God's wounds! That was truly disturbing.

She knew she shouldn't care. She couldn't have Gellir herself. So what did it matter who he married?

And yet it troubled her.

She caught her lip under her teeth and placed the cut stems in the basket.

It might not be her affair. But the truth was she liked Gellir. Maybe she couldn't have him as a husband. But she remembered how decent and honorable he'd been, even as a young lad. He'd looked after her. Maybe it was right that she look after him.

She couldn't let him marry so carelessly. With so little forethought.

Her own parents had made that mistake. One reckless roll in the straw had sealed their fate. They'd wedded in a rush when her mother's belly had grown too large to conceal. But theirs had never been a happy marriage. Her ma had driven her da away and then drunk herself to death.

Merraid couldn't let that happen to Gellir.

Gellir needed a wife who appreciated his good qualities. Who loved and admired his gallantry. His devotion. His generosity.

"So who's the first prospect?" Swannoc asked Ede. "Did ye hear?"

"Lady Forveleth," Ede said.

Swannoc's brows shot up. "The daughter o' Laird Aengus?"

"Aye."

Merraid tensed her jaw.

Lady Forveleth was young and attractive. She had lovely brown hair. Fair skin. Big brown eyes. But she was as vapid as a cow.

Surely Gellir would prefer someone with whom he could have meaningful conversation.

Would he be fooled by her looks? Would he be blinded by her beauty? Was he so eager to be wed that he'd overlook her shortcomings?

Merraid furrowed her brow.

As Gellir's friend, she couldn't let him make such a mistake. She couldn't let him be baited into a loveless marriage by a pretty face. She had to warn him.

"Is this enough?" Ede asked abruptly.

Merraid's eyes widened. She hadn't paid heed. The basket was overflowing with herbs. "Och! Aye."

When she stood up, Tom the kitchen lad was loping through the garden toward her. "Are ye finished? The cook is losin' patience."

"Aye," she said, handing him the basket, "here."

"And Merraid," he added over his shoulder as he hurried away with the basket, "Lady Feiyan said ye're to bring bath linens to the solar."

"Fine," she said, handing Swannoc her shears. "Ye two see what ye can find in the way o' berries and boughs to deck the tables."

The lasses scrambled down the garden path. Merraid dusted the dirt from her palms and headed toward the keep.

Ordinarily, Lady Feiyan bathed in the firth. She said the cool sea water was healing and invigorating. Merraid had grown accustomed to dips in the firth as well. But in spring, the water was icy cold. So the lady indulged in warm tub baths in her solar at least twice a sennight. No doubt she wanted to be freshly scrubbed for this evening's feast.

Merraid gathered a stack of linens and three vials of scented oil from the storeroom. Then she rushed upstairs to the lady's solar.

Backing through the solar door, she called out, "Which would ye prefer today, m'lady? Lavender? Rose? Or—"

As she turned toward the tub, the steam rising off the hot water swirled into an obscuring mist. But it wasn't enough to obscure the figure standing by the tub in linen undergarments. Who was definitely *not* Lady Feiyan.

# CHAPTER 3

Gellir expected Will at the door. The burly servant had already made a dozen trips to the solar to bring up buckets of water.

But when he heard Merraid's voice, he turned. She stopped in her tracks. Her eyes went as round as her mouth. The stack of linens teetered, shifting in her arms. Despite her best juggling efforts, they tumbled to the floor. The sound of shattering glass made him grimace. A pungent floral scent permeated the air.

She took a step forward.

"Stay back!" He thrust his hand out in warning.

She recoiled, her eyes widening. *"Ye stay back!"* she replied in a squeak.

"You don't want to cut yourself on broken glass," he explained.

But it wasn't the glass that alarmed her. It was his state of undress. Her mortified gaze flew wildly around the solar, like a trapped bird wondering where to land.

"My apologies for my appearance." He quirked up the corner of his mouth. Four years ago, he'd been reduced to his undergarments in front of this very same lass. "But then I suppose 'tis naught you haven't seen before."

Her brow clouded with misunderstanding. "What's that supposed to mean?" She planted her hands on her hips and lifted her chin. "Do ye think just because I'm a maidservant, I must be accustomed to consortin' with half-naked men?"

"Consort-..." He blinked, astonished. That wasn't what he thought at all. Besides, he doubted Merraid suffered much unwanted male attention, considering that wicked knee-to-the-groin defense of hers. "Nay, I only meant—"

"Because I assure ye I'm not." She narrowed her eyes at him. "I'm as pure as the day I was born, and—"

"I'm not saying you—"

"Anyone who claims otherwise—"

"Hold on, lass."

"Is a lyin' snake of a—"

"I'm saying no such thing."

From the passageway outside came a voice. "Is everythin' all right, sir?" It was Will. "I thought I heard somethin' break."

Merraid's eyes grew wide.

Gellir cleared his throat. "'Tis fine, Will," he called out. "I've got it."

Swiftly—before Will could intrude and start rumors that might compromise her reputation—Gellir swept past Merraid and slammed the door closed.

He should have guessed the maidservant would not take his assertive actions lightly. Mistaking his intentions and believing he meant to trap her in the solar with him, she took a deep breath, preparing to bellow for Will.

He couldn't let her do that.

Throwing caution aside, he lunged forward to clap a hand across her open mouth, holding the back of her head to keep her still and silent.

The minx instantly bit him.

Gasping in recoil, he pulled his tooth-marked hand away and stepped backward. Directly onto a shard of broken glass.

Intense pain shot up through his bare foot. He forgot all about his hand. He sucked a sharp breath between his teeth. Then he hobbled sideways until he could collapse into one of the chairs.

When he lifted his ankle upon his knee, he saw the shard. It protruded about an inch from his heel, like a bloody arrowhead.

The lass gasped when she saw it and grew instantly contrite. "Faith! Let me—"

"Stay back!" he shouted. If she interfered, someone was going to get hurt. He wasn't sure which of them it would be. But he didn't want to take chances.

"That looks nasty," she said.

It did. It also hurt like the devil.

She wrung her hands. "I could—"

"Nay."

"But if ye don't—"

Before she could finish, he wrenched the glass out with a growl. Blood began dripping from the wound.

She shook her head. "Like I was sayin'," she said, picking her way carefully through the broken vials and scattered linens, "if ye don't bandage it straightaway, ye'll bleed all o'er Lady Feiyan's solar."

He frowned, vexed that the state of Feiyan's solar took precedence over his wounded flesh.

She retrieved a length of linen, shaking it to be sure it was free of glass. Then she neared, kneeling carefully before him.

He held out a hand for the cloth.

"I'll do it," she said, slapping his hand away. "Ye'll only make a mess of it."

"Strong words," he grumbled, "coming from a lass who's made a mess of the solar floor." He waved a hand in front of his nose. "Smells like the stews of Edinburgh in here."

"Really?" She wrapped the linen around his foot. "And how would ye know what the stews o' Edinburgh smell like?"

"I've heard tell." He smirked, echoing her words. "As for me, I'm as pure as the day I was born."

She snorted.

That was a lie. It was impossible for a young man to resist the charms of maids who thrust themselves upon him day and night. But he was far less experienced than most believed. It has been long enough that being close to Merraid was causing him to respond in an inappropriate manner.

Once his foot was bandaged, she rose and moved away to salvage the dry linens.

"Woodruff 'tis," she said, wagging the one unbroken vial before uncorking it and pouring a few drops into the water. Then she popped the cork back in and placed the stack of dry linens beside the tub. "Don't expect me to bathe ye," she said. "Ye're a grown man. Ye can bathe yourself."

He chuckled. "Are you always so hospitable?"

She shrugged. "I've learned to keep my distance."

He nodded. "You're afraid you might succumb to temptation?"

"Aye," she replied. "The temptation to hold your head under the water."

That made him grin.

She dragged a chair beside the tub, turning it so it faced away, toward the door. Then she sat down and gestured with a wave of her hand for him to continue.

"Go on. Enjoy your bath. Someone has to stay here and make sure the tournament champion doesn't drown himself."

He was pleased she intended to stay, despite the disconcerting effect she was having on him. Merraid had been a clear-headed lass and a loyal friend. And in this chess game of marriage he was playing against the king, it was good to have an ally.

Merraid was grateful Gellir couldn't see her face as she heard him undress and sink into the water with a sigh of pleasure. Her memory was sharp enough to recall in great detail every inch of Gellir's magnificent body. He might possess battle scars that weren't there before. But he was at the peak of perfection when it came to his manly form.

She dared not think about it too deeply. She was on a mission now. A mission with a serious purpose. She had to save Gellir from himself.

"How well do ye know Lady Forveleth?" she asked him.

"The young woman I'm to sup with?"

"Aye."

"I don't know her at all."

"Well, I do."

"And?"

"Ye won't like her."

He barked out a laugh. "And how do you know that?"

"Well," she allowed, unwilling to outright lie to him, "she *is* bonnie."

"Mm?"

"And sweet."

"Aye?"

"And she has a gentle nature."

"Sounds dreadful," he said dryly.

"And she'll likely give ye lots o' bairns."

He gave an audible shudder. "God forbid."

"But she's goin' to bore ye silly."

"Bore me?" He snickered. "Not if we'll be making lots of bairns."

"I'm serious. She's...like a child."

"Wait." For the first time, he sounded concerned. "How old is she?"

"A few years older than me," she confessed.

He gave a relieved sigh.

"But she thinks like a child," she said. "She has no wit or wisdom."

"I'm not choosing an advisor. I'm only choosing a wife."

"Only?" she said. "Just what do ye think a wife is for?"

"Mostly to appease the king and continue the Rivenloch line."

"That's it?"

"What more is there?"

That angered her enough to make her whip around in the chair. She was only distracted for an instant by the recognition once again that, aye, his body was knightly perfection. Then she railed at him.

"A wife is more than a pawn or a brood mare. A good wife is a helpmate and a counselor. She must manage the keep while her husband is at war. Raise moral, respectful children. Defend her husband's honor. And aye, advise him in uncertain times."

"Where did you hear that?"

"I didn't have to hear it. I see it every day in your own cousin."

He scowled. "That's different. Feiyan is...special."

"Don't ye want your wife to be special as well?"

She glimpsed momentary doubt in his silvery eyes before they flattened and he looked away. "It doesn't matter," he said, running the wet linen over one magnificent arm. "I'll be away fighting the king's battles most of the time anyway. And I can afford a steward and all the nursemaids a wife requires."

His resignation troubled her.

"Ye know, for a fierce warrior, ye're certainly quick to surrender when it comes to betrothal."

"I've learned to choose my battles."

She frowned. So he didn't consider the matter of his bride a worthwhile fight. Bloody hell. If she'd known how detached he'd be about the woman he meant to marry, she wouldn't have wasted time trying to mold herself into the wife she thought he desired.

She turned away so he wouldn't see her hurt and frustration. Damn the Fates! *She* was special. *She* would have made him proud. She would have given him a brood of wee warriors. And she wouldn't have required a steward and nursemaids to raise them. She would have kept him so well entertained, he might have sent someone else to fight the king's battles.

Still, it was foolish to dwell on what could never be.

She was not destined to be Gellir's wife.

But she could still be his friend.

Despite his fierce reputation, Gellir was still very much the kindhearted lad she remembered. Generous and giving. Always thinking of others before himself. Always sacrificing his desires for the greater good.

Such magnanimity had served him well. It had earned him the respect of his clan. The loyalty of his fellow warriors. The gushing adoration of lasses. It was his benevolence to her, a mere servant, that had made Merraid fall in love with him.

But the occasion of his marriage was no time to be altruistic. He deserved better. He deserved the very best. And if he didn't know that, if he couldn't see what an important choice this was, then it was up to her to *make* him see.

"At least promise me ye'll take a look at all the blades in the shop ere ye settle on one," she said.

After a moment, he asked, "Why do you care so much?"

She turned to look at him. His hair was drenched now to the blackest shade of midnight. It curled along the curves of his massive shoulders. His heavy brows were furrowed. Beneath them, his eyes shone as softly as burnished silver. A drop of water trickled slowly down his cheek to kiss the corner of his inviting mouth.

Her breath caught.

*Because I love ye,* she thought.

Instead, she told him, "Someone has to watch your back."

He gave her a one-sided smile that went straight to her nether regions, flooding her with shame and desire.

"Fine," he agreed. "I promise I'll look at all the blades in the shop."

She gave him a brusque nod. Now that she'd secured his vow, she muttered an excuse about serving at the feast and took her leave. There was no point poking the coals of forbidden fire.

For Gellir, the supper dragged on and on. By the third course, he knew Merraid had been right. As the meddling maidservant served smoked haddock to the guests at the high table, she gave him a smug look to *prove* she'd been right.

True to Feiyan's promise, Lady Forveleth was as pretty as a daisy. She had flesh as pale as cream and lush hazelnut-hued tresses. She possessed a musical voice, light and soft. Wide eyes of dark brown. A sunny nature and a bright smile. And as Gellir sat beside her, she touched his forearm with her delicate fingers as if they were old acquaintances.

But already her childlike helplessness was wearing thin.

She waited for Gellir to place her napkin on her lap. To cut her mutton. To beckon a servant to refill her cup. She even expected him to—God help him—feed her from his fingers.

She babbled on to everyone about her jewels and her gowns and her pets until Laird Dougal nearly dozed off.

Then, her eyes twinkling, she leaned toward a very disinterested Feiyan to share a bit of mischievous gossip about her six lady's maids. Six! Gellir wondered wickedly if she had one maid to clean her teeth and another to wipe her arse.

Just as Gellir struggled to stifle a yawn, Merraid bent near to refill his cup, whispering, "Ask her about studyin' Latin."

He straightened. Ah, did the lady possess some intellectual curiosity after all?

He lifted his cup in a salute. *"Mirum est quod discis Latine loqui."*

Forveleth looked at him with the glazed stare of a deer. "I'm sorry. I...oh, is that Latin? Faith, I have such trouble with Latin." She giggled and bent near to confide, "Don't tell my da, but I'm actually havin' a servant take my lessons. What use will I have for Latin anyway? I'm certainly not goin' to be a nun. And I'm sure my husband," she said, coyly dipping her eyes, "will take care of any legal documents that require signin'."

Gellir felt the mutton congeal in his stomach. He gave her a weak smile. Then he took a bracing swallow of wine.

Oblivious to his disappointment, she blathered on about how silly she thought it was for a lady like her to learn skills she could easily hire others to do.

No one contradicted her. But Lady Feiyan's eyes grew cold. And Laird Dougal's fingers tightened on the cup of wine. All of his female kin were well-educated. It was a point of pride that Rivenloch women were as clever as they were fierce.

Gellir needed to turn the conversation before Feiyan throttled the lass. Surely there was some subject at which

Forveleth excelled. Some strength she possessed. Something that made her special.

He dabbed his mouth with his napkin and turned to her. "What would you say your greatest talent is, my lady?"

"Talent?" She wrinkled her nose as if he'd made a jest.

"Aye," said Feiyan, grateful for the change of subject. "Do you hawk? Sew?"

Laird Dougal chimed in. "Sing? Or play draughts?"

Forveleth caught her lip under her teeth and gave her head a little shake. Then a tiny crease appeared between her brows. "I suppose ye might say I've a talent for purchasin'."

"Purchasing?" Gellir asked. Now they were making progress. "So you purchase goods for the castle? Supplies and so forth?" That required careful accounting and skill so as not to create waste.

Her mouth made an "oh" of surprise. "Och, heavens, nay. All those figures and ledgers? I get dizzy just thinkin' about it. Nay, my father has a man who does that. I mean I have a talent for purchasin' goods at the market. Ribbons. Jewels. Scented oils."

His eyes flattened. "I see."

"I can find just the perfect shade o' ribbon to complement my tresses," she proudly gushed, "and I can spot which pendant is the highest quality..."

"And negotiate a reasonable price?" he guessed hopefully.

"Well, my servant does that," she admitted. "But I've managed to acquire quite a collection." She held up her pendant to show him the green cabochon. "'Tis an emerald. Is it not breathtakin'?"

He studied the piece. "Aye." Even more breathtaking if she'd known it was not an emerald, but some kind of glass. Of course, he wouldn't be so crass as to tell her.

He was beginning to realize, however, that marrying

Lady Forveleth would be a disaster. As Merraid had warned him, she had the emotional maturity of a child. What would happen when he marched off to battle, leaving her in charge of the keep? Would she let the stores of food run out? Allow their children to run amok like wild animals? Drain his coffers to purchase a worthless bauble?

How could he wield his sword like a tournament champion, distracted by the fear that his wife might at any moment hand over his castle in exchange for a ribbon in just the perfect shade?

It was a shame. She *was* quite beautiful. Her clan was well off and well respected. She and Gellir, with their complementary natures, even made an attractive couple. He was sun-bronzed, and she was fair. He was grim, and she was sunny. He was clever, and she was...

He shuddered, imagining a life of hand-feeding and coffer-guarding and caring for her as if she were a bairn in tailclouts. How would such a woman ever raise bairns of her own?

He scowled. He wondered if she even knew how they were made. Did she understand the intimacies between a man and a woman? Or would she run screaming from their marriage bed, crying to her maids that Grim Gellir had attacked her with a fleshy dagger?

The longer the evening wore on with music and entertainments, the more morose he became. After supper, Forveleth prattled on, drowning out the lute player. She frowned in confusion over the morality play. She gasped in exaggerated shock when the magician pulled a silk scarf from her sleeve.

All the while, Gellir remained polite. But he grew impatient with her naivete. And his smile grew thin. Each insipid giggle made the muscle of his jaw ache.

Clearly, he'd made a terrible mistake in thinking any lass would suffice for a wife. To be condemned to a woman who grated on his nerves and bored him to tears was unthinkable. How could he face a lifetime of such evenings?

"M'laird, here's the feverfew ye requested."

Gellir startled. It was Merraid. She leaned between him and Lady Forveleth and placed a vial on the table. As she withdrew her hand, she turned to him and added, "For your headache?"

For an instant, he stared mutely at her. Then he saw a conspiratorial glimmer in her sky blue eyes.

"Och. Aye." He pressed his fingers to his temple. "My thanks."

"Och nay, Sir Gellir," Lady Forveleth complained. "Do ye have a headache?"

"Alas, I fear so," he said, silently praising Merraid's genius. "I regret I must leave your sweet company."

Forveleth pursed her mouth in a disappointed pout.

He rose and lifted her hand to press a light kiss to the back of her knuckles. When he looked past her, his cousin Feiyan shot him a glare that could melt steel.

Let her scorch him with her eyes, he thought. Merraid was right. He needed to take more care in selecting a wife. Besides, didn't Feiyan agree? She'd said he should choose carefully as well. And she apparently had a whole host of prospects lined up from which to choose.

Bidding everyone good night, Gellir snapped up the vial of feverfew. He frowned and rubbed his brow once more for effect. He gave Merraid a clandestine wink before he retired in relief to his chamber.


The next morn, though Merraid's body moved easily through the familiar postures of the *taijiquan,* her mind was a hundred miles away. It wasn't the sun warming her. It was the memory of Gellir and his conspiratorial wink.

She swept her arm gradually to the left, as if smoothing the waves atop the sunlit firth.

At least Gellir had recognized Lady Forveleth at once for what she was. A wee lass in a woman's gown. A spoiled child. A loose-tongued bloviator, blithely oblivious to the feelings of others.

But that was only one prospect dodged. There were likely dozens of others.

She performed a deep lunge to the right. Then she twisted slowly toward the sea, bringing her arms together as if collecting all the gulls that circled above the waves.

Dame Joan knew every eligible female in the west of Scotland. No doubt she'd arranged a roster as long as her arm. Who was next on the list?

"There you are!" Lady Feiyan popped her head up from the stairwell, carrying her squirming three-year-old son on her hip.

"M'lady?" Merraid whirled and bobbed a curtsey.

"Sorry to interrupt your *taijiquan.* 'Twill be a busy day. Dame Godit is coming to dine with Gellir. Lady Margaret will go hawking with him in the afternoon. And Lady Affraic will be joining him for supper. I need every free hand I can get."

"Aye, m'lady." She dutifully dipped her gaze. But inside she was seething with outrage. Godit? Margaret? Affraic? Dame Joan's marriage candidates were completely wrong. Bad matches all. Something had to be done.

Feiyan shook her head, muttering, "I wish this marriage matter didn't require such haste." Then she retreated back down the stairs.

Merraid frowned. Why *did* it require such haste? Surely a man of Gellir's renown wasn't desperate. He was young. He was hale. He was rich. Why the rush?

She supposed it made no difference. It was up to her to save him from Dame Joan's prospective brides. And if it had to be done swiftly, she'd redouble her efforts.

She let down her skirts and rolled up her sleeves. It would be a busy day indeed. She had to save Gellir from Dame Joan's prospective brides.


"When you say 'old'..." Gellir said, speaking to Merraid between hacks at the straw-stuffed dummy in the middle of the lists.

As always, he'd arisen at dawn to begin training. An hour before anyone else. So it was a surprise, albeit a pleasant one, when Merraid appeared on the practice field. Her coppery hair had been burnished to gold by the rising sun, her walk brisk and confident, her manner urgent.

"Lady Godit is twice your age," Merraid told him.

He gave her a knowing smile as he swept his sword down. "Do you even know what twice my age is?"

"Forty-two," she said without hesitation.

He blinked, impressed. "You know your numbers?"

"Aye."

"How do you—"

"That's not important. What's important is she's forty-two. Forty-two!"

Gellir scowled, making another downward strike at the dummy's shoulder. That *was* a bit old for a bride.

"She's a widow?" he asked.

"Nay. She's ne'er been wed."

"Never? Why?"

"Men willin' to look past her pox scars are only after her wealth."

He sniffed. "I have no need of wealth." He took a swing at the dummy's head. "And I care naught about scars."

"I know," Merraid said tenderly. "That's what I..." She stopped short of saying *love about you* and kicked at a pebble on the ground. "My point is, at her age, 'tis possible she's beyond bearin' children."

He tightened his grip on the sword. That was a fair point. One of his duties to king and clan was to multiply the Rivenloch ranks.

"So what do you suggest?"

She spoke quietly, avoiding his eyes. "I've heard a marriage may be annulled if the bride proves barren."

"Annulled?" Gellir thought a man might as well drive a sword through a woman's heart. As if to demonstrate, he stabbed his blade into the dummy. "I would ne'er do such a thing."

Merraid's gaze flew to his and softened. "Then perhaps 'tis best to be truthful from the start. Lady Godit will understand."

Gellir nodded. He would be gentle but firm. "Thank you. I'm glad I can rely on your advice."

"O' course," she said. "And while I'm handin' out advice..." A mischievous gleam danced in her eyes. "Ye need to stop clenchin' your left fist when ye're about to strike a downward blow. It gives your intentions away."

His jaw was still open when the saucy minx sauntered away and disappeared beyond the stables.

When he finally regained his balance, he shook his head in wonder. Only Merraid would be so bold as to criticize the technique of a tournament champion.

He spun to strike a downward blow at the dummy and realized to his horror that she was right. He *did* clench his left fist.

# CHAPTER 4

**M**erraid felt sorry for Lady Godit. The lady was obliged to wear a veil over her pockmarked face so as not to offend. She had to guard against suitors who only ingratiated themselves to her for her fortune. All things considered, one would expect her to be a bitter shrew.

But she wasn't. All through dinner, the lady was polite. Calm. Reasonable. She made quiet conversation with Gellir and the others and praised the cook's efforts. Indeed, if she weren't quite so past her prime, Merraid considered she might have made a decent match for Gellir. Not perfect, but suitable.

As Merraid served sweetmeats to the diners, she saw Gellir beckon Godit near. He kissed her hand, never once flinching from her pox-scarred flesh. He murmured in words too soft to hear.

Lady Godit nodded.

He took her hand between his own. As he continued to speak, the lady's shoulders sank.

He reached out then and cupped her cheek through the veil.

She stiffened and looked as if she might pull away.

But he wouldn't let her. Instead, he spoke more

emphatically until she pressed her free hand against her breast, clearly moved by Gellir's words.

Merraid could guess what he was saying. He was telling her she was beautiful despite her scars. He was insisting she was worthy. He was apologizing for his duty to king and clan that prevented him from offering for her hand. He was telling her the truth.

Merraid's throat began to clog with emotion. Gellir was truly the embodiment of chivalry. A perfect knight. Whoever finally won his hand in this contest would be a lucky lady indeed.

The meal finished shortly thereafter. But while she helped to clear the tables, she kept thinking about poor Lady Godit, alone at forty-two. Merraid didn't want to end up like that.

There was plenty of time, she supposed. She was still young.

So was Gellir. Yet he seemed desperate to wed.

Should she worry? Granted, the marriage rules for nobles were much stricter than those for servants. Servants didn't have to consider wealth or clan alliances or childbearing when they chose a mate.

But Merraid wanted bairns. And a husband she could grow old with. A man who would willingly kiss her hand even when it was wrinkled, the way Gellir had kissed Godit's.

As she gathered the last of the linens, she wondered where she would find such a man. Then she shook off the thought like crumbs from a tablecloth. There was no time to waste worrying about her own future. Not while Gellir's was at stake.

She'd been instructed to cut fresh rushes for the mews. Gellir's next prospect, Lady Margaret, had a passion for hawking. But Merraid knew hawking was not all Lady

Margaret had a passion for. She wondered how long it would take Gellir to discover he could never win Margaret's heart.

An hour later, as Merraid approached the mews with her arms full of rushes, she spied Gellir. He was speaking with Raso the mewskeeper. A big hooded gyrfalcon perched on his gloved knuckles.

"Balachmòr will do ye proud, m'lord," Raso said. "He's the oldest, rather tame. But he's still got a good eye and a healthy appetite."

"Perfect. I fear I have little experience with falcons."

"Och," Raso said, spotting Merraid. "Ye've brought the rushes. Good."

Gellir turned to greet her, explaining, "I spent my youth hacking, not hawking."

"Ye'll do fine," she said, curiously charmed by his humble confession. "Balachmòr is a gentleman."

The mewskeeper took the rushes from her and entered the shadowy mews to spread them about. Merraid dusted off her skirts.

Gellir stroked the feathers under Balachmòr's chin. "So what can you tell me about Lady Margaret?"

"She's...lively."

"Lively?"

"Aye, and adventurous. She's loves to hunt and fish."

Gellir nodded. "What else?"

"Horseback ridin'. Archery. Swimmin'."

"So I shall have to train hard to keep her happy?"

Merraid gave him a sad smile. "I'm not sure any man could keep her happy."

"All right," he said with a sigh. "Tell me what's wrong with this one. Is she missing an eye? Does she limp? Is she the size of an ox?"

"Nothin's wrong with her. I just don't think she'll be happy with ye."

He frowned. "I think I've been insulted. You don't think I can keep a woman happy?" He blew gently toward the gyrfalcon's face, making it shiver.

Merraid knew how the bird felt. She was likewise affected by the soft, warm thrill of Gellir's breath upon her cheek. Gellir could certainly keep *her* happy.

"Not this one," she murmured.

"We shall see."

Gellir understood shortly after he was introduced to Lady Margaret what Merraid had been trying to tell him.

Laird Dougal and a small company of fellow falconers were waiting with him by the mews when the lady appeared across the courtyard with her retinue. She was a formidable woman with a bold manner.

When she bellowed out and waved wildly, her manner was so broad and boisterous, he was amazed she didn't startle the peregrine perched on her other hand. Even more amazed when she left her entourage and loped toward them. Her gown snapped and swirled behind her, and she strode as if she longed to be free of her flapping skirts.

*Lively* indeed, as Merraid had said. He couldn't help but wonder if she was as aggressive between the linens. That didn't necessarily seem a bad thing.

"Sir Gellir?" she called out.

Laird Dougal intercepted her with a small company of his nobles, coming between them at the last instant to make the introduction. "Sir Gellir, I'd like ye to meet Lady Margaret."

"My pleasure," the lady said, extending her free hand toward him.

The sudden movement startled Balachmòr. But Gellir managed to keep the gyrfalcon from biting off her fingers.

He pulled the bird out of range and clasped the lady's solid hand in his.

"M'lady?"

She nodded, withdrawing her hand. Then she scanned Dougal's company. "Where's Feiyan? Are ye hidin' your bonnie bride, Dougal?"

His reply was halting. "N-nay. She's...indisposed."

Gellir furrowed his brows. Indisposed? He'd seen Feiyan not an hour ago, fighting a Darragh warrior on the practice field. But perhaps, being with child, she tired easily.

"Indisposed?" Lady Margaret's face fell. "That's a shame. I was hopin' to show her my new glove." She pensively fingered the finely tooled leather beneath her peregrine's talons. "Perhaps later...when we return?"

Laird Dougal looked pained. "Maybe...next time?"

Her eyes dimmed, but she managed a nod. "Please tell her I hope she's feelin' better soon."

"I will."

When she lifted her chin again to face Gellir, she was beaming. But her broad smile couldn't hide the disappointment lingering in her eyes. "Shall we?"

She didn't wait for permission.

"Lead on," Laird Dougal said.

They proceeded out of the keep and toward the cliff of the firth, where seabirds were plentiful. Raso the mewskeeper had told him gyrfalcons like Balachmòr liked to hunt for crabs, and peregrines like Margaret's could take down gulls.

"I must confess," Gellir confided to Margaret as they crossed the sward, "I know little about falconry."

She narrowed her eyes at his gyrfalcon. "I know your bird. 'Tis one o' Feiyan's favorites. Balachmòr is a sweet old man. He'll be a good fit."

Gellir wished he could say as much for Lady Margaret.

But if what Merraid had hinted at and what he was beginning to suspect was true, no husband would ever be a good fit for her. Though she dared not reveal her secret, he guessed her preference was for more feminine company.

Gellir wouldn't breathe a word about it, of course. He was a man of chivalry. He would grant her the same courtesy and kindness he would any prospective bride. Even if he knew he could never be the kind of lover she desired.

She tried. She made a noble effort when they were alone at the cliff's edge.

"Ye do resemble your cousin a bit," she told him with a wistful smile, as if attempting to talk herself into caring for him.

"Ach, the Rivenloch curse," he jested.

"She's lovely, your cousin," she protested. "And ye have the same dark hair..." She turned to study his face. "The same wry mouth. And your eyes..." Heartache flashed like lightning through her gaze, gone as quickly as it had come. When she spoke again, her voice was thick with emotion. "Molten silver, like hers."

Gellir clasped her arm with his free hand. He could see she was trying to convince herself she might grow to like him. He also knew that wouldn't happen.

"But I'll never be Feiyan, aye?" he said in soft understanding.

Startled, she stiffened and looked away, her jaw tight. "I don't know what ye mean."

"I fear you wear your heart on your sleeve, m'lady," he chided.

She glanced up briefly and swiftly changed the subject. "Shall we release them now?"

Before he could answer, she loosened the peregrine's jesses and took off its hood.

He mimicked her actions, freeing his gyrfalcon.

The breeze rising up the cliff's edge ruffled Balachmòr's feathers. Then both birds lifted off together to sail into the updraft. In the space of a breath, they had dwindled into tiny specks high above the shore.

"'Tis amazin', isn't it..." Margaret said, gazing pensively at her falcon, hovering over the firth, "...the way they soar into the heavens like angels?"

"Mm."

"Sometimes I wish I could do that," she murmured. "Leap from the cliff...and just disappear."

Gellir heard the despair in her voice. Yet there was nothing he could say to make things better. Nobles lived in an unwavering world of inflexible rules. Neither of them could wed for love.

"You and I are pawns in a royal game," he said. "It seems neither of us is fated to follow our hearts."

Despite her bravely raised chin, her eyes welled with tears.

While the others were distracted, releasing their falcons, he took her by the shoulder. "Promise me you won't leap from a cliff."

When she turned to him, it was with a mask of courage. An expression she'd probably spent years perfecting. "Never fear," she said. "'Twill pass. It always does." She sniffed back her tears and confided, "Perhaps I'll find a husband who's as disinterested in me as I am in him."

Laird Dougal suddenly cried out, pointing to his falcon. "Look there!" The bird swooped upon on a seagull and was bringing it to ground in a tumbling flurry of wings.

The conversation between Gellir and Margaret was forgotten as everyone's birds began to hunt down prey, stalling and diving as gulls scattered across the sky and crabs skittered along the shore.

But Gellir knew from that moment he could never wed Lady Margaret. Knowing how she felt, he could never force himself upon her. And he would cut off his right hand before he would compel her to bear his children.

Merraid watched from the afternoon shadows of the courtyard wall as Gellir bid Lady Margaret farewell at the mews. She chewed at her lip, wondering what had happened.

Margaret had taken a keen interest in Lady Feiyan of late, more than friendship. The situation was awkward enough that Feiyan was compelled to avoid her to prevent a misunderstanding. Now Merraid feared Margaret might view wedding Gellir as a way to get close to his cousin. No doubt Margaret would be heartbroken to discover her new bridegroom intended to convey her to his home on the east coast of Scotland. A hundred miles from the lady she loved.

Once his gyrfalcon was returned to the mews, Gellir took Lady Margaret's free hand in both of his and spoke to her a long while. Merraid wished she could hear what he was saying.

At last Margaret nodded, and Gellir released her to place his left hand on her shoulder.

Margaret lifted her head proudly.

Gellir extended his right hand.

She extended hers and gave his hand a firm shake.

Then they parted ways.

The moment Margaret disappeared out the gate with her peregrine, Gellir turned and saw Merraid.

As he neared, she emerged from the shade. "How did it go?"

He raised a brow. "I think you know how it went."

"Ye were kind to her."

"You seem surprised."

She shrugged. "There are those who would condemn her."

"She's already condemned," he said. "Condemned to marry someone she cannot love."

Merraid nodded. She didn't mention that he might be in a similar predicament.

"Speaking of condemned," he added, "what's wrong with my next marriage hopeful?"


As she circled the high table at dinner, refilling the guests' cups with mead, Merraid knew full well the risk she was taking. She'd told Gellir she didn't know his next prospect well. But Lady Affraic's servants frequented the market. She'd had an earful from them.

The woman was of a suitable age and not uncomely. Her pleasant features were framed by a curtain of wavy brown hair. Frown lines were etched between her brows. But at the moment she was smiling. And her dark eyes showed intelligence.

She spoke easily with Gellir and his cousins, who seemed glad of her company.

But if the rumors were true, Lady Affraic had a terrible flaw of which Gellir would surely disapprove. And since she had yet to display that flaw, it was up to Merraid to provoke her into exposing it.

She waited until the serving lads brought forth the blancmange to finish the meal. Then, as Merraid refilled Lady Affraic's mead, she surreptitiously caught the edge of the blancmange bowl with the mead bottle, upending it into the lady's lap.

No sooner did the sticky white pudding plop onto Lady Affraic's golden velvet gown than she rose with a shriek of rage and dismay. She seized her pewter cup and flung out her arm, backhanding Merraid forcefully across the brow for her clumsiness.

Merraid saw the blow coming. She could have blocked

it. But she didn't. And from the dizzying pang of the impact, perhaps she should have.

Ignoring the gasps from the other diners at such violence, the lady doubled down on her outrage. Once again, Merraid allowed her to advance. Using the cup like a mailed fist, the woman gave Merraid another cracking punch, this one in the ribs.

Merraid retreated in pain. She staggered to the ground and dropped the mead bottle. The fired clay vessel shattered on the tiles, splashing mead everywhere. She wheezed, cradling her ribs.

"Cease!" Gellir barked, throwing his napkin on the table.

Merraid was sure that would stop her. After all, Lady Affraic was a guest here. Her own servants she might mistreat. But to batter the servants of another was in poor form.

Unfortunately, Affraic didn't seem to care about protocol. Or Gellir's command. She did *not* cease. Still red-faced and gnashing her teeth, she stepped away from the table to continue Merraid's punishment.

Rearing back one vengeful foot, she gave Merraid a vicious kick.

Despite preparing for the blow, the impact to Merraid's already bruised ribs made her groan in torment.

"Cease!" Gellir bellowed again, scraping back the bench as he rose.

It took all Merraid's willpower not to seize the lady's foot and propel her backward across the table. Instead, she let Affraic get in one final kick of revenge to her thigh. Then she curled into a protective ball.

Wasting no more words, Gellir pinned Affraic's arm behind her back. He forced her to drop the pewter cup. It clanged on the floor beside Merraid's head.

"Enough," he growled.

"How dare ye!" Lady Affraic went white with shock. "Unhand me!"

"I don't know how 'tis in your clan," he bit out, "but in Rivenloch, we don't beat the servants."

"Beat?" She blinked. When she realized the hall had gone quiet, she managed a nervous chuckle. "'Twas only a reprimand. No more than she deserved. Did ye see what she did? My gown is ruined."

"She intended you no harm," he insisted, though he gave Merraid an uncertain glance.

"Let me go," the lady hissed between her teeth, trying to wrest free without attracting more attention.

Gellir held her firm. "You will never again raise a hand to a servant."

Her eyes narrowed to simmering slits. "Fine."

When he released her, she couldn't help but mutter, "Spare the rod and spoil the child."

"Servants are not children," Gellir murmured. "But if that's how you feel, I don't think I wish to father any of yours."

Lady Affraic's rasping gasp filled the shocked silence.

An awkward and heated exchange followed between the lady and her hosts. Then Lady Affraic departed with her entourage before anyone got to enjoy the blancmange.

While Feiyan and Dougal bid her a stiff farewell, Gellir came to rescue Merraid.

"Are you all right?" he asked, helping her to her feet.

"I'll live."

Her head was throbbing. She'd have a lump there tomorrow. Her ribs ached when she breathed. And there was probably a sizable bruise where Affraic had kicked her in the thigh. But what hurt most was her pride.

She could have avoided those injuries. It frustrated her to appear so helpless. Especially to Gellir.

Unfortunately, fighting back wouldn't have served her

purpose. But now everyone knew the rumors were true. Lady Affraic was short-tempered and prone to brutality.

"Where are you hurt?" Gellir asked.

"I'm fine," she lied.

"Where are you hurt?" he said more insistently.

"My ribs," she admitted with a grimace. "And my leg. And there's a wee scratch…" She pressed her fingers to her forehead. They came back bloody.

"That's more than a wee scratch."

He snapped up his napkin from the table and tucked it into his belt. Then he wrapped an arm around her and helped her limp across the great hall. He grabbed a pitcher of water from a passing maid as they headed up the stairs.

"So I suppose ye'll be takin' Lady Affraic off your list o' prospects now?" Merraid asked.

He stopped on the step. Realization dawned on his face. "You conniver. You knew."

She stared at him blankly.

"You knew," he repeated. "You spilled the blancmange on purpose."

She feigned surprise. "Why would I spill perfectly good blancmange?"

"To incur her wrath. To make a point."

"And did it?"

He compressed his lips and shook his head in disgust. Then he continued up the steps with her, muttering, "You could have been gravely injured. Why didn't you just tell me she was a hothead?"

"I wasn't sure the rumors were true."

"That's a hell of a way to find out."

They topped the steps and hobbled along the hall. He shouldered open the door of the solar. There he settled her onto a chair by the hearth.

He whipped the rag from his belt and dipped it into the pitcher of water. Then he knelt before her to dab at the cut on her brow.

It stung. She winced.

"Sorry," he murmured.

If he'd known how many injuries she'd incurred in training—a twisted ankle, a slashed arm, a blow that left her senseless for half a day—he wouldn't have fretted over this wee scratch.

On the other hand, she had to admit it was pleasant to have him fretting over her.

This close, she could study the furrow between his brows. The stormy streaks in his gray eyes. The way his nostrils moved with every breath of air. She could smell his intoxicating scent of mead and leather and steel. And she wondered if his lips were still as warm and supple as they'd been all those years ago...

"There's a lump," he told her. "But I don't think 'twill leave a scar."

He'd said the same thing when she'd broken her nose. And he'd been right.

"It seems ye're always mendin' my injuries," she said softly.

His mouth quirked up in a half-smile. "Well, if you weren't so intent on getting them in the first place..."

She smiled back. "'Twas a necessary sacrifice."

"Was it?"

"Someone has to protect ye from schemin' bride-finders."

He chuckled. "I'm a grown man and a tournament champion. I don't think I need protection. Not from a scrap of a lass like you."

She gave him a playful shove that almost knocked him off his haunches. "This scrap of a lass tossed ye onto your arse in the armory."

He grinned. "Fair enough."

He leaned in to inspect his handiwork a final time.

She held her breath. He was inches from her face. Close enough to touch. Close enough to kiss.

As if she'd spoken her thoughts aloud, he lowered his gaze from her brow and looked into her eyes.

They never spoke. But she felt her heart melting as his expression slowly changed from amusement to affection. And then from affection to desire.

In another instant, she might have acted recklessly on her impulse. But the door flew open under Feiyan's hand.

"Merraid, are you all right?" Feiyan demanded, frowning in concern.

"Fine, m'lady."

"Nay, you're not fine," Gellir countered, then turned to his cousin. "That vicious wench could have killed Merraid."

Feiyan knew otherwise. But she said nothing. "I'll see to her injuries. You should get some rest. Three more—better—prospects are arriving on the morrow."

Gellir grumbled at that, but gave them each a salute and made his exit.

"Who are the three, m'lady?" Merraid asked when the door closed.

"Why do you wish to know?" Feiyan said. "So you can dump blancmange on their laps as well?"

Merraid tried—and failed—to look shocked at her accusation.

Feiyan clucked her tongue as she hunkered down to inspect Merraid's brow. "It took a lot of restraint for you to let her pummel you like that."

There was no point in denying it. "One more kick," she admitted, "and I might have fought back."

Feiyan nodded. She pushed Merraid's skirts up to examine her bruised thigh. It was red now. On the morrow it would be black and blue. "So why did you do it? Why did you goad her?"

"To show Gellir her nature." She pushed her skirts back down. "Your cousin doesn't seem the least bit concerned about his bride-to-be, m'lady. I vow he'd take more care in choosin' a weapon."

"Right," Feiyan said. "I told him as much myself."

"I fear he doesn't understand. He could be stuck for the rest o' his life with a nag. Or a wag-tongue. Or a…a servant-beater."

"Exactly."

"Someone has to protect him from himself."

"And that someone would be you?"

Merraid gulped and averted her gaze. "We're…friends. Four years ago, he looked after me. I owe him a debt. I should look after him. He deserves a wife worthy o' his love."

When Merraid looked up again, Feiyan was looking at her with those silvery eyes that sometimes seemed capable of peering into her soul. Then she spoke gently. "Dear Merraid, I know you've always had a soft spot in your heart for my cousin. It must be difficult for you, knowing he's to wed another. But surely you've known all along—"

"Aye, m'lady." Merraid's cheeks burned. "I'm not stupid. I know my place. Sir Gellir is meant for greater things. I only want him to be happy. To choose wisely."

"As do I. Believe me."

They were silent for a long moment.

Then Feiyan said, "You know, Merraid, you're of an age where you should start considering your *own* marriage."

"Me?"

"Aye. Why not? You want a husband and bairns, do you not?" She stroked her belly with fondness.

"Aye." She did. She wanted Gellir's babes. Handsome sons with thick dark hair and iron gray eyes.

"Then let me see to it," Feiyan offered. "While Dame Joan is seeking a bride for Gellir, she might inquire—"

"Nay! Thank ye, m'lady," Merraid said in a rush. "I can find my own bridegroom." Considering the candidates offered to Gellir, the last thing she needed was a ragtag bunch of marriage prospects rounded up by the clan gossip.

"Very well." She stood to give Merraid a final perusal of concern. "You're sure nothing's broken?"

"Aye," she said. Only her heart. "I may have cracked a rib. But 'twill mend with time."

"I'll leave you to heal then. I've had Ede and Swannoc take over your kitchen duties this eve. Meanwhile, think about what I said. You're young and bonnie. The village is full of handsome young lads."

"I'll do that, thank ye, m'lady," Merraid promised, though it was a promise she would find very hard to keep.

# CHAPTER 5

S trolling through the garden, Gellir fought to appear fascinated by Lady Dearbhorgaill, his latest bride offering, as she lectured on the plants they passed. But it was a losing battle. The lady had an intimate knowledge of every characteristic of every species they encountered. And she seemed determined to bestow that information upon him. Whether he wanted it or not.

He did not.

And the problem was made worse by the fact that something far more intriguing was happening just beyond the lady's shoulder.

He nodded as she rattled on about the propagation of lilies. But he let his eyes drift to the couple conversing beneath the apple tree.

The woman was Merraid. She'd removed her usual apron, revealing a plain blue kirtle that clung to her curves in a most provocative way. She was toying with the end of her marigold braid, which draped gracefully over one shoulder. As he watched, she smiled and dipped her eyes in gentle humor at something the man said.

Who was the rogue with her?

Gellir didn't know. But he didn't like him. The scoundrel was standing too close to Merraid. Cocking his blond head with interest. Grinning too broadly. A grin that showed off a row of white teeth that gleamed like a wolf's.

"Don't ye agree?" Lady Dearbhorgaill asked.

Gellir snapped his gaze back. He had no idea what she'd just asked him, so he mumbled in the affirmative.

Lady Dearbhorgaill beamed at him. "Then ye'll build a specularium to accommodate my experiments? How marvelous! I'll be able to study propagation of my lilies all the year round. Even in the chill of winter." She coyly lowered her eyes and amended the request. "That is, if we marry."

"Marry? Well. That is yet to be..."

What was he agreeing to?

And what kind of nonsense was that cocky rogue whispering in Merraid's ear?

Lady Dearbhorgaill clasped her hands dreamily together beneath her chin. "I could spend hours trimming roots, cutting stems, dividing bulbs..."

Why was Merraid not kicking the man in the ballocks for his impropriety? Did she feel somehow threatened by him? Was he threatening her?

He glowered.

Unfortunately, Lady Dearbhorgaill thought his frown was for her.

"O' course I wouldn't spend *all* my hours in the specularium," she said hastily. "I know in the past I've been accused o' bein' too singleminded in my flora pursuits. But I assure ye once we're wed, I'll...make time to be a good wife and mother to—"

"Will you excuse me a moment?"

He didn't wait for her reply. With a deep breath and clenched fists, he edged past Lady Dearbhorgaill. He marched toward Merraid, who was giggling now at whatever the man had said.

"What's going on here?" he bellowed, startling them.

The man's grin instantly disappeared. "N-naught, m'lord."

"Do you have business with this woman?"

The man blinked in confusion. "Business, m'lord?"

Gellir crossed smug arms over his chest. "Do you have any reason at all for engaging with her?"

"I...I..." he stammered.

He thought not. And he was just about to congratulate himself for coming to Merraid's rescue when she snarled and gave him a great shove.

He staggered back. "What the...?"

"Ye overweenin' arse," she spat. "What are ye tryin' to do?"

Both men were stunned. Gellir couldn't even summon up a reply.

"Never mind him, Robbie," she said to the man. "Go on with your tale."

But it was clear from the way Robbie was nervously licking his lips, he wasn't going to go on with his tale. In fact, he was probably going to go home with his tail betwixt his legs. Grim Gellir had that quelling effect on people.

"That's fine," Robbie said with an uneasy smile. "'Twasn't all that interestin' anyway. I'll be seein' ye, Mer-, m'lady." He gave her a brisk nod and hurried out through the garden gate.

At the slam of the gate, Merraid rounded on Gellir. "What was that all about?"

Gellir straightened. "I might ask you the same thing."

"And I'd say 'twas none o' your affair."

"Is that so?" He narrowed his eyes. "I happen to know how men think. I know what they're capable of. And I'm not going to stand idly by while a cunning knave takes advantage—"

"Takes advantage?" she said with a bark of a laugh. "Do ye honestly think I'd let a man take advantage o' me?"

Gellir had tasted firsthand Merraid's ability to defend

herself against attackers. But not all attacks were frontal. Some were insidious. Some came from unexpected quarters. Some came in the form of grinning, handsome youths with silver tongues.

But he couldn't explain that to her, any more than he could describe why he felt particularly protective where she was concerned.

From behind him, a voice called out, "Is everything all right, Gellir?"

He winced. He'd forgotten about Lady Dearbhorgaill. "Aye, m'lady," he called back. "Another moment." Then he turned to Merraid. "You're...my friend. 'Tis my duty—and my honor—to lend you my protection. Do not ask me to abandon chivalry."

He gave her a satisfied nod and strode towards Lady Dearbhorgaill, who was clandestinely digging in the dirt. He was sure he'd won the argument until Merraid called out, "And how do ye think ye'll protect me when ye're back home, a hundred miles from here?"

He stopped in his tracks. That was something he hadn't considered. Something he didn't want to consider.

Lady Dearbhorgaill popped up, her eyes wide. "A hundred miles from here? Is this not your home?"

"'Tis my cousin's keep. I live in the east, in the Lowlands."

"The Lowlands." The lady shuddered. Then she began shaking her head and worrying her hands. "Sweet Mary, that won't do. T'wont do at all, don't ye see? The climate is completely different. All my studies have been in the west. Och nay, I don't see how this can possibly work out." She continued muttering to herself, finally finishing with a sigh. "I thank ye so much for the lovely morn, m'lord," she said, coming forward to offer her hand. "But I fear we are incompatible." She brightened as she thought of a floral comparison. "Like marigolds and cabbage. Perfectly fine plants on their own, but alas..." She shrugged. Then she bustled past him, nodding at Merraid. "So sorry."

She hastened out the gate.


From the moment Merraid enticed Robbie the village chandler to the garden, she'd known exactly what she was doing. Gellir was sure to be there. It was common knowledge that his latest marriage prospect, Lady Dearbhorgaill, was obsessed with plants. In fact, most of the clan referred to her as Lady Daffodil.

She didn't mean to actively interfere, of course. She'd taken Feiyan's warning to heart. She only meant to keep an eye on Gellir.

Her other eye she focused on Robbie, whom she was trying valiantly to imagine as her bridegroom. Robbie was charming and quick-witted. He would make a suitable husband and an entertaining father. But she'd known him since she was a wee lass. She had trouble summoning up any feelings toward him that were more than brotherly.

Perhaps finding a husband would be a more difficult task than she anticipated. As she watched from the corner of her eye, she saw Gellir stifle a yawn while the lady droned on and on about a dead-looking vine. It gave her some satisfaction to note he was bored.

Then she returned her attention to Robbie. He'd always been pleasant to look upon. With straw-bright hair. And dancing blue eyes. He had a clever sense of humor. And an infectious laugh. He never treated her with disrespect, as some of the warriors were wont to do.

Sparks didn't ignite in her heart when he was near. But perhaps that would happen with time. Or maybe it was best to settle for a constant, low-burning hearth instead of the kind of wild fire that flared high and out of control whenever Gellir...

She bit her lip. She wouldn't think about Gellir. She would concentrate on Robbie. Robbie, who was light of heart and bright of smile. Not at all given to dark looks and grim scowls.

That was the moment Gellir suddenly strode up and began intimidating poor Robbie with his infamous frown and harsh inquisition.

Unfortunately, Robbie didn't have the courage to confront Gellir.

Merraid did.

Gellir was being ridiculous. Unreasonable. In fact, if she didn't know better, she'd say he was acting like a jealous suitor.

Of course, that wasn't true. He was only doing what he always did. Defending her when she didn't need it.

She didn't mince words, letting him know.

After Robbie fled and Lady Dearbhorgaill bid Gellir a hasty farewell, they were left alone in the walled garden.

As aggravating as Gellir's attempts to protect her were, in a way Merraid was flattered. Surely his misplaced concern for her stemmed from true friendship. It was the same way she felt about protecting him from unsuitable brides.

Yet she felt something more than friendship when she glanced up at his stormy eyes, still glittering from the thrill of chasing Robbie away. There was danger in them. Danger and intrigue.

She lowered her gaze past his flaring nostrils, settling on his wide, forbidding mouth.

Curiously, she felt no fear. Certain of his chivalry and sure he would do her no harm, Merraid found his dark looks not frightening, but fascinating.

Grim Gellir made a formidable enemy. But he was not *her* enemy. And that made her heart throb with strange excitement.

Surely he felt it too. The crackle of current between them. The intimate history they shared. The powerful attraction that drew them together like iron to a lodestone.

Yet she dared not let herself be drawn to him.

She reluctantly averted her gaze, fixing it on the bare branches of the apple tree.

"She'd probably prefer to cross-breed with a lily," Gellir muttered.

"What?"

"Weren't you going to ask me what I thought of Lady Dearbhorgaill?"

"Not...necessarily."

"Why else did you follow me into the garden?"

"I didn't follow ye."

He gave her a look that said he knew better.

She continued the deception anyway. "I was lookin' for a spot where Robbie and I could have a wee chat."

"A wee chat?" He arched a brow. "And what exactly was this wee chat about?"

She smirked. "Well, 'twasn't about a specularium and propagation."

"I'm serious. What did he want with you?"

She raised her chin. "I told ye 'tisn't your affair."

He looked like he might curse. Instead he demanded tightly, "'Tis my affair when it affects..." He hastily invented, "My cousin. In her condition, shouldn't you be helping her? Don't you have chores to do? What would Feiyan say about you meeting stray men in the garden when you're supposed to be working?"

She smugly crossed her arms. "'Twas Feiyan's idea."

"What?"

"Ye're not the only one of an age to wed, sirrah. Feiyan said I should be lookin' for a match as well."

"You?" he scoffed. "Why?" Then he lowered his brows. "Are you with child?"

She gasped in outrage. Was he serious? She reared back a hand to slap him across the face for his insolence. He caught her wrist before she could complete the blow.

"Forgive me," he murmured, repentant. "That was ill-mannered. I only wondered what the hurry was."

Her skin tingled where his fingers wrapped around her wrist. When she answered, her words came out like a breathy sigh. "I might ask ye the same thing. Brides are rushin' at ye from all quarters. Like blades in a melee."

His eyes dulled to the color of lead. He released her arm. But the heat of his touch lingered deliciously on her flesh.

"'Tis...complicated."

Merraid could tell from the tension in his mouth that he wanted to say more. But he wouldn't. Or couldn't.

She would have pressed him. But he was already stepping away, disconnecting from her.

"I have to go," he said. "I'm to ride with Lady Metylda this afternoon." Then he gave her a sidelong glance. "Is there anything I should know about her?"

She smirked. "Ye mean, does she wish ye to build her a stable so she can study the propagation o' horses?"

He gave her a frosty look.

"Nay," she replied. "I know naught about her."

He nodded and turned to go. Then he paused with his back to her. "Take care, Merraid. Not all men are decent. Find one who will be good to you. Who will treat you with the respect and honor you deserve. Take your time and choose wisely."

He left without waiting for her response. It was just as well. She would have told him to heed his own advice.

"Shall we be a bit naughty?" Lady Metylda asked. She gave Gellir a saucy wink.

They'd crested the hilltop and were far away from

onlookers. Naughty? Did she mean to seduce him here on the grass?

Under different circumstances, he might have considered her offer. She was lovely to look at. Pleasantly plump. Good-natured. And more than willing.

But he wasn't looking for a hilltop tryst. He was looking for a wife.

Apparently, that was not at all what she had in mind. Before he could answer, she let out a whoop and whipped her horse into a blazing, reckless run down the hillside.

"What the devil?"

That wasn't naughty. It was careless. On the uneven slope at that speed, one misstep and her horse would go down and break a leg, throwing her onto the ground or crushing her.

And now she'd given Gellir no choice but to chase after her before she got herself killed.

By some miracle, she made it safely to the foot of the hill, where she stopped and waited for him to arrive.

"'Tis heart-poundin', isn't it," she gushed, "ridin' like the wind?"

Gellir frowned. It was heart-pounding. But not in a good way. "'Tis dangerous."

"Pah!" she said. "Don't be so faint o' heart. What is life without a little danger?"

He bit back a growl. No one called Sir Gellir of Rivenloch faint of heart. But he was no fool. It was one thing to look danger in the face. It was another to invite it into one's home.

"Come on!" she shouted.

Once again she dug her heels into her horse's flanks, spurring the animal to an earth-pummeling run across the grass.

"Hold!" he yelled, even as he urged his horse to catch up to her.

He wished he'd taken Urramach. That steed was as fast as lightning. But he'd never imagined his riding companion would be a fool for speed. The old palfrey he'd borrowed from Feiyan was meant to be ridden for pleasure. It was no match for the demon Lady Metylda was astride.

"Wait!" he called out.

She giggled and called back playfully, "Catch me!"

The distance between them was increasing. His horse was already beginning to tire. But what concerned him was the lady didn't realize was she was headed straight for a bog. Disguised by a lovely green expanse of grass, the ground beneath was perilously soft.

"For the love of God, stop!" he bellowed.

She only laughed.

He urged the poor palfrey to a faster pace until she was wheezing. But still the lady outpaced him. He watched in horror as she flew straight for the marshy ground.

His stern commands did nothing to stop her. Instead, she taunted him by increasing her pace.

His heart collided against his ribs when he saw her horse stagger. And sink. And then he heard her shriek of fear.

"Shite," he muttered, spurring his already lathered horse forward, despite his better judgment.

"Help!" she cried as the horse sank in mud up to its knees.

Now Gellir had to use caution, lest his own horse meet the same fate.

"Help me!"

"I'm coming," he told her as he dismounted, several yards from the edge of the bog.

Her horse bucked and bristled. Lady Metylda squealed as the beast sank another foot and the hem of her gown brushed the mud.

He had to work quickly before the horse panicked in

earnest. He took a few quick paces toward her before his boots were sucked under. Having no other choice, he fell forward onto his belly to distribute his weight more evenly and began crawling on his elbows toward her.

The horse thrashed again, this time dislodging its rider. Lady Metylda slid from the saddle into the bog with a garbled wail.

"Lie flat'!" Gellir barked. "On your belly. Like me."

With a sob of dismay and a grimace of disgust, she did as she was told. "My gown!"

Her gown was the least of her worries. If she didn't follow his commands, she'd slip in over her head. But he didn't want to frighten her with the truth. "I'll buy you a new one," he promised. "Come toward me. Just a few more feet."

She struggled forward through the ooze until she was within reach.

"Take my hand," he said.

He managed to drag her across the muck to firmer ground. But by the time she was able to pull herself out, muddy and bedraggled, her animal was thrashing in panic, sinking deeper and deeper into the bog.

Gellir furrowed his brows and scoured the area. There was no tree nearby. No vine. No rope. Nothing to help pull a horse from a bog.

"Your gown," he said, eyeing the voluminous muddy folds.

"Aye, 'tis ruined."

"Nay, I need it."

"What?"

"Give it to me."

"What?"

"Now. Quick." He beckoned her with his fingers. "Take it off."

"I will not," she said, outraged.

An explanation wasted valuable time. So did gallantry. He drew his dagger, seized her gown, and began to cut, rending the cloth into a long strip to make a rope.

She shrieked at him. Shrill, angry protests that rivaled the panicked squeals of the horse, now sunk to its belly.

Ignoring Lady Metylda's furious curses, Gellir crawled carefully toward the horse again.

It was huffing with panic and fatigue.

"Easy there," he coaxed. "I've come to help you."

The animal seemed to understand. It let him approach. There was just enough room to sneak the doubled and twisted strip of cloth under the horse's barrel and around its legs. The rest would rely on pure strength.

Bracing himself as well as he could against the most solid bank of the bog, he hauled back on the makeshift rope, clucking to the horse to come toward him. Then his feet slipped, and the horse sank back again.

Coiling his fists tighter in the rope, he pulled once more, taking a step backward. This time the horse stepped forward. Another hard tug brought the animal a foot closer. Inch by inch, straining his shoulders and back, Gellir managed to gradually ease the horse out of the mud and finally onto hardened ground.

By the time the horse was safe, Gellir was drenched with sweat and muck, as exhausted as he was relieved. The horse looked traumatized and weary.

Lady Metylda was still spitting in fury.

But Gellir had no patience for her wrath. It was her carelessness that had caused this debacle and nearly cost the life of a good horse.

When he was finally able to struggle to his feet, he seized the reins of her steed. Then he made a decision that eliminated his chances of ever becoming her husband. "We're walking back."

# CHAPTER 6

Lorenzo, the cloth merchant from Florence, was fit, handsome, and unwed. He'd stopped by Castle Darragh with his wares. All the maidservants were agog over his wide smile. His glimmering eyes. His lush, curled hair. And the fashionable attire he wore, which delineated every tempting muscle. When he opened his mouth, no one could resist him. Even Lady Feiyan fell prey to his cunning persuasion, purchasing more than her usual yardage from the charming vendor.

Once Lady Feiyan's coffers were suitably drained, she tasked Merraid with accompanying the merchant to the neighboring villages to introduce him to possible patrons. The other lasses seethed with envy.

Merraid, however, felt nothing for the eye-catching merchant. Certainly Lorenzo knew how to wink and grin. He whispered the right sort of flattery to open ladies' purses. But there was little substance behind his merchant's mask. And as she discovered, ambling beside him along the path leaving the castle, when he wasn't selling something, he had very little to say.

That was fine. It was a lovely day for quiet walking. No late winter rain or early spring showers. Bright and cold and crisp. She didn't mind leaving the castle for the afternoon. It was better than pacing in worry, which she'd been doing since morning.

Where Gellir had gone, she couldn't follow. He was out riding with his next prospective bride. She'd overheard Lady Feiyan telling him the young woman was rather bonnie. But for Merraid, not knowing the bonnie young woman—or where they were, or what was going on—was driving her mad.

Fresh air and a brisk walk would do her good.

The cloth merchant, who'd been so eloquent as he coerced Lady Feiyan into purchasing just a few more ells of sendal, had fallen silent. Perhaps he had to rest his tongue.

She sighed as he hauled his cart of goods over the hard-packed road without a word. No doubt Lady Feiyan thought she was doing Merraid a favor by pairing her with an eligible, handsome, skilled merchant who might whisk her off her feet and into a happy marriage.

The lady would have been more successful trying to turn lead into gold.

As Merraid gazed into the distance where the road forked, she saw a pair of horses being led their way. She narrowed her eyes. The one on the left looked like Feiyan's palfrey. Hadn't that been the horse Gellir had borrowed?

She straightened. Could that be Gellir?

Surely not. The second horse and both travelers were covered head to toe in filth. They looked like gong farmers. Or horse thieves. Or beggars in sore need of a bath.

In any event, they'd likely be welcomed at Darragh. Laird Dougal and Lady Feiyan never turned away a soul in need.

But as the distance closed between them, Merraid felt a tingle of faint recognition. If that wasn't Gellir, it was someone of the same stature, with the same gait.

The second figure appeared to be female. She limped along in a soiled white underdress with mucky, torn rags wrapped around her. She was missing a shoe. And her hair was bedecked with clumps of mud.

When the first traveler raked his hair back with his hand, just like Gellir, Merraid froze with a loud gasp. She startled the cloth merchant, who dropped the handles of his cart.

"What is it, *signorina?*"

"Gellir," she breathed. But what had happened to him?

She strode forward again, fast enough that the cloth merchant, wresting his cart up, had to lope to keep up with her.

When she drew within hearing, she heard Gellir's companion railing at him.

"Ne'er have I been so humiliated!" the woman cried. "I shall tell my father about this, sirrah! He'll make ye pay for my shame." She bit out nastily, "Once he goes to the king, your reputation will be ruined."

Merraid's hackles rose. Whatever had happened, she was certain Gellir was not to blame. There must be a good reason for their filthy appearance. Gellir would sooner cut out his tongue than dishonor a woman.

She was close enough to feel the waves of fury roiling off of the lady. She may have once been bonnie underneath all that slime. Presently her face was contorted in a mask of ugly rage.

As for Gellir, even coated in grime, he looked noble. He trudged along with his head lowered, the weight of silent chivalry resting upon his shoulders.

When he offered no reply to the lady's threats, she continued to harangue him, oblivious to Merraid's approach.

"Ye're a monster, do ye hear me? Forcin' a titled lady to slog half-naked for miles like a bloody maidservant."

Merraid's hands tightened involuntarily into fists at the insult. Her blood grew hot. But she managed to keep a cool head, as she'd been trained to do in combat. After all, losing one's temper was a deadly mistake.

The woman continued. "Ye'll ne'er fight in another tournament, champion," she sneered, "and when I'm through draggin' your name through the mud, no woman will e'er wish be your bride."

That did it. That touched a spark to the tinder of Merraid's temper.

*Merraid* wished to be his bride, even if this shite-mouthed shrew of a wench did not.

"Ye're a vile fiend, Gellir Cameliard. A brute. A devil," the woman spat, punctuating each insult with a punch to his shoulder. "Loathsome. Despicable. Dishonora—"

Livid, Merraid surged forward all at once, intending to shove the abusive woman away from Gellir.

She would have succeeded too. But Gellir flung out an arm and caught her about the waist, pulling her back against his chest.

"Merraid?" he said, astonished to see her. "What are you—"

"Let me go." She strained against his arm. "I'll show this screechin' harpy 'dishonorable.'"

"What did ye call me?" the woman bellowed in shock.

"Ye heard me," Merraid bit out, struggling in Gellir's grip, which was as solid as steel. "Only a monster would sully the good name o' Sir Gellir Cameliard o' Rivenloch."

The woman gasped. "How dare ye insult me! Ye! A peasant! Ye're not fit to wipe my stable lad's arse. Ye're nothin'. Nobody."

Merraid felt Gellir tense. When he spoke, it was in a low growl that rumbled from his chest and sent a shiver up her spine.

"She's twenty times the woman you are, *Lady* Metylda."

Metylda purpled with rage as he continued.

"I vowed I would repay you for the loss of your gown.

I will keep that vow. But you will not return to Castle Darragh. And 'tis only mercy that keeps me from confiscating your mistreated horse."

Metylda's jaw dropped. "Mistreated? I hardly—"

"If you whisper any of this into the ear of the king, I will tell him how you willfully and recklessly risked the life of a fine steed. How you disobeyed my command to stop. How you drove the poor beast into a bog where I narrowly saved it—and you—from drowning. How you complained when the animal was too exhausted to carry you back. And how you disparaged me and mine at length." He snorted. "Indeed, 'twould be best for you if my name never crossed your lips again. My lady."

Merraid's heart had caught on the words "me and mine." Gellir was talking about *her*. Defending her.

She melted against him. He might never love her with the passion of a man for his wife. But his love for her as a friend was fierce.

Metylda was shaking with vitriol. "How do ye expect me to make my way home, lookin' like this?"

Lorenzo, who recognized opportunity when he saw it, dropped the handles of his cart and stepped forward.

"If I may be so bold?" he said. "I think I can be of assistance." He swept the cap from his head with a flourish and a bow. "I am Lorenzo, the celebrated cloth merchant of Firenze, at your service, *signorina.*"

Negotiations began at once to provide Lady Metylda with cloth for a new gown, at exorbitant expense, which would be added to Lady Feiyan's account. There was a tailor in the village who could sew the garment overnight. Metylda was gradually calmed and mollified by Lorenzo, who described in great detail how beautiful she was going to look in a gown of his new yellow silk from Lucca.

But Merraid only half listened.

Though she'd quit fighting him, Gellir still held her

close. Close enough to feel the heat of his chest against her back. Close enough to smell the earthy peat of the bog on him. Close enough to feel his warm breath tickling her neck.

It was unintentional, she was sure. He was only distracted and had forgotten to let her go.

She couldn't help wishing he would forget a while longer.

Gellir should release Merraid. He knew that. She'd calmed now. She wasn't going to attack Lady Metylda.

But somehow he didn't want to.

For the past few miles, Metylda's long litany of curses and threats against him had rolled off his back like rain off a duck. He was accustomed to contempt. He'd probably been cursed as a devil more times than Lucifer himself.

But when she'd called Merraid *nothing* and *nobody*, his iron resolve had cracked.

Merraid was not *nobody*. She was special. Unique. Brilliant.

She didn't deserve that kind of scorn.

And while she was in his arms, he felt like he could protect her from the world and its cruelty.

While she was in his arms, he felt right. As if this was where she belonged. As if he were home.

Still, once Lorenzo left with Lady Metylda, there was no more reason to cling to her. With a sigh of regret, he let her go.

"I got muck all over you," he apologized.

When she turned to him, she looked as shaken and breathless as he felt. She quickly lowered her eyes. "I lost my temper. Sometimes I have a hard time turnin' the other cheek."

He nodded and started down the road again, leading

Feiyan's palfrey. He gave a low whistle. "She certainly was a handful."

"The horse?"

"Lady Metylda."

Merraid fell in beside him. "So ye've crossed her off the bride-to-be list?"

"Definitely." Then he remembered how surprised he'd been to see Merraid. "By the way, how did you come to be on the road?"

He didn't know why he'd asked that. He was fairly certain he knew. Merraid had already made it known she was looking for a husband. His cousin had undoubtedly had a hand in introducing her to eligible candidates like this merchant. A too handsome, suspiciously well-dressed, slick-tongued foreigner who could probably wrap Merraid around his finger with a carefully chosen compliment.

"Lady Feiyan wanted to introduce Lorenzo to the neighboring nobles." She winked. "I cast the wrong lot."

"I doubt that," he said, looking stoically ahead. "He seems the sort of fellow who has ladies drooling about him, hanging on his every word."

Laughter was not the reaction he expected. It was a welcome surprise.

"Is that what ye think o' me?" she asked. "Ye don't know me very well then. It takes more than a bonnie face to turn my head."

"He seemed a man of fair means," he countered.

"Nor am I much moved by wealth."

Her answer pleased him. "Still, you can't deny the fellow's charm."

"He was charmin' enough when there was profit to be made. But his words were as empty as bubbles."

Hearing her wisdom convinced him there was no need to defend her further against the merchant's advances.

But if others tried to take advantage of Merraid's naiveté, her innocence, her good nature...

Gellir intended to protect her, no matter how independent she thought she was. He meant what he said. Merraid was his friend. Part of his clan. *Me and mine.*

As they continued along the road, Merraid mused, "Do ye suppose the two o' them will fall in love on the way to the tailor's?"

"Who? Lady Metylda and Lorenzo?"

"Aye."

He furrowed his brows. "I suppose she could keep him well employed, sewing new gowns every time she rides through a puddle."

"And he could keep her sufficiently flattered well into her dotage."

He snickered. "She did seem to like his flattery."

"And he liked the depth o' her coffers."

"My cousin's coffers," he corrected, "which I'll be replenishing."

She clucked her tongue. "Ye shouldn't have to pay for that gown. Ye said ye tried to warn her. 'Twas her fault she ignored ye."

"True, but I'm a man of my word. And 'tis worth the cost to be rid of her." He scowled. "She ran that poor horse down the hill and straight into the bog, laughing all the while."

"What kind o' person does that?"

"Not the kind of person I wish to wed." He shook his head. "She could have killed that horse. Hell, she could have killed *herself.*"

"She was very lucky ye were there."

Merraid's words haunted him all the way back to the keep.

It was true. Metylda would have drowned if not for him. If he hadn't been there at the right time, the right place...

But he *had* been. He had always gone where he was needed. Always defended the innocent. Always protected the helpless.

Whether she liked it or not, he considered Merraid one of those helpless innocents he was honor-bound to protect. Her father was long gone. She had no brothers. She needed someone like Gellir to make sure she stayed safe. To hold aggressors at bay. To stand as a barrier between lecherous suitors and her virtue. To weed out undesirables from the herd of rutting beasts who would surely come panting after her.

Chivalry was his calling. But what would happen when he returned to Rivenloch? When he could no longer be her knight in shining armor?

He had to make sure Merraid was well cared for, respected, cherished. And there was only one way to do that.

By the time they entered the gates of Darragh and he handed off the horse to Campbell for a thorough scrubbing, he'd made up his mind. He would insist that Feiyan let him screen all courters seeking to woo the maidservant.


"You want to what?" Feiyan stopped sparring and planted her *pang,* her staff from the Orient, in the ground.

Gellir halted as well, lowering his quarterstaff. He ran a hand back through his hair. It was still wet from his brisk dip in the firth to wash off the mud. "'Tis the only way she can be assured of a good match."

"Are you serious?"

"Of course."

She narrowed her eyes at him. "And you don't think that's a wee bit odd? You taking a personal interest in her affairs? The affairs of a maidservant? One you haven't seen in years?"

"I consider her a friend," he argued. "And so do you, I'm sure. If it weren't for Merraid, your husband might not have won back his castle."

"True," she agreed.

She lifted her *pang* again and came at him with a series of five angled blows. For a woman with child, she could move rather swiftly.

He managed to deflect four of them. But the fifth whacked his shoulder. He grimaced and stepped back.

She braced herself and motioned him to attack.

"Look," she said, "Merraid is..." He brought the *pang* straight down. She blocked it. "A grown woman now." He rammed his staff forward. She cast it aside. "Not a child." He sliced sideways toward her neck. She deflected the blow. "She doesn't..." He slipped both hands to the end of the staff and swung it at her head. She ducked under it. "Need your protection."

He waved her forward and held the quarterstaff defensively before him.

"I know how men think," he told her. She thrust toward his throat. He knocked her weapon upward. "The trickery they'll try." She jerked the bottom of the *pang* up, aiming between his legs. He lunged back out of reach. "I just want to keep her..." She advanced with three swift slices in a row. He blocked each one. "Safe."

The fourth blow struck him in the chest, knocking him onto his back in the dust of the yard. She towered over him, the end of her *pang* jammed against his throat.

"Are you sure you don't just 'want to keep her' for yourself?" She arched a brow.

He glowered at her. "God's eyes. Don't be ridiculous. Merraid is only a friend. She's like a little sister," he said, adding pointedly, "or a cousin."

"Are you sure about that?"

"Of course I'm sure."

But was he? Now that Feiyan had introduced that pesky possibility, it took up residence in his head.

Feiyan moved the *pang* from his throat and held out a hand to help him up. "You need to stop spying on each others' suitors to make sure they're good enough."

He grunted, dusting off his tabard.

"You're both adults," she said, retrieving his quarterstaff. "You can make your own decisions." She tossed the weapon to him. He almost missed it. "Neither of you needs protection," she said, resting the *pang* across the back of her neck and draping her hands over its ends. "What you need is to mind your own affairs. *You* need to secure a wife before the king weds you to a Sassenach. And *Merraid* needs to quit looking after you."

Then she left, telling him not to be late for dinner. But her words echoed in his thoughts.

*Looking after him.* Was that what Merraid was doing?

No one ever looked out for Sir Gellir of Rivenloch. No one ever offered. A tournament champion was supposed to be independent. Capable. In control.

Half the time, even he believed it.

But in his heart, he often felt alone, isolated, as if he were responsible for...everything.

That a wee maidservant would care about his happiness and wish to shoulder part of his burden warmed his heart.

Within an hour, however, that lovely warmth faded, replaced by icy dread.

Apparently, his efficient cousin had decided to hasten his selection of a bride by inviting a dozen prospects to dinner at once.


Merraid was aghast. The kitchen staff was expected to accommodate twelve bridal candidates and their guards?

How would they all fit? Did they even have enough victuals this early in spring to feed such a gathering? A feast like this would surely deplete the castle's winter stores.

As the seemingly endless stream of noblewomen arrived, the great hall of Darragh grew as crowded and noisy as the first spring fair. Merraid slipped through lavish gowns of russett velvet and golden sendal, scarlet brocade and azure fustian, like a needle stitching fabric.

The ladies greeted each other with sugary smiles that belied the hostility and competition brewing between them. Merraid wondered what kind of desperate race Gellir was engaged in that he would risk such a melee.

Somehow, they all managed to find a seat. Lady Feiyan had avoided conflict by assigning each lady a special place within view of Gellir.

When dinner began, and Merraid brought the first remove of salat to the high table, her breath caught. The sight of Gellir surrounded by fawning, beautiful women— fluttering their lashes, twittering like sparrows, touching his arm in faux fondness—was almost too much to bear.

Walking back to the castle with him earlier had stirred old feelings in her. Emotions she'd forgotten. Feelings she believed were long gone.

But she was wrong. They must have been there all along. Waiting like a sheathed sword for the right moment to strike.

It couldn't happen at a worse time.

Not only was Gellir unattainable. He was actively pursuing another. Or rather twelve others.

She had to admire Lady Feiyan's thriftiness when it came to time. Clearly the lady meant to force a decision as quickly as possible.

But she wondered again at the rush. A lass like Merraid might be considered a grape shriveled on the vine if she didn't marry young. But a man as desirable as Gellir

Cameliard could command an attractive, young bride well into his dotage.

She placed bowls of salat at the lower tables, where the ladies' guards sat. But she couldn't resist glancing now and then at Gellir and the brood of pigeons cooing around him.

She wasn't jealous. At least that was what she told herself. She was only concerned. Concerned that he might not choose wisely under such pressure.

"Are ye goin' to serve that, lass, or just keep wavin' it under my nose?"

Merraid snapped her gaze back to the table. The guardsman who'd murmured that taunt had a merry green gaze and a lock of black hair that drooped over his brow like the wayward tail of a kitten.

"Sorry," she mumbled, placing the salat before him.

"'Tis quite a spectacle, isn't it?" he asked, nodding toward the high table.

A spectacle. That was a good word for it.

"That's my lady to his left," he confided in a whisper. "Lady Maut." He shook his head sadly. "Frankly, I don't think she has a chance."

What a funny man he was. She gave him a quizzical look. "Why do ye say that?"

"Because the one on his right?" he said, gesturing with a tilt of his head and knocking his kitten-tail lock askew. "She looks like she could wallop the devil out o' Maut."

She gasped in amusement.

He continued, lowering his brows in mock gravity. "But I'm lookin' forward to the first bout between the second and third on his left. They've already exchanged minor blows off the field. Once they enter the real battle arena, fists raised..." He clucked his tongue.

Merraid stifled a laugh.

"The one next to Maut? She looks like a hair-puller. And the one next to her?" He whistled a breath between his teeth. "It would surprise me if she didn't have a habit o' scratchin' out eyes."

In the spirit of his jesting now, Merraid murmured, "What about the one on the end, the wee one?"

"Lady Gormal?" He arched a black brow. "She may look scrawny. But I'll wager she'll knock at least two o' the others flat on their arses."

Merraid fought the mirth twitching at her lips. "Sir, ye should guard your tongue," she warned, glancing around the table at the other ladies' guards.

"Och, them?" He waved to the other men, who waved back. "We're all wagerin' on the outcome o' the melee. Lads, what say ye? Shall we let the bonnie lass in on the wager?"

Merraid blinked.

Two of the guards said aye. Three nodded. One rubbed his hands together. "How much ye want in for, lass?"

When she hesitated, the merry-eyed man added, "A penny should suffice."

Wagering on which prospective bride would win the day was the silliest thing she'd heard in a long while. Silly. And hilarious. And irresistible.

He wiggled his brows. "So are ye in?"

"Absolutely."

Her wager was modest. But that wasn't the point. The point was that the guards understood how ridiculous the competition was. They were having fun at their mistresses' expense.

Of course, a battle never ensued. But by the end of dinner, surrounded by the merrymaking guards and the man who finally introduced himself as Henry, Merraid was sufficiently distracted to forget Gellir for a moment.

# CHAPTER 7

Gellir woke up in a foul mood.

It wasn't just that his cousin had tossed him into the ring of courtship. Like a Roman slave thrown to the lions.

It wasn't from the excess of ale he'd drunk, trying to take the edge off the shrill din of twelve females simultaneously vying for his attention.

It wasn't even from the disappointment of finding something mildly wrong about every one of them.

Nay. What chafed at him was the situation with Merraid. She'd left after dinner with a strange guardsman. One with hair as black as the devil. Eyes full of mischief. And a ready grin that said he enjoyed her company too well.

Gellir had had a strong drive to follow them. But he hadn't. He knew Feiyan was right. It wasn't his concern. Besides, he'd been just drunk enough to mistrust his judgment should his protection of Merraid come to serious blows.

But the sober light of morn hadn't changed his mood one whit. And when he was feeling this way, the only cure for it was fierce battle.

So he donned his mail. Seized his sword and targe from the armory wall. And marched to the practice field with fire in his belly.

The last person he expected to see as he rounded the courtyard wall and headed toward the field was Merraid. He surprised her as well. They both gave a startled gasp.

She clapped a hand to her bosom and giggled. "Gellir. I didn't expect to see ye for hours." She winked. "Ye were right sotted last night."

He tried to ignore the way her creamy skin glowed in the dawn's light. How the sun burnished her hair to lush copper. How her eyes sparkled like blue sapphires. How her laughter washed over him like a gently bubbling stream.

He narrowed his eyes at her and ground out, "I didn't expect to see *you* either. Did he finally wear you out?"

Her smile faded. "What?"

Engaging her was unwise. It wouldn't solve anything. And it would only give him more frustrations to work past on the field.

He tried to pass her.

She blocked his way. "What's that supposed to mean?"

He snorted. "You seemed...busy...last night, fraternizing with that guard."

"Frater-..." Her eyes glittered.

"Chatting," he clarified. "Giggling. Being overly friendly with—"

"I know what fraternizin' means." She gave him a cold glare. "But I'm surprised ye had a moment to notice. You were doin' quite a bit o' fraternizin' yourself."

He tightened his jaw. "At least I didn't leave with any of them."

She blushed. Her mouth fell open, which only increased his sense that she'd done exactly as he feared.

He should drop it. Press her no further. He had more important matters to attend to. And he was in a race against time.

He tried to sidestep her again.

Again she stood in his way.

"Ye know what ye sound like?" she said, crossing her arms. "Ye sound like a jealous husband."

He emitted a chuckle of a scoff. But it sounded forced, even to his own ears. "'Tisn't jealousy."

"Are ye sure?"

"Of course I'm sure," he said, trying to convince himself. "I was swimming in a sea of lovely, willing brides last night. Why would I be jealous?" Just because none of them compared to Merraid...

"Then what is it?"

He struggled with the truth and told her half of it. "I can't stand by and watch you throw away your affections on a man who isn't..."

"Isn't what?" she hissed. "Ye?"

Aye. But he wouldn't tell her that. "Isn't honorable."

"Henry *is* honorable."

Shite. The suitor had a name. Worse, it was the same name as his *other* nemesis, the king of England.

"Did he..." He didn't want to ask. But he had to know. "Did he touch you?"

"Not that 'tis any o' your business, sirrah, but aye. He took my hand and bowed o'er it when we were introduced."

"Did he kiss you?"

Why had he blurted that out? He didn't really want to know. Did he?

"Och aye," she said. "He kissed me and held my hand and took me to the stable and threw me in the hay and swived the holy hell out o' me. Is that what ye want to hear?"

Somehow her sarcasm was lost on him as his vision clouded with a red haze. "I'll break his neck!" he thundered, raising his sword and shield.

She seized his forearms. "Och, for the love o' Peter!

What are ye doin'? Don't be ridiculous. Do ye honestly think I'd let a man do all that?"

He glowered at her, considering her question. Nay, he didn't think she would. But that wasn't always a woman's option.

"What's to stop him?" he asked.

"Me!" she cried, incensed.

He shook off her hands. "You? With what? Fervent pleas and whispered prayers?"

Her eyes seethed with ire. "Have ye forgotten our skirmish in the armory so soon?"

He blinked. What did their skirmish have to do with it? "'Tisn't about that."

"Nay? Men are fore'er misjudgin' me. Always thinkin' they're stronger. Faster. Smarter. I thought ye might be different. I thought ye might understand, bein' from a clan o' warrior women. But ye're no different from the rest, are ye?" She began untying her apron. "So let's settle this once and for aye. I'm goin' to arm myself, and I'll meet ye on the field in a quarter hour."

His head was spinning. How had this escalated so fast? He was concerned about her ability to fend off seducers, not swordsmen. "What?"

"Ye heard me. A quarter hour. And if ye don't show up, I'll call ye coward from the high tower till all the clan knows it."

With that, she snatched off her apron and whirled, marching toward the armory.

Gellir opened his mouth and closed it. How had it come to this? This wasn't the outcome he wanted at all.

First, he didn't want to engage Merraid. At all. He'd rather forget last night happened.

Second, he'd already fought the lass. He hated fighting novices. And to be honest, with the exception of his clanswomen, he *really* hated fighting females. He always had to soften his blows to make sure he didn't harm them. And in his present state, frustrated and feeling the effects of last night's overindulgence, what he really needed most was to crack the devil out of something.

Third, her little challenge was going to garner a lot of attention. From the warriors of Darragh. From Laird Dougal. From his cousin. He was in no mood to be the subject of castle gossip for the next fortnight. It was bad enough that Feiyan had turned his search for a bride into the clan's favorite diversion.

His mood dark, he stormed past the stables. He vaulted over the wattle fence and charged toward the straw-stuffed dummy in the middle of the field. Again and again, he slashed and hacked at the dummy until it was reduced to shreds of canvas and a mound of scattered straw.

Sweat dripped from his brow. His chest heaved with every breath. His muscles trembled.

Now, with his temper calmed and his strength drained, he was ready to do what he had to do.

Lose the fight.

It was the only way to convince any men with designs on Merraid to keep their bloody hands off of her.

Merraid shivered into her chain mail and plucked up her double-sided *jian* and targe. The march to the armory had softened her anger. But she wouldn't back down from her challenge. Gellir didn't believe she could take care of herself? She'd prove him wrong.

Ultimately, of course, she planned to surrender. She'd already defeated Gellir once in front of the Darragh warriors. It was only right she give him a chance to regain his dignity.

But that didn't mean she wouldn't put up a good fight. She'd let him triumph. But she wouldn't make it easy for him. She meant to prove beyond doubt that she didn't need him. She was capable of defending her own honor.

By the time she arrived on the field, a handful of bystanders had gathered at the fence. No wonder. It appeared Gellir had engaged in some sort of vicious battle with the practice dummy. And won. Its innards were strewn across the field. And Gellir looked exhausted from the ordeal.

She entered the field through the gate and swished her blade through the air in salute, garnering the attention of the onlookers, who began mumbling among themselves.

She strode up to what was left of the dummy and tapped her sword against the post. "What's this? A warnin'?"

He gave her a grim smile. "A promise."

She arched a brow at him. "I'll be puttin' up more of a fight than he did."

"We'll see." He brought his blade down in a powerful, threatening slash that whistled through the air. "What do you say? Shall we make it more interesting?"

"More interestin'? How? Wear blindfolds? Tie one hand behind our backs?" She glanced toward the fence. The audience was growing quickly. "Whatever 'tis, ye'd best make it quick. I'm sure ye don't want more witnesses to your defeat."

He snorted. "Let them come. Unless *you're* afraid of utter humiliation." He raised his sword and casually sighted down the blade, checking the edge. "But nay, I meant shall we wager on the outcome?"

"What sort o' wager? Coin?"

"Nay, nothing so crass. What about a wager of honor?"

"Honor? What would ye wager then?"

"If I win, you'll do my bidding for a day. If you win, I'll do yours."

Her bidding? A dozen dangerous ideas flitted uninvited

through her head. Ideas that made the blood rush to her cheeks.

Perhaps it was a good thing she intended to lose.

"Fine," she managed to choke out. She whisked her *jian* through the air, as if to cut the tension between them.

They raised their blades in a brief salute. Then they began circling, their gazes fixed, sizing up the competition. Neither attacked.

After several tense moments, someone in the crowd yelled, "Get on with it!"

Others joined in, calling out, goading them to action.

Finally Gellir made a light thrust forward.

She easily blocked the ineffectual feint and returned with a lazy strike of her own.

Dodging her blow was child's play. He answered with a tap against her shoulder.

She deflected his blade with her targe and punched the shield slowly forward toward his face.

He ducked and thrust his sword from beneath the targe, not quite far enough to do any damage.

The crowd began to grumble. Merraid could see Gellir was intentionally holding back, afraid of hurting her.

Damn him. She was never going to lose this way. Not believably. She had to find a way to provoke him.

Throwing her shoulders back, she blew out a determined breath. "Is that all ye've got?" she scoffed. "I thought ye were the greatest warrior in the world!"

He didn't take the bait. But she saw his jaw tense. "I haven't yet begun."

"What are ye waitin' for?"

"Waiting for you to start."

He meant it as an insult. But she was used to insults. Feiyan had taught her to weather slurs with calm composure.

They began circling again. This time, she took the

offensive, advancing with a series of rapid diagonal slices. They were fast and showy, but light, not lethal. If any of them landed, there would be minimal damage.

He handily deflected them all and echoed her quip. "Is that all *you've* got?"

Merraid chuckled. This was going to take longer than she expected. "Hardly."

He came at her almost before she could finish the word. Not with his sword, but with unexpected punches of his targe. He moved from right to left, back and forth, forcing her to retreat.

He might have ultimately pinned her against the fence. But she ducked under the last blow and rolled forward. When she came up, her sword was aimed at his unprotected side.

Resisting her natural stabbing instincts, she pretended to trip and stumbled onto her knees.

Somehow, he tripped over her. In the next moment, he fell onto his back.

The onlookers hooted in disapproval. No one liked to watch a pair of clumsy combatants.

Merraid swore under her breath. She'd hoped to make this a quick battle. The longer it took, the bigger the audience would be. She still intended to let Gellir win. But she didn't want the entire clan to see her lose. She most especially didn't want Lady Feiyan to witness her defeat and disgrace.

Gellir muttered a curse. Damn the lass. What was taking so long? He'd fought Merraid before. She was a competent warrior. She could have gotten the best of him several times now. Yet she'd tripped over her own feet, obliging him to commit his own blunder lest he put her at a disadvantage.

Losing intentionally was turning out to be far more difficult than winning.

He'd have to rile her up somehow. Goad her into more aggressive action that would make her victory believable.

He popped up to his feet and offered his hand to her.

She slapped it away and scrambled up by herself.

He murmured, "We don't have to do this, Merraid. I have no wish to humiliate you in front of the whole clan."

Her jaw tightened. "What makes ye think ye'll win, sirrah?"

He shrugged. "'Tis inevitable. I'm a man. I'm stronger. Bigger. Swifter."

That did it. Her eyes blazed. "Ye think so?"

She answered with a volley of attacks that were so fast and fierce, he barely had time to defend himself. But when he finally found his footing again, he replied in kind. His blade clanged against her targe a dozen times before she slipped out of his reach and spun round, smacking him on the arse with the flat of her blade.

The onlookers' laughter made the blood rush in his ears. He meant to let Merraid win. He didn't mean to let her embarrass him.

Two could play at that game. He swung high with his sword, forcing her to raise her shield. Then he swept his targe low, knocking her off her feet and onto her backside.

This time he joined in the crowd's merriment.

He was still mid-laugh when she rocked back and sprang to her feet with acrobatic ease, giving him a hard shove that sent him staggering backwards.

Colliding with the fence kept him from falling. But when she rushed toward him—the point of her sword aimed at his heart—his eyes went wide. He was only narrowly able to deflect a skewering.

She crashed into him, and they grappled in that

awkward position for a moment, too close for swordplay, before he was able to push her away.

He expelled a harsh breath. The pesky maidservant had tried to run him through. This was no friendly battle. It was clear now that Feiyan had molded Merraid into an expert warrior.

He still meant to throw the fight. He still meant to send a message to the men of the clan. But he certainly didn't want to die for it.

Perhaps he didn't have to temper his blows so much after all. He meant what he'd said. Men were naturally bigger and stronger. But they weren't quite as conniving as women. If he wanted to avoid being slain, he'd have to use more clever tactics.

He faced Merraid again, who waited with her targe raised and sword ready. But before he could begin his next attack, he heard a bellow from the crowd.

"Hey now! What's goin' on here?"

It was Laird Dougal. The last man he wished to see.

"'Tis a friendly fight, my laird," he called out in assurance.

"Does she know that?" Laird Dougal jested.

The onlookers chuckled, and from the corner of his eye, he saw Merraid's gaze narrow. No doubt she'd heard her share of jests about the lowly maidservant who thought she was a noble warrior. It had to hurt, no matter how hardened she was to their ridicule. Their scorn made him even more determined to let her win.

To her, he murmured, "Pay no heed to them. Don't hold back. If I can't defend myself, I don't deserve the title of knight."

She seemed empowered by his words. She straightened her shoulders and bent her knees in readiness.

They engaged again. This time he unleashed his full strength. Their swords clashed and sparked and clanged.

With his long reach and superior power, he pressed her gradually back to the center of the field. He was in control now. Now he could manipulate the battle.

"Gellir Cameliard of Rivenloch!"

He jerked in surprise. It was Feiyan. In a foul mood.

"What the devil do you think you're doing?" she demanded.

He was afraid of that. In his absence, he'd asked his cousin to keep Merraid safe. Now here he was, sparring with her himself.

"'Twas my challenge, m'lady," Merraid called back.

"And you agreed?" Feiyan asked him in disapproval.

"I saw no harm in it," he replied. It was true enough. He didn't intend to hurt Merraid. He intended to lose.

Feiyan shook her head. "Try not to injure him, Merraid," she called out. "He has brides to impress."

Feiyan's confidence in her skills should have pleased Merraid. But Merraid's shoulders lowered, almost imperceptibly. Her feelings were clear. Gellir was an important noble with a bright future. Merraid was only a maid-servant. What happened to her was of little consequence.

"To hell with my brides," he murmured. "Let's give them a show, shall we?"

"Nay, she's right," Merraid said. "I should never have asked ye to—"

Gellir didn't let her finish. He lunged forward, swinging his blade in a low arc.

Quick on her feet, Merraid leaped up over the sword, spun in the air, and landed with a blind backward stab. He gasped and turned sideways. Her blade missed his belly by an inch.

She dove forward, rolling away from him.

He charged after her, raising his blade.

She whipped around and ran at him with the ferocity of a wild boar.

Fearful she might spit herself on his upraised sword, he lifted it out of the way. At the last moment, she slid into the dirt before him, skidding between his legs in a cloud of dust.

He pivoted to face her. To his surprise, she was already on her feet again, less than a foot in front of him.

Without warning, she punched him in the chin with her targe.

Hard.

# CHAPTER 8

Merraid felt the impact of the shivering targe as it struck Gellir, rocking his chin back. His head wobbled unsteadily on his neck. His eyes seemed to lose focus. He staggered onto one knee, dropping his sword.

"Och!" she cried. She hadn't meant to hit him that hard. "Are ye all right?"

He tried to answer. His words were muffled. "Och, aye, lassssssssss. Ahm fi—"

Then he fell back to the ground with a thud.

"Gellir!" Merraid cried, dropping to her knees beside him.

She'd never meant to hurt him. Bloody hell. She'd meant to lose the fight. What had she done?

She could hear the crowd murmuring in concern as she clapped frantically at his cheek, trying to revive him. She muttered under her breath. "Wake up now. Come on."

He didn't respond. She hadn't hit him *that* hard, had she?

"Shite," she whispered in panic, jostling his shoulders. "Come on, Gellir. Lady Feiyan will ne'er forgive me for bashin' ye. Laird Dougal will ne'er forgive me for shamin' ye. And the warriors, they'll ne'er forgive me for humiliatin' their champion. Twice." She let out a sob of despair.

"Please, Gellir. Ye've got to wake up."

His eyes were still closed when he grunted, "Fine. Seems you've won. So what's your bidding? What would you have me do?"

She gasped. "Ye faker."

"Nay," he said, wincing and rubbing his chin. "'Twas a good clout." He struggled up to his elbows. Then he waved to the silent crowd to let them know he was alive. "You won the match fairly."

There was a mix of cheering and booing from those gathered at the fence. As she feared, many were displeased to see their hero fall.

Lady Feiyan called out, "You haven't broken his nose, have you, Merraid?"

"Never fear, cousin!" Gellir yelled back. "A wee crook would only add character to my face."

"Och!" Feiyan cried. "Leave off your fighting then. We've got guests arriving after dinner. Merraid has chores to do."

"As you wish," he told her. Then he glanced up at Merraid. "Well, you've won. I'm at your command. What's your bidding?"

The way he was looking at her—his eyes misty and mysterious, his lips curved in a smile that was half irritation and half amusement—a dozen wicked thoughts coursed through her brain. Thoughts she dared not voice. Instead she lowered her gaze.

"What would your biddin' be if ye'd won?"

"My bidding?"

He reached up toward her. She took his hand to help him up. When he didn't immediately release her, she felt a blush warm her cheeks.

There was an awkward moment as their eyes met. Surely the smoldering she saw in his piercing gaze was only a reflection of her own desire. But for an instant, she feared he might blurt out something deliciously improper.

Like "a kiss." Or "a caress." Or "a tryst in the woods."

Then the smoke dissipated from his eyes, and he arched his brow. "I would bid you stop spying on me for a day."

She frowned. Disappointment effectively quashed her lust. "Spyin' on ye? I haven't been spyin' on ye."

She very much *had* been spying on him. But it wasn't because she was meddlesome, as he imagined. It was because she cared. She was trying to safeguard him.

He was a blind fool if he couldn't see that.

Damn his ungrateful hide. She'd exchanged serving duties with a kitchen lad just so she could watch over Gellir last night at supper. Manipulated her way into the garden the other day to keep an eye on him. Taken time out of her busy schedule to interrogate other servants, researching each prospective bride.

He had no idea what effort it took, what pains she'd gone to, looking after his welfare without neglecting her household duties.

Then inspiration hit her. She would show him how difficult it was.

"Ye'll do my biddin'?" she asked.

He placed a hand across his heart. "So I have vowed."

"Then ye can do my chores today."


Gellir had never been one to complain about hard labor. He was not as high-and-mighty as Merraid seemed to believe. He was always willing to help a crofter push his cart out of a rut. Chase after a lady's runaway palfrey. Help deliver a litter of pups. On the tournament circuit, he polished his own armor and cared for his own horse.

But he quickly learned Merraid's long list of tasks rivaled those of a king's squire.

It didn't help that the other servants snickered behind their hands at his clumsy efforts. Smoothing linens over trestle tables. Emptying a dozen chamberpots. Polishing wooden furnishings with beeswax. Carrying a basket of live eels to the kitchen.

With all Merraid's responsibilities, it was a wonder she found spare hours to perfect her fighting skills. How she carved out time to spy on him, he didn't know.

The Darragh warriors, apparently unable to stand the sight of their appointed hero subjected to such indignity, largely avoided crossing his path.

But Merraid stayed close to him all day. She seemed intent on lapping up every gloating drop of his humiliation.

"Ye missed a spot," she complained with an impish sparkle in her eye as he ran a waxy rag over the lid of Feiyan's oak chest.

He glared at her and swabbed across the wood...again.

"Don't break the eggs," she warned as he carefully counted out a dozen from the day's collection.

"I won't," he said, smugly tossing one in the air.

She caught it midflight, scowling as she handed it back to him.

When he entered the kitchen lads' quarters to empty chamberpots, she stopped him with a warning. "For this chamber, 'tis best to tie a scarf o'er your face."

"I need no—" His words cut off abruptly as the stench of waste hit him full in the face. He wrinkled his nose in disgust.

She handed him a scarf.

He finished that mortifying task. Then she said he had time to nibble a morsel before the cook would send him for herbs from the garden.

He declined. After chamberpot duty, he had little appetite.

"Ye should keep up your strength," she said. "Otherwise, ye won't eat until well after supper."

"Why not?"

"Ye have to clean up after everyone else first."

He sighed. There was just enough time to choke down a stale crust of bread and a cup of ale. Then, as she predicted, the cook put in a request for thyme and parsley.

Merraid found it highly amusing that he didn't know parsley from parsnips.

He grumbled back that she probably didn't know a bludgeon from a battleaxe.

He was wrong. And to rub salt in his wounds, as they cut herbs, she taught him the names of several weapons from the Orient. He knew none of them.

They delivered the herbs to the cook. Then they trudged up the stairs with besoms and buckets to sweep the hearths.

"Honestly," he told her as they entered the solar, "I don't know how you find the time to spy on me."

"I *make* the time." She began sweeping ashes into her bucket.

"Why?"

"Ye truly don't know?"

He shook his head.

"Ye're in such a hurry to claim a bride," she said, "that ye're bein' reckless."

"Reckless?" He started sweeping beside her. "You don't think I have good judgment?"

"Not when it comes to women."

He scoffed.

"Faith," she said, "'Tis like watchin' a great warrior snappin' up a blunt sword to go into battle."

He grinned. "You think I'm a great warrior?"

She swatted him with the bristle end of the besom. "Ye're a great-*headed* warrior."

He swatted her back. Ashes made a gray blob on the seat of her blue kirtle.

Her mouth went round. "Don't swat me." She swatted him again.

"Me? You started it." He swatted her again.

She picked up the besom in both hands, holding it horizontally before her like a quarterstaff. There was a gleam in her eye.

"Och," he said, "you're keen for a rematch, are you?"

He tossed aside the bucket. It clanged across the floor. Then he mimicked her stance with his besom.

She attacked first. With skillful lunges, she whipped the besom back and forth, driving him backwards toward the window.

"Ha!" she crowed as his back hit the shutters and he could retreat no more.

He pushed his staff forcefully against hers, casting her off. While she was scrambling backwards, he used the bristle end to sweep her apron up in front of her face.

She shrieked out in surprise and whacked her apron back down with one hand. Then she jabbed blindly forward with the handle of the besom.

"Whoa!" he cried, dodging out of the way.

At her second poke, he grabbed hold of her besom.

"A-ha!" he cried in triumph. He jerked the handle back.

Unwilling to let go of her weapon, she careened forward. And would have collided with him. But at the last minute, she dropped, skidding on her skirts and sliding onto the floor at his feet, besom still in hand.

"Let go," he warned.

"Nay," she said, laughter twitching at her lips.

"Let." He raised a brow. "Go."

"Never."

He'd warned her. While she lay helpless on the floor, stubbornly clinging to the handle of her makeshift quarterstaff, he angled the bristled heads of both besoms to bat repeatedly at her skirts, like a maidservant beating dust from a tapestry.

She squealed in dismay. But she couldn't help giggling at the absurdity of the situation.

"Surrender your weapon, wench!" he demanded with a grin.

"All right!" she cried at last, coughing at the rising cloud of ash. "'Tis yours!"

She let go of her besom. But she used his instant of inattention to seize his weapon with both hands, tearing it out of his grip. She rolled away with it and managed to scramble to her feet.

When she faced him, tendrils of her bright hair had come loose from her braid. They made a wild fringe around her glowing face. Her bosom heaved with each breath. Her nostrils flared. Her eyes were fiery with challenge. And her teeth were bared in triumphant delight.

She was beautiful.

Before he could fully absorb just how beautiful she was, the wicked lass dipped the bristles of the besom into the bucket of ashes, like a plasterer loading a brush with lime. Then she renewed her attack.

Now when their bristles tangled, they created a ghastly cloud of ash. But Merraid kept thrusting and blocking. Soon they were coughing and laughing as they continued their farcical battle.

He finally made some progress, backing her toward the hearth. But her eyes widened as she began to fall backwards over the bucket he'd dropped, waving her besom as she tried to catch her balance.

He reached for her arm, managing to keep her upright as the bucket clanged and rolled away against the hearthstones.

She wasted no time in thanking him. She immediately spun out of his grip, widening the distance between them.

In a show of intimidation, she began twirling the besom through the air. She traced swift, intricate patterns, as skilled as a quarterstaff master. While he stood thunder-struck, she whirled toward him in a graceful swirl of skirts. Then she swung the besom around in an upward arc.

Unfortunately, the bristles stretched out a few inches farther than she anticipated. She caught the clay pitcher on the table. It tipped. And rocked. And plunged off the edge.

Gellir dove for it. By some miracle, he managed to catch it in his hands just before it hit the floor.

Aghast at what she'd almost done, Merraid dropped the besom. She brought both hands to her mouth. Then she started laughing in relief at his dramatic rescue. Which made him laugh as well.

Shaking his head, he got up and replaced the pitcher.

She assumed the battle was over. "Shall we call it a draw ere we destroy Feiyan's solar?"

"A draw?" He wasn't going to let her off that easily.

Once the pitcher was safe, he seized his besom and kicked hers out of reach. Then he began sweeping at the ground before her. He brushed the hem of her skirts, forcing her back with a gaze full of amusement and dark promise.

"I don't believe in draws," he said.

"Ye cheated," she squeaked, retreating as the bristles grazed her toes.

"Cheated? Ha!" He laughed. "You're a fine fraud, calling *me* a cheat."

Inch by inch, he advanced with wide arcs of the besom.

She danced back to avoid the ashy bristles.

"We really have no time for this," she protested.

"You should have thought of that when you started this fight."

"Me?" Her wide blue eyes were anything but innocent.

"Fine," he said with a smile. "I'll hurry it up."

He swept furiously at her feet, forcing her to make a hasty retreat. Finally her back hit the plaster wall. He raised the handle of the besom sideways under her chin. Against her throat. Trapping her.

"I win."

Merraid narrowed her gaze.

Just because Gellir declared victory didn't mean it was true.

She had several options.

She could punch beneath his ribs and leave him breathless.

She could chop sharply at the ends of the besom and duck away.

She could drive her knee into his groin.

But what she most wanted to do was stand there in his power as he grinned down at her in triumph.

He was too close for decency. But she didn't want him to move.

Here she could feel the warm breath of exhilarating combat on her face. Share the glimmer of heady delight in his eyes. Hear the low chuckle of victory rumbling in his chest. Inhale the intoxicating scent of him—all clean sweat and worn leather and ash.

Beneath the wooden staff pressed against her throat, her pulse throbbed. Her blood—warmed by battle and laughter—surged in her veins. Her eyes grew wet with desire. Heavy with passion. Her breath slowed. Deepened. Stopped.

Then she made the mistake of lowering her gaze to his mouth.

A smile lurked at the corners of his lips. His straight, wide, inviting lips. Where they parted, she could glimpse the moist mystery within.

She could no more resist tasting him than she could pass by a luscious blackberry hanging ripe on a vine. She slipped her tongue between her lips, imagining the sweetness.

His eyes dipped to her mouth then. What he saw made his nostrils flare with the same yearning.

He hesitated only briefly. Then he eased forward. Closed his eyes. Slanted his mouth across hers in the gentlest, most tentative of kisses.

She dared not move. Like a blossom offered to a bee, she feared the slightest shiver, lest she frighten him away.

But soon his feather-light caresses tempted her to answer. She moved her mouth beneath his. Savoring the yielding softness of his lips. The sweet entreaty of his breath. The hungering movements of his jaw.

He groaned once, low in his throat. The sound catapulted her to new heights of longing. She deepened the kiss, drawing closer to let her tongue explore the inner recesses of his mouth.

His tongue circled hers in a slow and sultry dance of desire. But with each moment, the dance grew more eager. More fervent.

Her head spun with joy and arousal. What she remembered of his kiss before was nothing like this.

That had been the quick peck of a lad.

This was the measured seduction of a man.

Her ears began to ring in sensual vibration. Her breasts tingled with need. Current coursed through her, sparking a dangerous craving betwixt her thighs. Her fingers turned to claws as she clutched the front of his tabard in desperation.

Deep within her heart, a tiny voice screamed at her to stop. Gellir was not hers. He didn't belong to her. He would never belong to her.

But rapture muffled the sound. It felt so right. So perfect to be here in his arms. How could it be wrong?

A soft moan escaped her, driving him to more aggression.

He let go of the besom handle, caught now between their heaving chests, and delved his hands into her hair. Angling her head, he explored her more fully. He placed kisses at the corners of her lips. Swept his tongue over them. Boldly claimed her mouth with his own.

Breathless and overwhelmed, Merraid felt gloriously helpless in his embrace. It was a heady feeling to surrender willingly. Bathed in an invigorating sea of ecstasy, she had no desire to fight the current. In the next moment, she would have gladly drowned in his arms.

But the door swung open. They split faster than a tree hit by lightning. The besom clattered to the floor.

"What the devil?" Lady Feiyan stood in the open doorway, taking in the ruins of her solar.

# CHAPTER 9

**M**erraid's face flamed. She gulped guiltily.

Not so much because of the upturned buckets and ash everywhere. But because she'd had her hands and lips all over the lady's cousin.

Thinking the most inappropriate thoughts.

Feeling the most inappropriate feelings.

"This is my fault," Gellir volunteered at once. Of course he did. He was the most gallant gentleman she knew.

"Nay, 'twas *my* doin', m'lady," she argued.

There was no reason for him to take the blame. He was right. She *had* swatted him first. And there was no doubt in her mind that the kiss was her idea.

He continued. "Merraid was trying to show me how to sweep ashes from the hearth, and I knocked o'er the bucket."

Feiyan smirked. "Is that how you got an ash handprint on your backside?" she asked him.

Merraid froze in horror.

Then Feiyan turned to her. "And fingerprints on your face?"

Merraid lifted a hand to her cheek. She glanced at Gellir. He winced.

Before they could explain, Lady Feiyan raised her hands to stop them. "I don't want to know." She faced Gellir.

"Look, cousin, you can have all the mistresses you like after you're wed. But right now we need to *get* you wed."

Enraged, Gellir rose to her defense. "How dare you suggest—"

"Which is why I came," she said, waving away his comment. "The Graham sisters are arriving within the hour." She wrinkled her nose at him in disgust. "See if you can make yourself presentable."

He glared at Feiyan. Then he gave a bow of his head to Merraid. "My humblest apologies. I should ne'er have—"

"'Twasn't your fault. 'Twas I who—"

"Nay, 'twas me who should have—"

"Ye're not to blame for—"

"Go!" Feiyan said, pointing to the door.

Gellir glowered again at his cousin. Then he nodded at Merraid and left.

"And you," Feiyan continued. "To be honest, I'm disappointed, Merraid. You're better than this. You're too wise, too gifted to settle for being a nobleman's plaything. It pains me to see you squander your affections on a man you cannot have."

The truth felt like a punch in the gut. Merraid did know better. And hearing her transgression spoken aloud mortified her.

"Aye, m'lady."

Feiyan sighed. "I know my cousin is handsome and charming. He's the definition of chivalry. Brave. Courteous. Honorable. Women are drawn to him like flies to honey. Indeed, 'tis that way with *all* the Rivenloch men." She put a hand on Merraid's shoulder. "But you have to resist his charms. I *like* you, Merraid. And I don't want to see you get hurt."

Touched and ashamed, Merraid lowered her gaze and give the lady a quick nod.

"Which is why I've invited a guest for *you* tonight."

"What?"

Feiyan beamed at her. "Remember the guardsman you spoke to last night? Henry? The dark-haired fellow with the bright green eyes? He's agreed to return this eve, to court you properly."

Dread settled like a rock in the pit of her stomach. "Oh."

"So after you tidy up this mess," she said, "you should probably change into something less...ashy."

Merraid couldn't move for several moments after Feiyan left. She'd do the lady's bidding, of course. It would be rude to turn down her invitation.

But what she really wanted to do was disappear. Crawl under her bedsheets. Hide in the garderobe. Or maybe submerge herself in the firth.

The day had been delightful up to now. She'd enjoyed sharing her world with Gellir. She'd expected him to look down on her work. To treat it as something beneath him.

But he hadn't. After a bit of typical male stubbornness, he'd accepted her instruction. Heeded her advice. He'd never acted ashamed of his labors. And he'd treated the other servants with respect.

They'd been friends again, like that time long ago. Companions. Cohorts. Allies working together toward the same goal.

That, however, was the problem.

He'd made her forget he was a nobleman.

He'd made her forget she was a servant.

He'd made her feel like she was an equal.

But she wasn't.

She'd overstepped her bounds. Violated her position in the household. Worse, she'd been caught at it.

As she snatched up her besom and set her bucket to rights, she made a solemn vow.

Never again would she look at Gellir with longing.

To her, he would henceforth be Sir Gellir Cameliard.

Cousin of Lady Feiyan. Esteemed warrior of Rivenloch.

She'd distance herself from him, as painful as it would be.

She'd respect the boundaries between noble knight and humble servant.

She'd grow up and face reality.

A tear slipped from her eye. She wiped it away with the heel of her hand. It was just the sting of ashes. Nothing more.

She washed the smudges from her face. Stripped out of her ashy clothing. Changed into the worn surcoat of dull green wool Feiyan had given her.

She felt like herself again. Merraid the maidservant.

A lass who could easily avoid Sir Gellir Cameliard in the great hall.

Who could serve and clear supper without giving him a second glance.

Who could regard the pair of sweet-faced twin sisters who arrived to vie for his hand without the slightest twinge of jealousy.

Servants topped the trestle tables with linens. A musical consort practiced in the corner. A kitchen lad lit the candles around the hall. Merraid was sweeping rushes away to make a space for dancing when a familiar voice caught her ear.

"So what's the wagerin' on tonight?" he murmured. "Who'll take the first spill on the floor?"

She turned to see Henry. His eyes shone with glee. His stray curl dangled jauntily over his brow. She couldn't help but return his smile.

He truly was an amiable fellow.

And though she didn't think it possible, he made the evening bearable. Between his clever quips and warm-hearted teasing, Henry somehow distracted her from pining for the one she couldn't have.

As the guests arrived, he made up stories about each one. He danced and laughed with her. Together they drank and sang. They even wagered a kiss on who would be the first dancer to slip and fall. Both lost when a wee tot of a lad wandered into the midst of the dancers and was knocked down by a flinging skirt.

Later, in the moonlit courtyard, as he prepared to return to his keep, Henry turned to her with a soft smile. He fingered the braid draped over her shoulder.

"Ye know, neither of us winnin' that wager is the same as neither of us losin'."

She smiled back. "Is that so?"

"Och aye," he said with mock seriousness. "I think 'tis likely we owe each other a kiss."

She forced her expression to studious contemplation. "I see. Do ye think 'twould be best to pay the debt now or—"

Before she could finish, he stopped her mouth with his, pressing smiling lips to hers in a short, soft, sweet kiss. The touch was brief, but pleasant. Friendly. Respectful. Non-threatening.

"Shall I return to court ye, m'lady?" he murmured.

"Aye," she decided. "I'd like that."

He gave her a brief bow and disappeared into the night.

Later, when Merraid fell asleep, she dreamt of her own handfasting. The day was bright. The air was full of laughter. She was dressed in a lovely indigo gown borrowed from Lady Feiyan, who smiled on in approval. Laird Dougal himself wrapped the ribbons around the bride and groom's joined hands, speaking the declaration of marriage.

But when Merraid lifted her eyes to gaze upon the bridegroom to whom she'd tied her fate, it wasn't Henry's dancing green eyes that gazed back at her.

Her dream husband's eyes were forged of steel and silver.

Gellir and his brothers had grown up with the cautionary tenet—never court sisters. Apparently, his conniving cousin wasn't familiar with that rule. But if courting sisters was a mistake, courting *twin* sisters was a debacle of the worst sort.

All night, they vied for Gellir's attention with fluttered lashes and conspiratorial giggles. They sparred with each other, using sly snipes and cutting glares.

To make matters worse, they were dressed in matching crimson gowns. As they spun and wove their way through the dancing, Gellir lost track of which one was which. An unforgivable blunder in the realm of twins.

By the end of the evening, even Feiyan had to agree her strategy had been disastrous. The twins were fuming. Gellir was miserable. And after their taut farewell, he felt too agitated to retire.

Guilt had definitely settled on his shoulders today. Beginning with Merraid in the solar. He still felt on edge, to blame for what had happened.

Why had he trifled with the maidservant?

Why had he allowed temptation to get the better of him?

What the devil was wrong with him?

He sighed. He should be sleeping. But he was restless.

He donned his cloak and trudged up the steps, emerging on the wall walk surrounding the courtyard. Overhead, the moon seemed like a beacon shining down on him. Illuminating his flaws. Exposing his failures. Judging him.

Why was finding a wife so difficult for him?

After all, she had to fulfill just three simple requirements.

She must be Scottish.

She must give him bairns.

And she must be of noble bloodlines.

Was that so hard?

His heart had nothing to do with the decision. It didn't matter if she was ugly or fair. Short or tall. Brilliant or silly. Kindhearted or mean-spirited. Not really. He'd always followed the path that led him to success. Not the one that led to his heart.

Why suddenly did it matter so much to him what kind of woman he wed?

Unbidden, the image of Merraid appeared in his mind's eye. Merraid with her teasing smile. Her merry blue eyes. Her blushing face, streaked with ash from his careless fingers.

His clamped mouth softened.

She was the woman who touched his heart.

It didn't matter that she was a maidservant.

It didn't matter that they had no future.

She was the one he adored.

And he was certain she felt the same way.

Why else would she follow him about, watching over him like a sentinel?

Why else would she care so much about finding him a worthy bride?

God's eyes! *She* was a worthy bride.

She was beautiful and brilliant. Invigorating and inspiring. Clever and kind and devoted. All the things that would make her a loving wife and a perfect mother.

If only the dictates of the king didn't require Gellir's services as a political pawn, he wouldn't hesitate to offer for her hand.

But then a cloud passed in front of the moon, as if to eclipse his dreams.

For one dark space of time, he gave his mind free rein.

He envisioned following his heart—the king be damned—and stealing away with Merraid. He imagined kissing her again. Holding her. Caressing her. Peeling her clothes away, piece by piece. Worshiping every inch of her. Sinking into her welcome softness. Hearing her cry out in ecstasy. Celebrating his own.

For one lingering, bittersweet moment, he imagined a full life unfolding ahead of them. One with frolicking mock battles. And gentle surrenders. Swimming naked in icy lochs. Warming cups of mead by the hearth. Riding through the countryside. Stealing through the forest. Playing with children. So many children. Hundreds of kisses. Thousands of smiles.

He turned away as the cloud drifted past the face of the moon, lighting up the courtyard below.

Then he saw her.

Merraid.

The woman of his dreams.

But she wasn't his. She didn't belong to him. She belonged to the man who was laying claim to her even now.

Gellir clenched his fists. He growled in his throat. It took all his willpower not to bellow at the guardsman to keep his filthy hands off the lass.

But that wasn't Gellir's right. And he had to admit the truth. If Merraid didn't want a man's attentions, she could take care of herself. If she didn't like the way he was touching her—with such familiarity and intimacy—she'd toss the man on his arse in a heartbeat.

That she accepted the stranger's kiss so willingly meant it was what she desired. And that felt like a dagger stabbing his heart.

Wounded—and vexed that he'd let himself be wounded—Gellir shut his eyes against the sight. He wheeled back to face the moon. It now looked like the laughing mouth of a mischievous god, mocking his misfortune.

Sparring was a reliable cure for frustration and heartache. But it was too dark for swordplay. And clashing blades would draw attention.

Instead, he returned to the hall. He nabbed a jack and two bottles of ale from the buttery and headed to the stables. There, no one but the horses would bear witness to his grumbling.

In the end, even four pints of Darragh's strongest ale couldn't numb his emotions. But at last it conveyed him to the oblivion of sleep.

It was there Feiyan found him in the morning. He was sprawled in the hay with the empty jack tucked against his chest.

"There you are!" she cried. "I've been looking all over for you."

He groaned.

"Did you sleep here all night?" she demanded.

He winced. Was his cousin's voice always so loud and shrill?

"Gellir, wake up." She opened the door wider, blinding him with a sunbeam.

"Shite," he croaked, throwing his arm defensively over his offended eyes. "Go away."

His tongue felt thick in his mouth. His eyes were full of grit. His head throbbed.

"You drank yourself into a stupor, didn't you?" she scolded, grabbing the jack from him. "Look, I know 'twas my fault. 'Twas a mistake to make you choose between two sisters. Even worse, twins. Dougal won't let me hear the end of it."

God's bones. Why was she still talking? Didn't she know each word pummeled at his ears like an incessant, pounding bell?

He pressed the heel of his hand to his forehead, trying to ease the ache.

"I promise I won't make that mistake again," she said. "But you've got to do your part." She dug her fingers into his shoulder. "Come on. Pull yourself together. Get up."

"Leave me alone." Every muscle in his body was stiff. The last thing he wanted to do was move.

"I've seen what happens when I leave you alone," she quipped.

He growled.

"Besides, I've brought good news," she said.

He sighed. The only good news he wanted to hear was that some horrible tragedy had befallen the guard he'd seen kissing Merraid last night.

He instantly regretted that ignoble thought. Grimacing, he eased himself up until he was sitting in the straw.

"Fine." He scrubbed at his eyes. "What's your good news?"

"We've got a missive from Hew."

"Hew?" That brought him awake. Their cousin Hew was in the same predicament as Gellir. Hiding out from the machinations of the king. Blinking against the light, he looked up at her. "What news?"

"He may have found you a bride."

Merraid heard about the arrival of Gellir's next marriage candidate through the conduit of the servants long before Lady Feiyan formally announced it to her.

At first, the protocol seemed the same as all the others. There was to be a visit in two days' time. The lady would stay for a short while at the keep.

But there was a special gleam in Lady Feiyan's eyes. A lightness in her step. She wanted extra care taken with preparations for the lady's visit.

This candidate was different somehow.

"This is the one," Feiyan confided. She seemed to glow as she entered her bedchamber, where Merraid was preparing her bath. "I'm sure of it."

Merraid forced a smile to her lips as she poured a tiny bit of sandalwood oil into the warm water. "Aye?"

Feiyan sat on the edge of the bed to tug off her boots. "Aye. She's perfect."

Merraid nodded.

The one.

The one who would steal Gellir's heart.

The one who would become his smiling bride.

The one who would bear his name and his children.

The smile froze on her face as she swirled the oil into the bath. But she felt sick inside.

This was it.

Her.

The woman who would shred the last gossamer threads of Merraid's dreams.

Disappointment must have shown in her face. As Lady Feiyan peeled off her stockings, she said, "As for you, Merraid... I'm so glad you and Henry will be courting. He's delightful, isn't he?"

"Oh. Aye."

Henry *was* delightful. He was fun. He was charming. He was clever. He was attractive.

But he didn't set her heart to racing. He didn't melt her bones. He didn't leave her breathless. He didn't haunt her dreams.

"Perhaps there will be two spring weddings at Darragh?" Feiyan ventured.

Merraid gulped.

Who had said anything about marriage? She'd only met Henry. Besides, Merraid had a tournament to train for.

To change the subject, as Merraid prepared the bath,

she tortured herself further by asking, "What's her name, this perfect bride?"

Feiyan unbuckled her belt. "Lady Carenza."

She wished she hadn't asked. "'Tis a beautiful name."

"For a beautiful lady," Feiyan said. "Here, let me read you what our cousin Hew thinks about her."

She fetched the missive from the small chest on her table.

"He writes 'She is beautiful and clever, wise and sweet, helpful and generous. She has a gentle nature and a ready smile. A man could hope for no more perfect a wife.'"

Merraid couldn't even summon up a smile. She turned away and busied herself with stacking linens beside the tub.

"I know you were worried," Feiyan said gently. "Gellir is your friend. You wanted to be sure he found a good match. One deserving of him." She let out a contented sigh. "I think maybe this lady will make him truly happy."

Merraid nodded. But there was a knot of tears in her throat, choking off a reply.

"The best part is," Feiyan continued, "Gellir has already approved. He's grown weary of courting. And I think he's anxious to get back to jousting. He trusts Hew's judgment. So he's agreed to marry her."

Merraid bit her lip and blinked back tears. It was all happening too quickly. Gellir might well marry within the sennight. Then he'd return to Rivenloch with his bride. Merraid would likely never see him again.

"And Merraid," Feiyan said, "I need to ask you a special favor."

"Aye, m'lady?" she managed to choke out.

"Will you make her feel welcome? I know Gellir can be...grim...when he's restless. The last thing I want to do is frighten her off."

Merraid's heart sank. Of all the tasks Lady Feiyan could require of her, this was perhaps the most difficult.

"O' course, m'lady."

After that, nothing could cheer her. Not even the afternoon visit from Henry. He'd brought her an apple coffyn stolen from Lady Maut's kitchens. Naturally, she pretended to be delighted by his unexpected company. Pleased by his sweet pilfered pastry. But her smile didn't reach her eyes or come from her heart.

She sent Henry away after an hour, pleading a long list of chores to do. He seemed disappointed. But he politely bowed to her wishes.

She told herself there would be time later to court Henry properly. To exchange pleasantries and gifts. To make wagers on silly things. To hold his hand and kiss his lips and try to fall in love with him.

But for now, she had to fulfill her vow to Feiyan to make Gellir's new bride feel welcome. And she had to fulfill her vow to Gellir to ensure he made a good match. She only hoped Lady Carenza was as perfect as Hew described her. Gellir deserved nothing less.

Hoofbeats thundered beneath Gellir. His couched lance balanced effortlessly under his arm. His knees flexed with every gallop as he charged across the field.

This was what he needed. What he missed. All the silly courtship rituals—dancing, pleasure riding, hawking, strolling through the garden—had made him feel like he was going soft.

Riding full-tilt at a target made him feel alive again. Strong. And free. As if he hadn't just agreed to wed a woman, sight unseen, on the advice of his softhearted cousin Hew.

It had been a rash decision, he knew. But it was the only way he could purge his dangerous desire for Merraid. If he couldn't have the one he wanted—and it appeared her heart was already bending toward another—then he might as well let his cousin choose his wife.

His lance held. It knocked the target off the arm of the quintain. Two young lads scurried to replace it. He galloped to the end of the list and wheeled his mount about.

His cousin Hew had always left his heart unguarded. He'd had it broken half a dozen times. But Gellir supposed that meant he had experience. In general, his judgment seemed sound. All the lasses Hew pursued were attractive. Half of them were even good-natured.

The destrier stamped at the ground, eager to take another run.

Gellir knew how the horse felt. He itched to run as well. To flee Darragh. To go back out on the tournament circuit. To ignore the threat of the king. To forget the necessity of acquiring a wife.

"Ready, sir!" one of the lads shouted, backing out of the way.

He spurred the destrier into a charge and lowered his lance.

This time his weapon hit the target square, swinging it halfway round. The lads rushed to straighten it for his next run.

Again and again he returned until he had nearly demolished the target. After an hour, his arm and the horse were fatigued. His stomach grumbled for food.

He handed off the destrier to Campbell and headed toward the great hall.

He expected his exhausting day of tilting to numb him to anything but his aching muscles.

But then he glimpsed Merraid in the courtyard, sharing a coffyn with her fawning suitor. His heart cramped. He had to look away.

When his ears caught the guardsman's indulgent chuckle, he had to resist an ugly urge to march over and stuff the crust into the man's mouth. Anything to stop the sound.

This was why he had to leave Darragh, he told himself as he plodded toward the armory. Merraid brought out the worst in him. His affection for her had turned him into a monster. A brute who wished the most depraved sort of misfortune upon his rival.

Thankfully, it was the last he saw of the guard that day, saving the man from any pastry-related mishap.

But even brief glances at Merraid as she went about her day left Gellir feeling empty. He missed her meddling. He craved her conversation. By the end of the day, he was tempted to pick a fight with her—to draw blades or cross besoms—just to have some interaction.

The next morn he got his wish.

He arrived on the foggy practice field, sword in hand. Merraid was already there, sparring in the mist with his cousin Feiyan. They were using strange swords with slightly curved blades and no shields.

He should have turned around and walked away. They hadn't seen him. And no good could come of interacting with either of them.

But curiosity got the best of him. He watched them slice and hack at each other. Gracefully arcing and spinning. Almost like a dance.

He was used to seeing such maneuvers from Feiyan. But he'd never witnessed two masters of the intriguing art fighting together.

He was awestruck. Merraid twirled and lunged. Her swirling blade made whirlpools in the mist. Feiyan ducked under the sword and swept hers low. Merraid leaped over the slashing blade and rolled out of range. Then she sprang to her feet to attack again.

The blades struck rapidly and repeatedly. They whistled through the air, sliding together and snicking like scissors. In Scottish fights, men stood their ground, hacking at one another until someone tired. Feiyan and Merraid dove and flipped and skidded in the dirt. They used clever strategy instead of brute strength. It was fascinating. So fascinating, he didn't notice he'd been seen.

"Och, good!" Feiyan suddenly shouted. "You can take over, Gellir! Dougal needs me in the hall." She approached. Without permission, she pried the sword from his grip, replacing it with hers. "There. Merraid can teach you what you need to know about the *dao*." She waved and vanished into the mist. "See you at dinner."

# CHAPTER 10

This was unwise. Gellir knew it. And Merraid knew it. He could tell by the furrow between her brows.

"You don't have to..." he began.

"Nay. 'Tis fine, Sir Gellir. I am at your service." She bowed her head.

He scowled. Sir Gellir? Since when did she call him *Sir Gellir*? "Never mind. I'm sure you have better things—"

"Lady Feiyan wishes me to teach ye. Sir. That's what I shall do."

Her stiff decorum and that "sir" was making him testy. "I need no instruction," he said, adding a pointed, "my lady." How hard could it be? He waved the blade toward her. "Go on then. Attack me."

She lifted a skeptical brow. "As ye wish. Sir."

Did her lip quirk up then? He had no time to notice. In the next instant, her blade whipped around from the right side to kiss his neck.

He blinked. If the blade had been sharp, she could have beheaded him right then and there. He'd had no time to raise his own weapon.

She lowered the blade. "Again, sir?"

He stepped away and nodded.

This time, he blocked the slash aimed at his left knee. But the impact made the strange blade quiver in his grip. It

147

distracted him long enough to allow her a second attack. She reversed, spun, and sliced through the air. Before he could defend himself, the edge of her weapon found his throat again.

She clucked her tongue. "Twice now I could have killed ye, sir."

"Fine," he grumbled, moving her blade aside with a cautious thumb. Then he made an X in the air with his own sword. "Show me how to use this thing."

She agreed, though she remained aloof. And he was determined enough to master this new weapon to ignore her new primness.

"Scottish swordplay," she began, demonstrating, "is a series o' hacks. One after the other. Each has a beginnin' and an end. 'Tis like a sculptor chiselin' words into stone." She changed her movements into slow loops and lazy circles in the air. "But the fightin' from the Orient is a continuous flow. There's no beginnin'. No end. 'Tis more like a quill scrawlin' letters on parchment."

For the better part of an hour, Merraid taught him the basics of the Eastern style of warfare. He learned how to wield the lightweight, single-edged *dao*, which was capable of more speed and flexibility than a heavy Scottish sword.

He mimicked her motions, which matched the nature of the blade better as it flexed through the air.

"That's it," she said. "And when ye use it quickly, ye can feel the blade warpin' just a wee bit."

He nodded. "Making it less likely to break."

"Aye. The *dao* is made for speed, not strength. 'Tis used as both sword and shield. Strike at me slowly from the right. I'll show ye."

He did so. Her blade caught his, but then circled around it with a scrape of steel on steel. It didn't stop the blow directly as a shield would. It deflected it.

"Instead o' blockin' an opponent's strike, ye use its force and change its path."

"Let me try." He motioned her to strike at him.

She brought her *dao* down slowly. He snaked his blade around hers and cast it off in another direction. Then he returned with a slash that stopped short of her waist.

"Exactly!" Enthusiasm colored her voice.

They continued practicing the move, gradually moving faster and faster. Finally, he could do it at full speed.

From there, she taught him more complex maneuvers. Showy over-the-head circles. Sly under-the-arm thrusts. Levered behind-the-back attacks.

"That's it!" she cried when he successfully mastered a spinning backhand strike.

He grinned. It had been a long time since he'd felt this challenged and excited. He didn't want to stop. "Let's spar now."

Despite her determination to remain cool, her eyes lit up. "As ye wish. Sir."

Merraid dominated the battle. Which was no surprise. After all, she'd had years of training. But it was a pleasure to test his flexibility and his capacity to learn new techniques.

Indeed, he was enjoying himself so much that he completely lost track of time. He didn't notice the rest of the castle waking. Servants starting the day's work. Warriors emerging to spar on the field. Or the arrival of the last person he wished to see.

Merraid was in the middle of a thrilling acrobatic attack. Gellir was left breathless—nearly unable to defend himself—when he was interrupted by a harsh reprimand.

"What the bloody hell do ye think ye're doin', sirrah?"

Gellir's hackles rose. It was Henry. That pesky guard from Lady Maut's castle. The one who thought Merraid belonged to him.

Gellir resisted the urge to come round with his sword. He'd like to lop off the man's annoying curl—if not his head—for speaking to him with such insolence.

Merraid spoke before he could. "Henry!" she scolded.

But Henry's gaze was locked on him. Blind to Gellir's identity, he saw only a foe. "I'll ask ye again. What do ye think ye're doin'?"

Gellir narrowed his eyes.

The insolent guard came forward with a threatening hand on his hilt.

Merraid stepped in front of him. "Henry, stop!"

Henry's piercing gaze dropped to her. "Are ye all right, Merraid? What's he done to ye?"

Considering Merraid had the upper hand, Gellir couldn't help but snicker at that. The sound that enraged the guard.

"God's bones! What kind o' knight are ye, sirrah, attackin' a lass?"

Gellir opened his mouth to reply. But Merraid gave the guard a sobering shove backwards. "He wasn't attackin' me, Henry. We were sparrin'."

That didn't sit well with Henry either. He looked aghast at Merraid.

By now, the Darragh warriors who populated the field were alerted. Their intervention wouldn't be necessary, of course. Gellir could easily quell the guard alone. But Henry had proved one thing. He cared enough about Merraid to protect her with his life.

Gellir supposed he should be relieved.

Instead he was annoyed.

Henry muttered, "Was he forcin' ye to spar, lass?"

Laughter teased at the corners of Gellir's eyes. Henry didn't know her very well if he thought a man could force Merraid to do anything.

"Nay," she said. "'Twas my idea."

"Your idea?" Henry scoffed. "What do ye mean?"

"I mean, I'm a warrior, Henry. Ye might as well know it. I fight with a sword."

By his expression of horror and distaste, Henry obviously wasn't familiar with the Warrior Maids of Rivenloch. "By choice?"

"Aye." She placed a hand on Henry's chest. "Now will ye apologize to Sir Gellir for your discourtesy?"

"Sir..." Henry gulped. "Gellir?"

Merraid moved aside.

Henry took his hand off his hilt and nervously licked his lips. "I beg your forgiveness, m'laird. But when I saw wee Merraid—"

"You're forgiven." Gellir didn't need to hear the details or how desperate Henry was to save his beloved.

"Thank ye, m'laird." He bowed his head as he retreated. Then he faced Merraid and murmured under his breath. "As for ye, I don't know what to say, lass. A woman...with a sword..."

"Ye'll have to get used to it, Henry," she told him. "I've wielded a sword since I was a lass."

Henry's look of distaste was comical. At least it was to Gellir. He'd grown up savoring such confounded reactions to the women in his warrior clan.

But he could see Merraid was not amused. And he suddenly felt sorry for her.

Disappointment dampened Merraid's high spirits.

Why did Henry have to stumble onto the field just as she was crossing blades with Gellir?

She'd planned to tell him—eventually—about her unusual diversion. It wasn't something she ever meant to hide.

But she hadn't expected to have to defend herself so soon.

151

She hoped Henry might be different from the rest. She thought, given time, he might even be pleasantly surprised to discover her unique talents. Surprised and impressed.

But it seemed he was just like the others. Judgmental and disapproving.

She'd been having such fun, battling Gellir. She loved practicing her skills. And having an eager and dedicated student was a pleasure.

Henry's response had triggered old feelings of shame and inadequacy. True, she'd learned to keep up a brave face under criticism long ago. But his condemnation made a new cut in her already scarred heart.

"Come now. 'Tis a jest, isn't it?" Henry decided. "Ye saw me comin' from the parapet and—"

Gellir coughed.

"Nay," she told him. "'Tis true."

"Ye can't be serious," he insisted.

Gellir stepped forward. "She is. If ye doubt it, why not try your own hand?" He flipped the *dao* around and offered it to Henry, hilt-first.

Henry, of course, would have none of it. "Och, sir, I won't fight a woman." He shuddered.

"Are you afraid?" Gellir teased.

"Of a lass?" he replied. "O' course not."

The Darragh warriors laughed at that, confusing Henry.

"You should be," Gellir said. "She nearly took off my head. Twice."

Henry must have realized he stood on dangerous ground. He'd been issued a warning by a celebrated tournament champion. And he was surrounded by Merraid's allies. His frown of condemnation dissolved into an easy grin.

"Well now, I can see ye're havin' a wee bit o' fun at my expense. Far be it from me to stand in the way of a woman's... diversions. No matter how curious they seem."

He placed a humble hand over his heart and gave her an apologetic bow.

Gellir and the others chuckled, giving her a nod of reassurance, and dispersed. It had all been in good fun.

Until Henry reached out to coil a fond finger around the end of Merraid's braid. It was a gesture of affection. But it was also expressed ownership. He murmured for her ears only, "O' course, once we're wed, darlin', ye'll have my sword to defend ye. There will be no need to carry one o' your own. No need to engage in such violent sport. Not when there's more pleasurable sport to be had." With that, he tugged her forward by her braid and pressed a quick kiss on her mouth.

She should have stopped him the instant he touched her. She would have, if she hadn't been so stunned by his dismissive words. It wasn't until he claimed her lips that rage boiled up inside her.

She tore her lips away from him. Raising her *dao* between them, she sliced off the braid he'd grabbed, leaving him holding the severed lock. Then she planted her free hand over his face and gave him a great shove.

He stumbled backward, landing on his arse. He looked like an owl fallen from its perch. His eyes went round. He held her braid aloft, like some small prey in his claws.

The men of Darragh gasped.

Merraid was disgusted and hurt and disappointed all at once. She snatched the braid from his fist and stormed off the field.

Henry didn't follow.

And now she realized she'd probably never see him again. She'd humiliated him in front of all of Darragh. Henry had wrongly assumed Merraid was his for the taking. Nothing could be further from the truth.

She crossed the courtyard, clutching her braid.

The truth was he'd never be happy with a wife like Merraid.

Such was the curse of being an oddity.

It wasn't only that she was a woman warrior. She was a maidservant. That made her an anomaly.

The Rivenloch warrior maids at least had their clan name. Their reputation. Their long noble history to support them. No one questioned their unique authority. Men expected them to be fierce. Strong. Independent. Powerful.

But Merraid lived in a servant's world where lasses were obedient and subservient. Where husbands expected their wives to behave and be docile. Where men wielded weapons and women wielded besoms.

She shouldered her way through the door of the great hall. Servants were bustling about everywhere. Stoking the fire. Lighting candles. Transporting bread and linens and chamberpots. When they saw her charging across the hall—her *dao* in one hand, her braid in the other—they furrowed their brows in fear.

She realized she didn't exactly belong in this world either. As long as she was wearing her apron—sweeping out rushes, preparing baths, serving supper—the others considered her their friend. But when she tucked her skirts up for battle and wore a sword on her hip? They avoided her, as if she were some wild and unpredictable creature.

She headed toward the stairs, seeking refuge.

Such things had never troubled her before. Before, she'd never worried about conforming to expectations. She never thought of courtship or marriage. She didn't care what the men of the clan thought. She performed the duties expected of her as a maidservant. And indulged her love of combat with Lady Feiyan.

Her only dream had been perfecting her swordsmanship. Proving herself in the tournament.

What had happened to that carefree lass? Where had she gone? When had she disappeared?

Since Gellir had arrived, he'd muddied her plans. Her life had been turned upside down.

She entered the shadowy stairwell and dropped her braid on the floor. Her eyes welled with tears as she scowled down at what was left of her lopped-off tresses.

"Merraid."

She startled. Gellir must have followed her from the field. She bit her lip. She didn't want him to see her weeping.

"This is *your* fault, ye know," she blurted.

"*My* fault?"

She turned away and began to trudge up the steps. "Ever since ye returned, the clan has been obsessed with matchmakin' and marriage."

She heard him mutter on the step behind her, "At least 'tisn't *your* marriage they're obsessing over."

"Aren't they? After all, Lady Feiyan has decided I should be wed as well." A knot of sorrow rose in her throat. She dared not turn round and look at him. She'd burst into tears.

"Is that so awful?"

"'Tis—when ye're a maidservant who wields a sword."

He grabbed her arm to turn her toward him. "Listen to me. Henry is a fool. Any other man would consider himself lucky to have you."

The fierce, honest, blind sincerity in his eyes broke her. Her chin trembled, and her tears spilled over. Then, against her better judgment, she blurted out the truth. "*Have* me, perhaps. But there are no men who could *love* me."

Gellir felt her despair as if it were his own. It wrenched at his heart.

How could she think that? Surely it wasn't true. Did she not know what a lovely prize of a lass she was?

A dozen of her virtues sprang instantly to mind. Virtues he could recite off the top of his head. Merraid was kind. Sweet. Strong. Beautiful. Loving. Generous. Amusing. Bright. Graceful. Hard-working. Clever. And so much more.

He should say so. He could vanquish the desolation in her eyes by telling her exactly what he thought of her.

But that would be a mistake.

He had to keep his distance. Bite his tongue.

Showering her with praise would only complicate things.

Still, as he watched a devastated tear roll down her cheek, he knew he had to say something.

He brushed the droplet away with his thumb. "Listen, Merraid. We're not so different, you and I."

She sniffed, giving him a dubious look. She dragged the back of her hand across her nose.

"'Tis true," he said. "The more prospective brides I meet, the more convinced I am I'll ne'er find a woman I can love. Not truly. Not deeply."

"Are ye daft?" she asked. "They're clamorin' at your feet. Beggin' for your attentions."

He shook his head. "They love the *idea* of me. Marrying a tournament champion from a powerful clan. Becoming the lady of a castle with a laird close to royalty. Ne'er lacking for coin or status or worldly goods. They love the *idea.* But they don't really know me."

"Ye're so much more than your wealth and position," she argued. "Given time, the right woman would discover that."

He halted her with an upraised palm. If she started spilling out *her* list of *his* virtues, she'd make things worse.

"I don't have the luxury of time."

"But why?" she asked in irritation. "What's the bloody hurry? What secret have ye been keepin'?"

He sighed. He supposed he owed her the truth. "Can I trust you?"

"With your life."

"You cannot tell another soul."

"I won't breathe a word." She made the sign of the cross. "I swear."

He lowered his voice to a breath. "The king has been fighting alongside the English, against the French."

She nodded and whispered back, "At Toulouse."

He lifted a brow, impressed she knew that.

"Lady Feiyan has been grumblin' about it for weeks," she explained.

"Rumor says he wants to strengthen that alliance with marriages."

As the meaning of that dawned on her, her eyes widened. She sucked in a slow gasp. "With ye? With a Sassenach?"

"Not...yet."

Her tears forgotten, she straightened. New determination bloomed in her eyes. "Ye can't let that happen. We've got to get ye wed ere the king forces ye to..." She couldn't even finish the thought.

"So now you understand the rush. And why Feiyan has been hurling brides at me like battle spears." He lowered his eyes in resignation, emitting a humorless chuckle of irony. "You know, for a clan whose motto is 'Love conquers all,' they evidently don't think the legacy applies to me."

Merraid's heart sank at his sorrow. How heavy the weight of his marriage burden was. And how powerless it must feel to have his life arranged by the king. It was as if he were a pawn in a game of draughts.

At least Merraid had the freedom to not wed, if she so chose. She could remain a maid. Learn a trade. Or enter a convent. No one could force her to marry.

In that moment, she realized two things.

She realized, for all his fame and wealth and entitlement, Gellir had no freedom when it came to matters of love.

She also realized he needed her, now more than ever. They were friends, she and Gellir. And friends were supposed to help each other in times like these. When birth and death and marriage changed a person's life, a friend should be there to offer steadfast guidance and support.

She had to help him find a bride who loved him—a bride he could love—even if it broke her own heart.

"I won't let that happen," she vowed. "I won't let ye wed a woman ye don't love. Nor a woman who doesn't love ye for who ye are. I swear it."

He shook his head. "'Tisn't your duty, lass."

"I'm your friend," she insisted. "And friends don't let friends make poor choices."

A flicker of warmth entered his eyes. "I'll try to remember that," he said, offering her the lock of hair he'd swept up from the floor, "the next time you're tempted to court a knave who doesn't like maids with blades."

She sighed. That pretty much ruled out everyone. "Keep it," she said about the lock of hair. "'Twill remind ye o' my vow."

"A vow I'll only accept on one condition."

"What's that?"

He turned serious. "Promise me you won't be in the same hurry to wed. You have your whole life ahead of you. And you're beholden to no one. Not the king. Not Henry. Not Feiyan. Not even me." He chucked her under the chin. "You follow your heart, Merraid."

# CHAPTER 11

So this was the woman Gellir was supposed to marry. From the moment the petite, dark-haired, sweet-faced Lady Carenza of Dunlop rode through the gates of Darragh, Merraid knew Lady Feiyan was right.

Carenza was the one. The ideal bride for Gellir.

Everyone instantly loved her.

Merraid felt a pinprick of jealousy.

When the lady dismounted, she thanked Campbell for taking her horse, which made the young stable master blush.

When she picked her dainty way across the courtyard to meet Laird Dougal and Lady Feiyan, she offered her hand and a timid, sweet smile.

When she gazed round at the towers and gardens of Darragh, her wide-eyed and earnest admiration made the laird's chest swell with pride.

Lady Feiyan explained she'd sent Gellir off to fish. She meant to allow Carenza time to clean up and settle in before they met. Now she summoned Merraid to convey her to the solar and attend her bath.

Merraid complied, though she couldn't imagine the woman becoming any cleaner or more comfortable in her surroundings. Lady Carenza was poised. Prepared. Perfect.

Still, for Gellir's sake, it was up to Merraid to seek out a fatal flaw. A character deficiency. A nasty habit. Some well-concealed imperfection on her seemingly unblemished soul.

In the end, she could find nothing wrong with Lady Carenza. In fact, she liked the woman. A lot.

On the way to the solar, the lady asked Merraid about her life, her family, and the castle. Unlike most noble-women, who largely ignored maidservants, she took great interest in Merraid's thoughts.

She cooed over the steaming, fragrant bath that awaited her. And she placed a humble hand over her heart when she saw that Merraid had added lavender petals to the water.

"They're my favorite," she confided. She glided gracefully to the makeshift pallet to remove her boots.

Merraid knelt to assist her.

But the lady shooed her away. "There's no need for that. I'm perfectly capable of undressin'. Indeed, if ye have other chores to do, ye can leave me. I promise I won't drown."

"I have no other chores, m'lady." Merraid was sure Lady Feiyan wouldn't approve of her deserting their guest. Besides, she needed to see if the woman had an ugly scar. A flat bosom. A wart on her arse she should warn Gellir about.

Since Merraid didn't want to stare, she busied herself. Moving the candles. Poking at the fire. Rearranging the bath linens.

Lady Carenza took off each item of clothing with great care. Her leather girdle. Her linen hose. Her deep blue velvet surcoat. Her light blue woolen kirtle. And finally her linen underdress. She draped them on the pallet so they wouldn't wrinkle.

Then she sank into the tub.

Merraid could discern no physical flaw whatsoever. Not

a single blemish, freckle, or bruise. There was a feminine softness to her body. She was petite, but round in all the right places.

Merraid tried not to simmer with envy, recalling her own lean physique and unsightly scars. Some, like the hairline slash across the side of her neck and her crisscrossed knuckles, were from swordplay. Some, like the burn mark on the heel of her hand, were from the everyday hazards of work.

"Do ye need me to scrub your back, m'lady?" she asked.

"Nay, I can manage."

Merraid settled onto the edge of a chair beside the tub and clasped her hands, at a loss for what to do.

"So tell me..." The lady had spoken so softly, Merraid wondered if she was speaking to herself. "What's he like?"

"Who, m'lady?"

"Gellir Cameliard o' Rivenloch."

Was that hesitation she heard in the lady's voice? Worry? Dread?

How could she answer?

To Merraid, Gellir Cameliard was a shining paragon of men. A brave, magnificent warrior. A chivalrous knight without compare. A steadfast, loyal friend. A brilliant, honorable, devoted nobleman who would make his bride the luckiest woman in all Scotland.

She couldn't say that. Not without melting into tears.

"He's very tall. Striking. Dark-haired. With gray eyes."

"Is he as grim as they say?"

The question was so fearful, Merraid couldn't help but feel sorry for the lady. After all, she was just as much a victim of the king's manipulations as Gellir. Lady Carenza probably knew nothing about Gellir aside from his reputation as a fierce warrior.

Merraid had promised Lady Feiyan she'd help ensure a successful marriage. She'd promised Gellir she'd find a woman who could love him. She meant to keep those promises. Even if it shattered her heart.

"His enemies call him Grim Gellir for his ferocity in battle," she said. "But he's very kind and patient with those he cares for."

"Then I must hope he cares for me."

"He agreed to marry ye, m'lady."

"Men do much for position and power. But I would know his heart."

Merraid was confused. "M'lady," she ventured, "did ye not agree to marry him as well, without knowin' him?"

Her chuckle was soft and sad. "What else could I do but as my father commanded me?"

"Ye didn't wish to marry Sir Gellir?" Merraid asked gently.

The lady lowered her head and bit her lip. Merraid could see she was holding back tears. But instead of weeping, she forced a smile to her lips. "O' course I wished to marry. 'Tis every lady's dream, aye?" Her voice held a false brightness. "To wed a handsome knight. To live in a magnificent keep. To have a home full o' childr-" She broke off and buried her face in the wash cloth.

Pity welled up in Merraid's breast. Enough to make her set aside her own heart's pain. "There now, m'lady. Don't weep. All will be well. No one will be as devoted to ye as Sir Gellir."

For some reason, her words of reassurance made Lady Carenza break into sobs.

Merraid wrung her hands, unsure what to do.

When the lady finally regained her composure, she gazed up at Merraid with an apologetic smile. Her eyes were wet with tears and so blue, they were nearly violet. Naturally, Carenza was even beautiful when she wept.

"Forgive me," she said. "I'm bein' selfish and spoiled. I'm sure 'tis only nerves."

When Merraid's nerves were in need of calming, she did her *taijiquan*. But she wasn't going to suggest that to the lady.

"I could fetch ye a cup o' wine or strong ale," she offered.

"Nay, I must have my wits about me to meet my new..." She bit her trembling lip. "My new husband."

Merraid wondered now if that was such a good idea. Gellir could look formidable and grim when he chose to. He might react badly to a lass who burst into tears at the mere sight of him.

"Perhaps ye don't have to meet him tonight," she suggested. "I could say ye're weary from travelin'. That ye'd prefer to wait till morn."

Carenza chewed on her lip, tempted for a moment. Then she shook her head. "Nay, delay will only make matters worse. I mustn't be a coward. I must face my fate with courage and calm."

She rose from the bath. Her face was stoic now, like that of Athena, the goddess of strength and wisdom. Merraid wrapped a length of linen around her straightened shoulders.

She sighed as she stepped from the tub. Then she murmured wistfully, "Och, Merraid, so much of a woman's destiny lies in the hands o' men."

Merraid couldn't agree less. Lady Feiyan had taught her to be the mistress of her own destiny. In fact, with the messy exception of letting her emotions get the better of her where Gellir was concerned, Merraid's choices were her own.

"May I speak honestly, m'lady?" she asked.

"Please."

"Were ye betrothed against your will?"

She hesitated. "Nay, not really. 'Tis only..." She broke off, then searched Merraid's eyes with penetrating force. "Can I trust ye?"

"Aye."

"Ye must not breathe a word o' this to anyone."

"Ye have my word, m'lady."

"I intend to honor this betrothal," she vowed. "I'll be a willin' bride. And a loyal wife. I'll give him a happy home and bairns to fill it. I'll ne'er give him cause to regret our marriage. I'll stand by him through thick and thin. Good times and bad. I'll give myself to him freely. He will possess me, body and soul." She hesitated then, and Merraid saw pain and sorrow in her violet eyes. "But he will ne'er have my heart," she confessed, "for that belongs to another."

Merraid knew exactly how she felt. "I see."

Still, Lady Carenza had never met Sir Gellir. She'd never basked in his silvery gaze. Felt his oak-strong arms around her. Bathed in the sweet caress of his tongue.

"I swear I'll ne'er be unfaithful to him," the lady was quick to add. "Ye should know that."

She wanted to tell Carenza if she ever *were* unfaithful to Gellir, she'd have a very vexed maidservant to answer to. Instead, she said, "Ye've yet to meet Sir Gellir. Perhaps ye'll grow to care for him."

"Perhaps." By the sorrow in her face, she didn't believe that.

It was up to Merraid to make her believe. It would be unfair to Gellir to be shackled to a wife who felt nothing for him. Merraid had to make Carenza fall in love with Gellir.

It seemed like a ridiculously easy task.


When Gellir first glimpsed Lady Carenza, she was gliding across the great hall. He realized his cousin Hew hadn't exaggerated. The lady was as lovely as an angel. As she followed Feiyan across the floor, she moved with natural grace, nodding politely to those she passed. She was dark-haired and delicate, with a heart-shaped face and a shy smile.

Was it possible he *hadn't* made the worst mistake of his life after all?

"Gellir, you're back!" Feiyan called out. "Come meet Lady Carenza."

He pushed off from the wall.

Too late, he remembered his appearance.

Informed upon his return that his bride had arrived, he'd been directed to come to the great hall at once. So he'd come straight from fishing, not bothering to wash up. What was the point, after all? The marriage was already arranged, wasn't it? There was no need to impress his bride-to-be.

What did it matter that his clothing was sticky and damp? His hair full of salt and sand? What difference did it make if he reeked of fish and the sea? If the lady intended to marry him, she'd have to get used to the idea that he didn't always look and smell like a freshly bathed champion.

Still, he felt shame and regret when he saw her. Lady Carenza had obviously taken great pains with her own appearance. Her skin glowed. Her hair shone. Her sumptuous velvet gown was spotless. And she smelled of lavender.

Now he looked like a cad.

He extended his hand and grumbled, "Lady Carenza."

His regret was amplified by her subtle yet unmistakable shiver as she placed her delicate hand in his grimy paw.

He frowned, cursing himself for not taking the time to change into clean garments and wash his hands. This was no way to meet one's betrothed.

She mistook his frown for disapproval. After murmuring "Sir Gellir" in greeting, she nervously withdrew her hand.

"Sir Gellir has just returned from fishing," Feiyan explained, smiling gently at the lady. Then she wrinkled her nose and waved her hand in front of her face. "I fear you smell of the sea, cousin." Then she turned on him with a glare so sharp, pointed, and lethal, she could have slain him with it. "Perhaps you'd like to clean up before dinner?"

Feiyan's scolding was the last thing he needed. This was her fault. She was the one who'd sent him fishing to get rid of him. Did she expect he'd return smelling like a flower?

He glowered back at her.

Lady Carenza softly intervened, averting her eyes. "Prithee do not trouble yourself on my account, m'laird. My father says sweat is the sign of an honest man."

"Your father is wise," he said, arching a rancorous brow at Feiyan.

Foiled, Feiyan turned again toward Carenza with an encouraging smile. "Aye, and very kind, allowing our cousin Hew to reside at Castle Dunlop."

"How is Hew?" Gellir asked. Aside from Hew's recent missive extolling Lady Carenza's virtues, he hadn't heard from his cousin in over a year.

"He's...well," she replied.

Gellir scowled. "Aye?" He'd hoped for a little more than that. "Any news?"

She blanched and studied her clasped hands. "My clan is fond of him, and...and..."

"Silly Gellir," Feiyan said through a gritted-teeth smile, "you can ask him yourself at the wedding."

"What wedding?"

"*Your* wedding."

"Oh. Aye." He'd resigned himself to being married. But he'd overlooked the intricacies of *getting* married. "When will that be?"

"We thought just after Beltane?" Feiyan suggested, raising her brows at Carenza.

"The sooner, the better," he said. He was eager to get back on the tournament circuit. Then he remembered it was not his decision alone. "If 'tis your wish as well?" he asked Carenza.

She bowed her head. "Aye, m'laird."

"Call me Gellir. Please."

"Aye, Sir...Gellir."

He sighed. It didn't take a wise man to see the lady was anxious. Less than enthusiastic about wedding him. Which was awkward.

But who could blame her? She was meeting the worst version of Sir Gellir of Rivenloch. His brow was menacing. His voice was gruff. His hair was a tangle. Sand clung to his boots. Filth covered his hands. And he reeked of fish.

"I should clean up," he decided. "With your permission?"

"O' course, m'laird," Carenza replied, bowing her head to murmur the correction, "Gellir."

He quickly excused himself—ignoring Feiyan's glare of condemnation—and strode out of the great hall.

He was drawing a bucket of water out of the well when Merraid approached.

"Well?" she said.

"Well, what?"

She gave him a chiding cuff on the arm. "What do ye think o' Lady Carenza?"

He shrugged. "She's pleasant enough to look at."

"And?"

"She seems to have a kind enough nature."

"Aye? And?"

"She doesn't wish to be my wife."

"Did she say that?"

"She didn't have to."

"Well, to be fair," Merraid said, covering her nose, "the way ye smell right now, only a fishwife would want ye."

He lifted the bucket, showing her he intended to

remedy that. Then he sighed. "I'm not sure a bucket of water is enough to change her heart."

Merraid bit her lip. He was right.

As for Merraid, she'd love Gellir, whether he was bloody from battle, sweaty from labor, or covered in pig slop.

But changing Carenza's heart would take all the tools at her disposal. Still, a bucket of water was at least a good start.

"Give her time," she said. "She'll come around."

"To what end?" he scoffed. "'Tis as I've always said. Marriage is only a single move in a game of draughts."

He was absolutely wrong about that. Laird Dougal wouldn't be a heroic warrior without Lady Feiyan. Gellir's own father, Pagan, wouldn't be the man he was without his formidable wife, Deirdre. Indeed, in all the neighboring clans, the lairds who'd taken good wives prospered, while those wedded to nags faltered and failed. A man's wife could make or break him.

"I spent some time with her," Merraid said.

"And?"

"She's..." She rolled her eyes. "Perfect."

He chuckled. "I doubt that."

"She's everythin' Hew said she was. Kind. Courteous. Bright." She frowned. "She hasn't got a mark on her. No scars. No blemishes."

"Shite, lass. Did you open her mouth and take a good look at her teeth as well?" he mocked, shaking his head.

"Teeth?" she teased. "Well, there *is* that. The woman *has* no teeth."

"Out of my way," he ordered, heading across the court-yard with the bucket.

As they slogged toward the armory, Merraid confided, "I think she's a wee bit afraid o' ye."

He grunted. "She wouldn't be the first maid to quiver in the presence of Grim Gellir."

"But ye can be disarmin', even charmin', when ye want to be."

"I've already vowed to wed her. What's the point of charming her?"

She grabbed his arm, stopping him. "Ye're not even goin' to try?"

"We're going to be married. Forever. I don't think she's going to be afraid of me all her life." He jerked his arm away and resumed walking.

Peeved, she caught up with him. Seizing his arm in a more forceful grip, she hissed, "Shame on ye, Gellir Cameliard. She's weddin' a man she only knows by his fierce reputation. And she's tryin' to be brave. Surrounded by strangers. Not knowin' her future or the land she's goin' to. The least ye can do is put her at ease."

She wasn't afraid of his scorching glare. She mirrored it back at him until he lowered his gaze.

"Fine," he bit out. "At supper, I'll make every effort to...disarm and charm her."

She nodded in approval.

Then he added, "But prepare to be disappointed. I doubt she wanted this alliance any more than I did."

"Fair enough."

That was what she *said*. What she *thought* was Gellir was oblivious to the force of his charm. One wink of his eye, a touch of his hand, the music of his laughter, and Carenza would fall under his power like a pup having its belly rubbed.

Unfortunately, Carenza never came to supper. She claimed to feel unwell and remained in her chamber.

Gellir presumed her illness was due to nerves. Lady Feiyan claimed it was his fault for frightening the lass.

Which only furrowed his brow further and made his mood more morose.

Finally the glowering cousins parted. Supper was cleared away. Merraid took it upon herself to carry a trencher of thin pottage up to Carenza.

Entering the chamber, she expected to find Carenza looking as lovely as ever. Perhaps suffering from a mild case of anxiety.

She was wrong. The lady was curled into a miserable ball on the bed. Her pale face had a greenish cast. Her brow shone with sweat. Her lips were white. Her eyes looked dull.

Merraid gasped. Carenza looked sickly, almost as if she'd...

"Ye didn't take...poison, did ye?" she whispered.

"What?" Carenza croaked. "Nay. 'Twill pass. It always does."

"Ye've had this before?"

She nodded.

"I have wormwood or mint that may ease—"

"Nay. Prithee don't fret o'er me. I'll be right on the morrow."

But Merraid wasn't so sure. "Ye need to keep up your strength, m'lady. Here, I've brought broth and bread. 'Twill settle your stomach."

Carenza's brow wrinkled in distress as she fought off nausea.

"Perhaps ye'd prefer a bit o' cheese?" she tried. "Or an oatcake?"

Carenza closed her eyes and shook her head.

Merraid bit her lip. She couldn't let Gellir's bride worsen on her watch. What else could she offer?

Carenza opened her eyes. "Maybe...pickled eels?"

"Pickled eels?"

"Aye," she said hopefully. "Ye wouldn't have any, would ye?"

For someone suffering from nausea, it was an odd request. Merraid had trouble eating pickled eels when she *wasn't* feeling ill. Still, if it gave the lady sustenance and made her happy, Merraid would pickle the eels herself.

"I'll see what I can find," she promised.

# CHAPTER 12

Mud squeezed between Gellir's toes as he waded toward the eel net set in the murky brown shallows of the pond. He lifted the net. It was empty.

"'Tis two days now," he bit out. Choosing a spot in the shade of an elm, he submerged the net again and anchored it with a rock. "'Tis clear she's avoiding me."

He crossed his arms over his chest, daring Merraid to contradict him.

Merraid shrugged, unaffected by his peeved gaze. "Then 'tis up to ye to make her feel welcome."

"Pah! She obviously doesn't want this alliance any more than I do."

The words were bitter in his mouth. He'd die before he'd admit it. But under the armor guarding his heart lurked a wee lad who yearned for the kind of loving marriage his parents had. He'd always said it made no difference. But the idea of a loveless marriage weighed heavily on him now.

"Ye great tomfool," she said, "how could she not want this alliance? Ye're the finest warrior in Scotland. Born into a distinguished and wealthy clan. And," she added, stealing a glance at his bare legs, "ye have knees that would turn any lady's head."

He smirked. Even if that wasn't true, it was good to hear her say so. "Apparently, I've turned the lady's stomach." He sighed and muttered, "Maybe she's deathly ill and will die ere she has to suffer my presence again."

Merraid gave him a chiding punch in the shoulder. "Do not wish such things," she scolded. "She'll be well soon enough."

"She'll either be well...or well pickled." Why the lady insisted pickled eels were the cure for her sickness, he didn't know. But his bride's appetite was the reason he was up to his knees in icy water. He was attempting to catch more of the slithery black beasts to replenish Feiyan's stores.

"I've been thinkin'," Merraid said, watching him from her perch on a mossy boulder. "What would ye do if Carenza had ne'er come to Darragh? If she lived in a faraway land? And ye couldn't meet face-to-face?"

He shrugged. "We would correspond by missives, I suppose."

"Right. Ye'd have to woo her with words, aye?" She brightened. "So that's what ye should do. Ye should send a missive to her."

"A missive?" He arched a brow at her. "Why? I could just shout at her through the door."

"Silly cad," she sneered, throwing a pebble that hit him in the chest. Then she wrapped her arms around her bent legs and gazed dreamily across the loch. "Nay, ye must write her beautiful verse. Somethin' extollin' her virtues and expressin' your love."

"Verses?" He shuddered. She may as well suggest he eat beetles. "I don't write verses."

"I do."

He frowned. "You do?"

Because he was destined to be laird, Gellir had learned to read and write. Mostly legal agreements and royal

173

orders. But only a few of his fellow warriors were literate. And aside from his clanswomen, he could count on one hand the lasses he knew who could read.

"Is there anything you can't do?" he asked sincerely.

She smiled, clearly pleased by his praise. Then she answered, "I can't catch eels."

He snorted. "Apparently, neither can I."

He retrieved the net. It came up empty again.

She rested her chin atop her knees, contemplating the rushes growing at the edge of the loch.

"The missive would have to be in your hand," she informed him.

He shook his head. "I told you I can't write verses."

"But that's the beauty of it. Ye won't have to. I'll help ye. I'll recite the words. Ye can write them on the parchment."

He lowered his brows. "It sounds deceitful."

"It sounds romantic. And this way, she won't be afraid o' ye the next time ye meet."

She had a point. This marriage had been rushed. They'd had little time to get to know each other. He had to convince his bride he wasn't a filthy brute. Only then would she recover from her illness and agree to meet him in the flesh.

"Very well," he said. "If I can ever manage to fill this basket, we'll write her a missive, aye?"

"Aye." Her eyes lit up with mischief. She scrambled down from the boulder. Then she pointed to a clump of rushes about five yards from where he stood.

"There," she said. "The eels usually hide at the bottom o' the thick rushes."

The little minx had known it all along. "I thought you said you couldn't catch eels."

She gave him the saucy, wicked smile he'd come to cherish. A smile that lingered in his mind's eye. Even after he filled the basket. Even after they trudged back to Darragh.

He wondered if his bride-to-be had a smile like that. A smile that quickened his heart. That warmed him from head to toe. That made him feel treasured and adored and alive. A smile impossible to resist.

"I long to gaze into your lovely eyes..."

Merraid ambled past the barrels in the storeroom. The candle flickered on Gellir's makeshift table, fashioned out of a crate. They needed privacy for this clandestine endeavor. Somewhere no one would interrupt them. And the ale cellar was the most private place she could think of.

Gellir dipped the quill in ink. "I long...to gaze...into... your lovely eyes," he recited as he carefully scrawled the letters onto the parchment. "Go on."

"Like sparklin' gems set in the midnight skies."

He nodded. "Like sparkling gems...set in...the midnight skies," he said, copying down the words. "That's quite good."

Of course it was good. It was inspired. All she had to do was draw on her own feelings for Gellir. Use words that would charm Lady Carenza. Express his affection in a way that was polite yet persuasive. Assure the lady she was making the right decision in marrying him. And make it rhyme.

"Aye?" he prompted.

She cleared her throat. "To see the light of love there, sweet and wise..."

"To see...the light...of love...there?"

"Sweet and wise."

"Sweet...and...wise. Aye, I think I've got the pattern of the rhyme now. Don't tell me," he said. "And swiftly delve between your lovely thighs?"

His coarse jest was so unexpected, Merraid burst into laughter. Covering her mouth in amused horror, she gave him a punitive kick.

"Shh!" he warned.

"Ye scoundrel," she hissed. "Now ye've made the next line go right out o' my head."

He grinned. Then he cleared his throat and whispered, "Here's what we have so far. I long to gaze into your lovely eyes, like sparkling gems set in the midnight skies, to see the light of love there, sweet and wise..."

"Ah. And hear the tender music o' your sighs."

As he began writing the words, Merraid heard a muffled sound beyond the door.

"Hist!" she said, freezing. Was someone there?

They remained motionless for several moments. She heard nothing else.

"Maybe 'twas a mouse," she breathed.

He nodded, then finished penning the line.

She began pacing again. It helped her to think.

"I long to glimpse your smile..."

He copied silently.

"So warm and bright," she said.

She tapped her lip. What rhymed with bright? Fight? Might? Shite?

Light, she decided. "As welcome as the winter sun's first light."

"Ooh," he cooed in approval. "You do have a way with words."

She blushed. It wasn't hard to write about love when the object of your affections was right in front of you. Gellir's smiles *were* nearly as rare as winter sun. But she secretly treasured every one.

He crossed the final T and looked up. "Aye?"

"To listen to your laughter takin' flight..."

He dipped the quill and wrote carefully. When he

finished the line, he sighed. "You're sure this is going to work?"

"O' course." What woman didn't like to be wooed with words?

He nodded. "Go on."

"Like flocks o' sparrows," she said, smiling at the imagery, "chasin' off the night."

He moved the page up so he could continue writing. "Flocks of sparrows," he echoed as he transferred her words onto the page.

She tucked her bottom lip under her teeth. Good verse was like effective fishing. The lady had been lured with compliments. Now it was time to set the hook with subtle seduction.

"I long to take your hand and hold ye near," she said, running a fingertip along the top of a barrel.

He raised a skeptical brow, but she nodded.

When he finished, she continued, ambling thoughtfully toward the door. "To whisper words dispellin' all your fear..."

He wrote the line. Then he rested the quill in the ink bottle to flex his cramped hand. He obviously wasn't in the habit of writing long missives. Picking up the quill again, he told her, "All right."

She leaned back against the door, letting the words spill directly from her heart. "And murmur soft devotions in your ear..." she choked out.

"In...your...ear." He seemed to copy the words by rote, paying little heed to their meaning. She supposed that was just as well. "Aye?"

"In breathless wait," she murmured, "for what my heart would hear."

Her eyes blurred as emotion washed over her. Merraid knew exactly what her heart wanted to hear from Gellir. That he didn't care what king and clan demanded. That he loved her. That he couldn't live without her.

But those were words Gellir would never say. And if the truth be told, his uncompromising sense of chivalry was what she loved best about him. She wouldn't have him any other way.

"Is that all?" he inquired after her long pause.

"Oh. Nay." She pressed her palms into her eyes, scrubbing away the burgeoning tears. "Let me think." The hook was set. Now came gently coaxing the fish out of familiar waters. Into his waiting hands.

"I long to make ye mine," she said, her voice cracking as she added, "my dearest heart."

He hesitated, then whispered, "You don't think that's too..." He grimaced. "Too intimate?"

She shook her head. He'd be swiving the lady within the fortnight. If he thought her *verse* was too intimate...

He inked the quill. But he looked uneasy as he transferred the personal sentiments to the page.

She turned away, facing the door, and crossed her arms protectively over her aching heart. "'Tis anguish...every moment we're apart."

The air was so still, she could hear the scratching of his quill as it carved her feelings onto the parchment.

"Go on?" he said.

She swallowed back her sorrow and continued. "Since ye alone have power to make me whole..."

He silently recorded her words. "Aye?" he breathed.

She let out a soundless sigh and finished the verse. "I pray ye spare my poor tormented soul." She kicked idly at the barrel nearest the door, mumbling, "That should do it."

He didn't reply until he'd penned the final word. "Good," he murmured. "If this doesn't convince her, nothing will."

Forcing a shaky smile to her face, she put away her strained emotions. Just before she could turn toward him, she heard a scuffle of retreat beyond the door. Someone *had* been there.

Behind her, Gellir came to his feet. "Was that…"

"Shite," she whispered, trying to recall every incriminating word she'd said.

"Do you think they heard—"

"Nay."

She said it as much to convince herself as Gellir. If someone had been listening, they probably couldn't make out her words through the door. Or if they heard her words, they wouldn't recognize her voice. Or if they knew it was Merraid, they'd never guess who she was addressing.

At least, that was her hope.

"Still," she said, turning to him, "we should be cautious. I'll leave first."

"I'll wait till the parchment dries."

"Good." She stepped toward the door and put a hand on the latch.

"And Merraid?"

She hesitated.

"Thank you," he said. "You've said what I could not."

She answered around the lump in her throat. "Let's hope it works."


Merraid arrived later to bring Carenza her supper. The lady was sitting up in bed, the missive clutched to her breast.

"Merraid, you're here." The poor woman still looked pale and sickly. A feeble smile graced her face.

"I've brought your supper." She approached with the tray, giving the lady a furtive glance.

Would she mention the missive? Had she read it? Did she hate it? Love it?

"Och dear, more eels?" Carenza wrinkled her nose. "I fear I've eaten my fill o' them. I don't think I could take another bite."

Merraid bit the inside of her cheek. Poor Gellir had spent all morn, freezing his arse in the pond, to catch the vile things. "Shall I bring ye somethin' else, m'lady?"

"In a moment. Just put the tray here," she said, indicating the bedside table. "I've received a missive from Sir Gellir. And 'tis..." She let out a sigh. "Let me read it to ye."

Merraid set the tray down. Was that a sigh of disgust or a sigh of pleasure? It was hard to tell.

But as she read the verse aloud, it was clear the lady understood the passion with which Merraid had written it. It broke Merraid's heart to hear her words from another's lips. But the sentiment had exactly the intended effect. Carenza's fears regarding Gellir had melted away. Her heart had softened toward him.

"Lovely," the lady said, tears in her voice. "Just lovely."

"I told ye he was a good man," Merraid choked out. She picked up the tray. She needed to leave before tears started in her own eyes.

"He is, isn't he?" To Merraid's surprise, Carenza's voice was now full of misery. "He's *too* good."

"*Too* good, m'lady?"

"Any man who can express such tenderness, such devotion..." She shook her head. "He deserves far better than me."

Merraid's eyes widened. "Better than..." If Carenza were any other lady, Merraid would suspect her of fishing for compliments. But the beautiful young woman seemed to be truly blind to her own charms. Merraid set the tray back down. It was time for a bit of harsh truth.

"Hear me well, m'lady. O'er the last sennight, more than a dozen perfectly qualified brides have been presented to Sir Gellir. To my reckonin', every one has fallen short. But ye... Ye're perfect. Bonnie. Sweet. Kind. Soft-spoken. Well-mannered. He could ask for no one better suited to be his wife." Her voice caught on the last words. She hoped Carenza didn't notice.

"Generous praise indeed, Merraid, and I thank ye," she said, her voice breaking in despair, "but I told ye my heart belongs to another."

"In time, I'm certain ye'll have a change o' heart. Meanwhile, ye've done the noble thing. Ye've promised to marry him. Ye've vowed to be faithful and true. 'Tis good enough. And once ye're properly wed...once ye give him a bairn..."

The lady choked out a sob.

"Och, there now," Merraid cooed in sympathy, taking the lady's hand and clasping it in her own. "Ye've naught to fret about."

But the lady continued to weep until Merraid's pity slowly grew into irritation. How could the woman be anything but delighted at the prospect of wedding a man like Gellir?

"I'll bring ye a posset o' warm milk, aye?" She gave Carenza's hand a farewell pat. "I'm sure once ye're past this sickness, the world will seem a rosier place." She added pointedly, "And ye'll see what a lucky lass ye are."

She returned the eels to the kitchen and fetched a posset from the cook. But she summoned Swannoc to take the drink to Carenza. She didn't think she could face the distraught lady again this eve. Not while her own misery tore at her heart.

Instead, she escaped to the one place she could express her frustration.

A half hour with her sword in her hand and a new straw-stuffed dummy in need of hacking gave her the satisfaction she sought.

Exhausted, she sheathed and left through the practice field gate. The sky had grown dark. So dark she didn't notice the figure watching her from the shadows of the stable.

When he stepped out, she went swiftly for her weapon. Only a hand seizing her wrist stopped her from drawing the blade.

"Merraid."

"Gellir?"

She couldn't see his face. But she let out a relieved breath and released her grip on her weapon.

He did *not* release his grip on her wrist. Her flesh tingled where he touched her.

"I've been looking all over for you."

"Ye have?" There was a foolish fluttering in her breast.

"Aye," he said. "How did it go? Did she get the missive?"

She? Of course. He wanted to know about Carenza. Disappointed, Merraid pulled her arm out of his grasp. "Aye. She was...pleased."

"Pleased. That's good, aye? Pleased?"

"Aye."

"So she's ready to meet with me?"

Merraid hesitated. "She's still feelin' poorly."

"You brought her the eels?"

She didn't want to tell him Carenza had refused the eels. "Mm-hmm."

He sighed in impatience. "How much longer do you think—"

"I think we should write another missive," she blurted out.

Merraid could have bitten her tongue. Why had she said that? It was pure torture. Spilling out her emotions. Reciting vulnerable words of devotion. Knowing they'd be delivered to another. Another who may as easily cry as coo over the sentiments.

"All right," he agreed, more readily than she expected. "The armory is empty. I'll fetch a quill and parchment and meet you there."

Now? She hadn't meant now. But she supposed now was as good a time as any. After all, his wedding date was not so far away. And there was still work to be done. Just because Merraid had fallen instantly in love with Gellir didn't mean Carenza would.

"Fine."

She made her way to the armory and hung up her sword. She lit a candle on the flame of one of the sconces. Then she placed it on a bench he could use for a makeshift table.

While she waited, Merraid racked her brain for inspiration. Should Gellir flatter Carenza with more praise? Should he boast about his own prowess and virility? Should he paint a picture of her future as his wife? What words would change her heart?

She let out a heavy breath, closing her eyes and muttering, "Think, think, think."

She opened her eyes as Gellir swept into the armory. The candlelight flickered across his face. Illuminating his coal-black hair. His strong, swarthy jaw. His noble nose. His grim, delicious mouth. His creased brow. His shining, silvery eyes.

And she was instantly inspired.

# ChAPTER 13

As Gellir carefully set Merraid's words to the page, he couldn't help but feel unworthy of her talents. Her gift was astonishing. Never had he heard words of such honor and eloquence. To think they had come from a maidservant...

"Can you read that back to me?" she asked as she ran a fingertip along the curved edge of the grinding wheel.

He nodded. "Dear heart, I fear mere words cannot express The measure of the love I would confess. Each passing hour, deprived of your sweet smile I languish here in woebegone exile."

"Is that all right?"

Gellir grunted. He wasn't sure he was languishing. But he supposed it couldn't hurt to make his bride think so.

"My soul despairs," she said, giving the wheel a spin and watching it whirl, "to know ye suffer so."

His quill hesitated over the parchment. Despairs? That seemed even stronger than languishing. He raised dubious brows. But in the end, he faithfully reproduced her verse. He only hoped the gushing missive wouldn't fall into the wrong hands.

"Next?" he asked.

The wheel slowed to a halt. "I curse the devil's deed that laid ye low."

He wrote, then paused, debating whether to capitalize "devil." In the end, he decided it was probably *a* devil, not *the* Devil. "Laid...you...low."

"And pray ye take my strength to help ye heal..."

He nodded in approval. Strength was good. Much better than despair. Or languishing. "Help...you...heal."

She leaned back against the grinding wheel, closing her eyes and hugging herself. "That I may soon my own true love reveal."

For a moment, he couldn't tear his gaze away. Merraid looked so beautiful. So vulnerable. So damned desirable. His loins stirred, threatening to reveal his own true love all too boldly.

He dipped the quill, almost knocking over the vial of ink. "Shite."

Her eyes opened. He righted the vial. But now he'd completely forgotten her words.

"Sorry," he said. "Again?"

"That I may soon...my own true love...reveal."

"Right."

He managed to finish the line while she sauntered toward the door, stopping here and there to straighten a targe on the wall.

"More?"

"They say that absence makes the heart grow fond," she continued. "That trust and patience form the strongest bond."

"Wait. Slower, I pray you," he pleaded. His hand was beginning to cramp. "They say that absence... makes the heart...grow fond..."

"That trust and patience..." she repeated.

He copied down the words. "Form the tightest bond?"

"Strongest bond."

"Strongest...bond."

He looked up. Merraid stood in profile against the flickering flame of the wall sconce. Golden light haloed her bright hair as tendrils escaped her shortened braid, making her look like an angel of fire. He wondered if the same unsteady blaze burned inside her body.

"But I grow restless in our time apart," she said.

Scraping the quill across the parchment, he asked himself if he'd grow restless when he was no longer able to match wits with the maidservant each day.

"Our...time...apart," he echoed.

"Bereft o' hope to ease my achin' heart."

The more she recited, the more the emotions resonated in him. But it wasn't the way he felt about Lady Carenza. After all, he'd met the woman only briefly. He hardly knew her.

Nay, the sweet smile, the restlessness, the aching heart described how he felt about Merraid, knowing he was leaving her behind.

She continued. "A glance, a word, a smile would ease my pain."

He formed the letters on the missive meant for Carenza. But it was Merraid's face he imagined. Her grin of mischief. Her arched brow. Her gentle smile. Her twinkle-eyed laughter.

"Aye?" he croaked, dipping the quill.

"But since the Fates command us to abstain..."

The Fates. He cursed the Fates that steered him away from Merraid. That forced him to wed a lass repulsed by him.

"To...abstain..." he repeated.

He looked up. Merraid tapped at her lower lip. She gazed sightlessly at the flagstone floor, deep in thought.

Finally she murmured, "I'm forced to...woo? Court?" Her brow creased. "Court," she decided. Then she intoned, "Alas! I'm forced to court with awkward prose..."

"Awkward prose?" he protested. "Your prose is anything but awkward."

She gave him an indulgent smile. "'Tis kind o' ye to say so."

"'Tisn't kindness."

"Humility is best, I think," she explained. "No one likes a braggart."

That was true enough. He copied down the line. "Awkward," he read back, shaking his head, "prose."

She turned away from him then, facing the wall. She mumbled something he didn't catch.

"What's that?" he asked.

She turned her head slightly over her shoulder and murmured again. Her voice was too soft to discern her words.

"I didn't catch that. Could you speak a bit—"

"The one I long to hold in passion's throes," she blurted out. Then, aghast at her own daring, she whipped her head back toward the wall.

Startled, he dropped the quill. It made a blotch on the parchment. He gasped, picking it up before it could do too much damage.

Did he hear a second gasp in the darkness? Or was it just the echo of his own?

He wasn't sure. He was still reeling from the image her words had conjured. *Holding her in passion's throes.*

Merraid misunderstood his gasp for disapproval.

She bristled. "'Twas the only thing I could think of," she hissed in her defense. "'Tisn't easy, writin' verse. What would ye have me say? 'That I should like to grab and tweak her nose'?"

For an instant, he was stunned silent.

Then a bark of laughter erupted out of him. "Tweak her nose?" God's bones. What had made her think of that?

The picture of him tweaking Carenza's nose made more laughter rumble deep in his chest. The kind of laughter that bubbled up inside him only on rare occasions.

Like when Hew splayed himself in the mud at the feet of a lass he was trying to impress. Or when Adam did a brilliant impression of Father James, reading scripture after polishing off a jack of ale.

He wondered how Lady Carenza would respond if he grabbed her by the nose. The idea made him laugh even harder.

He was unused to laughter. There was a reason he was called Grim Gellir. When a man was known as the greatest swordsman in Scotland, there was little time for levity.

But on occasion, when something struck him by surprise, chuckles rippled and burst forth like ale kept too long in the barrel. And this was such an occasion.

The sound made Merraid swing about. She wrongly assumed he was laughing at her. Flushing with humiliation, she planted her hands on her hips. Her brows slammed together in anger.

" Tweak her nose'?" he repeated, tossing his head back and laughing in earnest. "Och, lass, that's priceless!"

She saw now he wasn't mocking her. Disarmed, she lowered her hands from her hips. Her brow smoothed, and her lips began to twitch. She couldn't stay angry with him.

"Well," she said, "'twas that or...'pinch her toes'."

He roared, which made her giggle. Soon they were laughing together.

"What about 'tie her hose'?" he suggested.

She gave him a chiding shove, which set off a new round of snickers.

"Or 'wash her clothes'?" she offered.

He tried to stifle a laugh with the back of his hand and failed.

"Well, shite!" she spat.

"What?"

"Now I've forgotten the line."

He managed to get his laughing under control. "I remember it."

He did remember it. Because the words were sensual. And intimate. And shocking. The kind of words exchanged only between lovers.

*The one I long to hold in passion's throes.*

He remembered. Because he felt that kind of longing.

But it wasn't for his bride.

It was for the woman who made him laugh.

It was late when Merraid left the armory. But she was too rattled to do more than toss and turn on her pallet. She feigned sleep when young Swannoc and Ede, finished with their chores, climbed into the straw pallet next to her. And it was a long while before she could calm the lusty beating of her heart.

When she finally drifted off, her dreams were spiced with desire. Images of Gellir at his bath. Whispered words of seduction. Memories of his sweet and tender kiss.

The next morn she woke late. Too late to perform the ritual of her *taijiquan*. It was Swannoc and Ede who jabbed her awake, telling her Lady Feiyan had a task for them in the garden.

Merraid quickly dressed and braided her hair. After the disturbing night she'd had, she was glad to be assigned work away from the keep. The second missive would be delivered to Gellir's bride-to-be this morn. And Merraid wasn't sure she was up to hearing the lady recite the erotic words she'd written.

An hour later, on her hands and knees in the dirt, Merraid forgot all about Lady Carenza and Sir Gellir. The sun felt pleasantly warm on her back. The soil was pleasantly cool under her fingers. There was a certain satisfaction in planting last year's dried peas in the earth, knowing the spring rain would make them sprout and grow into new vines to feed the clan all summer long.

She used a stick to poke holes in the dirt, keeping the rows straight and the spacing even. Meanwhile, birds twittered from the forest, and Swannoc and Ede kept up a soft patter of conversation.

"I think she hates him," Ede said, dropping a pea into the hole Merraid had made.

Swannoc covered it with soil. "What makes ye say that?"

"Davy took her another missive," Ede told her, "and he said she burst into tears when she read it."

Merraid frowned. "What are ye talkin' about?"

"Lady Carenza," Ede said, wrinkling her nose. "I don't think she likes Sir Gellir. Not at all."

"She should tell him," Swannoc decided, "before 'tis too late."

"What?" Merraid said, sitting back on her heels. "'Tis nonsense. O' course she likes him."

"Then why was she cryin'?" Ede asked.

"Maybe he told her he doesn't love her," Swannoc suggested.

"Don't be ridiculous," Merraid scolded. "O' course he loves her. Cryin'? They were likely tears o' joy."

Ede scoffed, then leaned close to Swannoc to confide, "I think she's a Weepy Winifred."

Swannoc shuddered. "There's naught worse than a grown woman who bawls like a bairn."

Ede clucked her tongue. "Sir Gellir isn't goin' to like that."

Swannoc nodded in agreement. "Men hate lasses who sob all day."

"He doesn't hate her," Merraid insisted. "He *chose* her."

Ede shrugged. "That was before he found out she was a Weepy Winifred."

Merraid thinned her lips. "Just because her eyes welled a bit..."

"'Burst into tears,' Davy said." Ede crossed her arms authoritatively.

"Once..."

Ede held up two fingers. "Twice."

"That doesn't mean she hates him." Ede rolled her eyes, and Merraid scowled back at her. "She's probably just afraid."

Swannoc arched a brow. "Men doubly hate cowardly lasses."

"'Tis true," Ede agreed.

"They should break off the betrothal now," Swannoc said.

"What?" Merraid stabbed her spade into the ground. "Ye don't even know what ye're talkin' about. Ye two should mind your own affairs and keep your noses out of it."

"We just want what's best for Sir Gellir," Swannoc explained. "He needs a bride who's strong."

"And brave," Ede said.

"One who can take care of a keep while he's off fightin'."

"Not a Weepy Wi-"

"Enough!" Merraid snapped. "Sir Gellir's made his choice. 'Tis up to all of us to see this weddin' through."

Swannoc and Ede exchanged disappointed glances.

"The clouds are gatherin'," she said, "so let's get the peas in ere the rain starts. And I'll hear no more gossip about who hates who."

But even though the lasses complied, retreating into silence, they'd planted a seed of doubt in Merraid's brain. One that ruined her concentration and made the last row of peas skew crooked.

Were they right? Did Lady Carenza dislike Sir Gellir? Was she not suited to him? Was Merraid doing a bad thing? Encouraging a marriage that would become unbearable for both of them?

She had to find out for herself.

191

After she finished planting, she fetched oatcakes and butter from the kitchens. Then she knocked softly on Lady Carenza's door.

"How are ye feelin', m'lady?"

Though her pallor looked healthier, the lady's eyes were red and swollen. Perhaps Ede was right. Perhaps she *was* a Weeping Winifred.

"Better," Carenza said with a wan smile.

"Good enough to eat a bit o' somethin'?" She set the tray on the bedside table.

The lady nodded, but didn't touch the food.

Against her better judgment, Merraid said, "I hear ye got another missive from Sir Gellir."

The lady's chin trembled. She nodded again.

Merraid gave her an encouraging smile. "He must care about ye a great deal."

The lady's eyes filled with tears.

Merraid bit her lip. Bloody hell. What had she said? Why was the lady upset?

"He's a most decent man," the lady choked out. "So noble. So kind." And then she did the inexplicable, just as Davy had reported. She covered her face and burst into tears.

"Och dear, m'lady," Merraid said, wringing her hands, at a loss as to what to do. "Whate'er troubles ye?" Then, suddenly inspired, she asked, "Is it your monthly courses?"

The lady paled and gasped.

Merraid bit her tongue. Perhaps that was too intimate a subject for the noblewoman to discuss.

Too upset to reply with words, the lady waved away Merraid's concern.

Moments later, when she finally got her sobs under control, she apologized. "Prithee forgive me for this foolishness. I fear my sickness...and Sir Gellir's lovely words...and these upcoming nuptials...have made me overwrought."

Merraid nodded. "Beggin' your pardon, m'lady, but perhaps meetin' him face to face would dispel your—"

"Nay!" she burst out. "I mean... I do not wish him to see me like this. All blubbering and sickly and fraught with emotion. Men despise such weakness." She lowered her eyes. "I'm sure ye understand."

"Aye."

"On the morrow perhaps." She nodded at the oatcakes and struggled to smile. "I'll fill my belly and get plenty of sleep. Once I have my temperament under control, I'm sure I'll be happy to converse with my husband-to-be."

Merraid hoped so. She was in danger of running out of verses.

"Moved?" Gellir murmured around the bite of hard cheese he'd pilfered from the buttery shelf.

"Aye," Merraid confided. "She was *quite* moved by the missive." He didn't need to know the truth—that Lady Carenza had been moved to *tears*.

"You don't think 'tis too soon to send another?"

"Nay," she said, patting her satchel, which contained a bit of parchment, a sharpened quill, and a bottle of ink. "We must forge the blade while the steel is hot."

Gellir had to reassure Lady Carenza that her tender emotions were not only acceptable to him, but welcome. That was the only way the lady would have the courage to face him. The only way she'd fall in love with him.

Merraid dragged a stool across the floor of the buttery. Moving aside a wheel of cheese and several bottles of wine, she cleared a space on the lowest shelf. Then she smoothed the parchment atop the shelf and set the quill and ink beside it. She gestured to him to take a seat.

He glanced around the chamber in recognition. "Is this where...?"

He remembered. She smiled. "Where ye looked after a wee maidservant with a broken nose? Aye."

It seemed like half a lifetime ago. But she recalled that day in the buttery as clearly as the day it had happened. The fierce battle. The close quarters. Fighting for her life. Throwing cheeses. Throwing punches. Being saved.

"You were attacked by those wretched brutes," he recalled.

"Fergus and Morris," she said. "And ye came to my rescue."

"Not soon enough to save your nose."

She shrugged. "And afterward..."

He scowled. "My cousin stole my clothes."

"To disguise herself." Merraid winked. "I can't say I was unhappy about that."

He clucked his tongue. "You know, a polite lass would put it right out of her head."

"I'm not a polite lass."

He smirked.

Besides, she thought, that memory had sustained her while Gellir spent four long years traipsing across Scotland. Fighting in tournaments. Putting *her* out of *his* head.

It was that memory—of Gellir's kindness and honor and empathy—that would inspire her now as she dictated what she hoped was the last missive he'd need to seal his marriage to Lady Carenza.

Gellir hoped he wouldn't have to transcribe too many more missives to the lass.

For one thing, he had a fierce reputation to uphold. He didn't mind revealing his thoughts to the one he meant to wed. But if anyone should intercept his tender notes... He shuddered. The thought of his fellow warriors chuckling over such softhearted sentiments was too awful to consider.

And for another? Hearing words of powerful passion and deep devotion, knowing they came from Merraid's lips, her heart, her brain... That fascinated and—what word had she used?—*moved* him, more than he wished to admit.

Years ago, in this very place, he'd been coerced to bare himself to the young maidservant. Now it seemed she exposed her heart to him, leaving herself likewise vulnerable. When she spoke, he felt as if he peered into her very soul. And what he saw there made his pulse race and his breath catch.

He was beginning to have feelings he should not. Feelings for Merraid. Feelings that were sinful. Tempting. Destructive. For a man loyal to the king, such feelings were distracting. For a man promised to another, they were deadly.

Perspiring despite the cool air of the buttery, he settled onto the stool. He opened the ink, dipped the quill, and braced himself.

She began with, "If ever I give cause to make ye grieve..."

Merraid had already given him cause to grieve by bringing him here, where lusty memories danced about like taunting tongues of flame.

But it was too late to change that. With a sigh, he copied down her words.

"Go on," he said.

"I pray ye to forgive my careless tongue."

He nearly strangled on that line. A vision of what he'd like to do to the lass with his careless tongue blinded him for a moment. His quill hovered over the parchment.

She didn't seem to notice. She picked up a cheese, sniffed it, and put it back.

He wrote down the line without repeating it. "Aye?"

She tapped her lip. "'Tis true...nay...I know...nay...I *fear*. Aye. I fear I wear my heart upon my sleeve."

He frowned. He didn't like fear so much. Fear indicated weakness.

But if the words *moved* his bride, as Merraid reported, he supposed he could be forgiven a moment of weakness.

"All right."

She hesitated a moment, then murmured the next line over her shoulder. "And cannot bear to leave my love unsung."

That was exactly what he was being forced to do. Leave his love unsung. Deny his feelings for Merraid. It felt wrong. And yet he supposed that silence was just the price of chivalry. He was not the first to suffer unrequited affection.

"Love...unsung," he finished.

She picked up a bottle of wine, blowing the dust from its shoulders. "For though at first I may seem hard as steel..."

His eyes widened. She obviously didn't intend the lusty reference. But the beast in his braies understood it all too well. Even now he swelled to steely hardness.

When he finished the line, he nodded for her to go on.

"'Tis only armor for my tender heart."

As he copied down the words, he felt a twinge of remorse. He hoped Carenza wouldn't expect him to continue writing verse for her after they were wed. He had no talent for it. And he couln't very well invite Merraid along to be his scribe.

The lass dictated two more lines of the verse. Then she asked him to read them back.

He cleared his throat and read, "My knightly pride forbids me to reveal...the gentleness I would to you impart."

"One more verse should do," she said softly.

He sighed, grateful. Looking at her in the candlelight, he

tried to recall the wee lass with the bloody nose. Then he'd assured her the injury wouldn't leave a scar. He'd been right. Her nose was straight. Her face was beautiful.

"I yearn to give ye comfort in my arms," she murmured, casting her gaze toward the floor.

He swallowed hard and lowered his gaze to the page as he wrote.

"Aye?" he rasped out.

"To catch your mournful tears upon my cheek."

Mournful tears? He hardly thought his bride-to-be would be mourning. After all, she was winning the hand of a respected warrior. Marrying into a legendary clan.

But when he completed the line and looked up at Merraid, he saw her eyes were shimmering with unshed tears. Before he could wonder why, she turned aside and delivered the next line.

"To soothe and save and shield ye from all harms..."

Gellir nodded in satisfaction. That was his life's purpose. Even as a younger lad, defending a wee maidservant from tyrants and tormenters, he'd known it was his calling to protect the innocent and helpless.

"And welcome ye with warmth when next we speak," she finished.

He gazed down at the parchment as he wrote and asked her bluntly, "Do you think the warmth will be returned?"

"How could she resist?" she said. "Ye're everythin' a woman could ask for. An undefeated tournament champion. A noble as rich as Midas." There was sorrow in her voice as she added, "But ye're more than that. Ye're kind. Decent. Honorable. Surely she'll see that at once."

Gellir had been flattered before. By ladies seeking his bed. Or his coin. They remarked on his dark good looks. They applauded his prowess on the field of battle. They raved over his brain. His brawn. His bravery. Some even called him a god.

Their praises had always felt as lasting as the night mist on a loch, burning away at dawn. They were brief, empty, meaningless.

But the simple observations Merraid made—calling him kind, decent, honorable—affected him more than they should. And that she thought he was "everything a woman could ask for" moved him beyond words.

That was how a wife should feel about her husband. It was the way his parents felt about each other. And it was how he wanted to feel about his bride.

Maybe once they were better acquainted, his heart would warm to her. Maybe time would draw them closer together. But at the moment, he didn't feel moved by Lady Carenza. And despite Merraid's optimism, he wasn't sure he would ever feel that way.

# CHAPTER 14

The next morn, Merraid went to the kitchens to fetch breakfast for Lady Carenza. A bowl of apple frumenty. Warm. Rich. Sweet-spiced. Gellir's last missive hadn't coaxed the lady from her sickbed. Perhaps she'd be tempted by a tasty breakfast.

She was winding her way across the crowded great hall toward the stairs when Lady Feiyan pulled her aside.

"How goes it?" she murmured. "Do you think our butterfly will emerge today?"

"Lady Carenza?" She hoped so. But according to Ede, Davy had reported more tears last night.

Lady Feiyan nodded. "Poor Gellir is beginning to believe she doesn't find him attractive."

"Gellir?" Merraid choked out.

Their brows rose in simultaneous amazement.

"I know," Feiyan said, shaking her head. "'Tis as if the man's ne'er looked in a mirror."

Merraid grinned. That was true. Lasses sighed and fainted at his feet. But Gellir was driven by his own purpose and ambition. He carried on, blithely unaware of their attentions. She should know. He'd been blithely unaware of hers.

"Here," Lady Feiyan said. She loosed the blue ribbon from her braid. Tied it into a bow. Set it on the tray beside the frumenty. "Tell her 'tis a gift from her betrothed." She winked.

"And that he said it matches her eyes?"

"Absolutely." She nodded toward the stairs. "Go."

She'd just reached the steps when she was mobbed by Swannoc, Ede, and Davy.

"Wait!" Ede cried, moving to block the path.

Merraid frowned. "What?"

"Don't do it."

"Don't do what?"

"Don't go up to Lady Carenza's chamber."

"Why not?"

"She's...not awake."

Ede was a bad liar. "Is that so? And how would ye know that?"

Ede gave Swannoc a desperate look.

Swannoc glanced at the platter. "What she means to say is the lady's not goin' to like the frumenty."

Bloody hell. What were they up to? "Well, she's not goin' to like it cold. That's for certain. Now out o' my way."

Davy crossed his arms and tried to deepend his voice. "I'm afraid I can't let ye do that."

If he were a grown man, Merraid would have tossed him on his arse for his impertinence. But he was only a young lad. She narrowed threatening eyes at him. "Ye're not goin' to stop me."

Davy nervously licked his lips. He'd no doubt seen her best greater men than he. "I'm just tryin' to help," he mumbled.

He looked to Swannoc for assistance.

"I heard her say she hates frumenty," Swannoc said.

"Hates frumenty?" Merraid said, arching a dubious brow. "A Scotswoman?"

"Aye, especially..." Swannoc insisted, glancing again at the platter. "Apple frumenty."

Now she knew they were lying. "Stand aside."

Ede gave Davy a fretful look.

"'Tis poison!" Davy blurted out.

"What?"

Davy clapped his hand over his mouth. Even Swannoc and Ede stared at him, aghast.

For one instant, Merraid wondered if that was true. But she'd fetched the frumenty herself. From a communal cauldron. No one had been poisoned this morn.

"Don't be ridiculous." She closed her eyes to smoldering slits. "What are ye up to, ye three?"

"Nothin'," Swannoc said.

"She made me do it," he said, glancing at Swannoc.

Swannoc punched him in the shoulder.

"Just...don't go up there," Ede begged.

"What have ye done?"

"'Twas *her* idea," Davy said, nodding at Swannoc and staying safely out of range.

Swannoc had to settle for giving him a cutting glare.

"Don't be vexed, Merraid," Ede pleaded. "We didn't mean any harm. But hearin' the words o' love ye spoke to Sir Gellir—"

"Ede!" Swannoc snapped.

Davy gasped.

Merraid's breath stopped. "What?" she whispered. "What did ye say?"

Ede's face crumpled as she blinked at Swannoc. "She may as well know."

"Know what?"

Swannoc murmured, "We heard ye."

What were they talking about?

Ede ducked her chin. "I heard ye in the storeroom two days ago."

"And I was passin' by the armory yesterday," Davy said.

Swannoc added, "I was goin' to the buttery last night to fetch a bite o' cheese when…"

Merraid felt sick. The sound she'd heard in the storeroom. The gasp she'd heard in the armory. "Ye were listenin' at doors?"

"We didn't mean to," Davy said.

Shite. This was a disaster. Now everyone would know. Everyone would realize it was Merraid—not Sir Gellir—who'd written the verses for Lady Carenza. And once she found out…

"Shite."

"Och, Merraid," Ede cried, touching her arm in sympathy. "Ye shouldn't have to hide your love."

Swannoc nodded, placing a hand on Merraid's shoulder. "Not when 'tis so deep and so pure."

"Lady Carenza must be told," Ede decided. "She has to know how ye feel."

Davy furrowed earnest brows. "Ye're a better match for him anyway. He can't wed that Sobbin' Sybil."

"There has to be a way to make this right," Ede insisted.

Swannoc intoned, *"Amor vincit omnia.* 'Tis the Rivenloch creed. Love conquers all."

"Even when romance seems hopeless," Ede said.

Merraid blinked. For the love of Mary… Things were even more twisted than she thought. The servants had not only overheard her dictating the missives to Carenza. They believed the words were Merraid's confession of her love for Gellir.

In a way, that was true. She'd poured her heart into every word.

To be honest, she was touched by the servants' reaction. Their intentions were noble. They wished to help two star-crossed lovers. They naively believed the power of love could bridge the chasm between a commoner and a noble.

But they were wrong. And she had to think of a way to discourage their matchmaking efforts.

She took a step back, shaking off their hands.

"Ye've got it all wrong," she scoffed. "I don't have feelin's for Sir Gellir. I asked him to copy my words down... for someone else."

"Someone else?" Ede said. She looked crestfallen.

"What someone else?" Davy asked.

Merraid sniffed. "'Tisn't your affair."

"But ye sounded so sincere," Ede said.

"I was. But my words weren't for Sir Gellir."

"I don't believe ye," Swannoc decided.

"I don't care whether ye believe me or not. 'Tis true."

The young maidservant gave her a sly look. "Why would ye need Sir Gellir to copy your words when ye can make your own letters?"

Swannoc was a savvy lass.

But Merraid was a quick thinker.

"My scribin' is pitiful. I didn't want to waste the laird's good parchment."

By her silence, Swannoc believed that. Fortunately, it didn't occur to her that anyone Merraid would woo probably couldn't read.

"Now will ye get out o' my way and let me bring the lady her breakfast?"

Davy stood his ground and gave the other two a nervous glance.

"Och nay," Ede wailed, wringing her hands.

"What is it?" Merraid had a bad feeling they'd already made mischief. "What have ye done, ye three?"

Swannoc straightened. "Ye have to understand we were tryin' to help ye."

"'Twas Swan's idea," Davy said.

Swannoc glared at him. "Tongue-wagger."

Ede gaped at Davy. "Besides, ye were the one who set them loose."

Davy replied, "Only because ye're scared o' mice."

All three froze, glancing in horror at Merraid.

"Mice?" Merraid repeated. *"Mice?"*

"I said we should use kittens," Ede said in her defense.

Davy scoffed. "Kittens? No one's scared o' kittens."

"Let me see if I have this right," Merraid said between clenched teeth. "The three o' ye loosed mice in Lady Carenza's chamber."

Davy proudly announced, "'Twas mostly me. Even Swan was too skittish to pick up the wee beasties."

Merraid blew out a determined breath. She'd have to decide their punishment later. For now, she had to go to Lady Carenza, who was no doubt standing atop her pallet, shrieking in fright.

"Out o' my way," she growled, elbowing the others aside to climb the stairs. "I'll deal with ye later."

The last thing she expected to see when she swung open Carenza's door was the lady kneeling in the middle of the chamber, cradling one of the wee beasties in the palm of her hand.

Spotting Merraid's tray, she murmured to the mouse, "That's Merraid, come with breakfast. And if ye're very good, I may give ye a wee bite."

Of *course* Lady Carenza was friendly to animals. Merraid shouldn't be surprised. The lady was friendly to everyone. Everyone except Sir Gellir.

Merraid set the tray on the table, lowered her head, and clasped her hands before her, looking remorseful. Out of the corner of her eye, she saw three more mice skittering along the wall. One more headed toward the hearth.

"M'lady, I must apologize for Davy and Ede and Swannoc. I assure ye their mischief will be punished."

"I fear I foiled their plot," she said, smiling. "Ye see, I

have a soft spot in my heart for wee furry creatures." She set the mouse down on the floor. It darted off to join its three companions. "And I understand" she said, coming to her feet. "I lost my mother when I was a lass, and I was sure my father's new wife would ruin my life. I gave her a welcome gift too," she confided, "only mine was frogs."

Merraid grinned at that. "Frogs?"

"Much more effective. Especially when you put them between the bedlinens." She winked.

Merraid's grin widened, even as her heart cracked. Damn it, she didn't want to like Carenza. But she did. The lady was so perfect, she was even perfectly mischievous. Gellir would adore her.

Gellir wished he could adore Carenza as much as everyone else did.

Maybe it was because none of them had to wed the lady.

She had finally emerged from her sickbed. Healthy and restored. She'd murmured her thanks for the blue ribbon in her hair, though he couldn't remember giving her such a thing.

What followed was a sennight in which they were to become acquainted before the wedding would take place.

He'd been accused of being too fierce. Unapproachable. For a warrior—a man whose greatest strengths were the depth of his courage and the might of his arm—it was hard to accept that the battle for his bride couldn't be won by force.

But he took Merraid's advice. He softened his manner. He did all the right things. Said all the right things. He was polite. Considerate. Gallant. Gentle.

Somehow that made things worse. Instead of cowering in fear from him, his bride dissolved into tears at the slightest show of tenderness.

Seven days made no difference. They still didn't wish to marry.

Merraid insisted their reluctance was because that wasn't enough time to truly know a person.

His cousin Feiyan thought he and Carenza must be blind not to recognize each other's virtues.

Neither of them knew how he felt about Merraid. How seven days had been more than enough to know *her*. How his fondness for Carenza paled in comparison with his fascination with the spirited maidservant. How he despaired of ever having a genuinely blissful union.

Still, he was on a path from which he dared not stray. Rivenloch's allegiance and the plight of Scotland depended upon this marriage. A marriage that would take place in just over a sennight.

Tonight, however, no one was focused on his wedding. Not even pesky Feiyan.

Tonight was Beltane.

As a lad, each year, Gellir had looked forward to the gigantic blazing bonfires of Beltane. He and his cousins helped to drive the cattle between the two fires and dared each other to leap over the flames. His wee brother Ian had once thrown a powder onto the fire that had made it spark and smoke. Their mother had put a quick end to that. But the night of Beltane had always seemed full of magic and mayhem.

As a grown man, however, Gellir had little enthusiasm for superstition. He was more concerned about the real threat of war and poverty than he was of faeries and curses. He didn't believe the ancient rituals protected crops, purified cattle, and ensured fertility. His clan had celebrated Beltane for centuries, after all, and yet some years the harvest was poor.

Still, it was a night of wild excitement and mad rulebreaking. Men drank themselves into brawls. Lads singed their arses on the flames. Lasses dipped their lashes and raised their hems. And some took the celebration of unbridled fertility as permission to cast seed about indiscriminately. It was said that bairns conceived on Beltane were blessed. More than one couple welcomed a bairn nine months after Beltane. Some legitimate. Some not.

This morn, however, Gellir had been compelled to participate in a far less thrilling ritual. Once a fearsome tournament champion, he was currently traipsing through a meadow with a basket of flowers.

According to tradition, it was a man's duty to deck his ladylove's window with garlands of blossoms on Beltane. And neither Feiyan nor Merraid was going to let him get away with anything short of full and enthusiastic compliance.

So he begrudgingly gathered the yellow, white, and violet blooms that dotted the lush meadow. They seemed like they would please Carenza.

He sighed. She would likely show her pleasure by collapsing in tears.

After that, he'd be required to join the rest of the clansmen in gathering the nine woods required for the bonfire. He smiled as he remembered how he and his clever cousin Adam had worked out a method for remembering them. HOARY BABE. Holly. Oak. Alder. Rowan. Yew. Briar. Aspen. Birch. And Elder.

He snapped off one final blossom before trudging across the soggy ground toward the keep. He wished Adam were here now. He could disguise himself as Gellir and take Gellir's place at the wedding. Perhaps *he* could make Lady Carenza happy.

And who would make Gellir happy?

Coppery hair and clear blue eyes danced through his imagination.

He furrowed his brows. Merraid was so maddeningly close, yet completely out of reach.

The worst part was she would never know how he felt. He would marry Carenza. Take her to Rivenloch. Make bairns with her. Grow old with her. And Merraid would never know that for one sweet and glorious spring, his whole heart had belonged to her.

How could he endure that?

How could he leave her without telling her the truth?

His fist tightened on the basket. He glanced down and spied an odd blossom tucked among the violet, yellow, and white. A single marigold, scooped up in haste. A curiosity.

Merraid was like that. Unique. Brilliant. One of a kind.

In that instant, gazing down at the lovely orange petals—bold, bright, and brazen—he made up his mind.

He *was* going to bare his heart.

On this mystical night, full of flames and faeries and fertility rites, before he had to wed the woman he didn't love—the woman who didn't love him—he had to tell Merraid how he felt.

# CHAPTER 15

**M**erraid loved Beltane. There was nothing quite as exhilarating as an enormous bonfire. Unless it was *two* bonfires.

The flames leapt high into the air as the cowherds guided the cattle carefully between the blazes. The animals' black bulks were stark against the bright fire. They lowed in confusion as tongues of flame threatened to lick the fur from their hide. Purified when they made the passage three times, the beasts were then driven to the summer pasture.

Even more exciting was watching the men trying to leap over the bonfires. More than a few caught fire and had to roll in the sod to douse the flames. Indeed, many a maidservant secretly cursed Beltane for all the burned clothes in need of mending afterward.

But Merraid didn't mind. It was all good fun.

What she *did* mind were the drunken lads who used the excuse of Beltane to flex their own fertility. The combination—free-flowing ale, uncontrolled fire, and rituals encouraging fruitfulness—was dangerous. Especially for lasses who were tipsy themselves and not inclined to resist the advances of enthusiastic knaves.

Which was why Merraid had appointed herself their protector on Beltane. She abstained from ale to keep a

209

clear head and watched carefully over any stray lambs who were in danger of being devoured by wolves.

It was what Gellir had done for her four years ago. Saving her from brutes who saw her, not as a young lady deserving of respect, but simply a vessel for their lust. Gellir had devoted himself to helping the helpless. And that had been inspiring.

Her vigilance this eve also kept her from dwelling too much on how magnificent Gellir looked silhouetted in front of the towering flames. The blaze rose high above his broad shoulders and gilded the top of his dark hair. If she squinted just right, she could imagine he was a great black dragon, breathing the fire to life.

But as she gazed on in amusement, a shadow of guilt crept over her. Her smile drooped. She shouldn't be staring at another woman's bridegroom.

Where was Lady Carenza anyway? Why was she not standing beside him?

The lady was one of the stray lambs Merraid should be looking after. Friendly and vulnerable were a bad combination. That Carenza was also beautiful made her an even more desirable target.

Scouring the clearing, she saw no sign of Lady Carenza. But she found Feiyan, watching the fires with Laird Dougal.

"Pardon, m'lady, but have ye seen Lady Carenza?"

"Och aye, she went to bed hours ago."

"To bed?"

"Aye. She was feeling poorly again. I fear Beltane was too much excitement for her."

Merraid nodded. But she had to admit she was disappointed. If Carenza collapsed every time there was a wee bit of excitement, Gellir would lead a dull life indeed. God forbid the lady should ever see him fight in a tournament. One scratch might well be her undoing.

She hoped someone had returned with the lady to light

her fire. All the hearths and candles had been extinguished in preparation for Beltane.

The clan folk were dispersing now. The less adventurous—those who weren't creeping off into the forest for mischief—plucked flaming branches from the bonfires to rekindle their hearths with new summer fire.

Her brow creased. She should probably make sure the lady was safe. In another sennight, Carenza would be in Gellir's care, body and soul. But for now, she was still Merraid's responsibility. The last thing Merraid needed was for Gellir's bride to freeze to death before the wedding because no one had fired up her hearth.

She approached the crackling bonfire with caution and pried loose a modest sized branch to serve as a torch. Then she began the trek back to the castle.

She had just stepped onto the path leading through the forest when Gellir swept up behind her.

"Merraid."

Foolish pleasure flushed her cheeks at the sound of his voice. Hiding it as best she could, she turned toward him. But the grave expression on his face sobered her at once.

Something was wrong. Had something happened to Carenza after all? Had she been attacked? Had she frozen to death? Had she run off?

"Aye?" she whispered, her heart pounding.

"I have somethin' t' tell you."

Now she detected the ale on his breath. The slurring of his words. The subtle swaying of his body.

"Ye're sotted."

"Aye," he said grimly, "that I am."

Relief let her breathe. Amusement tugged a grin from the corner of her mouth. She'd never seen Gellir drunk before. He was a man of control. Restraint. Honor. It was against his nature to let ale cloud his judgment.

On the other hand, it *was* Beltane. If ever the driven,

disciplined warrior deserved a night of excess, it was this night.

"Is that what ye wished to tell me? That ye're sotted?"

"Nay."

"What is it then?"

His brows darkened, lowering over his steely eyes like gathering thunderheads. She'd never seen him so grim.

He worked his mouth and cast a mistrustful glance over his shoulder. For someone with something to tell her, he didn't seem to be in a hurry to spit it out.

"Not here," he decided.

Behind him, the laird and lady were making their way toward the path.

Gellir seized her wrist, took the torch from her, and tugged her forward.

Ordinarily, her first instinct when a man grabbed her was to resist. But this was Gellir. She trusted him. Even if he *was* drunk.

She let him guide her through the wood.

They traveled at such a brisk pace, she had to struggle to keep up. The flaming brand was soon reduced to a glowing ember. If not for the well-worn path, it would have been easy to get lost in the trees.

"This way," he murmured, turning off down the trail that led to the pond and not the castle.

"But the keep is—"

"I know."

Where was he taking her? And why? It was a long way off course. She was weary. Carenza needed tending. And it was late.

Eventually they reached the pond. By then she was out of breath. And out of patience.

"What do ye have to tell me, Gellir?" she asked, yanking her wrist out of his grip. "Or did ye just want to go for a midnight swim?"

The brief hurt that creased his brow made her regret her harsh words.

"Sorry," she muttered, meaning it. If he'd taken her this far from the others, he must have something important to say. "What is it?" she asked gently, clasping his forearm. "What troubles ye?"

He looked directly at her then, as if steeling his nerves for what he would say. She was shaken by the intensity of his gaze. It was compelling. And forbidden. And dangerous. Yet she was powerless to look away.

He drew up to his full height and let out a sharp exhale. Bracing himself the way she'd seen him do before a sword battle.

"I have t'tell you," he decided. His jaw was resolute. His mouth was firm. His eyes were stern. "If I don't tell y' now... I ne'er will."

A warm and wary tingling started at the back of her neck. What did he mean to say?

"Y' deserve t'know," he murmured.

Her eyes melted under the scorching heat of his. The warmth wound its way around her throat. Smoldered on her cheeks. Ignited in her ears.

"Y' deserve..." His gaze burned her with yearning. "So much more."

There was no mistaking his message. Nor what the "so much more" left unspoken. Too much ale had stripped his mask away. Raw passion blazed in his eyes.

The same desire burned in her. And she longed to answer him. Hell, she'd longed for him for years.

But she wasn't drunk. And he wasn't himself. The craving they felt now would be gone in a moment. If they yielded to their baser instincts, the guilt they'd endure would last a lifetime.

She knew the two words that would sober him. Two words that would break the spell of lust. Reverse the wicked curse of desire the Beltane faeries cast upon them all.

She had to utter them. Before it was too late.

They came out like an incantation. "Lady Carenza."

But they changed nothing.

Gellir didn't shrink in remorse. He didn't even avert his gaze.

"She doesn't love me," he explained.

His words sounded so bleak it made her heart ache.

"She will," she promised.

"Nay." His eyes flattened. "Her heart isn't mine t' have."

"Did she tell ye that?" Damn Carenza. She'd promised Merraid that she'd never reveal that to Gellir. If she'd broken her word...

"She didn't have t' tell me." He shook his head. "Doesn't matter. I don't love her either."

Merraid blinked. That was hard to imagine. Everyone in the clan loved Carenza. Even the mice. "If ye just give it time—"

"I love *you*, Merraid," he gushed.

"What?"

There it was. The words he shouldn't have said.

Everything stopped. Her heart. Her breath. The air.

"I said—"

"I heard what ye said," she whispered, wishing urgently to silence him. It wasn't true. It couldn't be true. He was only caught up in the lust of Beltane.

"I mean it," he assured her, taking her by the shoulder. "I love you."

Her heart fluttered in panic. What if, on this magical night, his perilous whispered words drifted on the breeze? What if mischievous faeries carried them aloft? Strengthening them until they found their way into Lady Carenza's ear? Magnifying them until they echoed over the land?

She couldn't let that happen. She couldn't let careless, drunken murmurs be the cause of pain and heartbreak.

"Ye're drunk," she told him. "Ye don't know what ye're sayin'." She cast off his hand and snatched the torch away. "'Twouldn't be the first time a sotted lad tried to steal a kiss off a lass with those words." She said it as much to convince herself as to chide him. Because she very badly wanted to kiss him.

"I don't want a kiss. I swear."

"Och aye?" She raised a doubtful brow. Then she summoned up a glare. "Ye weren't hopin' for a quick Beltane tryst, were ye?"

He frowned. "I may be sotted. But I still have my honor. You know that."

She supposed she did.

"I jus' thought y'd want to know the truth," he said. "After all, we're friends, aye?"

"Aye."

"And friends should have no secrets 'tween them." He nodded. "So I want y' to know where my heart is."

Merraid bit her lip. Was it possible? Was his confession more than an impulsive outburst? Not just a lusty knave's trick designed to get under her skirts?

"Y' needn't fret," he said. "I know m' place. I'll do m' duty. I'll wed the one I'm told t' wed. I'll be a good husband to her. She'll want for naught. Jewels. Bairns... Mice." He quirked up a corner of his mouth. "But all the while I'll know the truth. And I want y' to know it as well." He looked deep into her eyes. "Know that I loved you once upon a time, Merraid. Jus' know that I loved you."

Her heart melted into a puddle.

"T'night," he continued, "when love runs wild and free, I'd open m' heart to you. That's all. I'm not askin' for a kiss. Or a tryst. I'm not even askin' y' to return the words. I just think y' should know how much y've meant to me. How much of a friend to me y've been. My *best* friend." He blew out a long breath then, as if his outpouring of emotion had drained him. "I'll ne'er love another the way I love you, Merraid. And I jus' want to have the memory o' you and the Beltane fire t' keep me warm when—"

Merraid would never be sure in that moment if she kissed him out of yearning or just to shut him up.

Either way, she successfully stopped his words. Words that were too powerful. Words that made her pulse race. Words that made her begin to hope, which was the most hazardous thing of all.

For one long moment, he stood frozen as she pressed her lips against his ale-flavored mouth.

She fooled herself into thinking that would be the end of it. She'd silence his reckless and futile declaration. He'd apologize for his outburst. And they would never speak of it again.

But in the next instant, everything changed.

Tentatively at first, he began to respond to her kiss. He moved his lips, coaxing hers apart. His breath sighed softly into her mouth. He tilted his head, teasing her jaw wider, deepening the kiss.

Current bolted through her as he touched the tip of his tongue to hers. She made a small moan of pleasure, which startled her and aroused him.

Capturing her chin between his thumb and finger, he trespassed farther. Delving in with his warm tongue to wage a sensual war with hers.

She yielded to his exploration and clasped his jaw between her hands, drawing him closer to make an exploration of her own. He tasted of ale and fire and fervor. An elixir both delicious and dangerous. Her thirst was great. She drank deep.

Drowning in a whirlpool of desire and curiosity, she forgot all about Carenza and Beltane. She thought only of Gellir. The lad he'd been. The man he was. Her friend. Her hero. Holding him. Kissing him. Loving him.

His deep growl of desire called to something primitive inside her. It summoned forth a woman of raw lust and raging need.

He dropped the dying torch to the forest floor, enfolding her in his arms. She answered him with a sigh of sweet surrender.

He pulled her closer. Against his hard warrior's chest. And his soft, throbbing heart.

She wrapped her arms around his neck. Threaded her fingers through his long, lush locks. Pressed her aching breasts against him. Melted into his embrace.

They feasted on each other like insatiable, ravenous beasts, unable to gorge themselves quickly enough. And yet she wanted more. So much more.

It felt right. He felt right. As if their love was meant to be.

Would it be so unforgivable to express that love with a tryst? Just once?

In a sennight, Gellir would be wedded to someone else. Someone he didn't love. Someone who didn't love him. Someone who would take her hero from her forever.

Was it so wrong to want one unforgettable night with him?

It didn't feel wrong. It would harm nobody. No one need know.

Merraid would have her virginity taken by a man she adored and admired. A man who'd take care with her and treat her tenderly.

In a sennight, they would part ways and never speak of it. But they would have one lovely memory to sustain them in melancholy moments.

Still, Gellir was a man of honor. Of rules. And codes. And chivalry.

Convincing him to ignore his conscience and follow his heart was a challenge.

But Merraid never backed down from a challenge.

As he continued to kiss her—sometimes with tenderness, sometimes with ferocity—a warm and sensuous vibration began to halo her head. Her aroused breath turned to gasps of longing. Her nipples tightened. And betwixt her thighs swelled a sharp yet pleasant craving.

She could feel the change in him as well. His breathing grew ragged as he dug desperate fingers into her back. His heart pounded, pulsing visibly in his corded throat. And when he lowered his hands, boldly grasping her buttocks and hauling her forward, she felt the shocking steel of his roused cock against her belly.

He wanted her. Nothing could be more seductive.

And just as he'd given her proof of his longing, she wanted to return the favor. She reached down to guide his hand slowly over her hip, across her ribs, and higher, until he cupped her breast.

His shaky sigh sent a thrill of power through her. He spread his fingers across the linen, warming the flesh beneath. Then he brushed his thumb across her nipple, awakening it like lightning.

She sobbed at the sensation. And yet it was still not enough.

With reckless abandon, she dragged down the neck edge of her kirtle and underdress, exposing her breast first to the cold night air. Then to the man who sought to warm her within the comforting palm of his hand.

His mouth tore away from hers, and she gasped at the sudden emptiness. But he resumed, leaving a trail of kisses along her jaw. Down the side of her neck. Warming her blood. Making her shiver with delight. He traced her collar bone with his lips and then ventured lower. Knowing where he was bound, she waited in breathless anticipation.

With the edge of his thumb, he flicked her puckered nipple and then lowered his head to enclose the sensitive nubbin within his mouth. The wet heat of his swirling tongue washed over her like a heavenly wave. The pressure as he sucked gently drew a rasping gasp from her.

Her head swam. Her knees weakened. She felt a dull ache deep in her womb. And an envious throbbing in her other nipple.

As if he could read her thoughts, he reached up with his free hand and slid his fingers under the shoulder of her kirtle. Inch by inch, he eased the garment down, placing a kiss each time another bit of skin was revealed.

She closed her eyes tightly in simultaneous frustration and pleasure.

When her nipple popped free of its confines, he swooped down on it at once, bathing it with adoring attention while fondling its twin.

Her legs trembled beneath her, threatening to collapse. Her head grew dizzy with bliss. Lost in a fog of lust and longing, she was utterly at his mercy.

How had she become so defenseless? With a sword in her hand, she had always managed to stand up to men. To give as good as she got. How could she be so easily conquered with a kiss and a caress?

Perhaps it was time to fight fire with fire.

While he pleasured her breasts, she slipped one intrepid hand between them and over his braies. There she found and captured his cock.

The harsh gasp he sucked in gave her a heady thrill.

He made no move to prevent her. So she rubbed her hand experimentally over him. The thick hardness sheathed in his braies reminded her of the wooden haft of a fine sword. Curious to know more, she gripped him, running her palm over his length.

He groaned and reared back his head, squeezing his eyes shut as if in pain.

But she knew it was only the pain of yearning. The same pain she endured.

Letting her fingers crawl upwards, she found the lacings of his braies and pulled loose the tie. Then she delved beneath the cloth to find the treasure below.

He shuddered when she plunged her fingers through his coarse curls and enveloped his naked flesh.

She expected his steely strength. But his velvety warmth was astonishing. Powerful and fragile at the same time.

He throbbed in the palm of her hand.

She felt an answering throb where her legs joined.

His breathing was strained and rapid.

Her smile was sultry and triumphant.

But her victory didn't last long.

While she fondled his enticing length, he shocked her by sliding a firm hand between her thighs. She squeaked in surprise. But as he glided his hand over the crevice there, her protest soon turned into mews of approval.

He knew precisely where she ached. Exactly what kind of pressure to exert.

Still, he wasn't finished. Despite her continued attentions to his pulsing member, he kept enough of his wits about him to begin inching up her kirtle. He gathered her skirts in his fist, lifting the hem higher and higher. Exposing her ankles. Her knees. Her thighs.

When he ran out of fabric, he slipped his fingers through the down guarding her womanhood and pressed the heel of his hand against the bone there.

It was instinct that made her grind against him. But though she sought relief, her lusty craving only worsened.

"I need ye," she gasped out.

"I know," he said.

"Swive me," she begged. "Swive me now."

"Och lass, I dare not."

"Just this once," she pleaded.

"But I'm bound to another."

"Your hand is bound. Your heart is your own." When he hesitated, she forged ahead. "We needn't tell a soul. No harm need come to anyone."

"'Tis reckless," he warned, removing his hand from betwixt her legs.

"'Tis more reckless for me to trust a stranger with my maidenhead." She knew if she appealed to the protector in him, he'd find it hard to refuse. "Once ye're gone, 'twill be in the hands of fate."

He sighed, wrestling with his morals.

"I trust ye," she said. "I know ye'll be kind. And gentle. And sweet. Unless..." She dipped her eyes. "Do ye not desire me?"

He smirked. His cock was still hard in her hand. "You know I do."

"And ye admitted ye love me."

"I do."

"Then know this," she said, placing his hand over her beating heart and gazing up at him with dewy eyes. "Know that I have loved ye since the first time I saw ye. For four long years, I ne'er forgot ye. And even if I can't have ye, I'll love ye fore'er."

Clearly touched, he lowered his head, resting his brow on hers.

"On this night of all nights," she whispered, "when all may be forgiven, can we not have a wee taste o' heaven?"

# CHAPTER 16

Even sotted, Gellir was sober enough to know he was making a mistake.

He told himself he was doing it for Merraid. To save her from suffering. To guard against clumsy knaves who might snatch her virginity without the proper gentleness. He convinced himself swiving her would be his one final act of protection before he left her side forever.

That's what he told himself.

But he didn't believe it.

In truth, he wanted this as much as she did.

He longed for a taste of paradise. Just once, he wanted to make love with someone who genuinely cared for him. Someone for whom it was not just a marital duty, but an expression of affection. Of adoration. Of trust.

So when she whispered that entreaty—looking up at him with a hopeful smile, reminding him it was Beltane, when all turned a blind eye to indiscretions—he was powerless to tell her nay.

"If I do this," he murmured, "it must ne'er happen again."

She nodded, promising, "I won't ask."

So she claimed. But they were the words of a lass who'd never been swived. He wouldn't be surprised if she broke that promise.

Carefully, reluctantly, he extricated her hand from his braies. He tugged her kirtle back up over her breasts so she wouldn't grow cold while he gathered leaves to make a soft bed.

The forest pool at midnight was not the best spot for a tryst. The air was chill. The ground was hard. But at least here they'd not be discovered.

Once he'd mounded the leaves, he swirled off his cloak to make a coverlet. Then he swept her off her feet, laying her gently atop the makeshift pallet. Though the torch had gone out, the half-moon's reflection on the water cast enough light that he could see her gazing up at him with adoring eyes.

How he loved her. And to see that love reflected back at him... He wished with all his heart that his wife would one day look at him the way Merraid looked at him now.

But he dared not think more about Carenza. Guilt already weighed on him like an anvil. What he did was sinful. He knew that. Never mind that he'd had plenty of lovers before Merraid. He was now betrothed. He should be true to his bride-to-be.

Why then did Merraid feel like his one true love?

"Come to me," Merraid murmured.

That sweet encouragement made him forget about everything except the lovely wee maidservant who shared his heart and welcomed his caresses.

Gazing down at the beautiful lass, he knew his greatest challenge would be keeping his own desires in check while he aroused hers. When she'd thrust her hand down his braies, he'd hardened faster than molten steel plunged in icy water.

Thankfully, he knew a few secrets. Secrets that would soon have her begging for his touch.

Moving her skirts out of the way, he nudged her knees apart and knelt between them. Leaning forward, he swept her hair back from her brow and placed a kiss there. He slipped his fingers into her tresses to cradle her head as he kissed each eyelid.

She giggled playfully and lifted her hands to clutch at his leine.

"Nay," he said, prying her fingers loose. "Keep your hands still."

"But I want to touch ye."

"I know," he said. "But do not. Just lie back. Close your eyes."

She sighed.

He nuzzled her temple and blew a soft breath into her ear.

She shivered.

"Do you like that?" he murmured against her hair.

She nodded.

"What about this?"

He turned her head aside and kissed the lobe of her ear. Then he captured it between his lips and licked at the tender flesh.

She made a sound of pleasure deep in her throat.

He opened his lips then and, with the tip of his tongue, traced the delicate shell and recesses of her ear.

She writhed in lusty torment and snatched again at his leine.

He murmured in her ear, "Let go."

She did so with difficulty.

When he turned her head to the other side, she stiffened, bracing for his touch, and made fists of her hands.

He smiled, running his tongue up the side of her neck, blowing on her flesh to make her shiver. When he bathed her ear, she arched up against him, making a strangled squeal in her throat.

He answered with a soft chuckle.

But her eager response was stretching his restraint to the limit. He felt the demanding beast stirring in his braies.

He moved lower, nudging her surcoat down with his chin, taking care not to scratch her silky bosom with his rough stubble. With nimble fingers, he peeled the cloth from her shoulders. Slipped it down till it perched on the tips of her nipples.

She strained against the fabric, keen to be free of it.

But he trapped her there and bent his head, slowly lashing her exposed flesh with his hair. He delved under the taut edge of the cloth with his tongue, finding and arousing each nipple with a teasing thrust.

She arched again. This time, he released his grip, and her breasts emerged from their prison.

He lavished kisses upon the creamy globes, marveling at their delicious softness. While he distracted her with licking and suckling, he simultaneously tortured himself with anticipation as he used one hand to slowly drag her skirts up, stopping only when he exposed the small recess of her navel.

Meanwhile, she defied his command. Her fingers crept up to weave through his hair. She held him firm against her breasts.

He pulled his head out of her grasp. Chided her with a cluck of his tongue.

"If you can't obey..." he warned. He intertwined his fingers with hers to hold them still.

Then he moved past the rucked surcoat to circle her navel with his tongue. He felt the uneasy hitch of her belly as he widened the circles, sweeping the upper margin of the soft curls hiding her vulnerable womanhood.

The farther he ventured, the tighter she gripped his hands. But he refused to let go. And he refused to cease.

As he nuzzled her with his chin, inhaling her intoxicating, womanly scent, she panicked.

"Nay," she hissed. "Ye mustn't."

"Mustn't I?" He grinned. "Why not?"

Merraid opened her mouth. And shut it. Twice. She couldn't think of a single good reason.

She could hardly think at all.

From his first kiss, she'd floated in a mist of passion and wonder.

Now, like a master warrior, Gellir kept deflecting the energy of her desire. With dizzying speed and nimbleness, he steered her from frustration to fulfillment, from agony to ecstasy. And like a novice opponent, she was completely outmatched.

All she knew was what he threatened now felt wicked. Forbidden. She both wanted and did not want it.

At her silence, he promised, "'Twill make it better."

She still felt uncertain.

"If you want me to stop," he said, "I'll stop."

She bit her lip. She didn't exactly want him to stop.

"You'll let me know." His hot breath ruffled her curls.

Deciding she trusted him, she nodded, lying her head back and closing her eyes, bracing for the worst.

Nothing could have prepared her for the divine shock as his tongue parted her nether lips. Intruded upon her most secret place. Swept across her flesh in arousing exploration.

She gasped and squeezed his fingers between her own.

Weighting her thighs apart with his arms, he continued his onslaught. Licking. Circling. Sucking.

Her head rocked across his cloak as waves of pleasure washed over her, each rising higher than the last. When she felt as if she could endure no more, he gave her hands one last squeeze and released her. With a final kiss, he withdrew his mouth as well, letting his fingers take its place.

His thumb danced over her swollen nub with expert grace while he eased a moistened finger farther and farther inside her.

He must have hauled down his braies with his other hand. She was too enrapt in her own rising passion to notice.

"Are you ready?" he asked, strain clear in his voice.

"Aye," she gasped. "Och aye."

He moved up to loom over her. Slipping his finger out, he replaced it with the tip of his cock. As he pressed inward, she could feel his thick member stretching her. Then he resumed kneading her slick folds. She was swiftly drawn into a haze of such erotic bliss that she scarcely noticed the sting of her maidenhead tearing.

He paused then, shuddering with the effort.

She peered up at him, wondering at the lusty torment on his face. The sweat of restraint on his brow. The beautiful awe in his eyes.

And she fell in love with him all over again.

He'd stopped to give her respite.

But she didn't want to stop.

She rocked her hips forward, seeking the sweet pressure that would carry her to the heights of desire. Then she withdrew, relishing the lovely friction of his flesh sliding against hers. Again she thrust forward, sheathing his warm cock like a dagger.

He growled at the sensation. A growl that sounded like a leashed beast. A growl that rose from the depths of his primal soul.

Stirred by the seductive sound, she continued. Easing forward. Pulling back. Driving deep. Compelled by some primitive rhythm, she moved beneath him until he at last joined her in the erotic dance.

Where their bodies joined, each stroke of their flesh was like flint on steel, sparking a fire. Gone was the night chill. Every inch of her burned with a growing passion that threatened to consume her in an explosive blaze.

Then, when she thought she could endure no more, when the heat of their union was intense beyond bearing, when she feared they would go up in flame and turn to ash, there came over her a sudden stillness.

Time stopped. She couldn't move. Couldn't breathe.

Yet within her still body, the flame of desire continued to rise, burning brighter and brighter. At last it erupted into a brilliant, blinding flash of light.

He must have felt it too. He groaned as she cried out. They were shaken by the same tremors. He clung to her, shielding her from harm as they dropped from the sky like falling stars.

For several moments, the only sound was their mingled breath, ragged and chaotic. The only scent was the sweat and musk of lovemaking. The only sensation was flesh upon flesh.

Gradually, the outside world returned. The soft lapping of the pond on the shore. The pungent pine in the air. The bed of leaves, his woolen cloak, and the solid earth beneath.

"Are you all right?" he finally asked.

There were no words to describe how right she felt. She nodded.

"Did I hurt you?"

She shook her head.

He sighed in relief. Wary of his great weight, he carefully withdrew to nestle beside her.

She frowned in dismay, wishing they never had to part.

Merraid thought trysting with Gellir would purge her desire for him. After all, once she made love to him, she'd no longer have to dream about her magnificent hero. No longer have to wonder about his kiss. His caress. No longer have to imagine how his worshipful arms would feel around her. How his cock would feel inside of her.

228

But she was wrong.

He'd only whetted her appetite for more. Given her a delicious taste of what she'd be missing from now on. And made her realize what a unique treasure he was.

Bittersweet tears gathered in her eyes. She would never again know his embrace. Never again experience the thrill of bursting into flame in his arms. Never again feel the miracle of their two bodies made one.

Eventually, her breathing calmed. Her heartbeat slowed. The chill of the night began to intrude upon their warmth.

She shivered once. He snagged the edge of his cloak and pulled it up over her bare shoulders.

"Thank ye," she whispered.

"Of course," he said. "I can't have you freezing to death. Not on the night we welcome summer."

"Nay, I meant for..." She left it unspoken.

"Och. Aye. 'Twas my honor." He added, "And my pleasure."

She let out a dreamy sigh. Was there any man more noble and gallant than Gellir?

But suddenly his earlier words pricked at something in her memory.

*Can't have you freezing to death.*

Shite. She'd completely forgotten about Lady Carenza.

As it turned out, when Merraid crept in to check on her an hour later, someone *had* lit the lady's hearth. A wee, cheery flame danced there, reflecting golden light on Carenza's peacefully slumbering face.

But as she gazed at the lass—the perfect, sweet, innocent lass everybody loved—guilt sat on Merraid's shoulders like a yoke on an ox.

It was a sin, what she had done. Swiving another woman's man. And no matter how much it had seemed like the right decision at the time, she knew now it was wrong.

She should never have pressured Gellir into trysting with her. Hell, he hadn't even been sober. He couldn't be held accountable for his actions.

It was all her fault. What she'd done was unforgivable. And Lady Feiyan was right. Merraid was better than that.

From now on, she vowed, she would do everything in her power to make certain Gellir's wedding went smoothly. For Lady Carenza's sake.

Things were not going smoothly with Lady Carenza. Not at all. And Gellir didn't know what to do.

Kneeling on the hard stone of Darragh's chapel—behind Lady Feiyan and Laird Dougal—he stared up at the stained glass in back of the chaplain, as if the saint depicted there might offer an answer.

But he heard no usable advice. Not from Carenza, murmuring prayers beside him. Not from the stained glass saint. And not from the minister, who droned on and on in Latin.

Gellir had tried everything. Bringing her flowers. Taking her riding. Impressing her with his sword skills.

Carenza could not be coaxed from her deep despair. Which made his mood even darker than usual.

On the morrow, they would wed. They'd be handfasted in the courtyard. Then, on this very spot in the chapel, they would seal their vows before God.

He suspected it would not be a joyous affair. For Carenza or him. Even the imminent arrival of his clan could not dispel the gloomy pall cast upon this marriage.

At first, he was troubled by the fear that Carenza had somehow found out about his Beltane tryst with Merraid. That it was the cause of her melancholy. That she had good reason to doubt his devotion and loyalty.

But she made no mention of it.

Nonetheless, if she ever *did* happen to find out—if by some tragic chance she learned what he'd done and confronted him with it—he vowed he would tell her the truth.

*Most* of the truth.

He would *never* disclose his affection for Merraid. Carenza wouldn't understand. But he didn't intend to let his feelings for the maidservant stand between them.

He would declare the tryst had been his fault. Aye, he'd been drunk. But not so drunk he couldn't take responsibility for his actions. He'd known full well what he was doing. He'd let lust and chivalry get the best of him. He'd let his cock make decisions for him instead of using his head.

In his heart, he'd also believed he was giving a gift of charity to a friend. Sparing Merraid the pain of losing her virginity to an incautious stranger. But he wouldn't tell Carenza that either.

Merraid was not to blame for any of it. Caught up in the spirit of Beltane, Merraid had simply turned to the one she could trust to initiate her. She'd chosen Gellir specifically because she knew he was leaving, that nothing would ever come of it.

There was more about the night he'd never reveal. How Merraid had made him feel treasured. How he'd always look back on Beltane with fondness and joy and gratitude. How he'd hold the memory fast in his heart. To remind him of what was possible. To remind him that precious love could thrive between a noble knight and a maidservant. To remind him that there existed in the world a woman who could make him feel like a god.

But he acknowledged the truth. No matter how amazing the night had seemed, he'd been unfaithful. If Carenza found out, he would take responsibility for his actions. And if she could not forgive him for his behavior, he'd make whatever amends she demanded.

For now, however, he'd try to forget about that night. And, as he'd managed to do since Beltane, he'd avoid Merraid.

She seemed to be of the same mind. He'd scarcely seen her in a sennight. She'd kept busy, readying Carenza for the wedding.

The chaplain at long last finished the lengthy prayer.

Gellir came to his feet and gave Carenza his hand, helping her up.

She gave him a brief smile of thanks that dissolved the instant she lowered her eyes. She may as well have stepped on his heart, crushing it beneath her heel.


It was late. Merraid was exhausted.

It was one thing to make wedding preparations. Choosing a suitable gown for the bride. Selecting her jewels. Planning the feast. Laundering linens. Strewing fresh flowers among the rushes.

It was quite another to have to deal with a nervous bride-to-be.

Gellir had done everything humanly possible to let her become accustomed to the idea of marrying him. For a sennight, he'd courted her with conversation and long walks. Hawking and archery. A ride at dawn along the froth of the firth. A late night stroll to gaze at the stars. He'd been gentle. Sweet. Accommodating.

Why then was his bride still so afraid of him?

The closer it grew to the hour of the wedding, the more agitated Carenza became. She should have gone to bed hours ago. Yet she paced hastily back and forth across her chamber, making the flames flicker madly.

"I'm sorry," the lady muttered for the hundredth time. "Ye needn't stay."

"I'm not leavin', m'lady," Merraid promised. "I said I'd get ye through this, and I meant it."

"Ye're a good friend," she said with a bleak smile.

She didn't feel like a good friend. She felt like the worst sort of betrayer.

Ever since that incredible Beltane night, she hadn't been able to look at Lady Carenza without the bitter taste of shame filling her mouth. The least she could do was stay up with the lady until she exhausted herself with worry.

She'd offered every reassurance she could. She'd told her what a beautiful couple she and Gellir were going to make. She'd regaled the lady with glorious stories about her bridegroom's bravery and humorous tales about his childhood. She'd raved over Carenza's lovely and lovable nature. She'd extolled the virtues of the clan she'd be marrying into and shared what she'd heard about the magnificent Rivenloch castle.

Nothing calmed Lady Carenza. She chewed at her lip and continued to pace.

Then, all at once, a fresh possibility occurred to Merraid.

Perhaps the lady was afraid of the wedding night.

Perhaps she knew nothing about what was to occur in the marriage bed. What it would be like to make love to a man like Sir Gellir.

Merraid gulped. She knew *exactly* what it was like.

Should she share her experience? Not specifically, of course. But generally? Would that help to ease Lady Carenza's worries?

"M'lady," she ventured, "are ye fretful about what's to come 'tween the sheets?"

The lady suddenly stopped pacing.

Perhaps Merraid was onto something. She continued. "Because I have a wee bit of experience."

The lady stood frozen, facing the window.

Merraid licked her lips, unsure how to proceed. "It can be quite...pleasurable. There's only a wee bit o' pain at first and then..."

She paused when the lady's shoulders began to quake. Was it from fear? Or was she weeping?

"And then," Merraid remembered, "'tis like...like a beautiful journey...with grand adventures along the way."

Carenza's shoulders shook harder. Merraid decided she was crying. It was just as well. Maybe she'd tire herself that way and get some sleep before the morrow.

"There's naught to fret about," Merraid said, "e'en if 'tis your first—"

When the lady wheeled about, Merraid was startled speechless. Carenza wasn't crying. She was laughing.

"My first?" Lady Carenza said with a giggle.

Perplexed, Merraid could only stare, which amused the lady all the more. A particularly loud laugh burst from Carenza's mouth, and she covered it with both hands.

Merraid frowned.

When Carenza was finally able to catch her breath, she clapped a hand to her breast. "Och, Merraid," she said fondly, "whate'er will I do without ye?"

Just about the time Merraid was feeling like the butt of some jest she didn't understand, Carenza's face crumpled, and her laughter evolved into sobs.

"Och nay, nay, m'lady," Merraid said, rushing forward to comfort her with pats to her hand.

"I have to tell ye, Merraid," she sobbed. "I have to tell someone."

A shiver of apprehension ran up her spine at those words. Nonetheless, she replied, "What is it, m'lady?"

"I've done a terrible thing," she confessed.

In the realm of terrible things, Merraid was fairly sure sleeping with someone else's bridegroom was worse.

How bad could the transgression of a perfect bride be? Had Carenza had impure thoughts? Lied about her age? Accidentally stepped on one of her pet mice?

"Come sit, m'lady," Merraid said, patting the pallet.

Carenza sank down onto the edge of the bed and stared at her clasped hands.

"What is it?" Merraid asked. "What's this terrible thing ye've done?"

"Ye mustn't tell a soul."

"Ye can trust me, m'lady." Who could deny those tear-filled violet eyes?

Between sobs, Carenza said, "Ye remember...I told ye... my heart...belongs to another?"

"Aye."

Her brow creased. More tears squeezed from her eyes.

"Well, I've got somethin' else that belongs to him," she said, placing a hand on her belly. "I'm carryin' his bairn."

# CHAPTER 17

Merraid couldn't speak.

Her mind reeled.

How the devil had this happened?

To be sure, she knew how it had happened. Obviously, the lady had no fear of the marriage bed. But how had someone as pure and sweet and innocent as Lady Carenza managed to get herself with child?

A dark voice in her head answered that for her. The same way Merraid had managed to tryst with Sir Gellir and might well be carrying *his* child.

Carenza's revelation explained a lot. Why she wished to avoid Gellir. Why she seemed so sickly. Why her emotions were in turmoil. Why she craved pickled eels.

"Och, what shall I do?" the lady despaired.

Merraid worried her fingers while her mind whirred. "How far along are ye? Two months? Three?"

Carenza shrugged and bit her lip.

Shite. If Carenza didn't know, she must have swived the man on numerous occasions. No wonder she'd laughed at Merraid's advice, meant for a virgin. Still, if her condition wasn't too advanced...

"Perhaps he doesn't need to find out," she suggested.

The lady sighed in defeat. "I can't keep it from him. I have to tell him."

Merraid wasn't so sure about that. How would Gellir feel, knowing the bairn wasn't his? Knowing he might have been tricked into marrying Lady Carenza?

He would undoubtedly forgive her for her indiscretion. After all, *he'd* taken lovers ere *he* was betrothed. And even one afterwards, she reminded herself.

But would he suspect Carenza had been foisted onto him because of her condition? Had her father pushed her into marriage because he knew her secret?

He would be furious to discover he'd been manipulated.

Of course, Gellir would never blame the child. A man of his character would take in any bairn born under his roof. He was a good man. A generous man. He would raise the child as his own.

But in his soul, he would know that his firstborn, the one destined to be laird after him, was not a child born of their love. It would be a reminder that Carenza's heart once belonged to another. And might still. And that would crush him.

"What if ye bide your time? At least wait till the bairn comes?" she suggested. "Ye wouldn't be the first bride to give birth early in a marriage. And if the father looks anythin' like Gellir...?"

She shook her head. "Nay."

Merraid's face fell. Of course he didn't.

"I must tell him," Carenza repeated, wiping at her tears and speaking with new resolve. "Gellir is a decent, kind, honorable man. I won't start our marriage off with a lie."

Ordinarily, Merraid would agree. But if that lie saved Gellir's feelings...

"Will ye tell him before the weddin'?"

"I can't. My father didn't know my condition when he promised me to Gellir. And this alliance is so important to him. Gellir might refuse to marry me. 'Tis his right. But if he does..."

"The alliance will be broken. And your bairn will be born a bastard."

A sob escaped Carenza. "Aye."

Merraid didn't mention that Gellir needed the alliance as much as she did. His bride might be with child, but at least she wasn't English.

"So ye'll tell him after the vows are exchanged?"

"Aye, ere we consummate the marriage."

Merraid frowned. "Ye don't mean to tell him on his weddin' night?"

"What else can I do? I won't give him myself to him—body and soul—knowing there's a lie between us."

"But... Ye can't tell him then. Not on his weddin' night." Merraid could think of nothing more tragic.

"I can't share his bed in good faith if he doesn't know."

Merraid had to admire the lady's integrity. It was damned inconvenient. But she had to admire it.

The lady shook her head. "I should have told him long ago. But I didn't have the courage. And once he started writing those beautiful letters to me, I didn't have the heart."

Merraid's eyes flattened. She wished she'd never interfered. Never made that promise to Lady Feiyan that she'd grease the wheels of romance.

The only thing she could do now was soften the blow to Gellir's heart.

"What if..." she said, worrying her lip under her teeth. "What if ye wait to consummate the marriage till ye arrive at Rivenloch?"

"Rivenloch?" Carenza exclaimed. "'Tis a sennight's journey or more. Will that not strain his husbandly patience?"

"Ye could tell him ye're sufferin' from your courses."

"I won't lie to him. I can't."

Merraid sighed. She was right, of course. Morally. But if a lie eased the way...

"What if I find a way to delay him where ye won't have to lie?" Merraid said. "By the time ye arrive at his home, ye'll be long wedded and well-acquainted. Perhaps the news won't hit him so hard then."

"Perhaps. But ye'll come with me, aye?"

"Come with ye?"

"To Rivenloch. Ye'll be there when I tell him."

Merraid's brows slammed together. Being near to Gellir? Stirring that fire? It was a terrible idea. "Nay. I can't do that."

"Ye can," the lady insisted, tightening her grip. "Ye've got to."

Of course she couldn't go to Rivenloch. That was absurd. Even if a tiny glimmer of hope stirred in her brain at the thought of seeing the formidable castle with its grand tiltyard and enormous armory.

"I'm needed here," she argued. "Lady Feiyan—"

"I need ye more. *Gellir* needs ye. Ye can go as...as my handmaiden."

"I cannot, m'lady," Merraid said, pulling her arm away. As tempted as she was, she knew it wasn't right. "Ye'll be fine. Ye'll see. Just don't..." She bit back her words.

"Don't what?"

"Promise me ye won't tell him on your weddin' night." Gellir deserved at least one night with the possibility of a blissful union with his new wife.

"But if you aren't coming to Rivenloch, if ye won't be there to soften the blow..." She shook her head. "I must do the honorable thing. Ye don't know him, Merraid. Ye don't know him like I do."

Merraid lifted a brow at that.

"The things he said to me," Carenza sobbed, laying a hand over her heart. "His beautiful verses. His lovely words. So honest. So true. So kind. I cannot bear the thought of deceiving him. Even for one moment."

Shite.

The whole clever scheme of courting Carenza with verse had just blown up in Merraid's face like one of Sung Li's legendary fireworks.

"I know he'll be upset," Carenza whispered. "And I cannot blame him."

He would be upset. But he wouldn't hurt her. "He'd ne'er do ye harm."

"I know," she said. "But *I'll* be hurting *him*. And that I cannot bear."

Merraid shook her head. What a coil. And it was partially her fault. She wished she'd never written those verses.

Carenza repeated, "Ye must come with me."

"Why? What can I do?" She had a momentary vision of standing between the newly wedded couple with her *dao* drawn.

"Ye're his friend," she said, placing a hand on Merraid's shoulder. "Ye can be there after..." Her face fell. "After I've broken his heart."

Merraid's shoulders sank. She wasn't sure which would be worse. His broken heart. Or his offended pride. Either way, Lady Carenza was right. She could calm Gellir down when he was vexed. Soothe his spirits when he was wounded.

But leaving her clan. Leaving Lady Feiyan. Traveling all the way to Rivenloch...

"I don't know," she said.

"I need ye," the lady pleaded. *"He* needs ye."


"Are ye mad?" Gellir, sweaty from the morn's practice, strode across the courtyard toward the great hall. "That's the last thing I need."

Merraid scrambled to keep up with him, dodging past

busy servants and flocks of hens. "'Tis what *I* told her as well."

"We cannot," he muttered. "We dare not."

"Agreed." She slowed her pace. "Although..."

He sighed and stopped to face her. "What?"

"'Twould only be for a wee bit. Just until she settles in."

"Absolutely not."

"O' course," she said. "I'm only passin' along her wishes."

Shite. Asking him directly was not going to work. But she'd made a solemn vow to Lady Carenza that she would accompany her to Rivenloch. She was going to have to think of another way. Some way to convince him—or coerce him—into taking her along. But how?

Merraid made the mistake of looking up into his eyes then. They were gray as storm clouds. Hard as steel. In her mind's eye, however, she remembered them softening with affection. Melting with lust.

It was only for an instant. After all, they were surrounded by the castle folk. She couldn't be seen, staring at another woman's bridegroom.

But in that instant, her breath caught, and her heart opened. A deluge of emotions rained down upon her. Her spirit soared like it had on the night of Beltane. When the whole world stopped.

In that instant, she remembered the strength of his arms around her.

The sweet exploration of his kiss.

The tempting torment of his tongue.

The welcome weight of his strong body.

The velvet heat of his cock deep inside her.

The breathlessness of their joining. Body. Heart. Soul.

In that instant, she glimpsed his emotions as well.

His smoldering passion. His tortured withholding. His sharp desire. The ecstasy of his release. The honesty of his love.

The memories were so vivid, so palpable, for that instant she couldn't breathe.

Then, behind them, the castle gates suddenly burst open.

Merraid took a startled step away from Gellir.

"Here he is!" Lady Feiyan cried.

The gates swung wider. Like a pack of rambunctious hounds, scattering the servants in their wake, Gellir's clansmen spilled into the courtyard. They surrounded Gellir, clapping him on the shoulder and all talking at once. Merraid found their enthusiasm dizzying.

"'Tis about time, champion!"

"Congratulations, lad!"

"I'm so happy for you, cousin."

"I thought you'd never find a wench."

"Who, Gellir? The greatest swordsman in all Scotland?"

"Oho! Not for long! Brand's a close second."

"Is this her? Is this your bride?"

They all silenced and looked at Merraid.

"Nay," said a well-muscled, dark-haired young man with a familiar face. "I know her. I know you. You're that maidservant. Merraid, aye?"

She squinted at him. He'd grown since the last time she'd seen him. But she was sure it was Feiyan's brother Adam, who had cleverly disguised his way into the castle with Gellir four year ago. "The rat-catcher?"

Everyone laughed.

"Aye," Adam said, grinning and bowing. "At your service."

"Gellir." The statuesque blonde woman who came forward was Deirdre, Gellir's mother and the Laird of Rivenloch, the fierce warrior in command of the forces that had saved Castle Darragh. "Where's your lovely bride?"

Gellir hesitated. Carenza had been crying in her chamber all morn.

Merraid saved him. "Och, he hasn't seen her, m'lady. At Darragh, 'tis considered bad luck for the bridegroom to see his bride before the weddin'."

That wasn't true at all. But it made Laird Deirdre laugh.

"'Tis a good thing Sir Pagan didn't get to see *his* bride before the wedding," she said.

Everyone chuckled, and her husband Pagan smiled with good humor. "I've got no regrets."

Merraid had heard the story from Lady Feiyan. To save her sister from marriage to Pagan, Deirdre had disguised herself, tricking him into marrying *her* instead.

Another group of guests flooded through the gates. Deirdre introduced Lady Carenza's father and her clan from Dunlop.

"Hew," Gellir called out to a man lurking behind the rest. "'Tis been too long."

"Gellir." The crowd parted to reveal Gellir's tawny-haired cousin, the one who'd been living at Dunlop, in hiding like Gellir. The man was tall and broad-shouldered, with a warrior's build and a handsome face to stir a maiden's heart. But he had no smile for Gellir. Bitterness smoldered in his eyes. "'Twould seem your fate is sealed. I've only to await mine now."

"Och, Hew." An auburn-haired woman with a bow slung over her shoulder rolled her eyes. "I'm sure there are a few good lasses left in Scotland who haven't yet broken your heart."

Subtle pain streaked across his eyes for an instant and then vanished. "Not all of us can find love at first sight, sister."

The great bear of a man beside the female archer burst out laughing at that. "First sight, was it? Ye mean after she sought to steal my keep? Or after I held her hostage?"

Merraid remembered their story too. Jenefer of Rivenloch was the hot-tempered lass who had battled with

Highlander Morgan Mor mac Giric over a castle. They'd ultimately settled the matter, not by combat, but by marrying and sharing the keep.

A sweet-faced lass patted Hew's arm in sympathy. She was a few years younger than Merraid, with tresses as pale as wheat and earnest brows. "Don't mind them, cousin. I know you'll find..." She sighed. "The One."

"He always does," Jenefer quipped, which earned her a simmering glare from Hew.

A lanky lad with light hair frowned thoughtfully. "I could do the calculations. Determine how many lasses he's courted as a fraction of all the available lasses in Scotland..."

"Ian!" the earnest lass scolded. "You can't find love with numbers. Love is..." She pressed a hand to her bosom. "Part fate and part heart."

"So..." Ian said. "Fart?"

Everyone roared at that.

Merraid loved Gellir's siblings at once. By their words, she realized the earnest lass was his little sister Isabel, who was an incurable romantic, and the calculating lad was his youngest brother Ian. She was suddenly glad she intended to go to Rivenloch with them. One way or another.

When the laughter died down, Gellir addressed Hew. "I owe you my gratitude, cousin." His words were stilted, though Merraid was likely the only one who could tell. "You were right. Lady Carenza is a jewel. She will make a fine wife."

Hew nodded, accepting the thanks. But his brow was furrowed and his jaw was clenched. Perhaps he was more sensitive to the others' ridicule than they realized. Perhaps, unlike Gellir, he knew the importance of choosing a compatible bride.

Deirdre spoke to Lady Feiyan. "Perhaps you'll take us on a tour of the castle?" she suggested, scanning the courtyard. "It looks like you've made some improvements."

The clans dispersed then. Some followed Deirdre. The Laird of Dunlop accompanied Laird Dougal to the stables. Brand was itching to see the armory. Isabel wished to see the tunnel to the beach where Lady Feiyan and Laird Dougal had fallen in love. Ian wanted to visit the firth to test several model ships he'd made. Gellir excused himself to prepare for the wedding.

Merraid glanced up at the window where Lady Carenza was no doubt weeping into her hands. How she would convince Gellir to let her come to Rivenloch, she didn't know. But she didn't have much time.

# CHAPTER 18

"**C**ome," Gellir replied to the knock on the solar door. He figured it was a servant summoning him to his wedding, now that he was bathed and dressed in his finest indigo velvet.

He was half right. It was a servant. A particularly pesky maidservant. Merraid seemed to be here to torment him one last time.

And torment him, she did. Scanning him from head to toe with bold admiration. Gazing at him with breathless awe and naked longing.

The mere sight of her made his heart race. Desire stirred between his thighs.

"Ye look..." she said in a strained voice, "quite suitable."

His brow creased as she closed the door behind her. He dared not encourage her attentions. So he turned his back, picked up a comb from the table, and ran it back through his damp hair.

"Why have you come?" he choked out.

"I have to speak with ye about goin' to Rivenloch."

"I thought we agreed 'tis a bad idea."

"We did," she said, "but Carenza did not. She's been beggin' me all day to come with her."

He grunted, threw the comb onto the table, and pounded the back of his fist once against the stones of the hearth.

Merraid sighed. She sauntered along the solar wall, running an idle hand over the weapons Feiyan had hung there. "Perhaps we could vow ne'er to be alone together."

He didn't answer. He picked up the fireplace poker and jabbed at the peat coals. The fiery sparks mirrored his mood.

Having beautiful Merraid underfoot at Rivenloch while he tried to make a difficult marriage work was unthinkable. He'd spent the last sennight trying to purge thoughts of the winsome maidservant—panting beneath him, kissing him, letting him sink his aching cock into her warm, welcoming womb—from his brain.

"She's afraid," Merraid said. "That's all."

"She won't be afraid after tonight," he growled. Then he lowered his eyes and his voice. *"You* should know that."

Her tiny shocked gasp made him regret his words. He didn't dare look at her, for fear he'd detect a smoldering memory in her eyes.

He scowled at the fire. The heat and smoke irritated his eyes. Still, it was better to keep his gaze on the flames than stoke the fires of his love for the temptress before him.

"I'd only stay for a short while," she countered, "just until she's used to bein' a wife."

There was no way he was going to grant his bride her request. Inviting Merraid to Rivenloch as her handmaiden was as foolish as welcoming a fox into a doocot.

"Nay," he grunted.

Merraid made no reply. But he noted the tense twisting of her mouth as she ran her fingers over the various daggers and shackles and flails on the wall. She was displeased.

"Hear me, Merraid." As he spoke the words, he engraved the plans into his mind. "In another hour, the deed will be done. Carenza and I will be wedded. I will consummate the marriage. Here. Tonight. As is my right.

On the morrow, my bride and I will leave for Rivenloch. Alone."

"But—"

"Nay." He held up a hand. "That's final."

It would be so much easier to say aye. It was what his bride wanted. It was what Merraid wanted. But he knew better. Merraid's proximity would lead to nothing but dishonor and disaster. He had to stay firm. No matter how alluring the proposition was.

From the corner of his eye, he saw Merraid pull a halberd away from the wall to inspect it.

"What if I told ye she doesn't intend to swive ye tonight?"

The fire popped, as startled as he. "What?"

"She might not," she said with a shrug, replacing the halberd.

"She will. She'll be my wife. 'Tis my right."

"Ye'd take her against her will?"

"Are you so certain 'twill be against her will?" He closed his eyes to smoky slits.

She blinked and averted her gaze, fumbling with the shackles hung on the wall.

"What if I said she was...in her monthly courses?" she asked.

He crossed his arms over his chest in challenge. "Is she?"

She hesitated long enough to make him doubt her claim.

"All I know is," she finally blurted, "she doesn't want ye to bed her tonight."

He furrowed his brows, staring hard at her. There was a glimmer of desperation in her gaze. A reckless prayer of hope on her trembling lips. Desire casting a sinful shadow on her soul. Now he understood.

"Nay," he said softly, "I think 'tis *you* who doesn't want to me to bed her."

By the crease in her brow, he saw he'd hit upon the truth.

But she denied it. "Don't be ridiculous!" she hissed. "Ye're marryin' a great lady. One the whole clan adores. What kind of a friend would I be to ruin that?"

He gave her a tender smile. "The kind who would do whatever it took to make sure I was happy."

She gulped. Then she came near. Looked up at him with liquid blue eyes. Gave him a faltering smile that was sad and beautiful and caring. "I do care for ye. And I want ye to be happy. But ye must believe me when I say I want her to be happy as well." She placed one hand on his chest and whispered, "Is there truly no way I can change your mind?"

Beneath her hand, his heart beat like a prisoner pounding to be free. The truth struck him with the force of a battering ram.

Bloody hell. *This* was the woman who made him happy. The woman he loved. This fresh-faced, fiery-haired, foul-mouthed runt of a maidservant.

*She* was the one who made his heart race.

Who left him breathless.

Who held his joy in the palm of her hand.

But it was not to be.

They both knew that.

Still, it was up to him to say the words she could not.

"We have to say farewell," he murmured. "We have to end this."

Her eyes teared.

He felt a choking lump in his throat.

"Don't you see?" he said. "'Twill destroy me, having you so near...and ne'er being able to...to touch you." He shook his head. "God knows I'll ne'er have a...a friend," he choked out, giving her a shaky smile, "quite like you."

She caught her lip under her teeth and lowered her gaze.

He blew out a sharp breath then, dammed his tears, and straightened. "But I've made a vow to my clan. To my king. To my country. To my wife. I won't break that vow. Not even for you, Merraid."

As miserable as he felt, having to make that statement, at least he had closure. He may have broken Merraid's heart. But in life, as in battle, it was always best to make a clean break. To take swift, decisive strikes rather than dragging out a man's death unnecessarily.

In the end, there was always less suffering. Less guilt. Less torment.

He reached up to give Merraid's hand one last fond squeeze, congratulating himself for handling the matter in such a forthright manner, when he felt the icy clasp of iron around his wrist.

"What the...?"

It took an instant to realize it was a shackle.

Another instant to see its twin enclosed Merraid's wrist.


Desperate times called for desperate measures. That was what Merraid told herself as she braced for his anger.

To be honest, she'd acted completely on impulse. It was a simple fact that as long as she was shackled to Gellir, there could be no consummation of his marriage. And that meant Carenza wouldn't need to tell him the truth about her condition. At least not tonight.

What would happen after that, she didn't know. But if she could stave off the confrontation until they got to Rivenloch, she felt like she might at least have more time for diplomacy.

She wasn't prepared for the depth of Gellir's fury.

When he realized what she'd done, his eyes widened. His brows lowered like angry thunderclouds. His nostrils flared. His chest heaved. He ground his teeth. Stabbed her with his eyes. Took a great breath, as if preparing to lash her with a ferocious gale of fury.

Now she knew why they called him Grim Gellir.

Before he could roar out his wrath, there was a rapid knocking at the door.

He exhaled sharply, the wind knocked out of his angry sails. Then he thrust their shackled hands down, hiding them in the folds of her skirt.

"Come," he bit out between clenched teeth.

Lady Feiyan rushed into the solar, frantically glancing around the chamber. "Where is Lady Carenza?"

Merraid's heart leaped into her throat. "Is she not in her chamber?" When Merraid had last seen her, the lady had been alternately weeping and pacing before the hearth.

Lady Feiyan shook her head.

"Have ye tried the chapel?"

"Aye."

"The garden?"

"Aye."

"The wall walk?" Merraid's words trailed off as she wondered if Carenza was distraught enough to do something dire. Something deadly.

"I've looked everywhere," Feiyan murmured. "She's nowhere to be found."

Gellir's sigh was full of defeat. "She's run away."

"I'm sure she's here," Merraid said, only half sure. "Maybe she felt ill. Maybe she's closeted in a garderobe somewhere."

"We've got to find her. Quickly. And quietly." Feiyan shook her head. "I can't have the Laird of Dunlop finding out we've lost his daughter."

"I'll check the garderobes," Merraid offered.

Lady Feiyan nodded and left.

Merraid turned to Gellir to assure him, "She wouldn't run away." At least, she was *fairly* certain Carenza wouldn't do that. She seemed like a woman of honor.

Still, Gellir looked crestfallen. Who could blame him? He'd had lasses pursuing him half his life. And the one lass he needed to fall in love with him was incapable of feeling anything for him but heartbreak.

They searched every garderobe in the castle, not an easy task in shackles. Then they checked all the outbuildings. The gardens. The orchards. The tiltyard. The stables. The underground passage to the firth.

She was nowhere to be found. And the clans were already gathering at the chapel for the ceremony. The Laird of Dunlop had a worried furrow between his brows. He no doubt suspected something was amiss with his daughter, whom he hadn't seen since his arrival.

Merraid had never seen Gellir look so downtrodden. His eyes were flat and emotionless. His shoulders were stiff. His jaw was tense.

"Let's check the armory one more time," she murmured, eager to get him away from the suspicious gaze of the bride's father.

The armory was empty except for Hew, who started when he saw them, knocking a targe from the wall.

"Gellir," he said, picking up the targe. "Aren't you supposed to be in the chapel?"

Merraid thought she could well ask Hew the same thing.

Gellir smirked. "I have to find my bride first."

Hew blinked. "What do you mean?"

"I fear I've lost her." There was so much deep meaning and pain in that phrase, Merraid felt her throat thicken.

"Lost her?" Hew awkwardly licked his lips, as if he didn't know what to say. "I'm sure she's around here some-where. Have you checked the keep?"

"Aye," Gellir said. "We've looked everywhere."

"Ye haven't seen her, have ye?" Merraid said to Hew. "I mean, since ye arrived?"

"Why would I have seen her?"

Merraid narrowed her eyes. That was a curious reply.

Gellir shook his head. "I'll need to let her father know she's missing. A wider search will have to be started."

"Nay!" Hew blurted.

Merraid frowned.

"I mean," Hew continued in a more casual tone, "I wouldn't do that. Her father can be a bit short-tempered. We don't have to let him know yet. Can we not ride out and look for her ourselves? Quietly? Just you and me, Gellir?"

"I'm afraid that's not possible," Gellir said, lifting up the shackles for Hew to see.

"What the—"

"Don't ask."

"Very well. I'll go alone then," Hew offered. He shouldered the targe and started collecting a few smaller weapons from the wall. "If I'm not back in an hour, *then* you can tell her father."

"Nay. Her father's temper can't be half as bad as yours," Gellir said, earning a scowl from Hew. "We have to find her ere she gets herself into trouble. We need all the eyes we can get. I'll send the whole clan."

"Fine, but wait an hour," Hew said, shoving more weapons into his belt. "Just give me that much time first."

He seemed rather passionate about his intentions.

"I'm not letting you go alone," Gellir said. "'Tis my fault she's run away."

Hew clasped Gellir's free forearm. "Cousin, you're in no shape to ride off across the countryside—in your wedding finery and shackled to a maidservant."

"'Tis no matter," Gellir insisted. "I'll manage. I have to find her. I have to find my bride."

"Can I not talk you out of it?" Hew asked.

Gellir shook his head once, nay.

Hew sighed. "Fine."

In the blink of an eye and without warning, Hew clapped a shackle around Gellir's wrist.

Gellir tried to grab the second cuff before Hew could attach it. But joined at the wrist to Merraid, he could only wrench her forward with his attempt. She staggered, and in the scuffle, Hew managed to fasten the other shackle around a bracket attached to the wall.

Merraid gasped. What had Hew done? And why?

She braced herself for Gellir's anger.

The heat coming off of him was a deadly cauldron of seething, simmering molten steel. His steady, burning gaze only flickered once, when Hew tucked the key to the shackles into his belt for safekeeping.

Like a caged bear, Gellir jerked hard at the shackles, startling Hew into stepping away to a safe distance.

Gellir's snarl was soft but lethal. "You're making a mistake, cousin."

"Nay," Hew declared. "For once I know I'm *not* making a mistake."

"Free me."

"Nay."

Gellir's mouth worked with rage. "I *demand* you free me."

Hew shook his head.

Gellir bit out, "Have you lost your mind?"

Hew lifted his chin, proud and fearless. "I don't expect you to understand."

"Enlighten me."

"I cannot let you wed Lady Carenza."

"'Tis not up to you."

"Aye, 'tis," he said, "as long as I have breath in my body."

"That won't be for long," Gellir threatened, rattling the shackles again.

"In my time at Dunlop, I've come to know Lady Carenza. She's kind. Gentle. Sweet. But she's..." He paused, shaking his head. "Not for you."

Gellir's eyes glittered with harnessed rage. "The contract signed by her father says otherwise."

Hew gulped. Breaking a marriage contract was a serious charge. Still he asserted, "Her heart belongs to another man."

That painful truth dimmed Gellir's gaze. Still, he managed to reply with a steady voice, strengthened by fact. "Her heart, her body, her clan, her holdings belong to the king and, by royal decree, to me. Would you challenge the king?"

Hew's face was grave. He had gone pale. His brow was deeply furrowed. His mouth twisted with the torture of indecision.

"Aye," he croaked at last. "If that's what it takes."

"Why?" Gellir asked, his tone incredulous. "Why would you risk the wrath of the king?"

Hew straightened then, like a noble champion about to die for his clan. "Because some things are more important than political alliances. Because lasses are not pawns to be sacrificed at the whim of the king. Because true love is precious and rare. And no one should come between a man and a woman who have been lucky enough to find it. *Amor vincit omnia.* Love conquers all."

Hew's passionate declaration melted Merraid's heart. Days ago, she might have uttered those very words to Gellir.

But now they only magnified Gellir's aggravation. "'Tisn't up to you to make that decision," he growled. "Not for me."

"I don't make it for you, cousin," he said. "I make it for her."

Merraid sighed. The rumors were true. Softhearted Hew had a crippling weakness for women. He couldn't resist playing hero. It was no wonder he'd had his heart broken so many times.

But Hew's vulnerability proved to be Gellir's frustration. Gellir was a man of honor and principle and loyalty. Love might conquer all. But it did not counter the will of king and country.

Merraid understood both sides.

She agreed with Hew about arranged marriages. She was even secretly grateful Hew had shackled Gellir. After all, it helped her accomplish her goal of stalling the wedding.

But she understood Gellir's unbending principles. In the end, she was *his* friend. And since she owed her allegiance to him, she had to aid him however she could.

Hew was out of Gellir's range.

But not hers.

And Hew likely assumed she was helpless, like the women he enjoyed rescuing. He'd never see the blow coming.

As he turned to go, Merraid stepped forward and swung out her leg, catching him in the belly with a hard kick.

He doubled over with an "oof." A dagger clattered to the floor. But his reflexes were fast. Before she could reach it, he scraped it up and scrambled back out of reach.

She lunged forward as far as the chain would allow, inches away, snarling and clawing at him with her free hand.

He frowned and shook his head, muttering, "Another warrior lass."

Then he grabbed one more axe from the wall and made his way toward the exit.

Before he left, he turned and spoke to Gellir. "If you care at all for Lady Carenza, do not follow me. 'Twas I who helped her escape. I told her where she could find safe haven. And I mean to reunite her with the one she loves."

"This is mad, Hew," Gellir hissed.

Hew gave him a curious smile. "Nay, 'tis the most sane thing I've done in a long time."

As he slipped out of the armory, Gellir bellowed out his name. Hew ignored him.

When he was gone, Gellir bit out an oath and kicked the wall. He cursed in pain when he forgot he was wearing soft velvet slippers instead of his usual leather boots.

Merraid bit her lip.

How long should she wait before telling him her secret? That Hew's dagger hadn't been the only thing she'd kicked out of his belt? That under her boot was the key to the shackles?

Perhaps it was best to let his temper cool. The last thing she wanted was for Gellir to race off after his cousin with violence on his mind. She'd wait perhaps an hour. Until Gellir's anger subsided and there was a good distance between him and the meddling cousin he wished to murder.

# CHAPTER 19

I f Gellir's hands hadn't been shackled, he would have punched the stone wall of the armory in frustration.

Part of him wanted to throttle his cousin.

Part of him wanted to haul Hew off to safety.

When they were younger, Gellir had always been the one to rescue Hew, who was always getting himself into trouble over a lass.

Sometimes Hew had pursued another man's mistress.

Sometimes he'd mistaken a harlot for an admirer.

Once he'd fallen in love with a nun.

With his heart laid bare and his cock as a compass, Hew was constantly wandering into dangerous quarters.

But this was a step too far.

First, Hew had never before interfered with Gellir's romantic pursuits. It was a hard and fast Rivenloch rule to never let courting come before clan.

Second, the fact that Hew felt the need to protect Lady Carenza from him...*his own cousin*... That was a blow to Gellir's pride.

But the situation was far worse than that. Hew was defying the king. What did he think would happen when King Malcolm found out Carenza was a runaway bride? That Hew had helped deliver her to another man?

Damn the fool! Malcolm would hunt Hew down. He would be punished. Carenza would probably be sent to a nunnery. God only knew what would happen to her lover. As for Gellir, all of Scotland would know he'd been spurned by his bride. And all of Rivenloch would have to bear the shame of what Hew had done.

Gellir had to stop him.

He jerked at the shackle yet again, hoping to find some weakness in the iron. But it held fast.

He could call out until someone found him. The heavy chain would eventually break under a sledgehammer. But he'd prefer to find a way to intercept Hew without alerting anyone to his sabotage. His cousin might be a fool, but he was a well-meaning fool.

Gellir had to protect him.

He had to protect the clan.

There was only one thing to do. One thing that would salvage Lady Carenza's honor and keep the king's eye off of Hew.

Gellir had to take the blame for Carenza's desertion.

He had to claim it was his idea to call off the wedding.

He'd say he had rejected her, and that was why she'd run away.

It wasn't a very convincing story. What man in his right mind would turn away a woman as beautiful and charming as Lady Carenza?

But he was Grim Gellir. He could speak the lie with a grave face. Especially considering what was at stake.

It would mean disappearing for a time. Avoiding the tournament circuit. Keeping to the shadows. He'd have to leave Darragh. Perhaps leave Scotland. Distance himself from the clan so as not to tarnish them with his dishonor. Live like a fugitive. Hide like an outlaw.

In a year or two, perhaps Gellir's transgression would be forgiven and forgotten.

Perhaps King Malcolm would awaken from his dream of an English alliance and would no longer seek to marry his Scottish nobles to the enemy.

By then, Lady Carenza would be wed to her lover. Hew would congratulate himself for having rescued another maiden in distress. Maybe Feiyan would assemble another round of marriageable noblewomen for Gellir's consideration.

Not that he was in a rush to resume courting.

He was sick of romance.

That so much sacrifice and heartache could come from a loveless alliance made him less than eager to swim in those waters again.

He expelled the last of his hope on a sigh of surrender.

"What are we goin' to do?" Merraid ventured.

He gave her a rueful smile. *"We're* not going to do anything."

As much mischief as the maidservant had caused, none of this was her fault. Hell, she'd even tried to stop Hew with the combat tactics she'd learned from Feiyan. In skirts. And a shackle. She'd acted like a friend. He believed she truly meant to see him happy.

"We've got to do somethin', she insisted. "Ye can't let your bride just...run off."

"I don't have a choice."

"Well," she said, biting the corner of her lip. "Actually, ye do."

He arched a dubious brow. "Do I?"

She worried her bottom lip under her teeth. "Ye promise ye won't be angry?"

He frowned. "About what?"

"Ye have to promise."

What was she up to? "You know I can't promise that."

"Well then, at least promise ye won't go chargin' off to kill your cousin?"

"Hew? I might beat the holy hell out of him, but I won't kill him. What's this about?"

"There may be a way…"

She lowered her eyes to the ground, lifted her skirts, and moved her boot aside. Under it was a key.

"Is that…?"

"The key to the shackles."

"How did you…?"

"I kicked it out of his belt."

For one instant, he felt a surge of admiration for the crafty lass. Then the truth hit him. "That was an hour ago."

"Ye were terribly angry."

He felt steam rising in his ears. She'd had the key all this time and hadn't said a word. If she thought he was angry *then*…

She added, "I was afraid ye'd do somethin' reckless. Somethin' ye wouldn't be able to undo."

He managed to bite back the oath simmering on the tip of his tongue. But it took all his willpower to keep his ire from boiling over. To be reasonable.

Merraid had done what she thought best under the circumstances.

She didn't realize he would never kill his own clansman. She only saw that having Hew's blood on his hands would irreparably damage him.

She didn't realize that Hew absconding with Carenza was tantamount to treason. She only saw that his cousin was rescuing a lovelorn lass.

She didn't realize that her delay in giving him the key, letting him go after Hew, and allowing him to retrieve Carenza changed his future forever.

It was too late now.

What was done was done.

And it was futile to blame Merraid for what she couldn't understand.

His anger dissolved, and he lifted a brow at her. "Are you going to give me the key now?"

"Ye vow he won't do anythin' rash?"

"Aye," he lied.

She picked up the key and handed it to him. He unlocked the cuff around his wrist and freed himself from the shackles.

"So what are we goin' to do?" she repeated.

"*You're* not going to do anything," he said.

"Ye can't go anywhere without me."

"Ah, but I know something you do not." He held up the key. "This works on all Darragh's shackles."

Before she could decide whether that news was good or bad, he inserted the key into the cuff around his wrist.

"You're going to stay out of trouble," he murmured, turning the key to open the cuff, "and look after Feiyan." Lowering his gaze to her mouth, remembering the taste of her kiss, he slipped his hand free. "Forget me," he said, memorizing the innocent blue of her eyes as he linked the two unlocked shackles. "Find a good man to marry." He closed the distance between them to brush her brow with a kiss. "And have a dozen children."

"Wait. Where are ye—"

The cuffs connected with a decisive click.

He was free.

And she was chained to the armory wall.


"Nay!" Merraid cried.

Panic and fury warred in her breast as Gellir shot her a look of apology.

Before she could fully understand what he'd done, he tucked the key into his belt and whirled away.

"Damn ye, Gellir!" she yelled after him, thrashing against her constraints and prying at the interlocked cuffs with her free hand. The chain jangling against the wall echoed the jangling of her nerves.

What was he doing?

Where was he going?

Did he mean to track down his cousin?

Would he return with Hew—bloody and battered and hanging his head in shame—and a sobbing Carenza?

Merraid didn't think so. What he'd said to her... *Look after Feiyan. Forget me. Find a good man...* Those were not the words of a man planning to return.

So what did he intend?

Surely his honor demanded he be wedded as the contract of marriage decreed—to the daughter of the Laird of Dunlop, at the pleasure of the king.

How could a loyal vassal walk away from that?

The idea was inconceivable, especially for a man like Gellir.

Yet it seemed that was exactly what he'd done.

She struggled with that impossibility for nearly an hour, until a handful of Darragh men came to see what had become of the bridegroom and found her chained in the armory.

Flinching against the sparks the armorer struck as he pounded his sledgehammer again and again to break the iron chain that bound her, Merraid struggled to accept the fact that Gellir was gone for good.

Lady Feiyan carefully questioned her after she was free. But Merraid feigned ignorance. She refused to betray Gellir's secrets. Nor would she reveal anything about her own misguided attempts at matchmaking—the love notes she'd dictated, the promise she'd made to Carenza to accompany her to Rivenloch, or her desperate plan to shackle herself to Gellir to keep that promise.

She wouldn't breathe a word about Carenza's secret bairn. Or about Hew's efforts to reunite her with her lover.

And she would never confess her own deep feelings for Gellir. Feelings that had led her to swive him on the night of Beltane.

Unwilling to expose so many unforgivable transgressions, she was tormented by uncertainty. Conflicting emotions raged inside her, alternating between remorse and anger, worry and woe. The hours dragged on, filling her with crushing guilt and immeasurable sorrow. Jaw-clenching fury and crippling anxiety.

The Laird of Dunlop was beside himself with worry. His face was ashen. His mouth was tense. He'd already lost his wife. He couldn't lose his daughter. Though he didn't blame the Rivenlochs for her disappearance, Merraid knew the fault would lie with them if Carenza wasn't found.

Laird Dougal assured him that the Darragh men would find his missing daughter. Laird Deirdre offered up the best trackers of Rivenloch. Several contingents were sent to search the surrounding countryside.

Hours crawled past. Eventually twilight descended. Clouds obscured the rising moon and painted the sky with an ominous glower. From the wall walk, Merraid watched the darkening woods, chewing on a fingernail. One by one, the groups of trackers returned. Their steps were downtrodden. Their shoulders slumped. Their faces sagged with disappointment.

"He'll be fine," came a soft voice beside her.

Merraid yelped and nearly jumped out of her surcoat. How long had Isabel been standing there?

"Och, sorry," Isabel exclaimed. "I didn't mean to frighten you."

Merraid was more frightened by the fact she'd let her guard down. She gave a quick curtsey. "I suppose my mind was far away, m'lady."

"Fretting over Gellir?" Isabel guessed.

Merraid frowned. "O'er...all o' them."

Isabel gave her a knowing glance. "But especially my brother."

Merraid looked away. She couldn't let Gellir's little sister see the emotions on her face. After all, her feelings for Gellir were too strong. Inappropriate. Sinful. "Nay, m'lady." But she couldn't resist adding, "Why would ye think that?"

"I have a gift," Isabel said with a shrug, twirling her blond braid around one finger. "I can see when there's a bond between two people."

"He's my friend," Merraid explained.

"Och aye. But he's more than that, isn't he?"

Merraid stiffened. "Nay, m'lady," she lied, feeling the heat rise in her cheeks as she spoke with vehement force. "Anythin' more would be improper. He's the heir o' Rivenloch and Lady Carenza's bridegroom. I'm only a maidservant."

"I see." Isabel nodded and leaned over the parapet, gazing into the distance. "Still, it may do your heart good to know he'll be fine. My brother is strong and resilient. He knows Scotland like he knows his scars. And he's guided by loyalty and honor."

Isabel turned her lovely fair face toward Merraid then and gave her a sweet smile of sympathy and understanding.

Merraid's return smile didn't reach her eyes. Knowing Gellir was guided by loyalty and honor was not the reassurance Isabel thought it was. Indeed, Merraid suspected it was loyalty and honor that were going to get him into trouble.

On the second morn, a missive from Hew arrived in the hands of a breathless messenger. Hew wrote that he had found Lady Carenza and wished to assure the Laird of Dunlop that she was safe and sound. Merraid noted he carefully omitted any mention about returning her. And if he stayed true to what he'd secretly declared in the armory, he didn't mean to return her at all. He intended to reunite the lady with her lover.

To Merraid's dismay, there was still no word of Gellir. And fretting over him left her so distracted—forgetting her duties, misplacing things, and pacing aimlessly across the great hall—that Feiyan ordered her to the tiltyard to work off her restless energy, tossing and catching a bag of chain mail. Feiyan chose Gellir's brother, Brand, to practice with her.

Brand could not have looked more displeased as he slogged onto the field. Notoriously obsessed with swordsmanship, he clearly thought doing such a menial exercise as tossing chain mail—with a lass, no less—was beneath him.

"If 'tis too heavy for ye, m'laird," Merraid teased, "I can find somethin' lighter. Perhaps a straw hat?"

Brand's eyes closed to dull slits. Her mockery was not lost on him. "Not a bad suggestion, since I'm likely to toss such a light bag right o'er your head."

Merraid smirked. He might resemble Gellir with his dark hair and grave demeanor, but this sullen, sulking braggart was nothing like his respectful and chivalrous brother.

She hefted the canvas bag of mail up to her chest and tossed it forward in a gentle arc.

He caught the bag and sent it back with a grumble.

She tossed it forward again, this time with a slightly more direct trajectory.

He grunted when he caught it and returned it with an arc that was so high, it fell short of her. By the satisfied narrowing of his eyes, she could see he'd done it on purpose, to make her pick it up.

"Is the distance too great for ye, m'laird?" she jested. "I could move closer."

His lips thinned at the insult. "Stand where you will. It makes no difference to me."

She retrieved the bag and threw it hard.

Surprised by the impact, he fell back a step. Then, humiliated, he returned the bag with a strength born of anger.

One of the secrets of Merraid's training was using an opponent's power against him. This she did now. Rather than absorb the impact of his forceful throw, she stepped swiftly aside, catching the corner of the bag and letting the momentum spin her about. When she swung back around, she released the bag toward him.

The immediate return gave him no time to brace for the impact. The bag hit him square in the chest, and he staggered back several steps.

She was prepared for his rage. She'd fought his kind before. Men who thought women were useless. Powerless. And when they were quickly disabused of that notion, they expressed their displeasure with violence.

So when Brand sneered and hurled the bag at her with all his might, she sidestepped it again and swung it back at him with the same force.

This time he was ready, but he still issued a grunt as the chain mail hit him in the belly.

They completed several more exchanges. Merraid dodged his aggressive throws and sent them back at him like a Greek discus. Brand clung stubbornly to his method of absorbing the force of her blows, and he hurled the bag back at her with ever-increasing anger.

To be honest, after a time, she grew bored and almost as irritated as Brand.

When he launched a particularly vehement throw, she stepped back and let it hit the ground.

"What do ye say we abandon this child's play, m'laird?" she suggested. "Draw swords and engage in a real fight?"

His eyes glittered as if he relished her murder. But enough Rivenloch nobility flowed in his veins to give her a civil answer. He snorted. "I don't want to hurt you."

"I doubt ye'll be able to," she replied, stepping atop the bag of chain mail and then hopping down as she drew her *jian*.

"Are you serious?" he scoffed. "I'm the brother of Scotland's tournament champion."

"And I'm the student o' Darragh's finest warrior."

He muttered something under his breath that sounded like, "'Tisn't saying much." Nonetheless he drew his sword.

Merraid swept her elegant blade through the air and prepared to engage him. She was used to being underestimated. She might not be able to topple this up-and-coming second-best warrior in all of Scotland. But she could hold her own against him.

He motioned her forward. "Go ahead then, wench. Give it your best ef-"

She struck before he could even finish the word. Her light blade whistled through the air and sliced across his leather hauberd.

He staggered back in astonishment, frowning at the light diagonal scar she'd etched into the leather.

"Your turn, m'laird," she said.

Still somewhat reluctant to engage her, he came at her with a slow and straightforward blow, one that was easy to turn aside.

She shook her head in disappointment. Then, distracting him with a flourish of her free hand, she thrust forward into the space between his flank and his arm. An inch to the left, and she would have thrust him through. Fortunately for Brand, her goal wasn't to kill him. Just to wake him up.

He was alert now. Realizing she was a serious opponent, he reset his position and braced himself for real battle.

This time when he attacked, Merraid noticed something familiar in his fighting style. The way he gripped his sword. How he lunged and thrust. The pattern of assault he used. He'd obviously learned from his older brother. Which did nothing to take her mind off of Gellir. But also made Brand somewhat predictable.

She easily tossed away his first thrust.

Glowering, he cast aside her subsequent lunge.

Then he attempted a knee-high sweep, which she foiled by jumping over his blade.

She quickly returned with another scratch to his hauberk, parallel to the first.

Muttering an oath under his breath at his scarred leather, he sliced once through the air and then made a rapid X strike.

"Ye learned that trick from Gellir," she remarked as she handily deflected the blows with the edge of her blade.

"And that's Feiyan's defense," he retorted.

"I learned from the best."

"You don't know her mother," he grumbled. "Or her mother's teacher."

His mention of the infamous Warrior Maids of Rivenloch suddenly made Merraid's enthusiasm for their match disappear. She would rather hear more about what it was like to grow up at Rivenloch. So to put a quick end to the fight, she launched a rapid figure eight attack until he was backed against the tiltyard fence with nowhere to go.

Pressing the sharp tip of her *jian* against his throat, she came close to him and murmured, "Shall we stop before too many witnesses gather, m'laird?"

He growled and quickly scanned the practice yard. Pride convinced him he'd ruin his reputation by repeatedly losing to a maidservant. So he gave her a brusque nod. "As you wish."

She didn't move her sword. "I have one condition for your surrender."

His brows slammed together. "Surrender?" he bit out.

"Fine," she said, wondering how such a bigoted man could have grown up in a clan full of warrior maids. "We'll call it our mutual decision to discontinue. But I still have a condition."

"I won't do your chores like Gellir," he said with a frown, obviously having heard of his brother's penance. "And I won't be your pet. If you mean to make a fool of me, I'd rather have my throat slit."

She rolled her eyes. What she'd heard about Brand's hostility toward women hadn't been an exaggeration. He didn't exactly despise them. He just had little use or patience for them.

"Don't worry, m'laird," she said with a smirk. "I won't make ye wear my dress or coo like a dove."

He looked aghast.

She withdrew her weapon and slid it into its sheath. "I only wish to hear what 'twas like at Rivenloch, growin' up in a clan o' warrior maids with Gellir for an older brother."

Brand was visibly relieved. Still, he sighed as he put away his sword and leaned against the fence. "There's not much to tell," he said, staring across the field. "Rivenloch is on the English border, so we've always been a warrior clan."

"But your mother is the laird," she said in awe. "She leads the clan and commands the warriors."

He shrugged.

"And the Warrior Maids o' Rivenloch... They're legendary."

His jaw tensed. "Och aye, I suppose."

"I grew up on tales o' their bravery. Everyone's heard o' them and—"

"And no one's heard o' the warrior lairds." His mouth had a bitter twist.

She blinked. Was that the reason behind Brand's harsh attitude toward women? Did he envy the warrior maids' fame?

"But your brother..."

"Gellir has managed to make a name for himself," he said tightly. "But he had to leave Rivenloch to get out from under the shadow of the Warrior Maids."

Merraid leaned against the fence beside him and murmured, "He was invisible."

"Aye."

"As are ye."

He nodded.

Merraid understood. A man in a clan of women warriors likely felt as out of place and useless as a maidservant who could hold her own with a sword.

"Tell me about your brother, m'laird," she said.

"Gellir? He was my inspiration, growing up. He kept my fighting skills sharp. Taught me how to ride a horse. Wield a blade. Use a targe. Gave me this scar," he said with a dry chuckle, pointing to a thin line across his cheekbone.

"Why do ye not go on the tournament circuit with him, m'laird?"

Her question hit a nerve. A muscle twitched in his cheek. "I've been commanded to remain at Rivenloch."

"By the king?"

"By the laird."

"Your mother?" Merraid scowled. Brand was the same age as she was. He was a noble and already a proper knight. Even she was allowed the freedom to leave the castle. She didn't need the laird's permission. "Why?"

"Because I'm next in line."

"For the lairdship?" That seemed overly redundant. If Laird Deirdre died an untimely death, Hallie would presumably inherit the title. Gellir was next in line after

271

Hallie. Brand was only a spare heir in the unlikely event that Deirdre, Hallie, and Gellir were killed prematurely.

"For marriage."

Merraid's brows shot up. "Marriage? God's eyes! Has the king threatened to marry *all* the Rivenloch men to English brides?"

"He hasn't actually threatened anyone. But better safe than..." He frowned. "Wait. Why would a maidservant know about that?"

"Gellir confided in me. We're...friends."

"So I've heard."

Her breath caught. "Ye have?"

He shook his head. "My sister Isabel won't leave it alone."

"What did she say?"

"Some nonsense about a bond between you," he said with a dubious roll of his eyes.

"Oh. Aye."

"She also said you were worried on his account."

"I suppose everyone's worried on his account."

"I'm not. And you needn't worry either," he said. "With a sword at his side, no one can conquer my brother. He'll be bested by neither man nor beast."

Merraid gave him a wan smile. Brand clearly admired his illustrious sibling.

But she wasn't worried about men or beasts.

She was worried about a king whose will had been challenged.

# CHAPTER 20

Forced to flee in great haste, Gellir had had no time to gather weapons or supplies. No time to even change out of his wedding attire. He tucked one precious souvenir of Darragh into his leine before he left. But he was ill-prepared for travel or combat.

His velvet tabard and silver jewelry ultimately did prove useful. When he reached the village, he sold them in exchange for the finest Toledo sword he could afford, a serviceable coat of used chain mail, humble rags, a pair of sturdy boots, and the purveyor's silence.

He spent the first day trudging northeast through the woods, getting as far away from Darragh as possible. Along the way, he performed small labors for food—cutting peat, moving stones, scouring pots—anything that required a strong back and a good work ethic.

Eventually he planned to take a false name and hire out as a free lance for whoever needed a swordsman to enforce a contract or settle a dispute.

He'd draw the line at committing murder, however. He still had his honor. He might give up his name. His clan. His dignity. But he would never surrender his honor.

Even when it meant finding shelter in a barn that first night, nestled in the straw amongst piglets and lambs.

On the second morn, he dug a burial plot in a monastery

orchard in exchange for use of a monk's quill, ink, and parchment. There he wrote a missive of confession to his cousin Feiyan. Then, concealing himself at a crossroads, he stopped a shire-reeve who was traveling past Darragh and begged him to deliver the missive to the castle.

As the shire-reeve continued down the western road, Gellir diverted east into the woods.

It had been a long while since he'd slept on the forest floor. A champion as esteemed as Sir Gellir Cameliard of Rivenloch was usually a highly desired guest, housed at the best castles. Even his tournament pavilions featured lavish appointments—feather pallets and soft bedlinens, rich victuals and freeflowing ale.

But as he gazed up at the cloud-ringed moon from his makeshift bed of moss and pine needles, though his body was restless, his mind and heart were at peace. Humility was the price of his gift to Rivenloch. His personal disgrace would preserve the collective honor of the clan. So the hard ground was of some comfort to him.

"Shite!"

The hiss of Merraid's impatient oath and the angry whirl of her skirts disturbed the thick morning fog as she abandoned the *taijiquan* for the third time. Her mind was unfocused. Her thoughts were scattered. Her limbs moved with a will of their own.

In her first attempt, she'd tripped over a crack in the walk.

Then she'd bumped her elbow on the stone wall.

This time she completely forgot the order of the movements.

She shook her arms and blew out her tension on a long breath as she paced back and forth along the wall walk, making tumultuous patterns in the mist.

The world was hidden to her eyes this morn. Except for the distant sounds of seabirds crying and the loch lapping on the shore, the castle might have been perched on a mountain of clouds.

The future was likewise obscured by mist. Merraid felt trapped in a veil of uncertainty and indecision. Frozen in time. Unable to move in any direction for fear of stepping off the edge of those clouds.

She tried to tell herself all would be well. So Isabel had told her. So Brand believed. Gellir's siblings placed great trust in his ability to survive.

But his future depended on more than his skill with a sword.

Did no one else understand that Gellir's highly developed sense of duty might be his undoing? That his honor might lead him to make a noble sacrifice? One that was irreversible? Or were they so blinded by his brilliance that they could not see the hero's path he might choose?

She swallowed hard, staring out at the impenetrable fog. Feeling isolated. Uncertain. Helpless.

Then, with a growl of exasperation, she closed her eyes and banished all self-destructive thoughts from her mind. There was no point in dwelling on what she didn't know. What she couldn't change.

Taking in a cool, calm breath, she bent her knees, opened her eyes to focus on the fog-shrouded firth, and started the *taijiquan* for the fourth time.

"Merraid!" Feiyan hissed.

Merraid spun around. The lady was out of breath from rushing up the steps. She clutched a missive in her hand. And her face was as white as the fog.

An icy dagger of fear stabbed Merraid in the heart. "Is he...?" she breathed.

Her terror must have shown on her face. Feiyan grabbed her forearm in reassurance. "Nay, he's fine. The missive is from him."

Merraid clapped a hand to her breast as she swayed on her feet. She hadn't realized how afraid she was until this instant. It felt as if she'd been holding her breath for three days.

"What news, m'lady?" she asked, though she'd already deduced what he'd done. It was what he'd always done. Sacrificed his own well-being for that of his clan.

As she'd predicted, Gellir had taken responsibility for the whole debacle in order to save Hew's honor and Carenza's reputation. His note only filled in the gaps.

"My beloved cousin, I pray you share the contents of this missive with the Laird of Dunlop," Feiyan read. "It is with deep regret that I inform you I have had a change of heart regarding my marriage. I have decided I am not yet ready to take a wife. I thereby release Lady Carenza from our betrothal arrangement."

Merraid felt ill. How it must have tormented him to make such a false confession.

"Furthermore," Feiyan continued to read, "I have learned the lady fled Castle Darragh in tears. I wish you to know I have sent my cousin Hew to retrieve her, as I trust he will keep her safe."

Merraid bit back tears. She wondered if Hew would ever recognize the great sacrifice Gellir had made for him.

"I intend to roam the countryside," Feiyan read, "to enjoy the last of my freedom, to lend my sword to whoever needs it, to follow the advice of Plautus and sow wild oats while I may."

Feiyan looked up to catch Merraid's eye. They didn't even need to speak. They both knew that was an outright lie. They also knew it was fruitless to try to disprove it. Once the clan heard his words, his fate would be sealed.

"Will ye share the missive with Rivenloch, m'lady?" Merraid asked.

"I can't keep it secret. Laird Deirdre deserves to know what's become of her son."

"But Gellir's honor..."

Feiyan nodded. Her lips were compressed. "I know." She lowered the missive. "At least he's safe."

Giving her arm a squeeze, Feiyan turned and trudged back down the steps.

But Gellir *wasn't* safe, donning the shame of his clan like a mantle over his armor. He'd simply decided he was better fortified than Hew to bear the weight of dishonor.

He wasn't wrong about that. Hew's nature was volatile. He was easily swayed by his passions. Gellir's integrity, however, was etched in stone.

Because of his stainless reputation, in time, Gellir's sins would be forgiven. If and when he eventually rejoined the tournament circuit, he'd be welcomed as a returning hero. His honor would be restored. His glory would be rekindled. He would be redeemed.

But Merraid couldn't help but wonder...

How long would it take?

How many weeks or months or years would Gellir spend as an outcast?

How long would he be forced to languish in loneliness and obscurity?

Would he ever feel it was safe to return?

That he even deserved redemption?

Perhaps, forever wary of the king's wrath and fearful of possible revenge upon his clan, Gellir would never return.

Her throat thickened with grief. She gripped the damp edge of the parapet, shivering in the forbidding cold. A gull swooped past the castle, doubling in her watery vision.

This couldn't be the end.

He couldn't be gone forever.

That would mean all her efforts had been for naught.

All her pining and patience, all her dedication and discipline, the hours she'd spent training for him, looking out for him, writing verse for him, coaxing his bride...

Still, deep within her sorrowing breast, where her hopes rapidly dwindled, a tiny spark of stubborn determination was kindled.

She couldn't sit back and let destiny take its course.

She was a woman of action.

She was done with waiting. She'd waited four years for Gellir Cameliard. She wasn't going to let four more precious years slip past.

Pushing away from the wall, she faced west, sniffed back her tears, and began the *taijiquan.*

She swept a hand across the horizon, as if clearing away all the obstacles in her path.

Transferring her weight from one leg to the other, she twisted and advanced with two slow punches. Clouted despair with her left fist. Knocked back uncertainty with her right.

Pivoting, she pressed her palm forward, shoving away self-doubt.

As she moved with new grace and confidence through the movements, the mist began to clear. She gazed out at the gray waves of the firth, kissed by the light of the sun breaking through the clouds. She felt its touch on her shoulder as well. Warming her. Invigorating her. Inspiring her.

Perhaps there was something she could do.

Perhaps she didn't have to wait for fate.

She lunged to the right, following with her arms as if brushing aside a cloak.

She'd wanted a chance to prove her worth.

She'd always imagined it would be in the tournament lists.

She lunged slowly to the left, bringing her arms forward.

But perhaps she could do something more meaningful.

Something to repay Lady Feiyan, who'd taught her everything she knew.

Something to earn Merraid the respect of the Rivenloch clan.

Something to show Gellir how much she cared for him.

Raising her arms high, she lifted her right knee, balancing.

She'd gotten Gellir into this coil. She'd meddled in his courtships. Spied on him. Manipulated conversations. Written love notes. Steered him toward what she imagined was his best prospect.

Lowering her knee with a stomp, she snapped her fists into a fighting position.

Gellir's self-exile was her fault. It was up to her to get him out of it.

She had an idea. But it would take careful planning.

With new resolve, she leaned forward onto her left leg, moving her right arm and leg in a wide, swift arc that spun her around.

A flash of movement startled her.

Someone ducked out of the way at the last instant, narrowly avoiding a kick to the head.

It was Adam. Feiyan's brother.

Her eyes widened. She staggered, nearly falling before he caught her.

"Och, m'laird!" She scrambled back out of his grasp, hastily untucked her hiked skirts, and bobbed a curtsey. "Forgive me. I didn't see ye there."

He shrugged, as if dodging lethal kicks was something he did every day. "I didn't mean to be seen."

Merraid didn't know what to say to that. But she was horrified that, for the second time in two days, one of Gellir's siblings had managed to sneak up on her. Stealth seemed to be a trait innate to the Rivenlochs.

He nodded at her. "You've been learning from Feiyan."

"Aye, m'laird." Belatedly, she realized why he'd managed to so skilfully evade her kick. Like Feiyan, he was the child of Lady Miriel, Sung Li's prize student. "Do ye know *taijiquan?*"

"Not much," he admitted with a one-sided smile. "Just enough to duck. And please don't call me 'my laird.' The last time we met, I was a rat-catcher."

She couldn't help but grin at that. "Did ye want somethin'?"

He sighed and ambled over to the parapet to gaze out at the firth. "Only to get away from the chaos in the courtyard."

"What's happenin'?"

He raised a brow. "The missive from Gellir?"

"Oh." She lowered her eyes. "Aye."

"Do you believe it?" he asked, still staring into the distance. "Do you believe he left to wander the country-side?"

She hesitated. How honest could she be with him? His expression was inscrutable.

"Nay," she breathed.

"Neither do I."

A forbidden thrill went through her, as if they shared a secret.

He continued. "Gellir would never defy the king like that."

"Nor abandon his bride."

"Right." He sniffed. "So what are we to do?"

"We?"

"You care about him, aye?"

Bloody hell. Did everyone in the Rivenloch clan know she had feelings for Gellir? Did they all have the sight, or were they just a brood of rumor-mongering wagtongues?

She gave him a reluctant nod.

"So you must be planning something," he reasoned.

She chewed thoughtfully at her lip. Should she trust him? What she schemed was a serious undertaking. One that could have dire consequences. She didn't want to put anyone else at risk. Still, it might be wise to have someone who was aware of her intentions, in case things went awry.

"If I tell ye," she decided, "will ye swear not to tell another soul?"

"If you wish."

She gulped. Imagining was one thing. Saying it out loud was another. "I'm goin' to Toulouse to beg an audience with the king. And I'm goin' to fight for Gellir's honor."

He arched a surprised brow.

She held her breath. Now that Adam had heard her audacious plot, she wondered if he would change his mind. Break his vow. Inform the others.

But his face betrayed no other emotion. He turned back to lean on the parapet and stared out at the surging firth. "You think you can convince him?"

She straightened, lifting a proud chin. "Aye."

"Then there's something you should know about the king."

She clenched her fists, prepared to defend her position. "I already know 'tis a reckless plan to stand up to Malcolm. I know the odds are against me. So say what ye will. But I won't let fear get in my way, even if it means—"

"He's not at Toulouse."

She blinked. "What?"

"The king. He's not at Toulouse. He left. He's gone to Perth."

She stared at him in wonder. Wasn't he going to condemn her rash plan? Or try to talk her out of slogging across Scotland to challenge King Malcolm?

Then he cocked his head, giving her a quick critical perusal from head to toe. "And he's unlikely to give an audience to a maidservant."

She narrowed her eyes in glittering determination. She'd had enough of being underestimated. "I don't intend to give him a choice in the—"

"So you'll need a disguise."

She froze, stunned speechless.

Did Adam approve of her plans?

He could have knocked her over with a puff of air.

"Perth is four days' journey," he continued, "if we go on foot. That's what I'd advise. Horses will only get in the way. As for attire..."

"Wait. We?" she said when she was able to find words. "Nay. Nay. I mean to go alone."

"Alone?" He seemed genuinely baffled. "That would be foolhardy."

"I don't want to get anyone else in trouble—"

"Trouble?" His eyes sparked to life, as if she'd just said his favorite word. "Look. You've obviously never done this kind of thing before. And I have. Countless times."

He wasn't wrong. His reputation for intrigue and impersonation were legendary.

But she shook her head. "I got him into this mess. 'Tis up to me to get him out of it. 'Tis somethin' I must do for him alone. As his friend."

"I'm his brother," he said pointedly. "Do you not think I might have an interest in rescuing him as well?"

He had a point. Still, as the son of a laird, there was much more at stake for him. "I can't ask ye to take such a risk."

"I don't think you *did* ask me." He pushed off from the wall and cast glances in both directions, looking for witnesses. "But time's wasting. If we're going to set out on this mission, we should do it while everyone's distracted, nattering away in the courtyard. Come on."

While she sputtered in indecision, he seized her hand and led her down the stairs. She was still breathless when they emerged in the great hall and he released her hand.

"Go to the buttery," he murmured. "I'll meet you there. I have an idea."

Several moments later, Adam returned. He was dressed in his armor and carrying a large satchel, into which he stuffed several cheeses.

"We'll take the tunnel," he said, nodding toward the back wall of the buttery, which was covered by a tapestry. He must have remembered it as the passage the Rivenloch forces had used to steal into the castle four years ago.

She caught him by the arm. "The gate at the bottom is locked now."

"Do you have the key?"

She shook her head.

"No matter," he said, grabbing a small torch from the wall to light the way. "I'm sure I can open it."

He was right. They navigated through the long tunnel—feeling their way over the rugged rock, past dripping, mossy walls, down the steep slope that led to the sea. When they reached the iron gate, he pulled a small leather bag of tools from the satchel. Using two slender steel picks with bent ends, he was able to work open the rusty lock.

Then he dug deeper into his satchel and pulled out a dull brown tunic and cowl.

"Put these on," he said. "You're going to be a monk."

He extinguished the torch by tucking it into the wet sand between two boulders at the mouth of the cave. Then, while he stood guard at the gate, she changed into the monk's robes. They dragged a bit, but the hood effectively hid her face.

After she'd changed, he took her servant's garb and stuffed it into the satchel. Then he donned his helm and pushed open the unlocked gate, which squeaked on its hinges.

She pulled the hood around her face and stepped out.

Making their way across the damp sand, they may have looked odd—a warrior and a monk strolling along the shore of the firth. But only a few fishermen witnessed their passage. And once they climbed back up the grassy slope and found their way through the forest to the main road, they looked as common as any pair of travelers.

Adam had warned her the journey to Perth would take four days. But Merraid wasn't about to complain. Once she began to experience the hazards of the road, she was glad she hadn't set out on horseback alone.

Thieves abounded in the woods. Fortunately, they were intimidated by Adam's armor and discouraged by the presence of his holy companion. But Merraid was certain a band of outlaws would have considered a lone maidservant an easy target. Of course, she would have disabused them of that notion with a few slashes of her *jian.* Still, fighting off villains would have wasted valuable time.

They walked all day, stopping by the roadside stream to rest, drink, and nibble at the cheese he'd brought. The skies had been only partly cloudy and blessedly free of rain. But as the last sliver of sun slid behind the horizon, she shivered with cold.

"Shall we stop for the day?" Adam asked.

"I can go on." She wouldn't let a bit of a chill get in the way of saving Gellir.

"We're making good progress. There's no need to suffer. Besides, I know a good keep nearby."

"A keep?"

"You didn't think we'd be sleeping on the ground, did you?"

Actually, that was exactly what she thought. It had never occurred to her to seek lodging. A maidservant with no coin wasn't likely to find accommodations.

"Come on," he said. "We'll stay with the Wallace clan."

She wondered how a man from the Lowlands of Scotland knew the Wallace clan. But an even more pressing matter concerned her.

"What if they ask me somethin'...holy?" Not only did she have a distinctly feminine voice, but she knew only a wee bit of Latin.

He gave her a sly grin that reminded her of Feiyan. "That's easy. You're a monk, aye? You've taken a vow of silence."

She smiled back at him. It was ingenious.

Using only his wits, he managed to secure a place for them by the hearth in the great hall of Wallace. Adam greeted the laird like an old friend, mentioning how well the new cathedral at St. Andrews was coming along because of his generous contribution. Even Merraid couldn't tell if that was true or not, but the laird seemed content for it to be so.

She slept soundly in the rushes, and they crept away at dawn to continue their journey.

By the end of the second day, Merraid's feet ached, and her lips were chapped. But she wouldn't complain. She'd walk barefoot over sharp rocks in a windstorm if it meant saving Gellir's honor.

Adam came through again. The Laird of Graham had a sizable keep, room at the hearth, and, by curious coincidence, had also donated funds for the cathedral at St. Andrews.

Their good fortune, however, turned sour on the third day.

Storm clouds glowered down from the beginning, turning from white to gray to black as their mood darkened. By midday, heavy with moisture, they released their store of rain in a torrent that threatened to beat the travelers into the mud.

Adam tried to shield her from the worst of it. But even

ducking into the roadside trees couldn't keep her from being soaked by day's end.

Thankfully, just before dark, Adam spied smoke from a wooden keep on a hillside nearby. He motioned her to follow him.

"What clan is it?" she called out over the din of the storm.

"I don't know."

She winced in disappointment. It appeared their luck had run out. But she would be grateful to sleep in a dovecot if she could only get out of the cursed rain.

As it turned out, Adam could foment connections out of thin air. Using hints and vague references, a bit of knowledge and a bit of guesswork, he managed to convince the laird—the head of Clan Drummond—that they were long-lost cousins who had fought side-by-side years ago in a clan battle.

Adam's skills were truly amazing. And terrifying.

Merraid decided the woman who made Adam fall in love with her would have to be clever indeed to match his brilliance. She'd also have to hang on for dear life, for Adam was not only bright, but dangerously impulsive.

Nonetheless, tonight Merraid was grateful for his shameless deceit.

As she drifted off within the folds of damp wool, steaming dry by the fire, she wondered how Gellir was faring.

She tried to imagine him nestled warmly in a friendly clan's keep.

But she thought it was more likely, considering his current disposition of self-sacrifice, he was shivering under the trees in the pouring rain, miserable in his drenched cloak.

She murmured a quick prayer that good fortune would find him and keep him safe.

# CHAPTER 21

Gellir shivered under the trees in the pouring rain, miserable in his drenched cloak.

At least the people he loved were safe and warm. By now, Hew would have taken Carenza to her lover. His clan were likely still at Darragh. And Merraid...

He pulled out the prize he'd tucked into his leine. Merraid's braid. He closed his eyes and brushed her hair against his lips, inhaling the floral scent, enjoying the silken texture, remembering her sunny countenance, her dancing eyes, her summery smile. The thought of her was enough to warm him in the midst of the storm.

Then he tucked his treasure away and opened his eyes. Through the punishing drops, he glimpsed a dim light in the dark distance.

Shelter?

With fingers made clumsy by the cold, he opened his leather purse and dug out two coins. It was all he had left from yesterday. Little work could be had in such foul weather. But it was enough to purchase an ale, a bit of pottage, and, if he ate slowly, an hour or two of respite from the rain.

He left the trees, scowling against the hammering of the storm as he trudged through the muck and mire.

Luck was with him. An alestake protruded from the

cottage, announcing the availability of freshly brewed ale, though the sign's wreath of ivy had fallen into the mud. He stomped the grime from his boots and pushed open the door. The blast of warmth from the cheery fire, the scent of hearty fare, and the pair of travelers huddled over cups of foamy ale made him sigh with relief.

He nodded in greeting and hung up his cloak and sword. A toothless old wench pulled out a three-legged stool for him at the wee table.

"Ye'll be wantin' pottage, no doubt," she said. "'Tis cold as the grave tonight." Before he could answer, she added, "And a hefty cup o' ale as well." She turned away, calling over her shoulder. "And ye won't want to venture out again till morn, I'm sure."

He opened his mouth to ask how much she'd be charging for all that.

"Don't bother," one of the travelers said. "She won't take nay for an answer."

"Aye," the other agreed. "A right captain o' the guard she is."

Gellir settled onto the free stool.

"I'm Walter," the first man said, wiping his hand on his thick black beard before extending it.

Gellir shook his hand. It was thick and callused, and beneath his woolen sleeve, Gellir glimpsed the dull silver of chain mail.

"You're a warrior," he said.

"That I am," Walter said, "as is my friend here."

"Robert," the second man chimed in, offering his hand. He nodded his shaggy blond head toward Gellir's sword. "And unless ye've pilfered that weapon from a passin' knight, ye're a fightin' man as well."

"Aye," Gellir said. "I'm...John."

"'Tis a bonnie blade, John," Walter said.

"It serves me well."

"It's earned ye a place to sleep tonight," Robert said with a wink.

Gellir frowned, confused.

Walter confided, "Methinks the old wench doesn't mind havin' a few well-armed lodgers to look after the place."

"Ah."

The old woman set a trencher of steaming pottage and a cup brimming with ale before him.

Gellir dug in eagerly. A crumb of horsebread and a wedge of hard cheese had been his only sustenance today. So the humble meal was as welcome as a royal feast.

"Where are ye headed?" Walter asked.

"East," Gellir said. It wasn't exactly a lie. But wandering aimlessly around the countryside seemed like a suspicious reply. "And you?"

"On our way home from Perth."

"What did you do there?" Gellir asked, stabbing a morsel of mutton with his knife.

Robert drew himself up proudly. "We marched with the king's guard."

"The king's guard?" Gellir frowned. "In Toulouse?"

"Nay," Walter said. "Malcolm landed in Scotland a fortnight ago." He arched a brow and added pointedly, "He needed extra defense for the journey to Perth."

"He's in Perth?"

"Aye," Robert said, shaking his head. "But we didn't stick around."

The two men exchanged meaningful glances.

Gellir stopped with his knife halfway to his mouth. "Why not?"

Walter scanned the corners of the cottage with suspicion, even though there were only the three of them. Then he whispered, "There's rumors of an uprisin'."

Gellir returned his knife to the trencher. "What kind of uprising?" he whispered back.

The old woman came in to poke at the fire, and they fell silent.

"Woolens are in there," she said, wagging a finger toward an oak chest, "and I'll thank ye to bank the fire ere ye bed down, aye?"

"O' course," Robert said. When she was gone again, he murmured, "A handful of earls are plottin' to lay siege."

"Because of Toulouse?" Gellir guessed. "Because of Malcolm's alliance with Henry?"

"Right," Walter said.

Gellir bit out an oath.

"Some o' them lost a good deal o' land to the Sassenachs," Robert muttered.

"So I can't say I blame them," Walter added.

Robert declined to comment further, taking a swig of ale instead.

Gellir rubbed thoughtfully at his chin. "Earls against the king. 'Twill divide Scotland."

"Pah!" Walter said. "No more than giving half o' her to the English will."

"What are their demands?" Gellir asked.

"They want their lands back, I wager," Robert said.

"Aye," said Walter.

Gellir took a thoughtful sip of his ale. That was a coil. He understood the earls' discontent. He even concurred with their demands. Like Rivenloch, some of their lands had belonged to the clans from the time of the Vikings and before.

But Gellir was a vassal to the king. He'd sworn an oath of loyalty to Malcolm.

His brow furrowed as he remembered the other oath he'd sworn. The one he'd broken. The one to wed Lady Carenza. That sin stained his soul like rust on chain mail.

Still, a warrior didn't toss away his armor simply because it was tarnished. It was up to him to repair it, polish it, and set it to rights so it could be useful again.

Was this his chance to redeem himself? To prove to King Malcolm the undying loyalty of the Rivenloch clan? If he challenged these earls in the name of the king, would it erase his past dishonor?

The effort might cost him his life. It seemed inevitable, considering he'd be brandishing his blade against several powerful earls.

But if his life was the price of his clan's honor, he would gladly pay it.

An hour later, as he bedded down in the rushes before the banked fire, he felt alive for the first time in days. He had purpose now. He was going to defend his king.

Perhaps he wasn't destiny's foe after all.

Perhaps fate had smiled on him.


"Something's not right," Adam murmured. His warm breath added fog to the frosty morning mist.

Merraid huddled beside him in the hawthorn near Perth Castle. They couldn't get too close. The motte-and-bailey castle was surrounded by a wide treeless expanse. Though such a keep was fortified by a courtyard wall, a deep ditch, and a wooden palisade, the cleared land made it easy for guards to spot attackers long before they drew near.

But at the moment, the grassy slope below Perth was filled with pavilions and soldiers.

"Is it a tournament?" Merraid asked.

He shook his head. "I don't think so."

"Perhaps a celebration o' the king's return?" she asked with heavy sarcasm.

"I fear not. Indeed..."

"What?"

"Let's take a closer look."

They crept through the fog and between the pavilions. Men-at-arms, horses, archers, and servants drifted in and out of the mist like fish swimming in a murky firth. Everyone was busy, but Merraid could only pick out snippets of conversation about supplies and weapons.

They gradually circled the entire expanse, passing by all the pavilions so Adam could identify the clan banners.

"Six clans are here," he told her. "I recognize Ferteth, the Earl of Strathearn. I don't know the others."

"Why have they come?"

He lifted a warning finger to his lips to caution her to silence. Then he called out to a passing archer. "Good sir, I've just come at the request of Strathearn." He gestured to Merraid. "Do you know what he wanted with this monk?"

The archer screwed up his face in consideration. "Mayhaps to bless the siege?"

"Ah, of course."

"'Tis a siege?" Merraid whispered when the archer was gone. "Against the king?" That seemed unlikely.

"I'll find out." Adam snagged an ale from the tray of a passing maidservant and approached a pair of soldiers drinking from their own cups. Raising his cup, he toasted, "Here's to our success! May the clans stay strong..."

The soldiers raised their cups in reply, and one of them added, "And may the king see the error of his ways!"

They all drank, and Adam gave them a salute of farewell.

Merraid was agog. How had this happened? How could King Malcolm's subjects rise up against him?

She knew Lady Feiyan had been unhappy with the king's behavior and the way he'd been sidling up to the English. But had things become so serious that clans were laying siege to their own liege?

Before she could begin interrogating everyone within sight, Adam dragged her back to the hawthorn to hide and consider their options.

By the time they reentered the woods, Merraid had already made up her mind. She wasn't going to let a siege deter her. She'd come a long distance to seek an audience with the king. She wasn't going to abandon her mission now. She was going to find a way into the keep. King Malcolm could deal with his disgruntled earls later. After he granted clemency to Gellir.

Adam had a different idea.

"We should go," he said.

"What do ye mean, go?"

"Leave."

"I'm not leavin'," she said. "Not when I've come so far."

"'Tis a bad time to ask the king for a favor."

"'Twas always a bad time for me," she admitted. "But I'm not goin' to let that stop me."

"How do you plan to gain entrance to the castle when 'tis under siege?"

She glowered at him. The one time she needed him to be daring and impulsive, and he was naysaying her with rhyme and reason.

He rubbed his jaw. "Unless..."

"Aye?"

"We could wait out the siege."

Her hopes collapsed. "That could be months."

"There's no other way."

There was one other way. A conniving maidservant's way. A few words whispered in the right ears could start a major battle among the clans. And while they were embroiled in their own skirmish, she might be able to slip into the keep.

But she quickly dismissed that idea. It was the sort of bold idea Lady Feiyan was always scolding her for. The sort of idea Feiyan called using a trebuchet to kill a fly.

So what would sly Feiyan do?

Merraid had been trained to use an opponent's power against them. To learn their weaknesses. To harness their strengths. To divert rather than stop blows. To use grace, balance, and redirection instead of brute force.

But even more key than battle skills, Feiyan had taught her to avoid conflict. If a matter could be solved by evasion, it was better to walk away from a fight. And if it could be solved through diplomacy, it was better to wield words than swords.

"What if I ended the siege?" she asked aloud.

"How would you do that?"

"By brokerin' peace."

She could tell by Adam's uncertain grimace that he didn't believe she had the skills for that. But he remained silent.

"Whose authority is higher than the king's?" she asked him.

"No one's."

"Ah, but ye're wrong."

He puzzled over that for an instant, then replied, "The church."

She grinned.

His furrowed brow was dubious. "You think the church can end the siege?"

"I do." She had a plan. One that even Lady Feiyan would approve. "But I'll need your help. And parchment. And a quill. And ink."

No sooner did she speak the words than Adam reached into his satchel and pulled out the requested items.

She stared at him in open-mouthed wonder.

He shrugged, explaining, "I come prepared."

"What else have ye got in there? A horse and cart?"

It would take some time to consider the perfect words. But Merraid knew if she could court a titled lady with romantic verse, she could sway six earls and a king with carefully crafted flattery. Especially if it came from the most powerful man in the world.

At midday, Gellir at last emerged from the woods on the main road to Perth. His breath caught at first sight of the castle. Surrounding the palisade, dozens of pavilions spread across the sward like heather blanketing the hills.

There were more of them than he'd expected. Enough to make him reconsider his brash intention to challenge the rebellious earls. Apparently they'd come, not as diplomats, but with their entire clan armies, ready to wage war.

In the end, it would make no difference. Gellir fully expected to die in the attempt. But his death would be in service to the king. Thus it would restore honor to Rivenloch.

Straightening his shoulders beneath the ragged coat of mail that was still rusty despite scrubbing it with sand, he took a deep breath and strode boldly across the mist-covered grass.

He immediately recognized the first banner.

"Ferteth!" he bellowed, unsheathing as he came.

Servants fled in the wake of his grim scowl and naked blade. Soldiers frowned and clapped hands on their swords. A scrawny lad scrambled into the finest pavilion to fetch the earl.

A moment later, Ferteth burst through the canvas flap with an indignant glower.

"What is the meaning of th-...." His eyes widened. "Gellir?"

Gellir would never attack an unarmed man. Especially Ferteth, who was as old as Gellir's father. But neither would he allow treason to go unpunished.

"In the name of the king," Gellir bit out, "I demand satisfaction."

The earl's face reddened with rage. "What? You would defend that Sassenach-lover?"

"I'm King Malcolm's vassal. As are you."

"He broke bread with the enemy," Ferteth sneered.

Gellir narrowed his eyes to slits. "Arm yourself," he growled.

"Bloody hell," Ferteth grumbled. "Donald, fetch me my sword and armor."

While Donald bowed into the pavilion to do Ferteth's bidding, another lad bolted away, probably off to spread the news of the challenge.

Before Ferteth could finish donning his chain mail, another earl burst from between the pavilions, carrying a bare blade in his hairy hand.

"Is it true, sirrah?" the new arrival demanded of Gellir. "Are you challenging us?"

"Aye," Gellir declared, eyeing the soldiers who had begun to gather. They hadn't unsheathed. Yet. Perhaps it would be a fair fight after all.

"James!" the second earl called over his shoulder. "Here!"

James, the third earl, arrived. He had a shock of red hair, blue fire in his eyes, and an iron grip on his sword.

"I know you!" he spat. "You're Deirdre's son! Good God, man! Does Rivenloch know what you're up to?"

Good, Gellir thought. At least they knew who he was. The king would know which clan was loyal. Which clan had come to his rescue.

The fourth earl was only half-dressed. He was young, fit, and fine-looking. And by the terrified expression on the sweet face of the disheveled lass trailing after him, he had good reason to be only half-dressed. He nonetheless carried a weapon.

While the fourth earl was catching his breath, a fifth stomped into the clearing. He was as big as an ox, with hair as black as peat. Drawing his sword, he let out a wordless bellow.

As if summoned by that bellow, a sixth earl scurried to join the others. He stood a full foot shorter than his companions, and his blade quivered in his pudgy hand. But he prepared for combat, pulling his visor down over his round face. Gellir wondered if the visor was to hide his flinches of fear.

Gellir blew out an uneasy breath as he scanned the warriors surrounding him now with their blades drawn. Even if he somehow managed to best the six earls, armies of their loyal clansmen stood behind them with their hands on their hilts, ready to finish him off.

"Look!" Merraid hissed from inside Adam's ill-fitting helm, stopping in her tracks halfway across the green. "'Tis the earls, aye?"

Adam, having exchanged his armor for Merraid's robes, pushed back the hood to take a closer look at the men gathering between the pavilions. "Aye."

She chuckled once. "They've already gathered. That's convenient."

"Not really. They've drawn their swords."

"Drawn their swords?" She raised her brows, and the helm slipped down over her eyes. She pushed it back up to peer at Adam through the slit. "Why?"

"I'm guessing they mean to…stab somebody?"

Merraid gasped. "'Tisn't the king in their midst, is it?"

"Hard to tell. Let's get closer."

Merraid's heart thumped in her breast. She bore no great love for King Malcolm. But if the earls killed him, she'd never get the chance to restore Gellir's honor.

Emboldened by her new disguise, she strode across the sward with manly confidence. Adam scrambled after her in his cowl, clutching the rolled parchment in his hand.

They'd just reached the back of the crowd when she glimpsed, in the midst of the earls, a dark head of hair she'd recognize anywhere.

For one terrifying instant, long enough to mouth the word, "Gellir," she froze.

Then the dull gleam of a steel blade rose above his head, and her body sprang to life.

Tearing away from Adam, shouldering soldiers aside, she drew her sword as she charged. Before the earl's blade could descend upon Gellir, she rushed in to knock it away with her weapon.

Whirling, she faced another earl's threatening slash, which she deflected from Gellir's chest. The third blow, struck by a young man who was only half-dressed, knocked her helm askew and narrowly clipped her shoulder before she could duck out of the way.

Gellir immediately understood he had an ally. "Back to back!" he shouted.

Adjusting her helm, she spun round. Their backs collided to create a two-faced enemy, harder to defeat.

Nonetheless, they were two against six. And should they manage to defeat the six, there were still their clansmen to contend with.

But she didn't dare think about that. Not while steel whistled and clanged and sparked all around her.

She lunged and lashed at one foe while the other two recovered. But their attacks came faster and faster. With her *jian,* she could have made minced meat out of the earls. Hampered by armor that didn't fit well and a Scottish sword she'd never used before, her defenses were slow and awkward.

"The king!" someone shouted.

She only had time for a quick glance, but high upon the parapets of Perth Castle, a noble figure watched the fight.

Reinvigorated by a royal audience, Merraid redoubled her efforts, pummeling the helm of the shortest earl and leaving a nasty scratch across the bare chest of the youngest.

She still couldn't see properly out of Adam's oversized helm, which kept slipping down over her eyes. But if she was going to be vanquished in this hopeless battle, she supposed it didn't matter if she tore it off and revealed her identity.

With her free arm, she wrenched the helm from her head and flung it hard at the spitting, furious, redhaired earl. As he dropped onto his arse and grabbed his nose in pain, she used her leg to sweep the short earl off his feet and onto the ground with a thud. And while the half-naked earl was gaping in wonder, she knocked him back with a punch to the chin that sent him to the land of dreams.

With three of them dispatched, she tossed back her braid and swiveled round to help Gellir with the last three.

"Merraid?" Gellir said, startled.

In that instant of distraction, the hairy bear of a man he was fighting charged forward.

But Gellir's incredulous eyes never left her as he handily jabbed the man's throat with the pommel of his sword.

It was a simple matter, once the bear was gagging and swaying on his feet, for Merraid to finish him with a swift sideways shove.

"What are you doing here?" Gellir asked in wonder. His expression was a curious mixture of disbelief and pleasure, horror and relief.

She gave him a quick wink. "Bein' your good friend."

But there was no time for chat. The second earl attacked.

He was an older gentleman, but an excellent fighter. And he seemed to have no qualms about fighting a woman.

Merraid thrust and dodged and deflected his attacks with great skill. Still the man met her, blow for blow. He would not go down easily.

Gellir, however, could be of little assistance. The earl he fought was a beast. He was at least six inches taller than Gellir, with shoulders as wide as an oxcart. His hair was black. His eyes were beady. And he was frothing at the mouth, practically choking on fury.

While Merraid leaped and kicked and finally began to weary her opponent, she could see that Gellir was getting nowhere with the beast.

Between blows of her own, she studied the hulking ox assailing Gellir. He might be able to pound a man into the ground with one fist. But he moved like a slug. He might have the shoulders of a blacksmith. But the weight of his body made him clumsy.

"Let me!" she decided, facing off against the beast, giving Gellir no choice in the matter as the old earl shifted to attack him.

She smiled at the frothing beast, which only goaded him into charging her. One quick sidestep, and he sailed past, colliding with the crowd like a ball striking ninepins.

Righted by his clansmen, he shivered with rage, raised his blade, and charged again.

Again, she sidled out of the way, and he crashed into the side of a pavilion, collapsing it.

While Gellir continued to do serious battle, she tangled with an oaf who seemed more like an unruly child. An enormous child, to be sure, but one who didn't understand anything but brute force.

But Merraid's training had taught her that the greater the power a foe had, the greater a weapon she had against him. And for a man of truly enormous power...

Once he extricated himself from the pavilion wall, he let out an animalistic growl and thundered toward her.

This time, instead of stepping away, she dove at his feet.

He tripped over her, dropping his sword, and fell with earth-shaking force onto his hands and knees.

She hopped up and waited for him to rise while Gellir backed his tiring opponent against a pavilion wall with a series of admirable, swift strikes.

When the beast found his footing, he didn't bother trying to locate his weapon, but recklessly charged her again.

She didn't need her sword either. She dropped it and charged in under him, aiming for his belt. Momentum carried him over her rounded shoulder, and he slammed to the ground on his back with such stunning force, it sapped the breath from him.

At that moment, Gellir gave the last remaining earl a hard clout to the helm with the butt of his sword that made the man slither to the ground.

Their enemies defeated, they faced each other, breathless and battered.

As they exchanged glances, she felt his gaze speak to her.

*I love you,* it said.

*I missed you.*

*I thought I'd never see you again.*

But then his eyes widened.

And that was when she saw it.

The clan armies around them were slowly advancing.

# CHAPTER 22

"*Audite! Audite!*" A monk standing near Gellir suddenly bellowed, throwing back the hood of his cowl and raising a rolled parchment in his hand.

Gellir could not have been more dumbfounded. It had been astonishing enough to find the cunning warrior fighting beside him was Merraid—a discovery that filled him with a mix of emotions ranging from shock to joy, from relief to terror.

Now his cousin Adam had shown up. In the guise of a monk.

What they planned, Gellir couldn't imagine. But Adam's outburst had effectively put a halt to their imminent massacre, so he was grateful for that.

"I have brought word from *Roma*," Adam announced with a thick Roman accent. "From His Holiness himself." He made the sign of the Cross.

The soldiers surrounding them gasped.

Gellir could only gape. Adam had certainly outdone himself this time. And he'd thought impersonating the *king* was audacious.

A missive from the Pope was rare indeed. In fact, Gellir couldn't remember *ever* seeing such a thing. Aside from an interest in the new cathedral being built at St. Andrews, he doubted the Pope thought much about Scotland at all.

From atop the parapets came the voice of the king. "You there! Did you say His Holiness?"

"Aye, Alexander III!" Adam called back. "Are you *Rex Scotiae?*"

"We are."

"Then it is for your ears as well, *domine.*"

The defeated earls began to rouse. The bedraggled lass tearfully dabbed at the young earl's bloody chest. Fertech took off his helm to rattle his brains back into place. The hairy man blinked back cobwebs. The redheaded earl cradled his broken nose. The short earl scrambled to his feet. And the beast managed, with the help of several bystanders, to peel himself off the ground.

The king cupped his hands around his mouth and yelled down, "Can we agree to a temporary truce to hear the words of His Holiness?"

"A truce?" Fertech growled under his breath. "With a Sassenach kiss-arse? Never."

But the remaining earls had other thoughts.

The short one whispered, "But Fertech, if His Holiness himself sent word..."

The youngest chimed in, "I for one have no wish to challenge the church."

The hairy one snorted. "And if the truce is only *temporary*, I'm for it. After all, we've been freezing our arses for a fortnight and gotten nowhere."

The redhead groaned, pressing tenderly at his cracked nose. "I suppose 'tis better than sitting here, bleeding to death." He punctuated his remark by hawking bloody spittle on the grass.

Fertech still wasn't convinced. "I won't bow before that traitor of an upstart."

"No one's asking you to, Fertech," the hairy one said. "We're only agreeing to a reprieve. Just so the missive can be read. Right?" He lifted one caterpillar of a brow at Adam.

Adam nodded.

"Fine," Fertech decided with a sigh. Then he called up to the king. "'Tis agreed, Your Grace. For now."

The king consulted with the men standing beside him, then announced, "We will open the palisade gate and meet the earls there."

Gellir gave Adam a clandestine glance. He wondered what his cousin intended. What was written on that parchment? What could His Faux Holiness have to say about a land conflict in faraway Scotland? And how much danger was Adam putting himself in, pretending to be the representative of the Pope?

Was the missive an attempt to challenge the authority of the king? Did it praise the efforts of the earls to recover their lands? Or was it a condemnation of the earls' demands and an affirmation of Malcolm's status as supreme monarch?

What side had Adam taken? And did he realize the grave responsibility he bore, espousing a holy opinion that came from God knew where?

He couldn't let his cousin endanger himself like that. The merest slip of Adam's tongue could betray him. The slightest wavering of his voice could bring his charade to an end. His words, spoken in the presence of the most powerful man in Scotland, could be used to denounce him.

Gellir reached out a hand, intending to grab Adam. To put an end to his cousin's playacting before he buried himself in political intrigue.

But Merraid prevented him, catching his arm in an iron grip. Despite the lovely blue of her eyes, the look she gave him was grave. Deadly. Forbidding. With the subtlety of a sharp blade sinking into soft flesh, she gave him a wordless warning.

Nay.

He should have ignored her. He should have pulled from her grasp and prevented Adam from joining the earls. But by the time he disengaged from her gaze, the entourage was halfway to the palisade gates.

When the clan armies followed after them to watch, he turned on Merraid, seizing her by the upper arms.

"What have you done?" he demanded in a sharp whisper.

With an easy outward flick of her elbows, she broke his hold on her and met his scowl with a scowl of her own. "Saved ye." She indignantly brushed the dust from her arms. "Ye could at least show a wee bit o' gratitude."

He sighed heavily. His shoulders sagged. He rubbed the back of his neck, frustrated with the pesky lass.

But in the end, he realized he couldn't blame her. She was only a maidservant. She didn't understand governance. Loyalty. The church. She didn't understand that a nobleman's life was not his own. Bloody hell. She couldn't even accept arranged marriage.

"I *am* grateful," he said, trying to muster up a smile. "'Tis only that I fear the two of you are wading into perilous waters." Then his smile faltered, and he shook his head in disbelief. "Feigning to be a messenger from His Holiness..."

"Don't fret," she said brightly. "Adam is brilliant. And once the earls hear my words—"

"*Your* words?" His heart plummeted. "*You* wrote the missive?"

"Aye," she beamed.

He felt ill. "What did you say...exactly?"

She creased her brow. "I can't remember exactly. But I put in a good quote from Aesop—'United we stand. Divided we fall.' And one from Alexander the Great—'remember, upon the conduct of each depends the fate of all.' And Publilius Syrus, who said 'where there is unity, there is always victory.'"

"You quoted," Gellir choked out, "a Greek storyteller, a Macedonian tyrant, and a Roman slave?"

She smiled proudly. "I told ye Lady Feiyan spared nothin' when it came to my learnin'."

Gellir had to sit down. Fortunately, there was a stool near one of the pavilions. He collapsed onto it.

It was too late to prevent what had already happened. He had to think of what to do next.

He couldn't abandon Adam. If the others discovered his secret, they'd eat him alive.

Then there was the matter of Merraid...

He looked up at her in concern.

"What's wrong?" she asked.

"You can't stay here."

"Why?"

"'Tis too dangerous."

"Ye don't understand. I've negotiated peace 'tween the earls and the king."

"Is that what you think?"

She looked affronted. "'Tis the truth."

He scoffed. And immediately knew scoffing was the wrong thing to do.

She turned on him with blazing anger in her eyes and her hands on her hips. "How dare ye! Was I not the one to broker a romance 'tween ye and your bride? Did I not employ just the right words to charm her tender heart? Did I not bait the hook with just the right phrases to lure her into your arms? Did I not season each syllable with just the right touch o' spice to keep her hungerin' for more?" She lowered her voice to add, "Ye think I can't broker peace 'tween a runt of a king and a half-dozen hotheaded earls?" Then she crossed her arms and shuddered with frustration. "'O ye o' little faith.' *That's,*" she said, arching her brow at him, "from a Nazarene woodworker."

At first he could only stare at her. She was quoting Jesus at him.

What a beautifully wild, naïve, outrageous, determined, carefree, fearless lass she was. Sweet as a flower. Clever as a fox. Generous to a fault. Wise beyond her years. Bright and bold and brimming with life.

A bemused smile slipped onto his lips as he realized the truth.

Merraid cared nothing for protocol. Proper behavior. Codes of honor. Rules of engagement. Everything she did came from her heart. From her soul. From what she knew was right. Not from what someone else had dictated.

The forthright, intrepid maidservant enjoyed a freedom he'd never tasted in a lifetime of honor, chivalry, loyalty, and responsibility. And he loved her for it.

A chuckle escaped him then.

"What?" she demanded, still miffed at him.

"I adore you, you know."

Merraid didn't think it was possible for a heart to both swell and crack at the same time.

Gellir's confession filled her with warmth and joy, even as it broke her into a million shards of despair.

It meant nothing.

Even if she managed to make peace between the king and the earls, it changed nothing between her and Gellir. He was still a nobleman. She was still a maidservant.

She had come here as his friend. To salvage his honor. To save him from his self-imposed exile. Nothing more.

She couldn't expect more. Not in a world that revolved around titles and rights, alliances and endowments. She had been born outside that world. And no matter how much training and education Lady Feiyan had so generously provided, no matter how Merraid longed to be part of

Gellir's world, Merraid would never be able to break through the imposing wall of stone that surrounded it.

She'd lost her illusions of belonging years ago. Knowing she would never fit inside the noble mold, she'd learned to be content with simply making her mark. With impressing those who dwelled within that world with her learning. With her skills. With her clever verse and her surprising strength. And that was enough.

At least she *thought* it was enough. Until she gazed into Gellir's loving eyes, melting now like liquid silver as he smiled at her.

Then she knew her heart would ache for him forever.

Forever she would remember his tender kiss. His gentle touch. His passionate embrace.

He had been her first. And she knew somehow he would always be her best.

*I adore you,* he'd said, pinning his heart upon his sleeve for her.

But one of them had to see reason. One of them had to be strong. It was up to her to break the bonds between them.

She kicked at the turf, saying flippantly, "Ye won't adore me if I've started a clan war, will ye?"

"Maybe," he murmured.

She didn't dare meet his eyes or she'd be lost. Instead, she picked up Adam's overstuffed satchel, which he'd left behind, and changed the subject. "Are ye hungry?"

"I wouldn't turn down a crumb."

She tossed him the satchel. "'Tis Adam's. I'm sure there's a crust o' bread in there, somewhere among the lockpicks and trebuchets."

He smirked. "Adam's strange hoard is the subject of much discussion at Rivenloch."

He dug in the satchel while Merraid watched for the king's arrival.

"Ye know," she said over her shoulder, "ye shouldn't have written that missive to Feiyan. Ye shouldn't have taken the blame."

"Better the fault should lie with me than with Hew."

"No one in your clan believes you've gone off to sow your wild oats."

He sniffed. "I just need Carenza's father to believe it."

She nodded. She suspected as much.

Damn his eyes. Gellir was too good for his own good. He would rather ruin his own reputation than sully the good names of Hew and Carenza or risk the honor of Rivenloch and Dunlop.

"What news of Hew?" he asked around a bite of bread. "Did he return?"

"Nay." She turned to him. "But he sent a missive. He said he found Carenza. And that she was safe."

He chewed and swallowed the bread. "He's not going to return her then." It was a statement, not a question.

"I suppose he means to reunite her with her lover."

Gellir shook his head. "Hew's soft heart will be his undoing."

There was a long silence before she murmured, "And what about you? What about your heart?"

He gave her a rueful smile. "'Twas never mine to give. You know that. I am a vassal of the king."

She bit her lip, holding back her opinions about a king who would wield such power over his subjects. Then she lifted her eyes toward the palisade gates. There he was now. Malcolm. Joining the earls to hear Adam's missive.

"He looks small among the others," she remarked. Though he was about her age, Malcolm was no taller than Fertech and as thin as a maid. He seemed only a young lad in his father's clothing, with a crown that was too heavy for his head.

Gellir rose to follow her gaze. "I suppose he is."

How could such an insignificant man hold Gellir's future in his hands? How did he have the authority to command earls? To steer the fate of a country?

It was no wonder the earls had rebelled when the young king started parceling out land to the enemy English. It left a bitter taste in her mouth to realize, now that Gellir had openly supported the king, it was even more likely Malcom would wed him to an English noblewoman.

The idea sickened her. Which made it even more critical for her plan to work.

"Listen," Gellir murmured, taking her chin between his finger and thumb and capturing her eyes with his own. "If your plan doesn't work..."

Placing her hands on his chest, she tried to protest. But he slid a silencing thumb across her lips.

"If the king isn't willing to bend..." he continued. "If the earls are too greedy or Adam's identity is revealed..." He looked at her with such intensity, she felt overwhelmed, as if a wild storm had torn the breath from her lungs. "I want you to know," he said, as if he meant to impress his words upon her soul, "'tis not your fault."

She felt her chin wobble. But she refused to cry. She might not be a maid of Rivenloch. But she'd be damned if she would weep in front of him. Not when she needed to be strong.

He brushed his thumb across her cheek. "I've always known my destiny was not mine to command."

She felt her grief curdling into anger. "Ballocks," she muttered. "'Tisn't fair."

He lowered his hand to capture both of hers, holding them against his chest and kissing the top of her knuckles. "Life seldom is."

Then, just as her heart was breaking for her noble hero who deserved love more than anyone, she heard, for the third time in a sennight, the all too familiar click of shackles closing.

# CHAPTER 23

Gellir hated to resort to such brutal tactics. He felt like the worst sort of betrayer. But he had to get Merraid to safety. And he knew very well she wasn't going to listen to reason.

Finding the shackles among Adam's things had been a stroke of good luck. On the other hand, considering his cousin could produce almost anything out of his infamous satchel, it should not have been surprising.

She still fought him, of course. She screamed with rage and flailed and kicked at him. It would have been easier to catch an eel with his bare hands than to subdue the wily, writhing lass who'd learned all of Feiyan's sly tricks.

In the end, with her arms bound and in overlarge chain mail that hampered her efforts, he managed to wrest her to the ground and pin her there with his weight. Then he used a piece of rope from Adam's satchel to bind her ankles.

She spat and cursed him to the devil. But what nearly unmanned him was the hurt he saw in her eyes. Hurt that no amount of vehement oaths could hide.

Eventually she silenced. Eventually she stopped struggling. Then she resorted to her deadliest weapon of all—impaling him with the sharp blue daggers of her eyes.

He told himself it didn't matter if she despised him.

Her hate was far less dangerous than her love.

Still, he strained to choke out his words. "Go, Merraid. Go back to Darragh. Live your life. Be free."

An angry tear slipped from the corner of her eye and dripped onto the ground. "Ye're makin' a mistake," she bit out.

"'Tis mine to make."

"So ye *want* to be married to a Sassenach?"

He blinked. That was what she was worried about? That he'd be wedded to an enemy against his will?

Shite. He doubted he'd live to be married. Malcolm wasn't going to compromise. He wasn't going to return the lands he'd given to England to the earls. Not after the English king had rewarded him with knighthood. And once the earls learned that, they would take their rage out on Gellir and probably tear him to pieces.

But he couldn't tell Merraid all that. He couldn't tell her her plan would never work.

"I don't care who I wed," he lied. Then, seeing the disappointment in her eyes, he decided it wasn't enough to encourage her to go. He had to push her away. Swallowing back regret and cursing the circumstances that drove him, he told her coldly, "I never have. 'Twas entertaining for a while—Feiyan bringing me prospects, you reviewing each one. But to be honest, as long as my bride spreads her legs and gives me bairns, she can be a Welsh hag for all I care."

"That's not true," she whispered.

It took all his willpower to ignore her. But he had to stay strong. He couldn't let her powers of persuasion divert him from his course.

He sighed. If she hated being bound, she was going to detest being gagged.

He used a silk veil from Adam's satchel, one that by chance matched the color of her glaring eyes. Though she resisted biting him, she didn't make the task easy.

Then, scanning the pavilions, he spotted a peasant beside a two-wheeled haycart, chewing on a piece of straw and watching the altercation with mild interest.

"You!" Gellir called out, gesturing him forward.

He dug in the satchel and found a few loose coins. "These are yours if you hide her in your haycart and take her to Kinross."

Merraid squealed in protest.

The man's eyes widened as he licked his lips and reached for the coins. Gellir closed his fist. Then he held up his sword. "This is yours if you fail." The man hesitated. "Do you understand?"

"Aye, sir."

He opened his hand and gave the coins to the man. Then he hefted up Merraid, carried her unceremoniously to the cart, and placed her among the sheaves of hay.

"Be safe," he wished her before shifting hay over her glowering face.


Merraid had no intention of riding all the way to Kinross in a haycart.

She might be shackled. And bound. And gagged. And half-buried in hay. But she was a fighter. One way or another, she meant to escape and return to Perth to speak to the king. And to rescue Gellir. Even if he didn't want rescuing.

The way the warp-wheeled cart limped along the rutted road impeded her efforts. She swore the man chose to trudge over every bump and pit along the way. Thankfully, he was too preoccupied with singing to notice her movements. And at last she thrashed her way free of the hay.

By then, they were already in the forest. The treetops peered down at her as she lay there, as if wondering how she'd come to be so helpless.

But helpless she was not. If she could manage to maneuver onto her knees, she could loop the chain of her shackles around the man's throat and force him to stop.

She twisted onto her belly. Then, using strength developed from her disciplined training, she slowly inched her hips up and slid her bound ankles forward until her knees were under her.

The wheels hit a rut, and she banged her knees on the bottom of the cart. But she bit back a curse and stayed rigid, determined not to lose the progress she'd made. Then, pushing against the wood with her shackled hands, she began to transfer her weight to her knees, uncurling her spine.

Balancing carefully, she straightened. Then, without a sound, she lifted her shackled hands above her. The oblivious humming haycart driver was inches away. All she needed to do was lunge forward. Drop the shackles down over his head. And pull the chain back against his throat.

In another instant, she could have done it.

But someone suddenly leaped down from the trees and shouted, "Halt!"

Shite. An outlaw.

The startled driver stopped abruptly and dropped the cart handles, which sent Merraid hurtling forward out of the cart and tumbling onto the road face-first.

She groaned in pain as her shin scraped on the edge of the wheel and her cuffed hands were crushed beneath her.

But she was more angry than hurt. The outlaw's timing could not have been worse. Why the devil would a thief want to rob a haycart?

With her cheek lodged in the dirt, she spit the dust from around her gag and opened one eye.

The black boots planted just inches before her were familiar. As was the voice.

"Merraid?" Feiyan pulled down the black mask obscuring her face and crouched beside her. "What are you doing here?"

Relief flooded her veins. Feiyan had come. She would understand. She would make Gellir see he was making a mistake.

Merraid grunted, indicating her gag. Feiyan reached behind her head to untie it.

"M'lady," she choked out, "ye have to save him."

"Save who?"

"Save *me,* m'lady," the haycart driver pleaded. "Don't take my passenger. The man who paid me for her will cut my throat."

"What man?" Feiyan asked.

He shrugged. "I don't know his name."

Feiyan nodded at Merraid. *"She* was about to cut your throat. That's why I stopped you."

The driver clutched his throat and gave Merraid a horrified leer.

"I wouldn't have," Merraid assured him, "and neither will Gellir."

"Gellir?" Feiyan scowled as she drew her dagger to sever the rope around Merraid's ankles. "What the hell is going on?"

"There's no time to waste, m'lady," Merraid said. "I can explain on the way."

"On the way?"

"To Perth."

Feiyan helped her up and nodded. "Perth. 'Tis what I feared."

She gave a loud whistle then, and out of the woods emerged the company of Rivenlochs from Darragh. Laird Deirdre and her husband Pagan led the clan. They were flanked by their young niece and nephew, Isabel and Ian. Hew's sister Jenefer followed, armed with her bow and arrows. Her husband Morgan carried an enormous broad-sword. Gellir's brother Brand tapped his fingers restlessly on the hilt of his sheathed sword. Behind them marched a dozen Rivenloch knights wielding swords and axes, war hammers and flails, bows and spears. They'd come prepared for war.

"Och, m'lady," Merraid said. "I think ye misunderstand. There's hope for peace."

"Aha!" Isabel smugly chimed in. "I told you. I said love would win the day, didn't I, Brand? And I just knew—"

Laird Deirdre jostled her shoulder to quiet her. Then she confronted Merraid. "Peace?"

"Aye, m'lady," Merraid replied. Explaining was going to take a while, and Gellir was in danger. So she nodded toward the road back to Perth. "Will ye not walk with me?"

Lady Deirdre agreed, motioning the others to follow.

Merraid didn't much like the idea of showing up at Perth with a contingent of armed clan warriors. Especially Rivenloch warriors, who had a fearsome reputation.

Perhaps by the time they arrived, there would be no need for fighting.

As they hurried down the road, Feiyan muttered to Merraid, "If 'tis so peaceful at Perth, then why did Gellir pay a man to cart you away?"

"Gellir doesn't believe 'tis possible, m'lady," she confided. Then she turned, skipping backwards to address the clan. "But I believe peace can be achieved. And so does Adam."

Feiyan stopped her. "Adam? What does my brother have to do with—"

"I knew it," Ian exclaimed. "Adam found some clever disguise, didn't he? And—"

Pagan scowled the lad into silence.

Feiyan wheeled Merraid around to resume walking. "I wondered where he'd gone off to this time."

Merraid explained to Laird Deirdre, "Adam came with me to Perth."

"Why Perth?" Deirdre asked, as if she already knew the answer, but wanted to hear it anyway.

"We were seekin' an audience with the king."

"Mm-hmm." Deirdre's lips were tight.

Merraid gulped. Clearly, the laird didn't approve of their plan. She turned to Feiyan. "M'lady, ye know how ye've always taught me that confrontation is a last resort?"

"Aye."

"Not to use a sword when ye can use fists?"

"Aye."

"And not to use fists when ye can use words?"

"Aye."

"Well, for the king, I used words."

Feiyan looked as if she was going to cast up her breakfast, something she'd done a few times in her pregnancy.

"What words?" Laird Deirdre's eyes had an icy calm.

Merraid's mouth went dry. The warrior maid's Viking origins were obvious now. No wonder she commanded an entire clan.

"What words?" she repeated.

Merraid told her, "The words o' the only man more powerful than the king."

Deirdre frowned.

Feiyan frowned.

All of Rivenloch frowned.

Merraid explained. "His Holiness?"

She expected Laird Deirdre would be impressed. Instead, the color drained from her face. "Where's Adam now?" she breathed.

"Och, he's safe, m'lady," Merraid rushed to assure her. "The monk's robes suit him well. And he's quite good at Latin. The king will ne'er suspect he's *not* the emissary from the Pope."

Deirdre's jaw tensed.

Feiyan paled.

Even Isabel and Ian gasped.

Then Deirdre called over her shoulder to the others, "Make haste!"

They sped along at a lope then, though Merraid couldn't understand why everyone was in such a panic.

After all, the king and the earls had already arranged a temporary truce.

Merraid had chosen the words of the edict wisely.

And Adam had played his role to perfection.

What could go wrong?

Gellir rubbed an anxious hand across his jaw.

So much could go wrong.

He paced at the back of the pack of soldiers, trying to get a better look at what transpired between the king and the earls.

He squinted at Adam, straining to make out what he was saying. In the midst of the two warring factions, his cousin held the parchment out like a shield, valiantly intoning what a maidservant had tried to pass off as the edict of His Holiness.

Damn it. He was too far away. If the earls turned on Adam, Gellir would never be able to get to him in time.

Finally, reaching the end of his decree, Adam lowered the parchment.

Gellir held his breath, praying no one would attack the messenger.

Much heated discussion followed.

The earls wagged their fingers.

The king raised his hands, silencing them.

The advisors consulted with the king.

The earls shook their heads.

The king held up a finger.

The advisors scratched their heads.

The earls rubbed their chins.

The king nodded.

And then, miraculously, the earls began clapping each other on the shoulder and grinning at Malcolm.

Gellir was too astounded to move. Even when the warriors around him realized they'd won—laughing and shouting and dancing in victory—he stood with his jaw agape.

Had Merraid done it? Had a maidservant made peace between the king and a pack of angry earls? How?

All he could imagine was she'd somehow managed to appeal to the young king's love of chivalry and his religious devotion.

Gellir looked up to see the earls returning. Their faces were wreathed in self-satisfied smiles.

Behind them came Adam in his monk's robes. Gellir dared not acknowledge his cousin, lest he reveal his guise. So as he passed, Gellir exchanged neither word nor glance, but furtively slipped the satchel into Adam's hands.

Behind Adam came the king with his entourage of advisors.

It had been a long while since Gellir had seen the young monarch. Though Malcolm was nearly Gellir's age, with his sweet face and weak stature, he always seemed somehow less a man and more a child.

Still, he was Gellir's king. As he approached, Gellir lowered his head in reverence.

Malcolm stopped before him. "Is this the man who fought so bravely on our behalf?" he asked of no one in particular.

"Aye, Your Grace," Fertech said. "'Tis Sir Gellir Cameliard of Rivenloch."

"Grim Gellir!" the king said in delight. "We should have known."

Gellir, like most Scots, squirmed at his use of the royal "we," meaning "God and I." Malcolm had doubtless learned that from the English monarch, who believed in the divine right of kings.

"The greatest warrior in all Scotland they've dubbed you," the king said. "And the very flower of chivalry." Gellir flushed at the praise. "But where is your companion? The wee one with the curious fighting style?"

Gellir opened his mouth, then closed it. He couldn't very well tell the king the truth—that he'd bound and gagged her and sent her away in a haycart.

"Here, Your Grace!"

The familiar cry made Gellir whip his head around.

Merraid?

How could she be here?

Hadn't he bound and gagged her and sent her away in a haycart?

321

# CHAPTER 24

Gellir's heart dropped. Clearly, the haycart driver had betrayed him, despite his dire warning.

He looked past Merraid then and saw the impressive band of warriors marching behind her. His mother and father. Feiyan and Brand. Jenefer and Morgan. A contingent of Rivenloch men. And his little brother and sister.

They must have freed Merraid.

But what were they doing here? And why were they so heavily armed? Did they mean to confront the king? Or wage war against the earls? Would they destroy the peace Merraid had orchestrated?

So far, they seemed peaceable enough. Laird Deirdre raised her hand, and the clan paused to respectfully lower their heads toward the king.

All but Merraid. She'd never seen the king up close before. And thrilled by his presence, she rushed excitedly forward. In another moment, she might have broken all protocol. Fallen to her knees at his feet. And seized his hand between her shackled own.

But Gellir quickly threw his arm out to stop her.

She sobered then, realizing her mistake, and bowed her head. "Your Grace."

"A lass?" Malcolm exclaimed. "No doubt a Rivenloch warrior maid." He nodded in recognition toward Laird Deirdre. Then he eyed her shackles. "But what's this? Have the earls taken you prisoner?"

Gellir felt a guilty flush rise in his cheeks.

But Merraid intervened to save his honor. She smiled, brazenly confiding, "They had to shackle me, Your Grace, ere they lost any more warriors."

Malcolm chuckled at that. "Now that peace has been forged," he decreed, "we shall have your chains removed."

How "we" were going to do that, Gellir didn't know. If there was a key to the shackles, it was in Adam's satchel, and Adam had disappeared.

Then the king stepped closer to murmur, "Lass, you fought bravely on our behalf against so many. Is there anything you would like as reward?"

She thought for a moment and then said, "Aye, Your Grace."

Gellir tensed.

She should have said nay.

She should have said that serving her king was reward enough.

That was what *he* would have said.

But she wasn't a noble knight. She was a maidservant who knew nothing of chivalry. Of humility. Of duty to one's king.

What would she ask for? Coin? Jewels? Land?

Shite. She was venturing into a world she didn't know. She was going to get herself into trouble. And there was nothing he could do.

Even as he had that thought, he knew deep in his heart, if Merraid needed rescuing, he would defy king and country to come to her aid.

Merraid had been waiting for this moment. She straightened, mustering up her courage. Now was her chance. Now was her opportunity to defend Gellir.

"We await your pleasure," the king said.

"I would...that is... May I speak with Your Grace in private?"

She felt Gellir stiffen beside her. But that was exactly the reason she wanted a *private* audience. For what she planned to divulge to the king, she didn't want Gellir or any other Rivenloch peering over her shoulder, telling her what a maidservant should and should not say.

By the glimmer in the king's eyes, he seemed amused rather than offended. "By all means." He gestured to Fertech's pavilion. "May we?"

"Of course, Your Grace," Fertech said.

She entered the pavilion, which was lavishly appointed for the long siege Fertech had expected.

The king followed with four of his men. Naturally, they wouldn't be completely alone. A king must always have at least two trusty men guarding his flank. And a *young* king was wise to keep a pair of older, experienced advisors nearby.

Malcolm seated himself, commanding the earl's chair as if it were his own. He summoned her near.

She knelt before him.

"What do you wish to say to us?"

Merraid had a challenging task before her. She had to combine the truth with diplomacy. She had to leave Hew's name out of the story. And she had to do it in as few words as possible so as not to waste the king's time.

"As ye may recall, the Laird o' Dunlop wrote to ye to secure Sir Gellir as bridegroom to his daughter."

"Lady Carenza," Malcolm replied. "She is a great beauty."

"Aye, Your Grace, and sweet and kind. Her father bid her wed at once. But what he didn't know was her heart belonged to another." She lowered her eyes. "And she was already with child."

The advisors grumbled in disapproval.

The king hushed them. "Go on."

"The lady wished to do the right thing. She wished to honor the betrothal. But she didn't have the heart to deceive her bridegroom. And so she ran away."

The king nodded.

"Once Sir Gellir learned his bride had fled to her true love," she continued, "he couldn't let her bear the shame o' her actions. Neither did he wish shame upon his clan. And so he wrote a missive, sayin' 'twas *he* who'd broken the betrothal."

"A noble sacrifice," the king said with an admiring sigh.

"Aye, Your Grace."

The king steepled his hands, considering her words. "What would you have us do?"

"Forgive them, Your Grace," she said. "That's all. Lady Carenza and Sir Gellir, they're goodhearted, both o' them. They meant to do right. 'Tis neither o' their fault the betrothal was broken. They shouldn't have to suffer disgrace and dishonor because of it."

The king narrowed his eyes at her. "You're a good friend to Grim Gellir."

"I try to be, Your Grace."

"You fought nobly for us by his side."

She humbly lowered her gaze.

The king didn't give her an answer. After their brief discourse, he simply rose and said to his men, "Shall we go? Ere the earls reconsider our newly won peace?"

Merraid managed to hide her disappointment. But she *was* disappointed. Was that it? Did Malcolm mean to do nothing?

When they emerged from the pavilion, the tension in the air was so palpable, Merraid expected lightning at any moment. Gellir's brow was as dark as a thunderhead. Laird Deirdre's fists were clenched. Feiyan had gone pale. Even young Isabel had a quivering hand over her mouth, as if she expected someone to lose their head.

She supposed they had a right to be upset. They couldn't know what secrets she'd revealed to the king. But though Merraid was impulsive, she wasn't a fool. They should have trusted her.

King Malcolm held up his hands then and announced, "We have been made aware that the betrothal between Lady Carenza of Dunlop and Sir Gellir Cameliard of Rivenloch has been broken."

The earls glanced around, unsure what they were supposed to do.

The Rivenloch warriors stiffened, poised for battle.

Malcolm continued. "By royal decree, let it forthwith be known that no dishonor shall stain either clan for this mutual...indiscretion."

A collective sigh filled the air. It felt as if a great weight had been lifted off Merraid's shoulders.

She'd done it.

She'd saved Gellir's honor.

Now he was free.

He could do what he loved best. Whether that was pursuing glory on the tournament field.

Or going home to Rivenloch with his head held high.

Or even resuming his search for a bride—whom his sister Isabel called The One.

While the crowd began to chatter in speculation, Merraid turned to look at Gellir. Her lips trembled in an uncertain smile. He had every right to be vexed with her for exposing the truth. But she hoped he would realize the outcome justified the deed.

What she didn't expect was the awe and disbelief and gratitude she saw in his gaze. No longer grim and foreboding, his face shone with an inner light. His clear and earnest eyes were full of admiration and respect. Adoration and pride and wonder.

"You did this for me," he murmured.

Her heart filled to overflowing at his precious words.

All her efforts had been worthwhile after all.

All the spying she'd done.

All the missives she'd written.

All the miles she'd trudged on his behalf.

She'd been able to give him the gift of redemption.

She'd never loved him more.

But she couldn't say that.

Instead she shrugged. "'Tis what friends are for."

Deep in her soul, she knew she was far more to Gellir. And a twinge of pain twisted her heart, reminding her he could never be hers. Still, she counted herself the luckiest woman in the world to be able to stand in the bright light of his affection. To call herself his friend.

"What about you, Grim Gellir?" the king sang out, interrupting her thoughts and halting the conversation around them. "What reward do you seek for your loyalty in defending us?"

Merraid knew chivalrous Gellir would ask for nothing. He would claim the mere honor of defending his king was reward enough. It was the way he was. Noble. Worthy. Gallant to a fault.

As she expected, he placed one hand across his heart and said, "I ask no reward for myself." Then he added, "But if it pleases Your Grace, I would request a special dispensation on behalf of your loyal subject." He indicated Merraid.

She was dumbstruck. She could hardly be called a loyal subject. She'd only met Malcolm. And before today, she'd had her ears filled with mostly disparaging comments from Feiyan about the Sassenach-loving Scottish king.

"A special dispensation?" the king asked.

Merraid wondered about that as well.

Gellir straightened and said, "Though Merraid of Darragh is of humble birth, she is of noble heart. I know she would be most grateful, Your Grace, if you bestowed upon her the honor of knighthood."

Merraid blinked. Surely she'd heard wrong. The murmurs around her said otherwise.

And to her surprise, the king smiled in approval. Indeed, he clasped his hands together with delight. "Brilliant! She shall be the first warrior maid knighted by our hand."

Merraid couldn't breathe. She couldn't move.

Only when Gellir grinned and gave her a nudge forward did she grasp the truth. She was going to become a knight.

She could hardly contain her pleasure as she tentatively approached the king.

She supposed she should have been prepared. This was why she'd trained so hard for the last four years, after all. And she *had* just proved her loyalty to the king.

Still, it was hard to believe her dream was coming true. And that Gellir had made it so.

Even harder to imagine the King of Scotland himself meant to knight her.

Before she could comprehend what was happening, Malcolm drew a magnificent jeweled sword. "Kneel."

She lowered herself onto her knees.

The king then lightly tapped her head with the flat of the blade. "In the name of God..." He tapped her left shoulder. "Saint George..." He tapped her right shoulder. "And Saint Michael..." He sheathed his sword and raised his gauntleted right hand. "We hereby lift you to the ranks of knighthood. Never again shall a gauntlet be raised against you without your answering for it." He then gave a hearty clout to the left side of her neck—not hard enough to knock her over, just hard enough to make her blink—and stepped back. "Rise."

She stood on shaky legs as the magnitude of what she'd just achieved struck her.

The king raised his arms to the crowd and proclaimed, "With these words, a knight is born."

Everyone cheered.

Then the king murmured to her, "Do you have a sword?"

Merraid furrowed her brow. She hadn't brought her *jian*. And she'd lost the weapon Adam had loaned her.

"Your Grace," Lady Feiyan said, approaching and unbuckling her own weapon.

Merraid's throat thickened. It meant everything to have Feiyan's approval.

The king took the swordbelt from Feiyan and handed it to Merraid. "This is for you," he said, "a sword from your sister in arms. Use it with wisdom, courage, and devotion."

Merraid buckled the swordbelt around her hips with trembling fingers while everyone around her cheered again. Even the earls she'd knocked to the ground.

She had never been happier.

Maybe it was Feiyan's sword she carried, but it was a symbol of *her* new responsibilities.

Maybe it was Adam's armor she wore, but it represented *her* new status.

And maybe she stood beside someone else's bride-groom, but he was beaming at her as if *she* were his whole world.

Gellir had never felt more proud. The dizzy smile on Merraid's face and the tears of overwhelming joy standing in her eyes—those brought him more pleasure than any glory on the tournament field.

This was the deep satisfaction that had been missing from his life. All the prizes he'd won, the victories he'd claimed, the honors he'd accrued. They felt hollow compared to the heady thrill he got from seeing his cherished friend achieve her hard-won goal.

The privilege of honor had come easily for Gellir. He was a man. A Rivenloch. The son of a laird.

But Merraid had had to work for every scrap of respect she received. Against all odds, she'd persevered. Despite her womanhood. Despite her humble birth. Despite her social standing. She'd risen to the challenge in a world that sought to thwart her at every turn. And though Gellir had played some small part in helping her take that final step, it was Merraid's triumph.

Caught up in sharing her victory, Gellir took little notice of what was happening around him. But eventually he noticed a quiet, heated discussion going through the Rivenloch ranks.

It appeared his sister Isabel was stirring up her usual mischief. She was arguing with their mother the laird in a frantic storm of hisses, waving her arms about wildly one moment and begging with clasped hands the next.

Feiyan and Jenefer kept chiming in with their muttered opinions, alternately frowning and crossing their arms, tilting their heads in indecision, and nodding.

The Rivenloch warriors mumbled together. Some shrugged. Some shook their heads.

Not wishing to be involved in what appeared to be delicate negotiations, Pagan, Morgan, and Brand stood aside.

Young Ian watched with calm interest, finally voicing a verdict that Laird Deirdre and everyone else could agree upon.

Isabel gave a wee squeal of victory. She rushed up to Gellir to whisper in his ear. After she spoke, she gave him a giddy grin, laughing aloud.

But he could only stare at her in wonder. Was what she said true?

He glanced over at the Rivenlochs. At the warriors. At his parents. All the clan stood of one accord. Laird Deirdre was beaming at him.

It *was* true.

He let his gaze drift back to Merraid. Beautiful, bright Merraid. Who made his heart swell. Who made his spirit soar. Who made his soul feel complete.

"Your Grace," he called out, "may I make one other request?"

"What is it?"

He locked eyes with Merraid as he addressed the king. "If she'll have me," he said, "I should very much like to be wedded to your newest noble knight."

Merraid's happy gasp was answer enough. And the rapture in her eyes was so compelling and so blinding that Gellir didn't much care whether the king approved or not.

# CHAPTER 25

A fortnight later, King Malcolm was still almost as excited about the wedding as Merraid.

He'd insisted it be held at Perth. Of course, that had more to do with his organization of a grand tournament on the day to follow. His advisors said such an event would serve to strengthen the newfound alliance between the king and the earls. But it also appealed to Malcolm's love of knightly displays, particularly by the legendary Rivenloch warriors.

It suited Merraid as well. This sunny morn, seeing the dozens of Rivenloch competitors riding through the gates of Perth stirred her love of battle to a fever pitch.

That wasn't the only love that had been stirred to a fever pitch. She and Gellir had been separated for the most part over the last fortnight. Between Merraid's rushed wedding preparations and training for the tournament and Gellir's fittings for armor and new wedding garments to replace those he'd sold, they hadn't had a moment together to let their new reality sink in.

Now, as Isabel flitted around her, pinning bluebells into the tiny braids framing her loose hair, Merraid felt a touch of worry.

What if Gellir changed his mind? What if he realized

he'd spoken in haste, in the heat of the moment, and didn't consider what he'd given up?

She looked down at the richly embroidered green velvet gown she'd been given by Laird Deirdre. Merraid had never worn such finery. She had no dowry. She owned no land. Her parentage was questionable. What sort of a strategic partnership was that?

Her concern must have shown on her face.

Isabel stopped before her. "What's this, sister?" She'd insisted on calling Merraid sister since the day she'd arranged the match. "Are you afraid?"

"Nay." Merraid wouldn't admit it if she was.

Though they'd been alone in the solar for an hour, Isabel glanced about to be sure no one was listening, then whispered, "Are you nervous about the marriage bed?"

Merraid almost choked. It was the same thing Merraid had asked Carenza. Carenza, who had a bairn in her belly at the time.

Isabel continued, "Because I know a bit about it."

Merraid lifted her brows in surprise.

"Och!" Isabel yelped. "Not because I've done it." She shuddered. "But I've got eyes. And some of the servants aren't too cautious."

Merraid didn't know what to say to that. Isabel was right. Merraid was a servant. And she'd certainly been less than cautious.

"Anyway," Isabel said, "I'll speak to Gellir and make sure—"

"Nay!" The last thing she needed was Gellir's little sister giving him marriage advice. "Nay, I'm fine."

Isabel cocked a dubious brow.

Merraid sighed. Gellir's sister could be meddlesome and dramatic. But she also had an inuitive sense about people. She'd foreseen more than one of the Rivenloch marriages. Perhaps Merraid could trust her.

"'Tis only that I fear your brother may harbor regrets."

"Regrets?" Isabel said, incredulous. "He's loved you since the battle at Darragh."

She scoffed. "I was only a silly wee lass to him then."

"Nay. He defended your honor. He comforted you in your time of need. He even gave up his spot in the battle just to look after you."

That was all true.

But Merraid shook her head. "He only did it because 'twas the right thing to do."

"Ballocks."

Isabel adjusted the sapphire pendant on Merraid's bosom, the one Gellir said matched her eyes. "I...*know* things. I *feel* them. I've always felt the connection between the two of you. I wasn't sure how 'twould happen. After all, 'tisn't every day the son of a laird weds a maidservant. But when Lady Carenza ran away, it all became clear." She clasped Merraid's hand and looked into her eyes. "I feel it in my bones. Your love was meant to be. For Gellir, you are The One."

Her words were strangely reassuring. "I hope ye're right."

Isabel suddenly uncovered Merraid's bare hand. "Och! The ring!" She dug in her satchel and pulled out a small gold ring with *Amor vincit omnia* inscribed on it, exactly as Merraid had always envisioned it. "Come on. They'll be waiting by the chapel. I'll have Ian give it to Gellir."

They whirled down the stairs in a flurry of dark green velvet and pale yellow sendal.

By the time they emerged onto the courtyard, at least a hundred clanfolk stood elbow to elbow, awaiting the ceremony. All of Rivenloch had come to see the next laird wed.

Gellir's aunt Helena had come with Colin—the husband she'd famously abducted—and Jenefer's siblings, Logan,

Nichola, and Neyll. The lady seemed uneasy, since her son Hew was yet to be found.

Lady Feiyan's mother Miriel had come with Rand—the husband she'd once robbed—and four of their children, Tian, Alexander, Gavand, and Merewen. They were unsurprised to learn their fifth, Adam, was currently missing.

Gellir's older sister Hallie had come with Colban—the husband she'd notoriously held for ransom.

Merraid had never abducted Gellir. Or robbed him. Or held him for ransom. But she could no longer deny the reality.

She was about to become part of the Rivenloch clan.

Her gaze lit upon Gellir, speaking with the priest by the chapel steps, and she froze.

His blue velvet finery was worth more than she'd earned in a lifetime.

He was tall and handsome, with a noble bearing that would turn the head of a queen.

The blood of Vikings ran in his veins.

He was a Rivenloch. The son of a laird. The champion of Scotland.

An ugly voice inside her whispered, *Why would he want you? Why would he want you when he could have anyone?*

Her heart, suddenly as heavy as an armorer's anvil, sank to the pit of her belly.

Her step faltered as she glanced down at her borrowed finery, at her work-roughened hands, at her bright, coarse, unruly hair.

She wasn't good enough for Gellir.

For one instant, she considered running away.

But then Gellir spotted her.

He halted mid-sentence, and his eyes quickly scanned her from head to toe.

His face slowly lit up with pleasure—as if they were the only two people in all the world.

Her worries suddenly vanished, and her heart grew light.

There was so much love in his eyes. So much happiness.

Isabel leaned near and whispered, "See? For you, he's The One." She gave Merraid a wink and skipped away like a butterfly leaving a flower.

All at once, with the way Gellir was staring at her, Merraid *felt* like a flower. As she walked forward, his adoration shifted ever so subtly into desire. His sparkling eyes were veiled by passion as he let his gaze roam the length of her.

She'd never felt more beautiful. More wanted.

That feeling persisted throughout the ceremony as they spoke the vows of marriage, gazing into each other's eyes.

As he eased the ring onto her finger with suggestive grace.

As the priest blessed their union with words that sealed their fate.

By the time they were expected to kiss, Merraid's pulse was racing. An exhilarating vibration sang through her body. And the heat engulfing her was not from the meager spring sun.

He captured her cheek in his sword-callused palm and tilted his head, lowering his lips to hers in the most gentle and respectful of caresses.

She knew that was proper. She knew their clanfolk surrounded them. Laird Deirdre was watching. The priest was watching. The King of Scotland was watching.

But she hadn't kissed him in a fortnight. She couldn't be blamed for wanting more than a quick peck.

Before he could slip away, she snagged his surcoat in her fists, crumpling the expensive velvet, and drew him closer. With a soft moan of need, she pressed his perfect mouth open with hers to deepen the kiss. Desire rose in her veins, and she fed it, letting her tongue play with his until she felt an urgent longing building betwixt her legs.

He groaned softly in reply, clutching her closer with an arm around her back, holding her against that part of him that hardened with need.

Somewhere in the distance, she heard rising laughter and the amused voice of the king.

"Perhaps you should make haste to your bridal chamber, Sir Gellir."

Gellir abruptly broke off the kiss. For one awful instant, she feared she'd humiliated him. Made a fool of him in front of his clan and his king. She feared he'd never forgive her.

But he only gave the king a brusque nod. "Your Grace."

Then he swept her off her feet, striding with her through the chuckling, cheering crowd, dissolving her fears.

The chamber was no doubt beautifully appointed. Perth was the residence of the king, after all. But as Gellir burst through the chamber door, carrying her in his arms, Merraid saw none of it. She only had eyes for her new husband.

He kicked the door closed behind them and murmured, "Och, wife, you are an irresistible temptation."

She shivered with passion as he carried her toward the bed.

There was supposed to be an hours-long feast, followed by entertainments. Afterward, her new clan sisters were supposed to undress her with great ceremony and prepare her to be bedded by her husband.

That obviously wasn't going to happen.

Gellir began ravishing her with his hungry mouth.

Breathless, she scrabbled at his surcoat, as if by sheer dint of will she could remove it.

He fell with her onto the bed. Kissing her. Caressing her. Groaning against her mouth.

His warm breath filled her with desire. His arousal, rigid against her thigh, drove her wild with yearning. Her breasts tingled as he squeezed them tenderly through her velvet gown. The ache between her thighs intensified as she arched and writhed upon the pallet.

She wanted him now. She could wait no longer.

Somehow he managed to tear loose long enough to whip up his surcoat and untie the laces of his braies.

Then he dragged her skirts up and knelt betwixt her legs.

She held her breath in mindless anticipation as his skilled fingers moved between her thighs to find the swollen fruit of her desire, ripe and aching for his touch.

With bold eagerness, he spread her nether lips and pressed the tip of his cock against her willing flesh.

Unable to endure any more, she surged upward, sheathing him like a welcome dagger inside her.

His deep groan sharpened her passion.

His thrusts, tentative at first, rapidly became more forceful, driving her to a frenzy.

Gasping and grunting, they collided again and again.

Every inch of her skin felt alive. Every pore seemed to sweat desire. Every breath took her a step closer to heaven.

And then she felt him squeeze and strain in all his muscular glory, catapulting her across the skies of yearning, until they both reached that infinite, shuddering place of pure ecstasy.

Then together, they floated gently back to earth.

For a long while afterward, they could do no more than lie in a boneless heap and gasp for breath, like combatants weary of war. Merraid had no wits left to think, much less speak.

Eventually, Gellir rolled off of her and drew her into his arms. She dozed for a long while, falling asleep with a smile on her face.

When she woke, the sun was already low in the sky, streaming in through the window. Gellir was on one elbow, looking down at her with amusement.

"What?" she asked drowsily.

"Sooner or later, we have to join the feast."

"Shite."

She'd much rather stay in bed with her new husband. Indeed, since she was awake now, she was keenly aware of his long, lean, muscular warrior's body pressed against hers.

"Don't look at me like that," he said.

"Like what?" she said, all innocence.

"Like you want to spend the rest of the night ravishing me."

"I do want to spend the rest o' the night ravishin' ye."

"Fine." He began to take his surcoat off over his head. "But don't blame me if you have no strength left for the tournament tomorrow."

"Och, the tournament!" She sat up. She'd almost forgotten. And now that he mentioned it, she probably should be a bit more judicious about how she expended her energy.

He laughed and let his surcoat fall back down.

"Ye're right," she said, standing up and smoothing her skirts. "We should go down to the feast. Do I look all right?"

Gellir grinned.

Her velvet surcoat was crumpled. So was her linen underdress. And her hair? Sprays of coppery tendrils and wee wilted flowers escaped the tangled nest of braids.

"You look lovely."

It was the truth.

He realized it had always been the truth.

Even four years ago, as a scrawny lass of fifteen—with

her freckled face and her wild orange hair and her broken nose—Merraid had had a beautiful heart.

A kind heart that had made her attend to his every want as she brought him breakfast. Bandaged his cuts. Polished his armor. Listened to his ideas.

A patient heart that had made her believe in his love and wait for his return.

A selfless heart that had made her sacrifice her own happiness by seeking a bride who would make him content.

A noble heart that had given her the courage to face the king and plead for his redemption.

And now?

Whether she wore a maidservant's apron or a suit of armor or a rumpled wedding gown, Merraid would always be the most beautiful woman in the world to him.

"Why are ye lookin' at me like that?" she asked.

"Because I love you."

She melted with a smile. He could feel her affection from across the room.

But as she passed him on her way to the door, she added, "Ye won't love me on the morrow when I've tossed ye on your arse in front o' the king and all your kin."

# CHAPTER 26

The day dawned perfectly on Merraid's first tournament. Fluffy clouds dotted the bright sky. Penants from a host of clans fluttered in a gentle breeze. The air was filled with sparrow song. The squeak of bowstrings. The restless stomps of horse hooves. The rustle of chain mail. The soft chatter of warriors on the field and spectators in the stands.

Merraid took a deep breath. Partly to drink in the familiar smells of the tournament—the dust of the arena, the aroma of hay, the tang of armor, the musk of leather—and partly to calm and center herself.

Her training had prepared her for this moment. She'd be unafraid. Self-assured. Confident, but not overconfident. Like the snake in Feiyan's story about the birth of *taijiquan,* she would remain steady and still until the moment came for a sudden strike.

"You will do well, cousin." Lady Feiyan said, coming up beside her in her black warrior's garb.

It was hard for Merraid to imagine she was now kin to Feiyan. Even harder to imagine Feiyan intended to compete in the tournament with a bairn in her belly.

As if she'd read Merraid's thoughts, Feiyan said, "I'll abide by Dougal's wishes and stay out of the hand-to-hand combat, but he can't keep me away from the archery."

Merraid smiled. "'Tis good news for me then. I didn't have a hope o' winnin', sparrin' against ye."

"You may be sparrin' against my mother," she warned.

"Lady Miriel herself?" That would be a challenge indeed.

"Aye. And she's got the wisdom of age." Feiyan gave her a sly grin. "But you've got the advantage of youth. And a few tricks my mother doesn't know."

Merraid wondered if that was true.

She also wondered if it was in poor form to defeat one's new clanfolk.

Before she could ask, Feiyan sidled away.

Moments later, the three sisters, the original warrior maids of Rivenloch, approached. Merraid, lost for words, could only stare in awe.

Laird Deirdre clapped a hand on her right shoulder and gazed at her with ice-blue eyes. "Remember, daughter, a stout heart is better than a sharp sword."

Lady Miriel slipped around her left side, arching a dark, slender brow. "You *do* have a sharp sword though, aye?"

Merraid nodded, touching the hilt of the *jian* Feiyan had given her.

Lady Helena crossed her arms over her chest, narrowing her eyes at Merraid and giving her a grim smile. "Unleash hell, lass."

Nodding brief salutes, they left. With their blessing, Merraid felt ready.

There was only one other warrior from whom she wished to hear.

As if she'd summoned him with her thoughts, Gellir murmured from behind her, "Be sure to save your strength."

"For the melee?"

"Nay," he said, whispering against her ear. "For the bedchamber."

His words sent a thrill through her. But she had no intention of holding back in the fighting.

"Not a chance," she told him. "I've waited four years for this. I'm goin' to leave it all on the tournament field. We have a lifetime o' lovemakin' ahead of us. Ye can bed me when ye recover from the arse-kickin' I'm about to give ye."

He chuckled at that. "Arse-kicking? You think so?"

"Aye." She'd defeated him before. She could do it again.

"Shall we make a wager on that?" He lowered half-hooded eyes to her lips.

She gulped. Faith, she hoped he wouldn't look at her like that when the tournament began. It would completely ruin her concentration.

"What kind o' wager?"

"We'll spar," he murmured. "And whoever wins reigns in the bedchamber tonight."

His breath sent a shiver through her. But she dared not let him distract her. "Fine."

"Good luck."

He departed with a glance meant to fire her blood. And it worked. Far too well.

Thankfully, the king arrived at that moment to take his place on the throne erected in the stands. There was a grand cheer, clapping, and stomping as Malcolm waved to the crowd. And as he announced the beginning of the tournament, Merraid forgot all about her tempting husband.

Merraid didn't compete in the events on horseback. She'd never ridden a horse. But it was exhilarating to watch the knights joust on their destriers, riding full-tilt at each other. To hear the thunder of hooves. The creak of the tack. The crack of the lances.

Gellir was the best of all of them, of course. Riding a destrier unfamiliar to him, he still charged along the fence with a bold aggression that intimidated his opponents and took her breath away. He unseated every man he met, even the unidentified knight who'd broken the lances of all his former challengers.

There was a break for bread and ale. And then the archery began.

Merraid had never fired a bow, so she contented herself with observing as contestants from near and far took aim at the ringed target. A warrior from Cathay shot with a jeweled bow. Two Moorish brothers used arrows with exotic feathers. A mystery archer in a green hood and a mask inspired murmurs of speculation, firing arrow after arrow in quick succession. And a German knight bested nearly all of them, shooting with smooth precision.

But none of them, not even Gellir, could beat Jenefer of Rivenloch. Her bow seemed like a natural extension of her arm. Needing no preparation, she simply lifted her weapon and fired with ease and accuracy.

Another respite followed with food and drink. But Merraid ate little. She fought better with an empty belly. And the swordfighting was next.

To accommodate dozens of warriors, six bouts occurred simultaneously, weeding out the weakest fighters.

Merraid's first two opponents were rather easy to defeat. They had never faced a woman in battle, so they were distracted by the novelty of it. They not only had to fight her. They had to fight their instinct not to harm ladies. She introduced them gently to the notion of defeat at the hands of a woman.

Meanwhile, Gellir battled against some of the foreign swordsmen. Even when one of the fighters from the Orient hacked at him with a wide, curved blade, he was able to knock it aside and swoop in with a shuddering blow from his trusty steel.

He jabbed the German after the man had tried to lop off his head, serving up a punishing poke to his arse that made him yelp in pain.

And while the French swordsman had a graceful and deadly style, he was no match for Gellir's succinct efficiency.

Logan and his sister Jenefer went head to head, but their familial ties were their downfall. Their bout erupted in a shouting match, which ultimately led to casting aside their swords and wrestling in the dust. They were banned from any more matches.

Merraid next had to face her new Rivenloch brother, Brand, who had no qualms about sparring with a lass. Indeed, some said he secretly disliked the whole notion of women warriors and was always eager to disabuse them of the notion that maids should wield blades. It was no easy task standing up to his relentless blows. He was cut from the same mold as Gellir, and he was just as devoted to swordsmanship.

But Feiyan had been right. Merraid knew a few maneuvers Brand could not anticipate. By the end of their bout, though she was covered in dust and gasping with effort, she finally managed to use his strength against him, flipping him to the ground and holding the point of her *jian* at his throat.

Gellir next fought against the great Morgan Mor mac Giric, Jenefer's husband. As broad-shouldered as Gellir was, the enormous Highlander was two hands wider. But in the end, Gellir proved the bigger they were, the harder they fell. When Morgan stumbled backward and hit the ground with a thud, Gellir moved in to force the surrender.

In the other matches, Deirdre and Pagan warred against each of the Moorish brothers. Colban fought an Italian knight. Dougal was matched with a grizzled old Highlander. And Colin and Rand crossed blades. Merraid didn't see who won.

Her last bout was with Tian, Miriel's son and Feiyan's brother, who had also trained under the great master,

Sung Li. There was no fooling him. And yet she found a certain satisfaction in sparring with someone who knew the movements so well. Their match was graceful. Lithe. Quick.

In the end, however, his reach won the day. She was forced to draw near to make contact, which left her vulnerable. When she strayed too close, he popped her sword from her grip in the blink of an eye, caught it in his free hand, and crossed the blades at her neck in victory.

It was hard to be upset. He was an amazing fighter. And their match had been fun. She yielded with a smile.

Retiring from the field, she watched as Gellir faced three more opponents.

One was his own father. Merraid noticed that a few times, he let Pagan have an advantage he hadn't earned, just to keep the match going. It was a kind and diplomatic gesture.

The second was his sister Hallie's husband, Colban. Raised in the Highlands, he had a rough fighting style, but Gellir was accustomed to defending against it. The match was short. Gellir emerged victorious.

His final bout was with the unknown lance-breaker from the joust. The man was equally as talented with a blade. His was a curious style all his own—a mixture of bold attacks and sly defenses. He was at once as strong as a bull and nimble as an acrobat.

Gellir had difficulty countering his ever-changing tactics, but eventually he wore the man down. When he staggered onto one knee, Gellir rushed in to flatten him.

With that final decisive blow, the king arose.

"We are pleased to announce the grand champion of the tournament is Sir Gellir Cameliard of Rivenloch."

A huge cheer arose, and garlands of flowers were tossed onto the field by spectators. Gellir waved once, acknowledging the praise. But then, with perfect chivalry, he helped the unknown knight to his feet, and Merraid's heart swelled with pride.

This was the man she'd married.

Sir Gellir Cameliard of Rivenloch might be a tournament champion. But he didn't live for warfare and glory. He lived to defend the helpless. To be strong for the weak. To protect the innocent and punish the guilty. He lived for the honor of serving others.

Her throat thickened as she gazed at her noble knight. The hero she'd carried in her heart all those years. The one she'd loved forever.

Now that she'd finally found him the perfect match, nothing could temper the way she felt about him.

Until he called out to the king. "Your Grace, I should like to make one more challenge."

The crowd cheered.

"Another?" the king said, laughing. "To whom?"

"To my bride."

The crowd gasped.

Merraid had forgotten their wager. She'd made that threat to toss Gellir into the dust mostly in jest. After all, he was a seasoned champion, and this was her first tournament. Her remark and the wager had been only a bit of boastful prattle.

Did he seriously mean to fight her?

"What say you, Lady Merraid?" asked the king. "Will you take up his challenge?"

What choice did she have? All of Rivenloch was watching. The warrior maids. Her teacher Feiyan. The king. Everyone wanted to see an epic battle between a man and his wife.

And maybe—just maybe—she *did* have a chance of beating him.

"Aye, Your Grace."

She replaced her helm and unsheathed her sword as she strode toward Gellir.

347

He gave her a sly smile just before he donned his helm and faced her at the ready.

Merraid would have to count on all her skills. Her agility. Her speed. Her reflexes. Her powers of misdirection.

The one thing she hadn't counted on was the support of all the Rivenloch ladies.

"Kick his arse!" someone cried.

"Throttle him!"

"Don't hold back, lass!"

"Give him all you've got!"

"Show him who's in charge!"

That last one was from Laird Deirdre, his own mother.

Bolstered by their encouragement, she blew out a steadying breath, bent her knees, and prepared to fight.

They slowly circled each other. Their first contacts were tenuous, as if they were testing the other's mettle.

Soon they became more aggressive, launching series of attacks that moved them back and forth across the field.

Before long, urged on by the crowd, they were exchanging blows that might have killed lesser fighters. But Merraid wasn't afraid. Indeed, she was fairly sure he was letting her seize the advantage. Allowing her to show off her skills. Matching her rhythm to ensure no one was seriously injured.

"Ye wouldn't be holdin' back, would ye?" she muttered as their swords tangled.

"Why would you think that?" He shoved her blade away.

"'Tisn't a real battle," she said, spinning and coming across with her *jian*, which he dodged. "'Tis more like ye're dancin' with me."

"Dancing? You think so?" He thrust at her, making her leap aside. "Thrusting forward." Then he dodged back from her attack. "Lunging back." He advanced. "Thrusting forward." Then he retreated from her strike. "Lunging back." He charged again, this time snaring her hilt with his and bending close enough to whisper, "I think 'tis more like swiving."

When he cast her off mid-gasp, she staggered and fell onto one knee. And that was when he dove in to set the tip of his blade at her throat.

There was a sigh of disappointment from the Rivenloch ladies and a cheer from everyone else.

"Do you ask for mercy?" Gellir teased.

"Never."

He laughed and took her hand to help her up, murmuring, "You'll be asking for mercy tonight."

His words sent a shiver of desire through her.

If it were up to Gellir, he would have left the tournament right then and there. Spirited Merraid away to their bridal chamber. And spent the rest of the day trysting with his wife.

He definitely would have skipped the melee. The melee was always his least favorite part of a tournament anyway. It was chaotic and dangerous, like a real war.

There was little room to move. No delineation between ally and foe. No clear strategy, other than every warrior for himself. Knights were expected to slash and clout and raze until they were the last warrior standing.

After a day of bouts, warriors were tired. They were careless. Some of them were drunk. Fighting in close quarters meant opportunities for accidental gouging and bruising and slices from stray blades.

If someone was going to get injured, it would be in the final free-for-all.

At Rivenloch, melees were usually conducted with blunted weapons, and even children could take part. He'd participated in his first melee when he was eight years of age. Only once had anyone been seriously hurt, and that was several years ago when Dougal had shown up with a sharpened blade, bent on revenge. Thankfully, there had been no lasting damage. Unless you counted being married to Feiyan.

Gellir feared this melee, however, might leave more than one widow.

Even worse, the king wished to take part.

Gellir prayed the combatants, especially those from foreign lands, understood Malcolm was to be protected at all costs.

After a brief break for ale and lamb coffyns, everyone assembled on the field. Gellir positioned himself beside Malcolm. After all, who could better protect the king than the tournament champion?

Most of the Rivenloch warriors followed his lead, gathering around the king. And though he would prefer she were completely off the field, Merraid stood with them, squeezing in beside Feiyan.

King Malcolm cried out, "Let the melee begin!"

A frenzy followed. Swords and targes clashed. Helms collided. Gauntlets scraped across breastplates. Gellir was shoved back and forth as the grunting and growling mob surged first one way and then the other.

All the while, he kept an eye on the king. He let Malcolm experience a harmless blow here and there. But he kept the worst of the attacks away from him.

The German knight was particularly aggressive. And one of the Moors had bloodlust in his eyes. So Gellir battled them back, hoping they would tire of targeting Malcolm.

His attention, however, was scattered. He couldn't help but worry about Merraid. She was a fine warrior. But she'd never been in a melee. Accustomed to space in which to swing her blade and leap out of range, she was no doubt struggling in the close-packed crowd.

Even now, he saw her elbowing warriors back as she tried to break free of them.

Was she in trouble?

He batted away the Moor's sword and glanced back at her.

She was beside Malcolm. And the German knight was closing in on the king.

Gellir shoved the Moor back and shouldered his way through the combatants toward the German.

He'd just caught Malcolm's eye when he lifted his gaze and suddenly glimpsed danger.

The flash of a steel blade.

Coming down over Merraid's head.

All at once, time seemed to stretch out.

He wasn't going to make it in time.

He was unable to move.

Unable to break free.

His heart sank like a stone through honey.

A gasp rasped slowly across his throat.

"Nay!" he cried, his voice strangely hollow.

Gellir had to block that sword.

He had to stop Merraid's attacker.

Even if he had to kill him.

On sheer instinct, with blind faith, he tightened his fist on his sword and, with agonizing sloth, thrust it forward.

Merraid saw the king's blade coming toward her.

In another instant, when it came within range, she'd deflect it with her *jian*.

Of course, she wouldn't reply to his attack. Feiyan had already informed her of the Rivenloch warriors' main task in this maelstrom of a melee. Protecting the king.

Then, from the corner of her eye, she spotted another threat.

A more serious threat.

A blade driving straight toward the king.

In an instant, instinct took over.

In one fluid move, she knocked the king's weapon away and turned to address the oncoming sword.

There wasn't time to deflect it.

So she did the only thing she could to protect the king.

She used her body to block the blade.

It wasn't the best option. But it was her only option.

It wasn't until she felt the sword pierce her side that she felt a twinge of regret.

She'd been slashed by a blade before. Her arms bore thin white scars from training with the *jian*. And once she'd been gouged in the thigh by a dagger when she wasn't paying attention.

But this was different. This was a blow with power behind it. A thrust that made her suck a sharp breath through her teeth.

The blade withdrew, and she had time for three thoughts as she clutched her bleeding side, wincing from the pain, and wilted onto the ground.

One, she wondered if she'd saved the king.

Two, she wondered if she was going to die.

And three, she wondered why Gellir had stabbed her.

# CHAPTER 27

"**M**erraid," Gellir breathed in horror. Dropping his crimson-stained blade as if it were on fire, he fell to his knees beside her. He felt sick. Distraught. Devastated.

"Merraid," he groaned.

God's eyes, what had he done?

He tore off his helm and cast it aside.

Blood trickled from between her gauntleted fingers as she pressed them against her side, trying to stanch the flow. How badly had he hurt her? Was she mortally wounded?

Guilt made his fingers tremble as he eased off her helm. Her hair spilled across the ground in bright contrast to her pale face as she barely clung to consciousness.

"Merraid," he begged, his voice breaking. "Stay with me, do you hear? Stay with me."

She didn't open her eyes, but she managed to croak, "The king. Is he all right?"

Gellir didn't know. And he didn't care.

He threw off his gauntlets. Reached under his chain mail. Tore off the bottom half of his linen undershirt. Wadding it into a ball, he moved her hands away and pressed hard against her wound.

She grimaced, letting out a weak whimper of pain that

tortured his heart. But he dared not let up, lest she bleed to death.

Meanwhile, the violent melee continued around them. Swords clashed. Spittle flew. Snarls erupted. Screams ensued. No one stopped for a bloody slash or a broken bone.

Merraid grabbed at his arm. Her voice was an insistent hoarse whisper. "The king."

If it would calm her, Gellir supposed he could see how the king fared. He glanced around and spied Malcolm, standing safely amidst a sea of Rivenloch warriors.

"He's fine."

She relaxed then, and in desperation, Gellir clapped at her cheek with his free hand, trying to keep her awake.

She bristled at his harsh touch and gave him a groggy gaze of accusation. "Why were ye tryin' to kill him?"

"Kill who?"

"The king."

Gellir wondered if she was delirious. He hadn't been trying to kill the king. He meant to kill the man whose sword had almost ended Merraid's life.

He took a breath to deny her accusation when he suddenly realized she was right.

It had been Malcolm's blade he'd seen. The blade arcing toward Merraid.

It had been the king he'd meant to stop.

Bloody hell. If Gellir had succeeded, he would have killed Malcolm.

Dizzied by the mortifying truth, he hardly noticed when Laird Deirdre came up beside him.

"Take her off the field," she commanded, blocking a claymore that swung near Gellir's head.

"We've got the king," Lady Helena assured him as she used her targe to shove a shaggy Highlander away from Malcolm.

Lady Miriel cleared a path for him with a graceful arc of her sword. "Go. We'll make things right."

While the warrior maids watched his back, he scooped Merraid into his arms and carried her away from the battle.

A month later, Merraid was still grateful to be alive. Even more grateful to be home.

She leaned out the window to gaze at the courtyard below. The late sun slanted across the thatched rooftops of the busy workshops. Craftsmen and crofters and servants crossed the daisy-studded grass. A flock of ducks waddled past the garden gate. Two kittens made chase around the well. Nearby, a litter of hound pups growled and snapped at each other, their tails wagging furiously. Along the wall, a pair of lads with wooden swords waged war. A flock of pink-cheeked lasses looked on, giggling.

It was hard to believe so little time had passed since she'd been wed—and stabbed—by her husband at Perth. Even harder to believe she already considered Rivenloch her home. It felt like home. Not just because the castle was all she could hope for with its enormous keep, magnificent armory, beautiful countryside, and vibrant courtyard. But because Gellir's kin had made her feel like a welcome part of their clan.

She received frequent visits from his siblings, who felt sorry she'd been confined to her bed while she healed. Isabel regaled her with tales of King Arthur and his knights. Ian shared his clever inventions, including a device to help sailors navigate the seas. And Brand demonstrated his warrior skills below her window, challenging a new victim each day for her entertainment.

Laird Deirdre and Pagan visited her as well, telling her charming stories about Gellir as a wee lad. How he'd saved the miller's daughter from a fierce kitten. How he'd stayed up all night to guard three-year-old Ian when he took ill. How he'd pummeled the Laird of Kerr's son when the lad had called the warrior sisters of Rivenloch changelings.

Merraid had shaken her head at that. She couldn't imagine speaking ill of the Rivenloch sisters. After all, it was the warrior maids who had come to her rescue after witnessing the horrible mishap during the melee at Perth. They claimed it was a random stray blade that had come too near the king, that Merraid had intercepted it to save Malcolm's life. Gellir had been relieved of blame. And Merraid had become the king's champion.

Of course, Gellir was her real hero. Since the return to Rivenloch, he'd seen to her every need with unflagging devotion.

*Almost* her every need. While he no longer felt crushing guilt for the grave mistake he'd made, he still treated Merraid like a crystal chalice that might shatter at the lightest tap.

Meanwhile, she grew restless.

Her cut had healed. She'd regained her strength. She was a bit stiff, but she could move without pain now. Most morns she was able to do *taijiquan*. For the last few days, she'd joined the clan in the great hall for supper.

She was anxious to take advantage of the beautiful summer weather. To take a walk in the meadow. Or bathe in the nearby pond. Or ride with Gellir through the forest. And she soon discovered that watching Brand spar in the courtyard whetted her appetite for combat.

That wasn't the only appetite whetted by neglect and nurtured by the summer sun. Which was why she'd invited Gellir to her chamber this afternoon.

A soft knock sounded on the door. There he was now.

"Come," she said.

He entered and closed the door behind him. "You wanted me?"

She smiled, leaning back against the ledge. He had no idea how much she wanted him. Especially the way he looked right now. Dusty from the tiltyard. His dark hair disheveled by the breeze. His swarthy skin kissed by the sun. His broad chest heaving from racing up the steps to her summons.

"'Tis been a full month now, husband."

He frowned, remembering. "Since I wounded you."

"Well. Aye." She pushed off the wall and sauntered closer. "But I was thinkin' o' somethin' else."

"Something else?"

She twisted the ring around her finger.

"Ah," he said. "Our marriage."

"Aye," she said, reaching out to flick a piece of straw from his leather hauberk. "And now that I'm healed..." She gave him a smoldering glance.

"Are you?" He raised a brow in smoky speculation.

She leaned forward to whisper in his ear. "Och aye."

She felt his shudder of desire. Glimpsed the spark of lust in his steely eyes. Saw the flare of his nostrils as he breathed in her scent.

She snaked one hand around his neck to tangle in his lush, damp curls, pulling him down to her. Closing her eyes, she pressed her lips against his, relishing their suppleness. The contrasting rasp of his stubbled chin. The musky, malty, salty taste of his mouth.

He returned the kiss, resting his hands lightly on her shoulders. Growling softly with desire. Exhaling his passion against her lips.

He smelled of battle, she realized. Sweat. Leather. Steel. Hot and manly. She gasped as lust filled her veins with erotic fire, igniting her senses. Her body remembered the ecstasy of swiving. And she wanted it again.

She curled her fingers over the top of his hauberk to haul him closer and deepen the kiss.

He responded, delving his tongue into her mouth as he threaded his fingers through her hair.

Suddenly ravenous, she began to feast on him with unfettered abandon. Her desire rose faster than a rain-swollen stream, and she couldn't stop it.

She longed to tear off his armor. Pin him to the bed. Have her way with him. And she didn't want to wait another moment.

"Wait," he suddenly choked out, ending the kiss. "Wait."

Breathless, she looked at him in confusion.

He caught her wrists and pried her hands away. Then he gazed at her with smoky amusement. "Are you trying to have your way with me?"

She chuckled once. "I thought that was fairly obvious."

He clucked his tongue. "If I recall, we had a wager at that tournament," he reminded her. "And I won. I believe I'm the one to have *my* way with *you.*"

"Fine," she said. At this point, she didn't care who swived whom, as long as it came to pass. "So what's your biddin'?"

"I want to go slowly," he said. "Undress you. Piece by piece. Worship every inch of you as you deserve."

Merraid swallowed hard. His words moved her. But she didn't know how long she could endure such torture.

Gellir wondered how long he could restrain himself. Part of him wanted to throw his lovely bride onto the bed and take her like a beast.

But that was how a man swived a lass who meant nothing to him.

And today, he wanted to make love to his wife.

He lowered onto one knee before her, catching the

embroidered hem of her blue woolen surcoat. Then he rose with reverence, lifting the garment higher and higher. She raised her arms to accommodate him. Carefully avoiding the intricate braids of her hair—Isabel's work, no doubt—he slipped the surcoat off over her head and set it aside at the foot of the bed.

Her white linen leine clung to her curves, and already he felt lust stirring in his body again.

Her eyes glazed with seductive anticipation.

He started at the top of her head, placing a kiss where her silky hair was swept back from her brow. "I love your bright, coppery tresses. They're like a beam of sunlight shining through the clouds."

He brushed her expressive brows with his thumbs and gazed into her eyes. "I love your brilliant blue eyes. The way they glimmer with joy. Glitter with rage. Glisten with tears. How they look into my soul and see my truth."

She seemed to soften a little at his words.

He ran his fingertip down the straight bridge of her nose and grinned. "I've always loved your freckled nose, even when 'twas broken and bloody."

Her chuckle was throaty.

He brushed his fingers across her supple pink lips and bent close to whisper against them. "I love your lips. The way they curve in a smile. And furl in a frown. The way they speak my name. The way they press gently against mine." He felt the shiver of her breath as he gave her the lightest of kisses. "The way you let me inside." He angled his head and tenderly urged her lips apart, venturing between them with his tongue. Tasting her sweet desire again and again.

She moaned faintly as he withdrew.

The beast of lust roared again within him. But he refused to feed it yet.

He grazed her smooth jaw with his knuckles, following

with his lips. Then he nuzzled the delicate shell of her ear. She shivered as he nibbled at the delicious side of her neck.

"I love your throat," he said. "So warm. So soft. The way your pulse throbs here when you're excited."

She was excited now. He could see her heart beat.

He could also see the deep rise and fall of her bosom as her breathing grew labored.

He let his fingers drift down to the gentle dip between the curve of her breasts. Then he pulled loose the tie holding the leine closed.

She arched up against him.

Sweet Saints, how he longed to nestle there in the warmth of her flesh.

Letting his thumbs slide beneath the neckline of her leine, he slipped the garment off of her shoulders.

"I love your arms," he murmured, stroking the round caps of her shoulder and gliding the linen lower. "The way they can wield a sword. Or a besom," he added with a smile, remembering their battle Feiyan's solar. "The way you wrap them around my neck. The way you'll cradle our children."

Hooking his fingers in the leine, he pulled it away to release her breasts and let the garment sag to her waist.

She blushed and lowered her eyes.

He tugged the sleeves off her wrists and clasped her hands in his.

"I love your hands. So small, yet so capable. So soft, yet so strong." He brought each one to his lips for a kiss. "Hands that toil and pray and seize and give. Hands that can make a fierce fist or a hold a butterfly on their palm."

He swept his hands up then to caress her bosom, first with the back of his knuckles, then cupping the creamy globes.

She sighed, squeezing her eyes tight.

"I love your breasts," he murmured. The beast in his

braies roared as he stroked her soft flesh, thumbing her rosy nipples to life. "So ripe. So sweet. So succulent."

He lowered his head to taste her luscious skin, licking circles around each taut bud.

She gasped and clenched her fists in his hair.

Taking care with her wound, he eased her leine down over her hips, letting it pool on the floor. For a moment, he could only stare at her in wonder.

How had this perfect woman have been under his eye all this time? How had he not seen her? How had he not pledged her his troth four years ago when they'd first met?

Then he swept her off her feet and placed her gently atop the pallet.

He took off her slippers and peeled off her stockings.

"I love your feet," he said, rubbing her arches. "The way you stand on tiptoe to kiss me." He grinned. "The way they sometimes kick my arse."

She giggled.

But when he moved his hands languorously up her calves, she stopped laughing.

"I love your legs," he said, grazing the back of her knees and making her arch up with pleasure. "So long. So strong." He moved his palms up her silken thighs, murmuring, "I love the way they wrap around me when we're making love."

Merraid moaned. She could endure no more. There was a throbbing ache between her thighs. An ache that demanded relief.

But he wasn't going to give it to her. Not yet.

Instead, he blew a gentle breath upon her curls. A warm breath that made her quiver.

"Do you like that?"

She nodded.

He flattened his hands on her thighs and nudged them apart.

She bit her lip. She felt so vulnerable.

But this wasn't a battle. There was no need to protect herself. It was safe to let him have his way with her.

Between the tender touches of his fingers and the agile dance of his tongue, she was lifted to a dizzying height of passion at a pace that took her breath away. When she erupted in spasms of joy, she felt thoroughly replete and cherished.

As she lay dazed in the aftermath, her satisfaction lasted only a short while.

Her beloved husband was staring down at her with such adoration and wonder, she couldn't resist him for long.

"Come to me, husband."

He needed no further encouragement.

Taking off his hauberk was the work of a moment. She licked her lips at the sight of his broad and muscular chest. When he dropped his braies, she could see he was aroused and ready.

Their joining was heavenly. Enchanting. Unifying.

She took his eager cock inside her, welcoming him in her wet embrace. Together they traveled through a sensual landscape of delights. Stealing through a quiet wood. Swimming in a rolling sea. Galloping hard across a rocky hill. And finally soaring high above the clouds.

There they discovered a beautiful release in each other's arms, tumbling gracefully back to earth.

Spent, they nestled in silence for a long time. But there was something Merraid wanted to tell him. Something she'd put off for days now.

"Gellir?" she whispered, easing up on her elbow to look down at him.

"Mm?" His eyes were still closed.

"Remember Beltane? The night we first made love?"

He smiled. "Mm-hmm."

"I think...somethin'...might have happened that night."

"You fell in love with me?"

She smirked. "Ye goose, I fell in love with ye four years ago. Nay, somethin' else."

"What?"

"Well... They say a bairn conceived on Beltane is blessed."

His eyes flew open. "Are you...?"

She nodded.

She knew he'd be happy. She didn't realize he'd be so overjoyed that he'd run naked to the window and shout the news to the world.

But she supposed she couldn't blame him. Especially when she heard all the cheers from the courtyard.

By winter, Grim Gellir Cameliard would be the proud father of the next child of the Rivenloch clan. And Merraid would have just enough time to get into shape for the grand spring tournament at Rivenoch.

# EPILOGUE

"**M**erraid! Merraid! Merraid!"

From the solar, Merraid could hear Isabel calling all the way up the spiraling steps. She exchanged an arched brow with Gellir. It had taken Merraid a while to grow accustomed to Isabel's enthusiastic nature. But after four months, she knew there was probably no cause for alarm.

By the time Isabel reached her, the lass was breathless. Grinning with excitement, she barged into the chamber, holding a sealed parchment in her hand.

"A missive!" she gushed.

Gellir pushed himself up from the chair.

Merraid remained seated. She was grateful for Isabel's energy. In her current condition, clambering down the stairs would have been exhausting. Even standing was too much effort.

She'd been out of sorts for a fortnight now. She'd grown too unwieldy to perform her *taijiquan* with her usual grace. Laird Deirdre had finally banned her from the tiltyard. And Gellir treated her like a queen, waiting on her, hand and foot.

Resigned to reading and embroidery and strolling through the dying fall garden, she was bored and restless. A mysterious missive was welcome.

Gellir reached out a hand for it.

Isabel pulled it back. "'Tis for Merraid," she announced smugly, handing it to her. But that didn't mean she didn't want to know what it said. She clasped her hands under her chin, eager to hear the news.

Merraid broke the seal and unfurled the parchment. She glanced at the bottom.

"'Tis from Lady Carenza."

Isabel squealed and clapped her hands together.

Gellir sat back down. "Is she well?"

Merraid scanned the missive. "I think so."

"What does it say?" he asked.

She read it aloud. "To Merraid, my dear and amiable friend, I bring you glad tidings from Dunlop. As you have always shown me perfect benevolence and patience, I pray you will receive this missive with cheer and good will. I must beg your forgiveness for the abrupt manner in which I left Castle Darragh, but I know you will understand, having confided in you my heart and my condition. As you know, shortly after, Gellir's kind cousin Hew conveyed me to safety, ensuring I was reunited with my dearest love."

At this, Isabel released a dreamy sigh.

Merraid continued. "I have since received word that you have been united with yours as well, and I wish you every happiness in your marriage."

She smiled at Gellir.

He smiled back.

"Go on," Isabel urged.

Merraid read, "I must confess, however, the news came as little surprise after Hew, chancing upon the heartfelt missives Gellir gave me, revealed that someone else must have penned them, since his cousin has no talent for verse. I knew at once who the author must be and realized that the verses were indeed from the heart—*your* heart."

Isabel gasped in shock. "What? *You* wrote them, Merraid? *You* wrote the love missives?"

Merraid frowned. She'd hoped that wee bit of deceit would remain secret.

But it was not to be. Indeed, in the next instant, Isabel wheeled about in a flurry and scurried from the solar to spread the news to all of Rivenloch.

"Isabel!" Merraid shouted after her. But the lass was already halfway down the steps.

"'Tis no matter," Gellir said with a shrug. "Once everyone knows you can compose verse, you may gain a new pastime to occupy the hours."

He had a point. Merraid did like composing verse. And if she didn't find something productive and engaging to do soon, she'd go out of her wits.

She returned to reading the missive. "It is my understanding that fortune has blessed us both, for not only have we wed magnificent men..." She paused to give Gellir an appreciative glance.

"Am I magnificent?" he teased.

"Most magnificent." She lowered her eyes to find her place. "...not only have we wed magnificent men, but we will shortly be delivered of the fruits of those marriages." Merraid wondered if anyone would count the months between their marriages and the births, for both she and Carenza would deliver early. "I know your Gellir will make a devoted parent, and no one looks forward to fatherhood more than my..."

She trailed off as she studied the next word. That couldn't be right. She narrowed her eyes at the writing.

"What?" Gellir asked. "What does it say?"

She shook her head. "I must be reading it wrong."

Gellir held out his hand for the parchment, and he quickly scanned it from the beginning. His eyes suddenly went round as he read the same word.

"Did you know about this?" he asked.

She shook her head.

He stood, thrusting the missive back at her. Then, with a glower of concern, he marched out of the solar.

Merraid struggled up out of the chair to peer down out of the solar window. Isabel was already in the courtyard, flitting from lass to lass with her bit of gossip.

She grinned. She had a feeling Isabel's big revelation about the writer of the verses would be lost in the wake of this new and far more startling development. It seemed Lady Carenza had married into the Rivenloch clan after all. And Merraid wanted a bird's eye view for the fireworks.

## The End

*Coming soon...*

# LAIRD OF FLINT

### The Warrior Lairds of Rivenloch, Book 2

*Crossing blades and breaking hearts in the Highlands of Scotland!*

# THANK YOU FOR READING MY BOOK!

Did you enjoy it? If so, I hope you'll post a review to let others know! There's no greater gift you can give an author than spreading your love of her books.

It's truly a pleasure and a privilege to be able to share my stories with you. Knowing that my words have made you laugh, sigh, or touched a secret place in your heart is what keeps the wind beneath my wings. I hope you enjoyed our brief journey together, and may ALL of your adventures have happy endings!

If you'd like to keep in touch, feel free to sign up for my monthly e-newsletter at www.glynnis.net, and you'll be the first to find out about my new releases, special discounts, prizes, promotions, and more!

*If you want to keep up with my daily escapades:*
Friend me at facebook.com/GlynnisCampbell
Like my Page at bit.ly/GlynnisCampbellFBPage
Follow me on Twitter @GlynnisCampbell
Follow me on Instagram @glynniscampbell
Follow me on Goodreads @glynnis_campbell
Follow me on Bookbub @glynnis-campbell
And if you're a super fan, join
facebook.com/GCReadersClan

# About the Author

I'm a *USA Today* bestselling author of swashbuckling action-adventure historical romances, mostly set in Scotland, with more than 20 award-winning books published in six languages.

But before my role as a medieval matchmaker, I sang in *The Pinups*, an all-girl band on CBS Records, and provided voices for the MTV animated series *The Maxx*, Blizzard's *Diablo* and *Starcraft* video games, and *Star Wars* audio-books.

I'm the wife of a rock star (if you want to know which one, contact me) and the mother of two young adults. I do my best writing on cruise ships, in Scottish castles, on my husband's tour bus, and at home in my sunny southern California garden.

I love transporting readers to a place where the bold heroes have endearing flaws, the women are stronger than they look, the land is lush and untamed, and chivalry is alive and well!

I'm always delighted to hear from my readers, so please feel free to email me at glynnis@glynnis.net. And if you're a super-fan who would like to join my inner circle, sign up at http://www.facebook.com/GCReadersClan, where you'll get glimpses behind the scenes, sneak peeks of works-in-progress, and extra special surprises.